# Praise for the novels of Melissa Hill

## *The Summer Villa*

"Emotional and cleverly crafted ▮▮▮▮▮▮▮▮▮▮▮▮▮▮▮▮▮
—*People*

"Another great read from the best-▮▮▮▮▮▮▮▮▮▮▮▮▮
—*Hello* magazine

"This emotive story will touch your heart."
—*My Weekly*

"Blissfully escapist."
—*Marie Claire*

"Addictive!"
—*GRAZIA*

## *Keep You Safe*

"Guaranteed to kick-start book club debates."
—*Good Housekeeping*

"I was completely gripped. Every parent will recognize the issues raised in this book."
—*USA TODAY* bestselling author Sarah Morgan

"Hill has her finger on the vaccination zeitgeist, offering savvy and well-researched points on a touchy subject. The driving pace and small-town setting make this perfect book-club bait, ideal for discussing tough decisions and happy endings with friends and loved ones. Fans of Meg Wolitzer and Emily Giffin will devour this introspective and enlightening novel."
—*Booklist*

## Also by Melissa Hill

### The Lakeview Series

*The Truth About You*
*All Because of You*
*Never Say Never*
*The Last to Know*
*The Guest List*
*Wishful Thinking*
*Not What You Think*
*Christmas at the Heartbreak Cafe*
*Summer at the Heartbreak Cafe*

### A Winter Escape

*A Weekend in Paris*
*Christmas in New York*

### Escape to the Island

*Santorini Summer*
*The Getaway*

*The Charm Bracelet*
*Something from Tiffany's*
*A Gift to Remember*
*Keep You Safe*
*Please Forgive Me*
*Before I Forget*
*Something You Should Know*
*The Hotel on Mulberry Lane*
*Fairytale on Fifth Avenue*

For additional books by Melissa Hill,
visit www.melissahill.ie.

# MELISSA HILL

# The Summer Villa

**mira**

mira™

ISBN-13: 978-0-7783-5998-2

The Summer Villa

Copyright © 2020 by Melissa Hill

This edition published by arrangement with Harlequin Books S.A.

For questions and comments about the quality of this book, please contact us at
CustomerService@Harlequin.com.

Mira
22 Adelaide St. West, 40th Floor
Toronto, Ontario M5H 4E3, Canada
BookClubbish.com

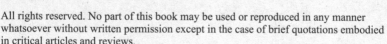

**Printed in U.S.A.**

To great friends, old and new.

# The Summer Villa

# *Prologue*

It was just a little white lie. A way to kick-start her freedom. And Kim Weston was now officially a runaway.

She couldn't help but laugh at the idea as she stared out the window of the airplane into the abyss around her. Thirty years old—an adult—and here she was, running away from home.

She'd boarded a flight from JFK earlier and watched as the sky turned from pale blue to black. They were already six hours into a nine-hour journey and she was tired but couldn't sleep.

There wasn't a star to be seen, no way to discriminate the ocean below from the sky above. Nothing but emptiness.

Ironic because it was exactly how Kim felt inside. She had no reason to, or so everyone told her.

She had everything—the luxurious Manhattan apartment,

a personal driver to take her wherever she wanted to go, generous expense accounts at all the best Fifth Avenue stores, and a black Amex to service every last one of her spending needs.

She and her friends were the crème de la crème of New York's Upper East Side society set and partied with celebrities and VIPs alike. By all accounts she had the quintessential dream life.

So why was she running away?

She could still hear her parents' voices in her head and her own guilt in her heart as she sat quietly nursing a vodka and orange juice.

Most of the cabin's passengers were asleep, and the crew was moving around less frequently, but Kim's mind simply wouldn't quit.

For once, she wasn't playing the role she'd been allotted. If she was expected to assume her part in the Weston family script for the rest of her life, then she needed a chance to play the rebel, even if only briefly.

Everything was planned to ensure that her parents wouldn't find her—at least not for a little while.

Her destination (and certainly choice of accommodation) wasn't somewhere Peter or Gloria would ever think to look for her, since it was so far removed from the kind of places the Westons usually frequented.

No five-star luxury hotel suite awaiting Kim when she arrived. Instead she was staying at a tumbledown villa she'd found on the internet, where she'd be sharing living space and possibly even a room with other guests. She shuddered involuntarily.

Kim was roughing it, in as much as someone like her could. The house had no on-site staff, apparently there was someone who'd come by daily to tidy and meet and greet, but that was it. No concierge, butler, in-house chef—nothing.

For once, she was going to have to cater for herself—in more ways than one.

That gave her some sense of unease; she wasn't exactly Martha Stewart, which was why she also planned to maybe enlist herself in an Italian cooking class, as suggested by the booking site she'd used. Failing that, she'd just survive on pizza and pasta. It was Italy after all.

And she could afford that much, for a little while at least.

It was early afternoon when the flight landed at Naples airport and the transfer service she'd arranged (her final luxury—she wasn't going to rough it entirely after a transatlantic economy flight) picked her up outside the terminal.

"Signorina Weston?" the driver holding the sign with her name on it queried as she approached.

"That's me."

"*Buongiorno.* Right this way," the young Italian man instructed as he directed Kim to a waiting black Mercedes.

She stepped outside of the terminal, her long slender legs clad in white jeans, which complemented her hot pink poncho. Sunglasses protected her eyes from the bright sun but she still held a hand to her forehead to shield them as she stared up at an almost cloudless Italian blue sky.

"I am Alfeo," the driver introduced himself as they walked, taking her luggage along with him. "How was your flight?"

"Long," she answered. She was bone-tired, a little cranky and not particularly in the mood for small talk.

Alfeo nodded and opened the car door for her. "The journey will take just over an hour and a half depending on traffic. But we can stop along the way if you need anything."

"That's fine," Kim replied as she slid into the back seat and tipped her head against the leather headrest. She closed her eyes, suddenly spent and exhausted from worrying now that she was here.

She was really doing this…

It seemed as if only a few minutes had passed when she was woken by Alfeo's voice announcing arrival at their destination.

Kim blinked several times as she tried to gather her bearings, then lowered the window to look out at her surroundings. They were parked down some kind of laneway, and up ahead she could make out a grubby wall of peach-colored plaster, and a paint-chipped wooden door—the only interruption on an otherwise blank facade.

Unimpressed, she regarded the weather-worn door and its tarnished brass ring, and hid a frown as she dragged manicured nails through her tousled blonde mane, pulling her hair partially over her shoulder.

Her heart fell. This place looked like a complete dump. She sincerely hoped the inside was a helluva lot better.

"This *is* Villa Dolce Vita, right?" she asked, casting a fatigued gaze at Alfeo as she stepped out onto the dusty gravel pathway.

"*Sì*. Villa Dolce Vita."

"I'll need your number," she stated as she walked toward him with her phone in hand. "Just in case."

Alfeo complied, assuring her that he'd be available whenever she needed, the suggestive grin on his face indicating he meant for more than just transportation. Were Italian men really such unabashed flirts?

"Can you maybe just help get my cases inside before you go?"

"Of course." He duly took her suitcases out of the boot, while Kim wandered further along the perimeter wall to where a break in the trees gave way to a view of the sea.

Realizing that they were on an elevated site, high above

the glittering Gulf of Naples, she glanced to her left to see a group of impossibly beautiful pastel-colored buildings and terra-cotta roofs, clinging and huddled together.

The setup immediately put her in mind of a huge piñata cake: the center of the green and gray mountain cut open to release a tumbling selection of irresistible pastel-colored candy.

*Now this is more like it...*

Further along down the coast, rock promontories jutted out above diverging bays, beaches and terraces, all presiding over cerulean waters. Hills dotted with lush vineyards, olive trees and citrus groves looked down over the colorful shops, cafés, hotels and historic buildings scattered below.

Sailboats dotted the clear blue waters and, looking down from where she stood, Kim could see snaking wooden steps leading all the way to the rocky shore below.

The whole thing was dizzying in every sense of the word.

By the time she returned to the villa entrance, Alfeo was gone, but the old wooden door had been left ajar.

Kim slipped through into the courtyard area to discover a hidden garden of sorts.

The dark pea gravel of outside gave way to a lighter-colored, more decorative kind, and she noticed heavy stone planters dotted throughout the small courtyard area, housing rows of mature lemon and olive trees.

Coupled with vibrant magenta bougainvillea tumbling down the edge of an old stone building—evidently the villa itself—the garden was a riot of color and, against the azure sky and glittering water on the bay, made for a picture-perfect entrance.

Citrus scent from the lemon trees followed as Kim walked to the front of the property, her senses now well and truly awakened.

The villa was of the same blotchy peach plaster as the outside wall, a pretty two-story house with a terra-cotta roof and rustic windows trimmed with dull cast-iron railings that had long since seen better days.

Turning to check out the view from the front of the house, Kim noticed a terraced area beneath the gardens, accessible by four or five stone steps leading down to a small pool bordering the edge of the entire site overlooking the panoramic bay.

Without the ornate bougainvillea-laden perimeter railings holding everything together, it was as if the entire site could easily slip right off the edge and plummet down to the rocky shore below.

OK, so this place was old, but surprisingly charming, and while Kim didn't have high hopes for the quality of accommodation, given the crumbling exteriors, she already felt a weird sense of calm at just being here.

It was as if Villa Dolce Vita had already cast a spell on her.

A chipped wooden front door with a ringed black-painted knocker at its center stood wide open, and Kim hesitated momentarily as she listened for noise from inside.

She wasn't sure if there were other guests staying there already or if anyone was even expecting her, but there was no going back now.

She took a deep breath. She was really here. Doing her own thing, finding her own path.

Time to take the plunge.

*Here goes nothing…*

# Chapter 1

Now

The word "transformation" was an understatement.

The once-crumbling Villa Dolce Vita was now one of the loveliest restorations on the Amalfi Coast area, in Kim's opinion at least. It was the perfect location for a wellness center and retreat, and was going to be the ultimate real-life showcase for her business, The Sweet Life.

In the two years since they'd bought it, Kim and her business partners had wholly achieved their intention to create a very subtle, yet contemporary architectural update that reinterpreted the character of the building, while staying faithful to its origins.

Outside, the cast-iron perimeter and window railings had all been lovingly restored, external plasterwork and sash windows replaced with weatherproof alternatives, and every last one of the terrace's limestone tiles and steps had been completely relaid to ensure a sleeker, less rickety poolside surface.

The gardens had been well-maintained throughout the years, and while they'd had no choice but to cut back some of the more aggressive bougainvillea so as to retouch the exterior plasterwork, and earmarked a patch previously overrun with dying trees for a grassy area, little other work had been required.

The remaining good olive and lemon trees still bore heavy fruit, and the familiar citrus scent now filled the warm summer air as Kim wound her way through the courtyard.

At last, the Villa Dolce Vita Wellness and Cultural Retreat was due to open next month and Kim couldn't wait.

"Just here," she said, as she supervised the delivery guys. The patio furniture some of the locals were carrying had been handpicked by Kim, each piece reflecting her own classic style as well as the influence of their Amalfi Coast surroundings.

"Giving orders already, I see," an amused male voice called out from behind her.

Kim smiled. "Someone once told me that if you want something done right you have to do it yourself."

"Yes, I think I have heard that one." Antonio Berger had been one of Kim's business partners for the past five years. More than two decades her senior, the Italian was more of a father figure and mentor, and encouraged her in every venture she pursued.

When she'd first met him and his wife, Emilia, on her first visit to Italy almost six years before, they'd been a welcome presence in her life and much-needed guides as she tried to navigate away from her upbringing and figure out what to do with her life.

Antonio, as ever, was dressed in a light-colored linen suit and square-front brown leather shoes. His salt-and-pepper hair was brushed back regally, accentuating his long face and square jaw, and his lively brown eyes lit up as he smiled at her.

"As always, you already seem to have everything covered," he commented, stepping back and casually slipping a hand into his trouser pocket as he regarded the villa's freshly renovated grandeur. "You certainly don't need me."

"I always need you," she answered with a grin. "So do you want the grand tour?"

The pair walked back toward the main house together. "You haven't been here since we bought it, have you?" she realized as she led him through the narrow hallway to the kitchen at the rear.

She smiled fondly as the memories of her arrival here all those years ago came rushing back.

How the kitchen had once been a cornucopia of blue, green and yellow with its grubby tiling, mismatched cheap units, and equally mismatched plates and cups on the open shelves. All the kitchen units were now bespoke in dark wood, complementing the ochres and light blue accents, and contrasting the wider openings and light tinted walls.

A brand-new staircase replaced the old heavy wooden steps and rails, completely redefining the formerly dark and dreary entryway. Constructed in white-coated metal, the stairs appeared as if suspended from a softly curved aperture above the main space, adding instant character and interest to the reception area.

The interiors felt lighter, brighter, and much more spacious, with blues and grays of the ocean incorporated primarily in the soft furnishings, bringing a restful classic feel that could be easily updated.

The color ochre recurred throughout, contrasting with new glass openings overhead and lighter shades on the walls. Bright terrazzo flooring had been installed throughout in place of the dark terra-cotta mishmash that had welcomed Kim six years before.

"Actually, no," he replied. "I meant to, but you know… with Emilia," he added gently, referring to his wife who had recently been diagnosed with dementia.

"How is she?"

Kim noted the way Antonio's chest rose and fell before he spoke. She couldn't imagine what it would be like to come to terms with the fact that the person you love will eventually lose all memory of you and the life you shared.

It was difficult enough for Kim to get her head around the decline of a sunny, vibrant woman into the confused and frightened soul she apparently was now.

Not that she'd seen Emilia recently, she thought guiltily, given how busy she'd been getting this place ready for the launch. The Bergers were based in Milan, while Kim lived in California, where her husband was from, and whenever she traveled to Italy to check on the renovation project, her short visits had been restricted to the Amalfi Coast.

"It is hard to say. Sometimes she is perfectly lucid, the same Emilia, while others…" he trailed off solemnly. "The doctors have been talking about residential care but I think that is premature," he added, almost to himself. Kim knew the very idea of it was killing him.

She stepped forward to give him another hug.

"It'll be lovely to see her at the party and once all of this is over, I'm looking forward to spending some quality time with you both."

He patted her back paternally. "It's OK, I'm coming to terms with it, and for the most part she is still my Emilia. We've had a good life and have been through a lot together. She gave me two beautiful children and almost forty years of true love," he said with a fond smile. "I would be nowhere else than by her side."

"Then I'm even more grateful that you carved out the time for me. I know it must've been a wrench to leave her."

He shook his head lightly. "No, no, she is excited about this. You needed me also, and of course she and I are not just your partners, but your friends, too. In any case," he teased, "perhaps she will not even miss me."

Though she knew he was joking, she could still hear the pain behind his words. Ever the optimist, she knew he was trying his utmost to not let his wife's diagnosis blight their lives or dampen their spirits.

Now he took both of her hands in his. "So how are you, *bella*?"

Kim smiled gamely but knew it didn't reach her eyes and Antonio would likely see through her own pretense just as easily. "Just OK," she answered, averting her gaze. "I'm a bit tired. There's been a lot going on and still loads to get through. At least I'm here on the ground now, the invites are out and the guest list is finalized…"

"Well, it's a long list. Are your friends going to make it? The ladies who were with you that summer?"

Kim had almost forgotten she'd first met Antonio the same time as Annie and Colette. The three had come together as strangers six years ago at the villa but in the ensuing years had managed to maintain their friendship, albeit at long-distance with their contact now sporadic.

She and Colette had been guests at each other's weddings, and she'd managed to meet up with Annie on a business trip to Dublin the year before last.

Of course, social media made it easy to keep track of each other's lives, but Kim missed the closeness they'd shared that summer. It would be so lovely to get the gang back together in person for a reunion. Here at the villa, especially.

"I hope so," Kim said, realizing that she needed to check in on the RSVPs. She'd sent invites to both women, asking them and their respective plus ones to next month's official Villa Dolce Vita Wellness and Cultural Retreat launch celebration, including flights and a hotel stay over a long weekend.

Once the party was done and the center officially open for reservations, Kim would be temporarily free from work obligations. She relished the chance of catching up with them here and revisiting some of their old haunts.

She hooked her arm in Antonio's. "Let's keep going. I've still got lots to show you. The bedrooms have been transformed, too, and wait till you see where we managed to slot in the massage area."

When he'd finished his tour of the accommodation area, and its new state-of-the-art wellness facilities, Antonio nodded with satisfaction. "You've done an amazing job, Kim. The investors will be more than happy."

"I just hope it's enough to get those reservations flooding in." She smiled. "Now, how about lunch? We can head down to Il Buco, maybe? I'm feeling in the mood for pizzaiola beef."

Antonio looked at her with a sad smile. "*Bella*, in all the time I've been here you have not once mentioned your husband. Gabe is coming next month, too, I hope?"

Kim's heart stuttered guiltily. "Of course. He and Lily are flying in soon, actually." Her three-year-old, a beautiful little girl she barely saw these days.

Gabriel's plan was to have some long overdue family time in Italy together before everything kicked off. Kim only hoped that things would run smoothly in the run-up to the launch so that she could carve out the necessary time.

Much like Antonio, her husband was an optimist at heart.

Now she could feel her mentor's eyes following her as they meandered back out to the courtyard and down the steps to the pool terrace perched on the edge of the property. When she turned to look at him, the expression on his face said it all.

"Don't..."

He smiled weakly. "I'm sorry but thirty-odd years of marriage has taught me well. I know trouble when I see it." He stepped closer, taking Kim's hand in his as he patted her knuckles. "Why don't we go to lunch and you tell me everything? All right?"

But Kim didn't want to talk about her personal life. She really didn't. She had enough on her mind.

"I won't take no for an answer," he insisted gently and she knew there was no point in refusing.

While she'd never been able to talk to her father, to trust or confide in him, Antonio was so much more reliable. He understood her, sometimes even better than she did herself.

Minutes later, Kim leaned her head back against the plush leather seats of Antonio's convertible Maserati as the car wound along the coast toward Sorrento. She gazed out over the water, catching sight of the magnificent island of Capri in the distance. She held her hand out, allowing the warm breeze to pass through her fingers as sunlight danced across the dazzling blue of the sea.

She would never, ever tire of this view and doubted there were many others in the world to compare.

This place had transformed her life six years ago.

Perhaps it could do the same again now.

# Chapter 2

## Then

She could hear them already. The authoritative voices of her folks filled the house as Peter and Gloria Weston returned from yet another trip abroad.

Kim turned her music up and rolled over on her bed.

It was Saturday, the weekend, and she was doing what she did best—nothing. Which seemed to be all her life was about.

A steady stream of nothing.

It was bad enough that they still ran her life from a distance; with them home she'd have no peace.

Kim was in no hurry to face that. She turned her back to her bedroom door and rolled over.

She was twenty-nine years old and was still living at home, despite spending four years at business school at Cornell. And for what? She wasn't exactly sure, other than the fact that it was her parents' will at the time, and their dime. She enjoyed her studies, but since then, hadn't had much opportunity to put her knowledge to work.

After graduation, her venture capitalist father had given her a position in his company, though he never seemed to let her do anything except put in the hours. And, of course, wine and dine any clients he sent her way.

She learned very early on in life to go along with what her folks wanted, or forfeit the luxury of their purse strings.

Kim liked her life, her Gucci bags and jaunts to the Caribbean, summers in the Hamptons and never-ending nights out in Manhattan. Or at least she did when she was in her teens and early twenties.

As time went on, things had begun to seem same-y and, well…boring. But as much as she disliked being a pawn in the games her parents played, she didn't really have the inclination or the means to deny them.

Now a hand on her shoulder was shaking her awake, though it was unnecessary as Kim wasn't sleeping. She groaned inwardly, feeling a bit like a teenager.

"Fast asleep in the middle of the day? How typical," her mother's voice chided as Kim grabbed her iPhone and paused Spotify.

"Nice to see you, too, Mother." She gave Gloria a mirthless grin that disappeared as quickly as it had appeared, and her mother gave her a deeply condescending glance in return.

Kim was used to those glances. She'd been getting them her entire life.

"Do you plan on staying in bed *all* day, Kimberley?"

"If I can help it, yes," she answered as she attempted to turn over. Attempted was as far as she got. "Tough night last night."

"I hope you took time out of your…busy partying schedule to meet with the tech people your father requested? They were only in town for a couple of days so it was very important to him that you entertain them."

There was always some up-and-coming entrepreneur or other business type she was expected to "entertain" on her parents' behalf—apparently because she was hot, blonde, and knew all the trendiest haunts in Manhattan.

Kim hated her ditzy socialite role; it all felt so fake and manipulative. She felt she was capable of so much more, but there was no arguing. She'd tried many times and it never worked out well.

"I took them to Hirohisa yesterday," she answered, rolling her eyes. "They loved it. Mr. Clarke had a lovely time and said he looked forward to seeing Daddy in San Francisco."

"Good," her mother replied. "Very good."

Gloria was sitting on the edge of the bed, just by Kim's hip. She always sat in the same place; it was the perfect vantage point—far enough from her daughter to avoid direct eye contact and close enough to corner her if she tried to move away.

Her mother took everything into consideration before she acted, which was probably the main reason for her parents' success. She weighed the odds, tested the waters and then launched her attack. In her mother's long history of battles (as Kim saw them), she had never failed in her conquests.

"Where's Dad?" Kim asked casually as she listened for noise within the house. It was silent, almost as if her father wasn't there.

"Downstairs on the phone. Your uncle called."

"Did he?" Kim said enthusiastically. Ted was the only good thing in their family as far as she was concerned. He wasn't the raging success her parents were—far less acclaimed in his field as a lowly accountant—but he was fun and Kim liked him a lot. Much more than her folks.

"I don't know why you're so happy about it; he's probably

just trying to get your father to loan him more money to invest in yet another harebrained financial scheme." She wrinkled her nose in disdain.

"Why do you never have anything good to say about Uncle Ted? He's your brother."

"I have no control over family—sadly. Ted made his choices and I've made mine. The results speak for themselves."

Her mother was always so goddamn controlled. Not once in Kim's entire life had she ever seen her overcome by emotion. Most of the time she wondered if Gloria actually had any for anyone or anything outside her work.

Not even her father seemed to move her. It was always the job. Kim wasn't sure if even that made her happy. There was no way of telling.

"Stop lazing around up here and come downstairs," her mother ordered with a solid pat on Kim's shoulder. "Your father and I need to speak with you about something."

Kim sighed heavily. "What is it? I was in the middle of something."

"Downstairs in two."

She watched as her mother swept out of the room as if nothing had transpired and Kim's protests meant diddly-squat. Which was exactly the case. It was just expected that she'd do as her mother demanded. Her words and opinions were meaningless in this house, in this family.

She picked up her phone again and texted her best friend, Natasha.

Meet at the club tonight? I know I'm seriously gonna need to blow off steam when this day is over. Ugh.

She slapped her phone down on the mattress and forced herself from her bed, realizing there was no putting it off.

She might as well find out whatever latest scheme her parents wanted her involved in. Probably just another skinny nerd with a great idea her father wanted Kim to show a good time by pretending to be Paris Hilton.

It was embarrassing, not to mention demeaning.

She might have legs up to her armpits and green eyes that could charm George Clooney, but that didn't mean she was dumb.

Minutes later, Kim sat, stunned.

Her parents had had a lot of shitty ideas about a lot of stuff, but this was by far the most outlandish scenario they'd ever come up with for her.

"Are you guys *serious*?" she asked for the second time, slightly dazed. "Or I am misunderstanding in some way?"

"Depends on what you understand," her mother answered coolly. "If you understand that you've had a very privileged life, with opportunities that you've repeatedly squandered, that you're not getting any younger, and that we feel it's time you got serious about your future—then yes, you understand us correctly."

"You actually want me not just to entertain but actually *seduce* some random stranger," Kim repeated hotly, her eyes wide.

"He's not a random stranger; you've already met Spencer Andrews. You just haven't had a chance to spend a whole lot of time with him, that's all. That's what this is about. A summer in England, all expenses paid, to spend quality time with Spencer—and Lord and Lady Andrews, of course."

"Seriously?" Kim's horrified gaze shifted to her father. "Dad, do you understand what you guys are actually asking of me?"

"It's not much what we're asking, and it's a potentially advantageous move for you, too." Peter leveled his gaze on her.

"We have paved a great path for you in life, Kimberley. We've always given you everything you could want—definitely more than most. Now it's your turn to make a move that could affect your future and ours, too, of course." He spoke as if he were giving her a choice, whereas Kim knew better. "And, honey, you know, like your mom pointed out, you're really not getting any younger. That pretty face won't last forever."

Kim was floored, not to mention wounded to the core. In all her life she'd never been made to feel like nothing more than a piece of ass. And by her own father!

Whenever she did take his business prospects out on the town to show them a good time, she never just left it at that. Instead she talked to them about their hopes and intentions, teased out their strategies, and subtly influenced them to choose Weston Inc.

She'd thought her father knew this and quietly appreciated it. But he hadn't even noticed.

"You actually expect me to do this? You actually expect me to coldly pursue a guy I barely know? With marriage as the endgame? I've never even been in a proper relationship with someone I like, so why would I want to be involved with someone I don't?"

She was trying her best to contain her anger and dismay. This was like something from a horror movie, playing out before her eyes. People didn't do this in real life. They didn't just pimp out their daughters as part of a freakin'…business move!

But, Kim realized, it was basically what her folks had always done. Except this time they wanted her to go a step further and actually try to land this English guy as a potential husband, taking her off their hands in the process.

"Dad," she pleaded softly. "Please, don't ask me to do this."

"Kim, don't act like a child," Gloria tsked. "Do you think the life this family has comes free of cost? There's a price and we all have to pay it. Your father paid it. I paid it. Now it's your turn. You can't expect us to bankroll you forever. It's high time you had a plan for the rest of your life and we think this is the perfect start."

Why had she thought her father would help her? He never had before. Whatever her mother wanted she got. It was clear that what Gloria wanted now was a familial connection with some kind of gentry and her father the backing of this English bigwig's multibillion company.

Capitalism at its finest. A merger of the purest kind and all it would cost was Kim's sanity.

Her heart sank. They were asking her to offer herself up for their futures. It wasn't about her. It was about them. It was always about them. She gritted her teeth.

"I'm not doing it," she told them, her chin lifting. It was pointless, she knew, but she wasn't going to just go along with something this twisted without a fight. "And you have no right to ask—"

"It's not a request, Kimberley." Gloria's tone brooked no nonsense. "Everything's already arranged."

"Well, you can just go and rearrange it then, because I'm not doing it. I'm not throwing away my life—my entire future—for one of your business deals. And it's disgusting that you'd even consider—"

"Maybe you might like to suggest an alternative career plan then?" her mother interjected, her voice dripping with sarcasm. "Because lazing around in bed till midday doesn't seem like much of a go-getter strategy to me."

"You seem to have forgotten that I was *working* late last night—with Dad's clients. Seriously, is that all I am to you two? Some built-in entertainment manager for Weston Inc.? I'm your daughter, for chrissakes! What about some consideration for my needs?"

Gloria harrumphed. "Your father and I have always ensured that your needs are more than catered for—with your expense accounts, generous salary and pretty much everything you could ever want."

"Except love..." Kim replied in a small voice. "And respect for what I might want or need."

"Honey, think about it," her father began, his tone softening, and she was hopeful that her words had finally got through and appealed to his better nature. "This is a solid plan. You're always saying you're bored of New York, so it's an ideal opportunity, to get out and explore new horizons. London is a great city—a summer there could well be exactly what you need."

"A summer there sounds fine, Dad; it's what I'm expected to do while there that makes me sick." She stood up. "You know what? I'm not doing this anymore. I've had enough of being a pawn in this family. I'll move out, get my own place, find a job where someone appreciates my actual talent and skills..."

"Find your own place—here in Manhattan? How on earth will you afford that?" Gloria gave a mirthless laugh. "I think you seriously overestimate those skills and talents if you expect to just randomly waltz into a job that pays the same kind of salary your father does."

The realization stopped Kim in her tracks. Her mother was right. She was damned if she did and damned if she didn't. She couldn't make it on her own. She didn't even know where to start. She was just a puppet and her folks held the strings; they always had.

Check. Mate.

As always, Kim was outplayed.

"When did you want me to leave for England?" she asked, defeated.

"Two weeks, when your father and I head to the Hamptons. I told you she'd make the right decision in the end," her mother commented snidely as she turned to her father. "Our daughter will always choose the easy life."

Peter didn't answer. Instead he got to his feet.

"I need a coffee," he commented absently as he left the room. That was it. Kim's dad had basically just whored out his only daughter, and all he could say was he needed coffee.

Tears filled her eyes as she stood up and headed for the door.

"I'll let the Andrewses know to expect you," her mother said to her back as Kim left. "You've made a very wise choice this time, Kimberley. Very wise indeed."

# Chapter 3

## Then

That night, as Kim and her friend Natasha made their way from club to club in Manhattan, she drank herself into oblivion, trying to put the disgusting sordidness of her parents' request—no, *demand*—out of her mind.

Part of her hoped that she'd just wander out on the street and have a cabdriver end her misery for her. She was too cowardly to do it herself.

Had she really acquiesced to this? Agreed to barter herself for her family in order to secure a future for herself?

"Hey, slow down—we're not eighteen anymore," Natasha encouraged, but Kim was hearing none of it.

"I'm fine," she slurred as she pushed her way again toward the bar.

"I think you've had enough, actually," her friend interjected as she attempted to get in her way. But Kim could be persistent and with the level of alcohol that now coursed through her veins, she felt unstoppable.

"Bartender!" she yelled as she slapped the top of the electric green counter.

"Seriously," Natasha insisted, grabbing her wrist, "you'll break your hand the way you're hitting that."

"So what," Kim snapped as she yanked it away. "What difference does it make? The Andrewses will just get a slightly bruised whore for a daughter-in-law."

*Daughter-in-law...* The word disgusted her and the notion of charming some guy into marriage made her want to throw up.

"Hey! Vodka," she shouted as she raised her glass above her head and waved frantically at the bartender. The guy, who knew Kim well, hustled over and grabbed the empty glass from her hand.

"Another one, princess?" He smirked. Normally Kim wouldn't have entertained his flirtations but today was different. "You sure?"

"Hey, if you're pouring then I'm drinking," she teased, leaning across the bar, practically falling over it, and kissing him.

"OK, enough," Natasha stated as she grabbed Kim by the hem of her skirt and heaved her backward. "What the hell are you doing?"

"My thing," Kim spat. "What I do best. Make guys like me," she drawled drunkenly.

Kim could see the look of disgust and annoyance in her friend's face but it was nothing compared to the feeling in her heart. Natasha would never know how she felt. She'd never know the betrayal, the hurt, and despair that Kim felt right then. Her life was over when it had never really begun. How could anyone call what she did living when every moment was for someone else, never herself?

And now she was about to cross a line over which she could never return.

Once she set foot on that plane and traversed the ocean, any hope of a normal life would be over. From what she remembered of them, the Andrewses were stuffy and pretentious, and Spencer was the most anal guy she'd ever met. Seduce him? That bit would be easy. But marry him? That was a whole other prospect.

She grabbed the vodka bottle from the bartender, and downed the remaining contents in one go. Clear liquid burned every inch of its way down as she hissed her approval.

"*That's* what I'm talkin' about."

"For crying out loud," Natasha sighed.

"What?" she snapped involuntarily.

Her friend cocked her head at her accusingly. Kim knew what that meant. She took a deep breath and sighed. She was acting out, behaving like a bratty teen. No wonder her parents wanted to marry her off.

"Sorry," she apologized.

Natasha shook her head sympathetically. "It's OK. I know you've got a lot going on right now. But this…" she indicated the bottle and Kim's ragged appearance, "this isn't you."

Her friend was right. This *wasn't* her. She tried to refocus, get herself back in the game, but all she could think of was the upcoming trip to England and the horrific scenario it presented.

Natasha slapped her hand across the bar. "So what're you going to do about it?"

Kim's head snapped up, her wide green eyes piercing her friend's dark gaze. "What can I do? It's all decided and I agreed. Case closed." Feeling dizzy now from the effects of the vodka, she stumbled against the bar a little. "I'm outta here."

She stumbled erratically through the crowds, her short skirt and skimpy top gaining the attention of most of the guys she passed, but she didn't notice. Her eyes were solely focused on the exit. She could hear Natasha following her but she didn't look back.

The moment they stepped outside, her friend grabbed Kim's arm and turned her around. "Oh, come on, quit the 'poor me' act. The Kim Weston I know doesn't just give in. So what—now you've decided to just turn into a wet mop and do what they want?"

"What does it matter?" Kim spat. "Everything stays the same. They always get what they want. So why bother fighting?"

"You're always saying that one day you'll finally stop letting them win and take a hold of your own life. This could be the day."

"Easy for you to say. Your folks are great. They don't pressure you. They let you find your own way and just be there for you if you need them. They love you. My parents only bother with me when they need to whore me out."

"Seriously?" Natasha rolled her eyes. "Kim, you're nearly thirty years old. No one is stopping you from having the life you want. You're just scared to actually go out and get it. You find excuse after excuse for why you can't walk away from your parents and this 'woe is me' attitude, but the truth is you're afraid to let go of the trappings that Mommy and Daddy's cash can buy."

The words were a fist to the gut. "So what if I am? You mean to tell me you wouldn't be scared if having what you want meant giving up everything you already have, your entire way of life?"

"Of course," Natasha answered. "I'd be terrified. We can't pretend that we haven't had an easy time. We've always had everything we've ever wanted. The best that money can buy. People kill for the types of lives we were born into."

Her words weren't helping Kim feel any better. "So what's all this talk about me being scared?"

"I'm saying it because there comes a time when you need to decide if what you want from life is more important than the trappings you'd forfeit for that freedom. Does having everything handed to you beat the ability to make your own choices? If it does, then go to England, Kim. Make Spencer what's-his-name fall head over heels for you. Get married, have two point five children, smile for the Christmas card photos and make your parents happy, while you—Kim Weston—are dying inside."

She could see the exact image in her mind as Natasha described it and it made her nauseous.

"Or," her friend continued, "take a bold step. Do something different and unexpected, and see where it takes you."

"Like what?"

"I don't know. Something no one would see coming, not even you. This may be your last chance, Kim. Take it. Before you commit your life to misery, take a chance that maybe there is something more out there for you. Maybe getting the life you want isn't so scary. I'll help you."

"How?"

"I don't know. It depends on what you want to do."

"I don't know what that is either," Kim answered with exasperation. "I just want to escape from all this."

Natasha's eyes lit up. "They why the hell don't you?"

"What do you mean?"

"I mean, why don't you escape? Here in New York your folks' shadow is always looming over you. Why don't you go somewhere they can't influence you?"

The prospect was intriguing. "Like where?"

A smile spread across her friend's tanned features and Kim's stomach began to knot. Was she really considering this? Yes, she was.

"Come on, let's head back to my place and sober you up a little first," she stated as she took Kim by the hand and went to hail a taxi. "Party Girl Kim is done."

# Chapter 4

Then

Natasha had her own Midtown apartment in the heart of everything. She was lucky, she got to live on her own but her parents still paid for it, so she had all of the freedom without the worry of bills and rent.

Kim often envied Natasha's situation, and she told her that. They'd been friends since middle school and had few secrets between them, but the distance in their lives was widening the older they got.

Tash couldn't understand what Kim went through, no matter how much she tried. She always had ideas to save her and simple solutions to whatever problem Kim faced, but it was easy to find an out when your feelings weren't in the mix, and your heart wasn't being torn by the choices you faced.

It was easy to rip a bandage off when you didn't have to feel the pain of the removal or bleed once it was done.

Now, the pair settled onto the couch as Natasha turned on her Dell and typed in her password. Kim nipped to the bathroom, pulled her blonde curls back in a scrunchie she had in her bag, and went to splash her face with water.

She wasn't that drunk; the act back at the bar was mostly borne out of despair, and more than that, Natasha's suggestion had sobered her up and got her thinking.

"So what are we doing?" she asked, coming back into the living room.

"We," her friend answered as she pulled up a search engine, "are going to find you the perfect escape, Kim Weston. So what are you feeling? Someplace down south, maybe? I hear Miami is fun."

"Too humid in summer," Kim answered.

"California?"

"We go there all the time."

"Hawaii then?" Natasha suggested as she turned to her. "You could surf or climb a volcano."

Kim didn't share her enthusiasm. "How about someplace I haven't been? Somewhere new?"

"OK, so why don't we let Google decide?" Natasha suggested with a laugh.

Kim frowned.

"Trust me," her friend assured as the "I Feel Lucky" prompt appeared and Tash duly pressed "enter." "There. What do you think?"

"Italy?"

"Yes. On the other side of the world, a whole ocean away from your folks' reach," she added with a satisfied smile. She pushed the laptop in Kim's direction and a flood of stunningly picturesque images filled her vision.

She knew Italy was beautiful. Her family had visited Venice once when she was six or seven and Kim had always wanted to go back. She remembered Gloria being annoyed with her because all she wanted to do was chase around after the pigeons in St. Mark's Square.

She flicked through the on-screen images of picture-postcard scenery: blue skies, historical sights, twinkling water and impossibly pretty villages, each one more appealing than the last.

The idea of running away to such a place was unbelievably alluring. Not to mention romantic.

"Looks incredible…" she muttered, as she continued her search.

"Good place to hide away for a while and maybe get your bearings?"

"Yes, but there's no way I can go."

"Why not?" Natasha challenged. "No one has to know and I certainly won't tell. What's stopping you?"

"How am I going to pay for it? If I use the Amex, Mom and Dad will know and they'd be on the next flight to drag me back before I even arrive," Kim pointed out.

Or more likely, have someone else do it. Her driver, probably.

"Not if you pay with mine." Natasha grabbed her purse and pulled out the little magic black rectangle.

Kim took the credit card from her friend and turned it over in her hands. She bit her lip. Could this tiny piece of plastic be the key to her escape? She grinned.

"How much can I spend?"

"Whatever you need," Natasha answered airily, as a satisfied grin spread across her face. "No one's going to check. I can cover your flight, hotel—everything. You'll need some cash for spending, though, or else your parents will be able to track you."

Clearly Natasha had been watching too much true crime on TV again, but Kim was thankful. If she did go ahead with this then she couldn't take the chance that her parents would find out.

"OK, but just coach flights, and nowhere expensive, OK? And I'll pay you back." She knew the money wouldn't matter to her friend but it did to Kim.

If this was going to be about finding her own way, then she needed to get her priorities straight from the get-go.

"Great! So let's find you someplace to stay," Natasha practically sang as she pulled the laptop closer. "Italy's a big country. Where would you like to go?"

"I don't know. Does it matter? Isn't the point of an escape to just go and see what happens?" Kim pointed out.

"Pin the tail on the donkey then," Natasha laughed.

"What?"

"On the map. Just close your eyes and pick a spot," she insisted.

Kim looked at her skeptically. "Seriously?"

"Just do it."

Kim did as she was bid and they both stared at the part of Italy she'd picked, a spot at the shin area of the boot-shaped map.

The Amalfi Coast looked and sounded amazing.

And the further along the plan progressed, the more hopeful Kim felt. A chance to take some time out, if only for a little while, was something she hadn't even realized she needed.

Either one last summer hurrah before life as she knew it ended, or the opportunity to find out what the alternatives could be. And perhaps, most importantly, a chance to outmaneuver her parents, have some fun and take charge of her life in the most spectacular way.

"All we need now is your flight. You're supposed to leave for England next month, right?"

"Yes," Kim confirmed.

"So find out the date and we book your flight to Italy for the same day, so your parents won't be suspicious."

Kim had to laugh. "You really think of everything, don't you? Espionage would suit you."

"Don't think I *haven't* considered it," her friend mused. She continued in her best James Bond voice. "Slater. Natasha Slater. Agent Nine-Inch Heels."

"Thanks, Tash," Kim said as her emotions took over. "For this…for everything."

"Of course." Her friend pulled her in for a hug. "You're my best friend and I want the best for you. Whatever that may be." She turned back to her computer. "Now, let's find a place for you to stay," she continued. "Somewhere fitting for Kim Weston's Italian Great Escape."

# Chapter 5

## Now

"So are you going to share what's on your mind?" Antonio asked as his Maserati made its way along the coast and deftly around the hairpin bends that used to so terrify Kim, but were as familiar to her now as Fifth Avenue used to be.

She turned to look at him, brushing back strands of her hair as it blew in the breeze.

In spite of his advancing years, he was still very handsome. There was something about him that reminded her a lot of her husband.

Both men had angular jaws and arresting eyes, but while Antonio's were brown, Gabriel's were piercing blue. Both also had Roman-shaped noses, reflecting their Italian roots. Gabe was American but his family was originally from Sicily, and the semblance of his ancestry still shone through.

Now, she visualized her husband's handsome face before her—his gentle eyes and brilliant smile. She hadn't seen that smile in weeks and she missed it.

"Nothing," she lied automatically, before adding, "nothing important."

"No trouble in paradise, I hope?"

"No trouble," she answered a little too quickly. "It's just… Lily is young and life has been…challenging lately."

"And of course that would have nothing at all to do with your frequent absences and workload…"

Kim loved Antonio's honesty, but sometimes she hated his candor.

"I need to work hard, you know that," she answered. "Lots of people relying on me—there are publicity engagements, photoshoots, interviews, you know the drill. Especially over the last eighteen months," Kim continued, referring to Villa Dolce Vita. "This new venture is the culmination of everything we've worked for, Antonio, the showcase for the brand. Obviously it's taken a huge amount of my time and effort. If we want Villa Dolce Vita to be all it can be, then I need to put in the necessary care and attention."

"But what about your family? Doesn't it also deserve your care and attention?"

His words were a jolt to her system and she didn't know how to answer. Kim supposed she'd never thought of it in those terms. She scoffed internally. The Sweet Life was all about mindfulness and finding balance in all things, yet she knew that, ironically, her own life once again was heavily off-kilter.

"*Bella?* Where did you go?"

Kim snapped back to reality as they pulled up close to the trattoria. "Sorry, what?"

Antonio laughed. "I said that I think there is a lot more

going on than what you are telling me. Let's talk about it properly over lunch."

But where to even begin? Kim wasn't sure she had the words to express the turmoil in her brain as she took a seat across from her mentor and friend inside the charming cliffside restaurant.

How could she confide in Antonio everything that was going on in her life just now, let alone the sense of dread she felt deep down?

To say nothing of the ugly truth that Kim was turning out to be a terrible mother. Just like her own.

Gloria had never cared about Kim. Never considered her daughter or what she wanted. The only thing her mother ever desired was her own ends. It didn't matter how they came, as long as she got them.

Kim realized a long time ago that she had been just another one of her mother's devices. Her father had wanted a child to carry on the Weston legacy. They'd hoped for a son but Kim was it, and her mother had lived with that as best she could. She made sure she had nannies and the housekeeper to tend to Kim's every scrape and need, while she jet-setted across the world. Success was all she cared about.

Kim never experienced what it was like to have a mother's love. And now it seemed she lacked the skills and knowledge to give it to her own flesh and blood. While she, too, relentlessly pursued success.

"*Bella?*" Antonio pressed when the waiter had poured the wine.

"It's just…most of the time I don't know what I'm doing," she admitted to Antonio, as tears filled her eyes. "With Lily, I mean."

His comforting gaze lingered on her momentarily before he focused on the glittering water. "Emilia and I were married for about five years when I began to question it—the marriage, I mean."

The confession came as a huge surprise. Kim could never have imagined that Antonio, the man whose love for his wife she thought unmatched, could ever have thought he'd made a mistake.

She didn't for one second regret marrying Gabriel; she adored him and almost from the moment they met knew he was her soul mate. But she was just as certain she was never cut out to be a mother, and when Lily arrived, her worst fears were realized.

Every day of her daughter's three-year-old life, she'd felt like a failure at it. And the worse she felt, the more she threw herself into her work, leaving her husband to care for their daughter pretty much alone while she built The Sweet Life into an international brand.

He never complained, never even seemed to notice that Kim was spending less and less time at home as the business grew. He'd been there from the start, so knew that this was her passion, and the reason she was pushing so hard to make this new venture a success.

But neither her husband nor Antonio knew that The Sweet Life had actually been built on lies.

And Kim was terrified of being uncovered as a fraud.

# Chapter 6

## Now

Colette Hargreaves yawned as she rolled over in bed. The blinds were open and it was after 7:00 a.m. She turned over, her copper hair falling across her shoulders as she looked around the bedroom.

Outwardly, everything was in its place, but she sensed something was missing.

"Ed?"

Silence answered her call and Colette swung her feet from beneath the sheets and onto the lush new carpeting they'd had laid during the most recent renovation of their London town house. Her husband was fond of hardwood, whereas she preferred carpet, so they'd made a compromise. Carpet in the bedroom and hardwood everywhere else.

She pulled a robe over her silk nightgown and tied a loose

knot at her waist as she slipped her feet into her slippers and headed for the door.

Their house was such a far cry from the tiny cottage she'd lived in growing up. Colette had left Brighton behind five years ago when she'd been offered a translator position at the Home Office.

A little while before that, Ed had asked her to marry him, and suddenly Colette was a Londoner with a comfortable house near Hyde Park.

Three bedrooms, living/dining area, a kitchen and outdoor terrace, and yet the house felt so empty. She walked into the living room and turned on the television before going into the kitchen to start breakfast.

She had just plated some eggs and bacon when Ed walked in, dripping with sweat, his sandy hair now dark against his forehead.

"Good morning, darling," he greeted, walking over and kissing her cheek. He pulled open the fridge and grabbed a bottle of his post-run shake.

Her husband was very concerned with his health, jogged seven days a week, and drank pre- and post-workout elixirs comprised of things Colette didn't want to think too much about.

"How was your run?" she asked as she set his plate on the white granite worktop. Her sister, Noelle, often joked that the brightest thing in the entire house was Colette's hair.

Ed's mother, Laura, had "helped" with the decorating (an understatement) and had declared bright colors gaudy and unsophisticated.

Colette hadn't wanted to argue. She was in a different world here, where the rules were set but often not shared, and one small misstep could have negative social or professional consequences.

The older woman also cautioned that people would look

to topple Colette because of Ed's profile within the London business world and that there would be several who would love nothing more than to see their relationship ruined.

Laura's intentions weren't malicious, Colette knew, but a heartfelt warning. Ed's mother was much like her, in a way. She'd come from a simpler life and had been propelled into this world by her own marriage. It had ended badly for many of the same reasons she now cautioned Colette about.

She'd left Ed's dad a few years later and made a place for herself on her own terms. She wanted Colette to do the same, without the broken marriage.

"It was good. I ran into Carter and Freddy in the park," Ed informed her as he continued to drink the contents of his bottle. "They said they had some news about that IPO I've been tracking."

When they first met, her husband was a lowly portfolio manager's assistant for a small investment firm in London. Now, he was the personal fund manager for seven- and eight-figure families, who paid him more than handsomely to manage their investments.

He'd gone from a tiny fish in a small pond to a great white in a lake of other investment managers just like him.

"And speaking of news—according to Mother there's another grandchild on the way." Ed's tone was casual but Colette noticed he wouldn't meet her gaze.

She was glad of it, because she knew there was no way she would have been able to hide her reaction. "Oh. Sarah's pregnant again?" She wasn't entirely sure how she'd even got the words out, the lump of disappointment in her throat was so huge. Or was it envy?

Colette wasn't sure how to describe the visceral, almost primal disappointment you experienced when someone else managed to achieve the very thing you wanted.

Five years of marriage and countless attempts, and still she and Ed had yet to conceive. There had been occasions when she thought she might be pregnant, but each time proved to be dodgy hormones or a faulty pregnancy test.

Ed was great about it, always encouraging, but she knew he was as disappointed as she was.

His brothers already had five (now soon to be six) offspring between them, and had been married years after them. Her own sister, Noelle, also had family; she lived in Germany with her husband and twin girls.

Sometimes it felt like Colette and Ed were the only ones with all these rooms and nothing to fill them.

"Could you put that in the microwave for me?" Ed said now, referring to breakfast. "Just the eggs, actually. I'm going to take a shower before I eat." He duly washed his bottle and set it out to drain, before coming over and kissing her on the cheek. It was his way of letting her know that he understood her disappointment, knowing she wouldn't want to make a big deal out of it.

Colette was grateful for it, but she sometimes wished they would talk more about the void in their lives, instead of pretending it didn't exist, the way Ed tended to sometimes.

"Of course," she answered. She'd just taken a seat at the kitchen island, hoping for a cozy breakfast together, but it seemed it was going to be another morning of eating on her own.

"Thanks." Ed kissed her forehead and jogged back out to the hallway. "It smells amazing."

"No problem," she said to his back, then turned to her own food and sighed.

He was so busy these days. Up early and to bed late so many nights. His clients could be demanding, and a call from someone meant he—or sometimes both of them, depending on the effort required—could be called away to the country for a weekend retreat, or invited to a party of rich elites.

It was something that both amazed Colette and made her uncomfortable. She'd adjusted, though: five years of marriage had done that, but in that other world the glaring differences between her and Ed's peers was more than evident.

He never complained or made her feel unworthy in any way. In fact, it was just the opposite. He was supremely proud of her and loved to talk about her accomplishments.

The translator position, which had started her career, had moved Colette along the path to her present job as project manager in the Department of International Development. It was a fantastic opportunity, which sometimes even allowed her to work for the United Nations. She was so lucky to be living her dream, at least in part.

Colette had the wonderful home, fantastic husband and an amazing job making a difference in the world, just as she'd always wanted.

There was just one thing missing.

An hour later, she was dressed in a stylish pencil skirt and heels. A string of pearls draped from her neck and a matching pair of earrings dangled from her ears.

Ed was on the couch going through the newspaper when she emerged downstairs again. This was often the way. Two ships passing in the night.

"Where are you off to?" he asked as he looked up.

"I told you on Wednesday that I was going shopping with your mum, then we're going to have lunch in Mayfair," she stated.

"You did, but I thought you said Saturday?"

"Ed, it *is* Saturday," she replied.

He looked perplexed. "It can't be." He closed the paper quickly, checking the date on front, then promptly jumped to his feet. "Damn! I was supposed to meet the boys at the tennis club for brunch. I can't believe it."

Colette watched as he picked up his phone and swiped quickly through his contact list.

She sighed. Her husband was wonderful, just too busy sometimes. If he wasn't dashing around the city for business, he was traveling around the world on business.

Sometimes his clients demanded he personally check out the companies in which they were interested in investing. It came with the trappings of the life they had. But still she wished that the pace of that life could just slow down a little now and again.

Leaving Ed to call his friends, she made her way out to the hallway, then stopped as the post on the bureau got her attention. Ed must have picked it up earlier when coming in from his run.

She stood, absently flipping through the envelopes to see if there was anything important. A crisp white envelope addressed to Colette and Ed Hargreaves caught her eye.

It wasn't so much the letter, but the fact that it wasn't addressed to "Mr. and Mrs. Ed"—her name was actually included this time. Turning the envelope over, she pried the flap open and unfolded a piece of paper emblazoned with a familiar logo.

*Enjoy La Dolce Vita!*

KIM WESTON AND THE SWEET LIFE FAMILY
CORDIALLY INVITE YOU TO JOIN US FOR
THE LAUNCH CELEBRATION OF

*Villa Dolce Vita Wellness
and Cultural Retreat*

ON THE GLORIOUS AMALFI COAST.

A smile spread wide across Colette's face as she skimmed over the invite, pushing her cheeks almost up as far as the lower rim of her reading glasses.

The timing of this almost made up for the disappointment of earlier. As if her old friend had somehow known she needed a boost.

Still smiling, she glanced back at the envelope and saw that there was something else inside. Two airplane tickets to Naples and a weekend reservation at a five-star Sorrento hotel, as well as a handwritten note.

*Can't wait for you guys to see what I've done with the place!*
*Perfect excuse for a long overdue reunion?*
*Kxx*

Her heart well and truly lifted, Colette walked back into the living room and held the invite out for her husband to read.

It had been a few years since Kim had announced her intentions to buy and restore the old villa, and the process had been less than easy.

From their (admittedly far too infrequent) phone catch-ups, she knew Kim had encountered obstacle after obstacle, from the Italian authorities to some of the locals, almost from the moment she let her grand plans be known.

However, as always, she hadn't wavered in her intentions, and now the invite was proof of her success.

"Isn't it wonderful? She really did it. I can't wait to see how it looks now," Colette prattled excitedly, as she waited for her husband's reaction. "And Kim, too, of course. And I wonder if Annie will come? Oh, I hope so. I haven't seen her in so long."

Colette and Kim had always made a conscious effort to stay in touch after their time in Italy, Annie less so. But the trio's was the kind of friendship that bucked time and place, and Colette knew that once they were together again, the preceding years would simply melt away and it would be as if they were never apart.

"Seriously?" Ed replied flatly. He looked up at her. "This is only a month away. I know you were looking forward to going back to Italy again, and it's great Kim seems to have finally got it all up and running, but do we really have time for this just now? You have that new project coming up, for starters."

Colette looked at him, puzzled. "We'd make time, of course," she answered. "I don't understand... We knew for ages that Kim's launch would likely be happening this summer. Why would I want to miss a trip like this?"

"It's just with everything we have going on, isn't the timing a bit off for a last-minute jaunt to Italy? And it's not as though you two are that close anymore."

"What? Of course the timing's not off," she replied, confused by his reaction. She'd thought Ed would be as excited as she was to return to the Amalfi Coast, where, in truth, their own love story began. And perhaps while there, the location might just work its magic again? And yes, while their lives had diverged considerably since their time in Italy, Colette considered Kim and Annie friends for life.

"OK. I'll see about making the necessary reservations," Ed answered. His mood still seemed off, though, and Colette was completely baffled by it.

"No need. Kim's already arranged everything," she announced as she handed the envelope to him. "We fly out a couple of days before the party and stay in Sorrento over the weekend. All we have to do is show up. It's really quite generous of her, actually."

Ed inspected the tickets carefully. "Well, that timing definitely doesn't work for me," he declared. "The IPO is that very week. I need to be here."

Disappointment filled her lungs as Colette inhaled deeply.

She leveled her gaze at her husband. How could he do this? He knew how important this was to her—and indeed to Kim.

"Ed, an old friend I care for and respect has offered to fly us both out to Italy for the grand launch of her latest business venture, and to reunite with old friends. Not only that, it happens to be the place where you and I met and fell in love. How could you possibly refuse? I don't usually say anything when it comes to your work but this time I have to dig my heels in."

"But we can always go again afterward, when it's not so busy…"

She put her hand on her hips. "Kim's put a huge amount of work into renovating a place that will always hold a special place in my heart. I really want to see how it looks now, and I so want the opportunity to catch up with her and Annie, too. She's pulled out all the stops, flying us over and putting us up in one of the nicest hotels in the area, and you're just going to refuse?"

"I'm not refusing—I just don't think we can sacrifice so much time to it, that's all," Ed replied, getting to his feet. He reached out to take her by the arm and sighed. "Yes, of course I know how much this means to you and I want to be there, too. It's just work is so hectic at the moment, darling." He kissed her forehead lightly.

"I know work is difficult; that's another reason why I think we need this trip. This isn't just for Kim's sake, Ed, it's for ours, too. We've hardly spent any time together lately." She stepped toward him and he pulled her close. "I miss you."

Colette didn't often let her insecurities show. She didn't like being a burden on others, especially her husband, who she knew needed her to be strong. How could she put her concerns on him when he had so many of his own?

"I'm sorry," he apologized again. "I promise, after things settle with this IPO thing, I will make a conscientious effort to devote more time for us." He turned back to the invite.

"Why don't we just fly over there on the day of the launch, instead of before? I'm sure Kim wouldn't mind; the important thing is we're there at all, isn't it?"

Colette nodded. "OK, sounds fair. But I meant what I said, Ed. This is important—an opportunity to spend time together in a more relaxing way."

*And with luck*, she added silently, *maybe the necessary break we need in order to conceive.*

"That's settled then, but first things first, OK? Once the IPO is over, everything will change, my love, I promise."

She didn't doubt his words and knew he had nothing but the best intentions. The problem was that things never got easier or settled when it came to his work. He just couldn't help himself. Being the best was both a blessing and a curse. He didn't know how to lose or to slow down.

She supposed it was why he was so successful, though. Ed always got what he wanted.

He always had to win.

## Chapter 7

Then

"Mum, what are you doing?" Colette asked, coming in the back door of her family's small terraced home in Brighton.

"What does it look like?" Miriam Turner replied in a voice raspy from chemotherapy.

It had been four years since her mum's diagnosis, though for Colette, it had felt like a lifetime.

She could only watch helplessly as cancer ravaged her mother's body, reducing her from a somewhat plump, pink-cheeked woman into the pale wraith she was now. Still, by some grace, Miriam maintained her smile despite it all.

"You're cooking? Why? Let me do it." Colette rushed to take over.

Before her illness, Miriam had worked tirelessly at the bakery she set up in the town with her husband, Emmett, and occupied what little free time she had volunteering at the church or hospital near their home.

She'd done her utmost to maintain her way of life for as long as she could, but eventually the chemotherapy and radiation treatment took its toll, her red hair turned light and thin, and eventually began to disappear.

It was then that Miriam had been forced to admit to herself that life wasn't going to be the same. The whole family had to. Eventually, she let Colette, her eldest, shave her head and handed over the responsibility for the house and business to a girl in her mid-twenties. It was a brave move for them both—until then Colette had spent most of her life in books, and was suddenly forced out into the real world.

The adjustment had been uncomfortable and had taken quite a bit of time, but at least her father was there to help her through it.

Until that changed, too.

A few months after Miriam was diagnosed, Emmett began to falter. He spent more and more time away from home, unable to watch his wife deteriorate. Everyone could see it, but no one ever thought he'd just up and leave. Less than a year after his wife's diagnosis and well into her treatment, he moved out.

And by the time another year had gone by, he'd initiated official separation proceedings.

Now, Miriam shooed her daughter away gently and smiled.

"Didn't you hear what the doctor said today?" she insisted as she continued stirring the contents of the pot she was standing over.

"Mum," Colette challenged, but her mother ignored her entirely.

"Set your stuff down. How was your walk?" she asked as

she carried on about her business while Colette stood there, dumbfounded as always at her mother's determination.

When Emmett left, Miriam had wished her former husband well and then refocused her energy on the rest of her family. Colette's younger sister, Noelle, was about to leave for university and had almost deferred her entry, but Miriam wouldn't hear of it.

By then, Colette had completed her own time at University of Essex. She missed her sister and she missed college life and her old friends.

Instead she'd stepped into the kind of responsibility she'd never imagined, especially after her father relinquished his share in the bakery, leaving the running of the business entirely up to her.

Miriam had arranged for someone to take over the bookkeeping and day-to-day administration, while Colette baked and worked on recipes with her mother's guidance, keeping things going when her mother no longer had the strength to stay involved.

Yesterday Miriam wouldn't have dared challenge her about housework, but today was different. Earlier, incredible news had been delivered by the oncologist. Her cancer was in remission.

Colette could hardly believe it. After four long years of relentless treatment, her mother had finally overcome the disease.

Even though they both could see Miriam looked much better than she had in years, Colette felt running the household was still her responsibility and one she took pride in.

But since today's news, her mother was apparently ready to dive right back into her life, starting with making dinner.

She slipped out of her jacket and hung it on a hook by the door. "It was good," she answered with a smile as she inspected the ends of her hair. "I went to the beach."

She twirled the large waves that had wound into curls at the end around her finger distractedly as she took a seat at the heavy wooden kitchen table. She couldn't remember the last time she'd just sat there and did nothing. It was weird.

"Why don't you go get changed into your pj's?" Miriam suggested as she glanced over her shoulder at her.

"Pj's? Mum, it's only dinnertime," she answered incredulously.

"Tonight you will do what I say," her mother insisted with a smile. "Go get changed, have a shower or a long bath, even, eat the lovely dinner I've prepared, then settle yourself on the couch to watch a movie and eat popcorn with me."

Miriam was often tired and went to bed early, while Colette stayed up and read or sometimes wrote in her diary. This would be the first time in years that the pair of them would do something so mundane or simple together, and the idea appealed enormously.

The water heater was working again, allowing Colette to enjoy a warm bath for a change. It had taken her several weeks to get the money together to pay for its repair, but now it was fine.

She lay in the warm water, thinking about the latest turn in events.

Remission. It was a word with a lot of power.

For years her whole life had become a routine centered entirely around Miriam's illness. Now it seemed that center was no more, and while of course she was thrilled by her mother's news, Colette couldn't deny she felt a bit lost, too.

Tears started in her eyes as she released the emotions she'd withheld for so long. Worry about her mother's illness, the pain of her father's abandonment and her sister's departure. Having no social life or companionship amid the pressure of running a business that was the sole means of her family's survival.

She'd buried those feelings deep inside and now as she lay in the warm water, they were spilling out uncontrollably.

At that moment, she needed to cry, needed to release herself, so that for the first time in what felt like forever, she could just be Colette Turner, a young woman with no clue about anything and afraid of everything.

Still, a burning question loomed in her mind.

*Now what?*

When Colette emerged, she toweled the damp from her hair and dressed in her favorite pair of Snoopy pajamas. She'd had them since she was a teenager and, though old and tatty, they were still a comfort—a reminder of a much simpler life.

When she returned to the kitchen a plate of beef stew with boiled potatoes and broccoli was waiting for her. There was even garlic bread.

"Mum, you outdid yourself," she exclaimed.

Oh, she couldn't wait. While she was a competent enough cook, her efforts weren't a patch on Miriam's, and she'd so missed her mother's cooking. Especially stew—her favorite. Her heart softened, knowing that her mother was going all out on purpose.

"It's long overdue, love," Miriam replied gently, taking a seat at the table across from her. "Besides, you deserve it. You've done so much for me over the last few years. This is just a small thing to start making it up to you."

"Oh, Mum, of course there's nothing to make up," she answered. "I just did what any daughter would do."

"And I'm so grateful, Colette," her mother responded. "I truly am. I don't know how I would have made it through this if it weren't for you."

She could feel her cheeks growing hot. She wasn't used to

being the center of attention, and even a compliment from her mother made her feel bashful. Miriam must've sensed this as she then changed the subject.

As expected, the food was delicious and Colette enjoyed every last morsel as she and her mother chatted about everything and nothing. It was incredible to see her so strong and bright, and she was hopeful that it would continue. She'd really missed being the daughter and her mother being her mum. It was nice to see the order put right again.

"Movie time, then?" she asked as she went to clear the table, but again Miriam shushed her away, insisting she'd do it.

"Movie time."

# Chapter 8

Then

That weekend, Noelle came home from uni to join in the celebrations, and there was a jovial feel in the house for the first time in years.

Again, Miriam fussed around the kitchen, this time insisting on baking fresh scones for her girls. And once more Colette floundered a little with this sudden reversal of roles, but since it made her mother happy, she was, too. She sat at the kitchen table with Noelle as the three caught up.

"Here you go." Her mum dropped a plate of warm currant scones on the table with a flourish. "Who's for a fresh cuppa?"

"Mum, there's really no need to run around after us like this." Noelle caught Colette's eye and smiled.

"Only the best for my girls." She grinned, looking at them both. "And it's about time."

"Mum, stop," Colette answered. "You're the one who deserves the best."

"And I got it," her mother replied fondly.

"The very best," Noelle agreed, nodding at Colette. "We'd all be lost without you, big sis."

She really didn't expect or want all this gratitude. And she wasn't sure how to react to it.

Then her sister and mother exchanged a conspiratorial glance. "But now we think the same effort should be spent on you."

Colette was confused. She eyed her family members suspiciously. "What do you mean?"

"Should we tell her now?" Noelle asked with a grin and Colette's brow furrowed, feeling left out all of a sudden. What was going on?

"What have you two been keeping from me?"

"What I faced was no more than others have faced before me. It was nothing special," her mother continued. "You, though, love, you were special. You stepped up when there was no one else."

"Don't..." Colette stopped her, unwilling to bring the mood down with a discussion about her father. "Anyway, I've told you loads of times, I don't want any thanks. I don't need any."

Miriam got to her feet and went to her eldest daughter. She crouched down and took Colette's hand in her own, rubbing the back of her knuckles with the pad of her thumb. "Love, the past four years *have* been difficult for us all, of course, but for you most of all."

"That's not true," Colette corrected. "You had to deal with chemo and radiation and all the worry that came with that..." She could never bring herself to say the horrible "C" word out loud.

Miriam looked at her tenderly. "I wish you'd stop interrupting me. I'm trying to tell you something but you refuse to let me."

"Sorry," she apologized as she resettled herself in her seat and gave her mother her full attention.

"Thank you," she said with a smile. "Now, where was I?"

"Difficult for everyone," Noelle insisted, her eyes watering.

"That's it. Colette, love, don't think for a second I don't appreciate the sacrifices you had to make. Like it or not, you had to move out of your comfort zone and take up the mantle in my place. You did what you had to in order for this family to be all right, and you never complained, never faltered in your determination to be there for me and do the best you could. Not once. In all the time I was going through treatment, or when I had to give the reins of the business over to you, you never failed me. You always did all you could. I'm more grateful for that than you'll ever know."

Her mother touched her cheek and Colette felt a rush of emotion. She didn't need the praise, or at least she didn't think so, but receiving it was nice all the same.

"Thanks." Her smile faltered a little when she realized Noelle in the meantime had left the room. She hoped all this hadn't made her sister uncomfortable, or worse, feel guilty for not being around for the worst of it.

But then she returned with an easy grin.

"Do you have it?" her mother asked, turning back to Noelle.

"Sorry, it was in my bag," her sister said, producing an A4 envelope. She was smiling when she handed it to their mother.

"Here you go." Miriam took the envelope and in turn handed it to Colette.

"What's this?" she asked, confused.

"Open it and see, silly," Noelle insisted.

Colette turned the envelope over in her hand, then proceeded to glide her finger under the seal to pry it open. Then she pulled the contents out and stared.

The brochures were a magnificent blaze of color and light, and the scenery they presented was simply stunning. Azure oceans and groups of pastel houses tumbling down mountainside forests filled the pages, interspersed with images of sailboats on the water and delicious-looking cuisine.

"Italy?" Colette questioned, turning to the front of the brochure.

"Yes, Italy," Noelle cheered. "You've always wanted to go there, haven't you? You studied the language after all."

"Well, yes," she replied hesitantly. "But I don't understand…"

"Open the white packet now," her mother chuckled.

Colette did as instructed, and pulled out a colorful green-and-red folder. Inside was an airline ticket with her name on it and the destination read "Naples." Her eyes grew wide and her jaw dropped in shock. It couldn't be.

Her gaze flew upward to her sister and mother, and her words came out as a whisper, so fragile that if spoken too loudly the dream she was obviously in would shatter and she'd be sent right back to reality.

"Really?"

"Yes," her mother replied tearfully, as she took both of Colette's hands in hers.

"We've made all the arrangements," Noelle added, excitement raising the tone of her voice to almost a squeal. "You leave at the end of the month. Three weeks on the Amalfi Coast in sunny Italy."

Colette couldn't speak. She shook her head. "I can't. I can't go."

"Why not?" Noelle asked, confused.

"Who will take care of Mum and the bakery? The summer season is our busiest, you know that. Who will take care of things around here?" It seemed as if her entire life had been her mother, the house and the business for so long that she couldn't imagine a day without having to attend to them. Not even a day without responsibilities.

"Love, I can take care of myself now."

"And I'll be home for the summer."

"But—"

"No buts," her sister interrupted. "You're going on this trip and that's that. I knew you'd try to find some reason not to. Didn't I tell you, Mum?"

"Yes, you did," their mother answered, a small smile on her face as she looked at each of them in turn. "Though we have to remember that for the past few years Colette's been the lady of the house here," she explained. "She's done it so much she's forgotten that she has a life of her own. And now the world is out there for her to discover."

"Mum," Colette said, realizing she was being well and truly cornered. Yes, the doctor said all was well with her illness, but it would take more than a couple of weeks until her mother was ready to take on the responsibilities of the life she'd been forced to relinquish. Was she really up to it? "Why do I have to go so soon?"

"Because Noelle will be home from university by then. And to be honest, it was quite difficult to find a place for you to stay—that part of Italy is very busy over the summer months, apparently. The travel agent said that this was basically all we could get."

Colette looked at her. So it seemed it was now or never. "Are you absolutely sure you'd be OK with this? With my leaving you on your own?"

"I'll be perfectly fine," her mother insisted. "Really."

"Hey, like I said, I'll be here, too," Noelle added with some annoyance. "Stop being such a worrier, Colette. I can take care of Mum just as well as you. Things are different now. We'll be fine, honestly. It's time you got out there and lived some of those dreams you're always banging on about."

"An escape," their mother said. "High time you had some fun back in your life and came out of your shell."

"And live it up a little, too," Noelle added with a grin. "Go and meet a nice Italian who'll show you a good time."

"Well, maybe not too much of *that*," her mother cautioned automatically, though unlike Noelle she knew well that her eldest wasn't much of a party person. "But, love, it is definitely time to see what's out there for you, don't you think?"

It sounded all too good to be true, and rather frightening, to be fair, Colette thought. She supposed she'd become quite dependent on her routine, so the idea of going somewhere outside of Brighton, let alone to a foreign country on her own, was a little overwhelming.

*Oh, come on*, a voice inside chided her. *You took care of your mum, a business, and a household. What's so scary about the Amalfi Coast?*

She looked again at the brochures and the ticket with her name on it. Italy had always been such a dream, and like Noelle said, she'd studied Language and International Relations in college, so she did already speak quite a bit of the language. She could view this as a chance for some practical application of her skills. A chance to try new things, meet new people and the opportunity to push herself out of her comfort zone and widen her worldview.

*You need this.*

Colette had worn the badge of responsibility like a true soldier, never faltering or complaining, but she was tired. She was weary of the routine, of having to always say no to social invitations or a chance to just be flighty or careless. For feeling as if her life was on hold with a terrible end awaiting her. The thought that her mother might die had been a shadow that always loomed in the back of her mind, clouding her decisions. Now that cloud was lifted. She could breathe again.

*An escape…*

"All right," she decided, smiling. "I'll do it."

## Chapter 9

Then

There was an incessant drilling sound that was annoying Annie O'Doherty to no end. It was Saturday morning. What the hell…?

"Oh, feck off!" She attempted to toss an errant pillow in the direction of the noise but when she turned over in the bed to grab one, she was met with an unexpected obstruction.

There, sleeping soundly beside her, was someone—a man— she didn't recognize.

Annie felt familiar discomfort rise up in her stomach as she tried to remember the previous night's events.

Damn. She'd done it again, the thing she'd sworn time and time again not to: come home with some random stranger.

She raised her head slightly, trying to avoid any sudden

movements that would alert Prince Charming to her presence, or indeed make her blinding headache even worse.

Now she had to figure out the best way to get this fella out of her flat without complication. This *was* her flat, yes?

She squinted around suspiciously at the messy room, discarded clothes scattered everywhere—Annie was more a floor-drobe than a wardrobe person—makeup littered all over the dressing table, and a hairdryer and straightening tongs hanging precariously from the radiator.

She'd remembered to turn the tongs off, which was good; it meant that she must have been sober before she went out.

And yep, this was definitely her room. Thank God for small mercies.

Annie raised the sheets a little to see she was wearing her pajamas, which was another good sign—she hoped. Gingerly, she shimmied her way off the bed, grabbed her dressing gown and threw it on.

She always did this to herself. She'd have a bad week at work, or a fight with her mam, and then she'd go on a binge.

Eileen called her a slut, floozy or whatever else her angry, inebriated self felt like. Theirs was a hugely dysfunctional relationship, she knew, but it was the only consistent one Annie had ever had. She could just imagine what her mam would have to say about this.

"Nothing else for it," she murmured, deciding to bite the bullet and wake up Prince Charming. "Hey, sunshine, time to get up!"

The words sent her bedfellow scrambling to his feet and it seemed to take him a while to realize he wasn't under attack.

"What the hell?"

"Time for you to get going," Annie muttered, unable to meet his eyes. She really had no idea who he was but she figured she must have hooked up with him in the late bar last night. "I've things to get on with and I need you to leave."

It was her day off, Annie recalled (hence the night out in the Dublin hotspots), so she didn't have anything pressing to do really, she just wanted him out.

The guy scratched his jaw and took a deep breath before flopping back down onto her bed.

"Another half hour, maybe? I'm wrecked," he protested, as he puffed up her pillow and stuffed it under his head, closing his eyes once more.

"Hey! I said I need you to leave, so off you go." Annie poked at his exposed leg. He was wearing boxers, another cause for relief in her books. He didn't seem her type at all either; he was bone-skinny with a bit of a culchie accent, so she had no idea how or why he'd ended up here.

But did she even have a type these days?

Still, if this gobshite thought he could grab a lie-in at her expense, he was sadly mistaken. She'd throw him out on his arse herself if he didn't skedaddle on his own, pronto.

Her persistence got his attention and he forced his eyes open once more.

"Hey, why don't you get back in and we can finish what we started last night?" he said suggestively, and Annie's hackles rose even more.

"Are you deaf? Get the feck out!" She grabbed the end of the duvet and yanked it off him. "I mean it." Then, grabbing his clothes, she marched across to the door of her flat (which didn't take long as it was a tiny studio) and flung it open, launching his stuff through. "Don't let it hit you on the way out."

Her unexpected guest looked completely bewildered. "What the hell? Why are you being so weird? You asked *me* back, remember? You were all over me."

Annie didn't remember—that was the problem—but she wasn't about to tell him that. "Look, I'm sorry but I told you already that I've got stuff to do and you're getting in the way. So please just go," she insisted.

She watched as her guest jumped up again and stepped out into the hallway, scrambling for his clothes. He pulled his shirt over his head, sticking his arms into the sleeves in one smooth movement, then eyed her angrily from the doorway.

"You're something else, you know."

"I know," she murmured airily, as she closed the door behind him, her heart racing a thousand beats a minute. She'd done a pretty good job convincing him of her bravado, but all the while she'd been terrified. A strange man in her bed and in her flat. It wouldn't be the first time things had gone awry.

"That's it. No more getting pissed out of your head, Annie… No more."

She walked to her bed and looked at the sheets with scorn, before yanking them off. She'd be doing a wash today for sure. Once all the bedding was off, she returned to the bare mattress and flopped down on the edge of it.

Annie O'Doherty was never supposed to live, but she had. Abandoned in the toilets at Connolly train station in the center of Dublin almost thirty years ago, she'd barely been breathing when she was found by a curious Irish Rail cleaner, who heard a noise from inside the ladies. There he found an infant, scarcely a few hours old, and had called for an ambulance.

Even before she had a name, Annie was making headlines for all the wrong reasons.

Placed into the Irish foster system from the start, she eventually found herself part of a family. Robert O'Doherty, her foster father, had doted on her. He was the reason she'd been chosen by them—a real-life orphan Annie.

He always said he saw something in her eyes, a spark, which

told him she was the right child for him and his wife, Eileen. They'd formally adopted her when she was five, and over the following twelve years she had the most amazing life she could imagine. They didn't have much money, just enough to get by, but after Robert suffered a heart attack and died, life was upended.

That's when Eileen started drinking and Annie had no choice but to rely on herself. Life had steadily declined after that. The tongue-lashings, accusations of theft, and even the added bonus of being accused of trying to seduce Eileen's boyfriends. As if she would stoop so low.

Now she sat on her bed thinking about just how badly her life sucked. She was thirty-two years old, working at a low-budget hairdressing salon for a woman who didn't know a perm from a curl, paying an exorbitant rent for her tiny Dublin shoebox, and nothing or no one stable in her life whatsoever.

Most of the friends she had during her teens were by now settled with families of their own, while Annie embarked on a string of disastrous hookups with lads who were only after the craic. That had suited her down to the ground all throughout her twenties, but now it was getting old—as was Annie.

These days she mostly went out on the town with some of her hot young coworkers from the salon, and was already starting to feel (and no doubt look) like the desperate old one.

Feeling a fresh wave of hangover-inspired exhaustion, Annie fell back on the bed and lay atop the exposed mattress. She stared at the cracks in the yellowed ceiling as she tried not to cry. She was frustrated and disillusioned.

Life was supposed to improve the older you got, wasn't it? Life was supposed to be a series of ups and downs. So when was her up coming? When was it her turn to have something good finally come her way?

Tears stung her eyes and she didn't try to stop them. It

wasn't every day that Annie allowed herself to feel her emotions. Pretending she didn't have any seemed to work best for her over the years, at least for a while, until the flood rose too high, smashed the dam and, like now, she had to release it.

She hated her life. She hated this dingy kip of a flat. She hated her job, her mother, this stupid city.

She hated everything.

"No more," she said firmly as she balled her fists at her sides. "No more. After today, you're making a change. Things are going to be better. You're going to make them better."

But even as she said the words, Annie knew she was kidding herself. She'd tried that mantra before.

And still, nothing ever changed.

# Chapter 10

## Then

"Good morning, Betty," Annie sang, as her first salon client of the day took a seat in the chair in front of her. "What'll it be today?" she asked as she danced about, getting the woman ready for her treatment.

She wrapped and secured an apron around her neck and draped a towel over that, clipping it in place.

"You're in great form today. Is it a fella who's responsible?" the older woman teased as her eyes followed Annie's every move.

Betty was one of her regulars. She always came for the same thing—a wash and set—despite Annie's angling to get her to try something new. She never did. Most of the women who came here were the same.

"No," she replied, rolling her eyes good-naturedly. "Why must it be a fella? Why can't we just be happy all on our own?"

Betty guffawed. "Sure, isn't that the only reason God created Adam?"

Annie rolled her eyes as she chuckled. "Maybe *you* can't be happy without a man, Betty Corcoran, but I certainly can." She looked at her client in the mirror as she began to run her fingers through her hair. "I make myself happy."

Betty sniggered.

"Don't mind that one," her boss, Rose, put in. "She's Not-So-Little Miss Sunshine these days," she said, taking a blatant aim at Annie's muffin-top—another thing she'd been meaning to fix by taking long walks in the evening after work. But she was always too tired.

The salon owner teased the hair of the blonde in front of her. Rose was lost in a time warp, still back in the eighties, where people liked their hair puffed up to the size of a football helmet. And the explanation for why all of the salon's clients were in their forties or older, Annie knew; no one else would be interested in getting their hair done by her.

"At least sun is better than rain," she quipped back at her boss. "So what color do you want?" she asked, turning her attention to Betty. "Same as last time?"

"I'm thinking something spicy for a change," she answered with a wicked grin.

Annie raised an eyebrow. "Spicy?"

Betty smirked. "I'm meeting my fancy man tonight," she boasted. "I want to look my best."

"In that case," she answered, "I think you'd look amazing with a richer burgundy shade. I can darken your eyebrows a little, too," Annie added as she turned toward her mixing station and began pulling colors from the cupboard.

People thought just a tube of solid hair dye could give you the right look, but that wasn't true. You needed the right mix to give the highlights and low tones. She grabbed a fire-engine red, a dark blonde, and a chestnut, with the addition of a drop of dark brown to make a tone that would be uniquely Betty. That was what Annie did.

She didn't "do" cookie-cutter clients. She made sure everyone who stepped away from her station was spectacular in their own right. She picked up the dyes, mixing them quickly in a fluorescent pink bowl with her medium brush.

"So where did you find this fancy man then?" she asked as she began applying dye to Betty's roots, starting at the back.

"At Tesco," she replied. "He was trying to pick the right peppers and I helped him find the best one."

Rose laughed. "Passion over peppers. Spicy indeed."

"I think we could all use a little of that," Annie said dreamily.

"Even you with your Ridey Rabbit?" Betty joked as she gave Annie a look in the mirror.

"Hey, that's not what I meant by making myself happy! And I never said I didn't want a fella either. I'm just tired of the eejits you get around here. I want someone real. Someone who gets me," Annie explained.

"Hear, hear," Felicity Finch piped up. She was one of Rose's oldest regulars (and Annie's favorite client) and was sitting in the corner waiting area reading a magazine. She folded the periodical and rested it on her knee. "Good for you, Annie. It's about time your generation realized there's more to life than mindless craic. Eventually, you need to get serious."

"Listen to you," Rose joked. "You sound like a schoolteacher, Felicity."

"No, I sound like wisdom," she replied. "I lived the wild life myself, Annie, but it gets boring after a while. I know what it's like. And I know the repercussions."

Annie's gaze shifted toward her. While her personality was typically lighthearted, the older woman's expression was now deadly serious. There was a look in her eyes that Annie could only describe as regret.

"I ran around like there was no tomorrow," Felicity continued, and Annie was discomfited by the fact that she seemed to be looking her right in the eye. "I loved men, and boy did they love me. I was practically the town bike—"

"Really, now…" Rose interrupted, but Felicity smiled, continuing her story as if she hadn't been interrupted.

"I don't mind. I had loads of men running after me, and I thought it was great. Mad craic altogether. Then I stopped being twenty and became thirty, and still I thought I could live the same life. Then thirty became forty," she explained. "And I started waking up with lads I didn't remember, in places that weren't my own. Then one day I was on the far side of forty-five and there was no one. All the men were settled and married. My friends had moved on and had families, whereas I had just me."

A hollow feeling began to fill Annie's stomach as she listened to a story that sounded way too familiar. It was as if the older woman could see right into her soul. She didn't want to be Felicity. She wanted a family, preferably while she was young enough to enjoy it. But there was no sign of that anywhere on the horizon just now.

It took her a moment to realize that her hand had stopped its work and was hovering just above Betty's head.

Everyone was looking at Felicity, surprised. No one had expected that story. She was a frequent customer but not one who routinely chitchatted about personal stuff like some of the others. Today she'd revealed more than any of them ever had.

Now Felicity's gaze met Annie's full-on and there was no mistaking the warning in them.

"Decide what you want and go for it, Annie. Don't think that tomorrow will always be there. You won't always be thirty, or even forty. One day, the way you lived in your younger years will catch up with you."

Annie got it. She understood. She already felt as if she'd lived as long as some of the women who came to the salon. She was tired.

Tired of meaninglessness, empty encounters, having no one she could call on to be there. She looked at Felicity, with her sad eyes, gray hair and wrinkled brow. Would she look like that in thirty years' time? Would she be telling someone else a similar cautionary tale in years to come?

Not if she could help it.

"Well, it just got very serious in here," Rose joked, breaking the stillness. Everyone laughed. Everyone but Annie.

Felicity's story had hit home.

That night, as she walked home, Annie's mind was racing while her body was weary. She'd seen a record number of clients that day, including several last-minute emergencies that she simply couldn't refuse. Why did people try to do their own hair when they'd never done it before?

She flopped onto her bed and once again stared up at the ceiling as she kicked her shoes off. Annie worked hard; she always did. She had to.

She was seventeen when she moved out and got her own place. Life with her mother had become unbearable, and after one of Eileen's boyfriends made a pass at her, she knew that it was time to get out of there.

Her mother hadn't protested and Annie believed she was happy to see her go. In fact, she was sure of it. She'd walked out the door and moved into a friend's place for a while, then bounced from one couch to another until she finished secondary school, by which time she was already helping out Rose. Fifteen years later she was now her longest-serving (and oldest) staff member.

Annie rolled onto her side. Fifteen years. In one respect, it was such a short time; in another, it was forever.

She was still young, but in those years she'd felt like she'd lived a thousand lives. She'd been wilder than most. Lack of parental supervision and the misguided belief that she was living the high life had seen her make mistake after mistake. She gave a hollow laugh at her silliness. Did she really think that being parentless had served her well? At the time she had. Now she knew better.

Sleep crept up on her. Annie didn't even realize when she'd started to drift off, but the sound of her mobile phone ringing had awakened her.

"What now…" she whined as she forced herself off the bed. She shuffled toward her coat pocket and took the phone out, answering grumpily. "Hello?"

"Hello, Annie." The voice on the other end was the last she'd expected to hear.

"Felicity? How did you get my number?"

Her mind was whirring like an out-of-control mechanism as she listened to the older woman speak.

"Annie, I've been keeping an eye on you over the years and you have a wonderful heart. I see a lot of myself in you—the younger me, I mean—and like I said in the salon, it's all too easy to stray off-path when you're young and foolish." She cleared her throat. "But I suspect you've already realized that yourself."

Annie was confused. "I'm not sure what you mean…"

"I can't say too much at the moment, and it's hard to explain, but, love, I'd like to do something for you. Something small as a thank-you for being so good to me over the years."

"For me?" Annie asked skeptically when the other woman finished her spiel. This was weird. "You don't have to do anything for me, Felicity. Really, I'm doing grand." She wasn't about to let on about her struggles.

"Please. Don't argue. Just…keep an eye out for something in the post from me soon. Can you let me know your address?"

Annie's brow furrowed afresh. "Felicity, no, I appreciate you thinking of me, but really, I don't need anything…"

Felicity was having none of it, insisting she pass on her address or she'd just get it from Rose at the salon anyway. Indeed, she seemed just as stubborn as Annie was.

"OK," she finally conceded, "but you really don't have to do this."

"I know that. But promise me this: just accept it, OK? For me."

Reluctantly agreeing, Annie said goodbye to Felicity, put down the phone and once again curled up in her bed. What was the woman on about?

*Just accept it?*

Accept what?

Annie rolled onto her back, her eyes staring up at the ceiling, now wide awake, her thoughts whirring.

"What are you up to, Felicity?"

*Chapter 11*

Now

The drive back from the restaurant in Sorrento had been a silent one. Kim knew Antonio wanted her to confide more in him but she couldn't.

She and Gabriel weren't him and Emilia. There were some major differences in their relationship. Kim idolized the older woman, who might soon no longer even remember her.

Right from the start, Emilia had inspired and encouraged her. She had facilitated everything that Kim had achieved with The Sweet Life, had pushed her out of her comfort zone, and encouraged her to break away from the hold her parents had on her.

After all these years, Kim wished she could thank whatever god was smiling on her the day she'd met her and Antonio. His wife was someone Kim admired and adored, but definitely not one she could compare with.

Emilia was the best of women.

"Are you going to be grumpy for the rest of the day? If so, I might as well fix us both a drink." Antonio's voice again interrupted her musings.

They were back at the villa now, sitting at a patio table outside on the terrace, next to the adjoining lawn that was to be the center's yoga area.

"I don't think my being grumpy is the reason you want a drink," Kim drawled, briefly checking her phone.

"Perhaps, but it is the reason I'm going to use."

Still his words brought a smile to her face. The Italian knew the right things to say at just the right time. He had for as long as she'd known him.

Having checked her email, she scrolled idly through her social media, noting with some satisfaction that her latest post—a pretty and artistic shot she'd taken earlier of the villa's lemon groves and the azure waters of the bay as a backdrop—had already racked up lots of activity.

She read a little way through some of the comments, before one in particular stopped her in her tracks.

The Sweet Life? That's a joke, considering. Don't you mean The FAKE Life?

Kim frowned.

Since the villa project had ramped up, lately she seemed to be getting some negative and downright nasty comments from people (although possibly even the same person using different identities, as online trolls often did).

Par for the course with social media, she knew, especially for an account with a following in the hundreds of thousands, and while Kim didn't usually pay too much attention, she didn't like the sound of this one.

*The Fake Life…*

It was unsettling, as it suggested something more sinister—personal, even—and because, in truth, it tapped into Kim's own deeply held insecurities.

"Are you OK, *bella*?" Antonio asked, frowning as he came back out with a decanter of rich amber that he'd stolen from the villa's freshly stocked kitchen.

"I'm…fine."

He studied her face and then his brows furrowed slightly as he noticed her faraway expression. He set the whiskey down on the patio table.

"OK, maybe this is something that should be spirit-free," he decided. He lowered himself onto the seat beside her, his knees pointed toward her. "Tell me what's going on."

Kim exhaled and looked out over the water. She wasn't going to tell Antonio about the comments; not until she could get a proper handle on it all herself.

Not to mention that he didn't really *get* social media, routinely joking that it was "not of his generation."

"You asked me earlier about Gabriel…" she began, though the strain to get the words out was considerable.

Antonio didn't interrupt. He sat quietly, his expression still, as he allowed her the time and comfort to say what she needed to.

"When I met Gabe, I really thought I'd hit the jackpot, that everything I'd ever dreamed about was actually happening. A kind, accomplished, wonderful man wanted me by his side and it had nothing to do with my parents. It was a bit surreal. He was so good to me, genuinely kind and caring. He understood my passion for what you, Emilia, and I had started. Eventually, he became my best friend." Kim could feel sadness start to rise up as she spoke and her eyes began to sting.

"You are speaking in the past tense, *bella*. Did that change? Did he stop being good to you?" Antonio queried hesitantly, as he placed a comforting hand on top of hers.

"No," Kim answered. "The very opposite, actually. Once we were married, he remained all those things and more. My biggest champion and supporter. I was so happy and felt I could take on the world with him at my side. We had everything, the rest of our lives to look forward to. Then I got pregnant."

She noted how her words affected Antonio. He shifted slightly, a disapproving expression passing over his face. She knew his view on children. He adored them, believed them a gift from God, something to cherish. Kim didn't get that line of thinking. Her parents obviously hadn't either.

"When I found out I was going to have a baby, I was scared out of my wits. I didn't know how to be a parent. I didn't even know where to start. Having a child had never been a consideration for me. Everything with the business was going so well and I was happier than I'd ever been in my life. Then there was this baby in the mix and I was supposed to be over the moon about it. Everyone else was. Gabriel was beside himself with joy." She shook her head as her eyes glassed over at the memory.

"Kim—" Antonio began but she stopped him.

"I know what you're going to say, but please hear me out," she pleaded. "I didn't really want the baby."

The words were horrible to say out loud, but nonetheless true. Kim hadn't wanted her own child. She felt terrible for it, but it didn't change what was. She might not have wanted Lily, but not having her wasn't an option either. Gabriel would never have forgiven her (nor could she have forgiven herself), and he assured her every day that she would be a great mother. Her fears would pass and she would see that she could do it.

But it hadn't happened.

"I carried Lily for all those months and every day I hoped to feel the excitement and happiness everyone said I would, but I didn't. The closer I got to her birth, the more scared I became. When she finally arrived, it was almost a confirmation that I shouldn't be a mother. She refused to nurse and cried whenever I picked her up. It was almost as if she didn't want me either." Kim took a deep breath as emotion began to overwhelm her. "It's like she knew."

"It is all right. Let it out." Antonio spoke gently, like a father to his child.

"She had colic. She'd cry and cry but nothing I did helped. Only Gabriel could get her to stop. He'd hold her in a special way and she'd just go quiet and fall asleep. It never worked for me, no matter how many times I tried. Eventually, I stopped trying and just left him to it."

"You let him take over caring for her because you felt you couldn't, and he would be better?"

Kim nodded solemnly.

"Babies sometimes reject breastfeeding. It is nothing strange and it certainly isn't personal," Antonio assured her.

"It felt like it."

"I can't imagine. I can, however, imagine a colicky child. I had one myself. Nothing worked. Nothing Emilia or I did worked, but we got past that. It wasn't us, it wasn't the baby. It was just a simple condition that Giuseppe got over, and I am sure Lily got over, too."

"After a while," Kim said with a sniffle.

"Did you try with her after that?" he asked gently.

"Not really," she replied with a shake of her head. "Things started getting even better with work, the collaboration offers were flying in, and Gabriel seemed happy to do it all, so I let him. I let him be mother and father to her. She doesn't need me, even now."

The soothing strokes on her back stopped as firm hands gripped her shoulders and Antonio turned her to face him. "Now that is nonsense. I have never heard a more foolish remark. Your daughter needs you, Kim. Your husband needs you. You can't just run away again and turn to work to escape what doesn't go according to plan in your life."

"But..."

He raised a finger to silence her. "No. Maybe I can understand that you didn't have an example to follow, and you felt lost and incapable because of it, but the Kim I know is not a quitter. Six years ago she did whatever she could to free herself of her parents' hold and established a thriving business all on her own."

"Not exactly. I had a lot of help," she interjected.

"I did very little," Antonio responded. "And Emilia simply opened your eyes to the potential of what you already had inside you. Yes, she might have got you some introductions in the beginning, but it was you who had your wonderful ideas and brought them to life in the first place. We had no part in that."

"I wouldn't say that..."

"I would. I would also say that you can't let your fears keep you from your happiness. Follow your own advice: take a chance. If you win, you will be happy; if you lose, you will be wise."

"Well, something like that," Kim replied with a smile, as he lobbed one of her very own quotes at her.

"You get my meaning," he continued. "You need to be that person now. It can't only be for some time but all of the time, or else you will never have the happiness you want to help others achieve. You'll forever be the person who came here to Italy as a runaway. Yes, the business is a great success and will continue to be so, but it will be hollow. I assure you. Don't fall into the trap of letting work achievements distract you from the truth. It's just somewhere to bury your head in the sand and hide from what frightens or challenges you."

"But I truly don't know how to be the mother Lily needs. I'm not sure I even know how to be the wife Gabe needs. I'm never there."

"Hush," Antonio silenced her. "Have you not been listening to a word I said? You can do this, Kim. But first you must be honest, not only with Gabriel, but yourself. Maybe start by admitting to him how you feel. I'm sure he'll understand."

Panic stabbed her heart the moment the words left her mentor's lips. "I can't tell Gabriel what I just told you—about Lily. He'd hate me. *I* hate me."

Antonio scoffed. "Gabriel loves you. Very much. He won't leave you, if that's what's bothering you. He's one of the most honest and honorable men that I have ever known. He is also no fool. I expect he knows a lot about what you've been keeping hidden from him, and is waiting for you to come to him when you're ready."

"Do you think?" Kim replied as a small glimmer of hope ignited in her chest. The fear of Gabriel leaving was one she hadn't had the courage to admit, but Antonio, as ever, had got to the bottom of her fears anyway.

"I think you won't know for sure until you talk to your husband. I can say all the right things in this situation, but it isn't my assurance you need."

"You're so perceptive it's annoying," Kim said with a smile as she rubbed the errant tears from her cheeks. Despite her efforts, they'd defied her.

"When Gabriel arrives, do you have plans to talk to him about this?"

"Not particularly," she admitted. "There's so much else going on right now…"

"I think it would be the perfect opportunity for you to talk. The publicity is in place and the renovations are complete—all's that left now is the party to celebrate Villa Dolce Vita's introduction to the world. Everything is ready, Kim. And I can keep any last-minute things covered while you have some important time together with your family."

Everything he was saying sounded good, but there was still so much for her to consider before her husband and daughter joined her here.

What if Antonio was right? But what if he was *wrong*? Gabriel was the best thing she'd ever had in her life and Kim was terrified of losing him.

Then Antonio patted his knees and sighed. "I'd better go. I have another meeting before I fly back to Milan this evening. We will talk again?"

"Sure. Please give Emilia my best. And tell her I can't wait to see her at the party."

She stood and walked Antonio out as far as the door of the courtyard. He hugged her one last time before heading back to his car.

"As you Americans say, you got this. And of course, honesty has always been your finest trait."

Kim looked up at the glorious blue sky and closed her eyes. If only he knew.

# Chapter 12

Then

Annie still couldn't believe it. It was so surreal that anything like this should ever happen to her.

She looked down over the crystal-clear water and rocky promontories as they flew overhead.

It was the first time she'd been on an airplane and, though excited, she found herself equally nervous. She tried to keep her eyes from looking down but there was a certain morbid curiosity to it. Besides, she had a window seat, so looking down was practically inevitable.

Still, her mind kept going to the reason she was here in the first place, and to the person who had made this all possible.

Felicity Finch was dead. She died just weeks after her chat with Annie, but she only found out a few weeks after that when a solicitor arrived at the salon looking for her. He stood out immediately.

Six feet tall with a pasty complexion and shiny bald head, Rose's place had never seen anyone like Patrick Campbell. No one knew who the man was or what he wanted, and the moment he asked for Annie she almost ran out the door. Had her mother sent him? Was he there to serve her with some trumped-up accusation of theft or worse?

The envelope he gave her was still in her handbag, along with Felicity's letter:

Dear Annie,

I hope the words we shared did something for you. I hope that you find the true way for yourself and not choose a path that will lead to pain and hurt. When I heard you talk in the salon all those times about what you really wanted from life, I knew I had to help you reach your goal. I had to do for you what no one ever did for me. Give you a chance.

I hope you can forgive me, but if you don't it won't really matter because by the time you read this I will already be gone, but I asked Rose all about your past. I was saddened to know that our paths were more similar than I imagined.

I, too, am a product of social services, but unlike you I fell into the hands of people who couldn't love me or treat me the way I wanted. I let that decide my future. I let their harsh words and the hurt from them blind me and make me into someone to be ashamed of. Someone whose lifestyle was their end. I don't want that to be you.

I know you have dreams, not to mention talent, too. You've always worked your magic on me and I've also seen the women who leave Rose's and how happy they look. You're being held back there. I know how difficult it is for someone of your age and background to make a move forward when there's so much against you. It was very difficult for me, and I went in all the wrong directions for help. I don't want you to do the same. That's why you'll find in this envelope the information on a small allowance fund I've set up for you. It will be under the guidance of my solicitor, and he will oversee the payments to you to help you get started with a salon of your own. You'll also find a ticket to my absolute favorite place on Earth and stay at a place owned by one of my dearest friends for as long as you like.

It's a magical part of the world with transformative powers.

I've also included some fun money. You need a break before you start your brand-new venture and, I hope, brand-new life. I'm sorry I won't be there to see your transformation, but I'm pretty sure you'll do me proud.

I wish you all the best in your future, Annie. I hope you'll remember me, and maybe one day do something good for someone else who might need it.

In the meantime, enjoy La Dolce Vita.

Felicity

Annie's eyes misted afresh as she read the words the older woman had written. How had someone who barely knew her, really, seen something in her that no one else did? She took a chance on her, a chance that no one in Annie's life had ever taken before, except her dad. Yet Felicity had done even more—she'd invested in her.

"You won't regret it," she whispered as she looked down at the coast of Italy. "I promise you won't."

"Did you say something?" The lady seated next to Annie gave her a strange look. She was in her late sixties, with mostly gray hair and small framed glasses. She wasn't smiling. In fact,

Annie had been sure up until the moment she spoke that she was sleeping.

She blushed. "Sorry, I was talking to myself."

"Maybe next time speak more softly," the woman muttered. "I was trying to sleep."

"Sorry," she repeated with a little grin, as she slouched down in her seat and turned her gaze back to the window.

She wondered what Italy would be like. She had never been on a foreign holiday before; hell, she had barely traveled outside of Dublin.

How would she get on in this strange new place?

# Chapter 13

Then

By the time they landed at Naples airport Annie was completely lost.

She didn't speak a word of Italian, and her head was completely muddled by the fast-moving crowds and general hubbub, but thanks to the English exit signs she was able to find her way to the baggage claim and out of Arrivals.

"You want a taxi?" a lightly accented voice called out.

"Yes. I need to get to a place called Villa Dolce Vita." She read out the address written on a piece of paper. "Do you know it?" she asked hopefully.

"Positano?" the man repeated. "But of course. It is a long journey, though."

Annie smiled as she said words she'd never before had the privilege of uttering: "I can pay."

The driver was dangerously fearless, she was sure of it. She'd never seen anyone weave in and out of traffic at such a pace, and for most of the drive—as he wound along roads that were so narrow and high she was certain they would drop off the side and go hurtling to the ground on every turn—her heart was in her mouth.

She was relieved and elated when they finally arrived at the villa and she could see the back of him. Though he was nice, in fairness. He had great English and didn't seem to bat an eyelid at her nonexistent Italian.

She supposed they were well used to tourists in these parts and it made her feel immediately at ease. Until they'd hit the road, that was.

The accommodation Felicity had chosen was surprisingly underwhelming. Granted, many of the houses around here looked fairly ancient and crumbling, but huddled closely on top of one another—as if fighting for space all the way down the mountain to the bejeweled sea—they looked like a pile of colorful kids' blocks with their pastel colors and terra-cotta roofs. The effect was startling.

The house looked to be situated just on the edge of a big town, and Annie could see lots of blue-and-white beach brollies and sun loungers laid out on the beach a little further along the coast, beneath all the houses and buildings, which was where the main action must be.

Annie supposed the crumbling buildings thing was the kind of old-world Italian charm that tourists seemed to love.

For her part, she couldn't wait to hit the beach and then visit some of the local watering holes—though from her vantage point, as she stood beneath the shade of a lemon tree and stared down at the water below, it was going to be one hell of a climb down to get there.

When she went into the house, dragging her suitcase behind her, a smiling woman introduced herself as Valentina. Annie immediately wondered if this was the good friend and villa owner Felicity had mentioned, but in broken English the woman told her that no, she was just there to do some cleaning and the occasional meet and greet.

While outside looked gorgeous with all the flowers and the trees and the amazing view, inside the place was a bit of a dive, to be honest—very old, though in fairness spotlessly clean, thanks to Valentina, Annie guessed.

And when the Italian woman led her to a dark, poky bedroom upstairs that was about a quarter of the size of her flat back home, she was a bit disappointed.

She'd had visions of cocktails out on the balcony over that lovely sea view, but at least it was nice and cool in there, and so small she knew she wouldn't have to share her room with anyone, which was a major plus.

There were a few other people already staying there; a German couple on their way out had greeted her politely on arrival, and Valentina introduced her to a small group of French backpackers eating lunch in the kitchen area, where there were so many mismatched tiles and creaky-looking pieces of furniture that Annie had to laugh.

Again, the language barrier was a slight problem but she got the sense that everyone pretty much did their own thing in places like this. The students did give her a helpful heads-up on a couple of hotspots in the town, though, which she planned on checking out later.

She wasn't going to waste too much time on pleasantries or making friends. Not when the sun was still high in the sky and the little pool outside looked so inviting.

Thanking Valentina for her impromptu tour, she trudged her suitcase up an ancient wooden staircase to the room.

Unpacking wouldn't take long; the only thing she needed

just now was her swimsuit and she'd put that in her carry-on luggage, just in case. She'd heard enough stories about lost luggage and she wasn't about to find herself in a foreign country with nothing.

The water in the pool was cool but a welcome relief from the afternoon heat, as she dived straight in and swam from one end to the other. It wasn't much of a length, just a small rectangle on the edge of the terrace overlooking the bay, but boy was it bliss.

She lingered by the edge now, looking through the chipped wrought iron railings dripping with pretty pink flowers, out over the side to the colorful buildings tumbling down from the green of the mountains to the water below.

"OK, I could get used to this," Annie mused happily as she ducked back under the water and swam across to the other side.

By evening she was ravenous, and finding some bits and pieces in the fridge, courtesy of the French students, who'd told her to help herself (or at least she hoped that's what they meant) since they were leaving the next day, Annie cobbled together a light meal of pasta and tomato sauce with crusty bread.

After that, she got ready to head out on the town, choosing a strapless black dress that showed off her freshly spray-tanned skin, though she had a nice little sun-kissed glow from the pool earlier, which made it look really natural.

She opted not to bother straightening her hair for a change; in this heat it was probably a waste of time and would end up frizzing anyway, so instead she just tied it up in a loose bun and let a few black tendrils frame her face.

Same for makeup, which would also surely melt off in the humidity, so she kept it basic, with just a smear of bright red lipstick to finish the look.

*There.* Annie admired herself in the mirror. The dress lifted her boobs and really made the most of her curves, and putting on a pair of silver sandals, she felt pretty confident that she could hold her own with any Italian glamour-puss.

She wasn't sure how those heels would hold up for the long walk back up the hill, but first things first. She couldn't wait to find out what the social life in this place was like. It was a popular holiday resort so she guessed it would be hopping.

Annie wasn't sure what she was expecting when she walked into Music on the Rocks—the late-night bar actually cut into a cave the students had told her about—but what greeted her was a scene like so many she'd encountered back home.

A room full of people, pulsing music, a neon bar and crowds of happy revelers. Her dress clung to her body in all the right places as she shimmied her way around the dance floor toward the bar, the short hem brushing sexily along her thighs to the beat.

She saw him the moment she reached the bar.

Tall with mussed-up dark blond hair and green eyes, the color of the sea. His cheeky smile was like sunshine the moment their eyes met.

Annie tried to pretend she hadn't noticed him, but the moment her eyes drifted in his direction, there was the ocean looking straight back at her.

His eyes were like deep pools that she wanted to dive right into. He didn't look Italian and seemed to be with a large group of lads, so she wondered if he was a tourist, too.

"Nope," she scolded herself, turning away with a bottle of water for the dance floor. "Not going there."

She'd decided not to drink tonight; not to drink too much while here at all, really. She didn't want to end up doing the same in Italy as she'd been doing back home, getting trashed and ending up with strangers.

She was on her own in an unfamiliar country after all, so she needed to keep her wits about her.

Annie loved to dance. It was an urge that started at her hips and took over her entire body. She couldn't help it. It was the most liberating thing you could do, at least in her mind, and it was something she indulged in whenever she could.

One moment she was on her own, giving it socks on the dance floor, and the next she could feel a presence behind her. Annie turned to find the guy from the bar, his body dangerously close to her own.

"Mind if I join you?" he asked in perfect English.

She turned to him with a grin. "Ah, you are a tourist."

"I wasn't sure if you were," he admitted with a small chuckle. "I'm glad because I'm absolute crap at Italian. I was just taking a chance."

He was *verrrry* cute.

"Glad you did," Annie replied flirtatiously as she turned her back to him and continued to dance. His hands reached her hips then as he joined in and Annie found herself having to repress the urge to lean into him.

*Take your time, girl. Take your time.*

The music played on and they continued to dance, chatting intermittently as they did. He was a Brit and he and his mates had just arrived the day before. This was also his first night out on the town.

Annie felt a slight thrill when she told him she was traveling alone and not on some girlie holiday; it made her feel sophisticated and mysterious—someone who did her own thing and controlled her own destiny.

Which of course she was now, thanks to Felicity Finch.

She wasn't particularly interested in pointless chitchat, though, not when there was dancing to be had instead.

A song she really loved came on, and she twirled in his arms, losing herself in the thrill and romance of the electrifying music and being in a foreign country, dancing with a handsome stranger.

"What's your name?" he asked eventually.

"Annie," she shouted above the music, as one of his friends appeared alongside him.

"Harry, we're moving on, mate. You coming?"

She smiled. Harry suited him. And now that she thought of it, he even looked a little bit like his princely namesake in England.

He looked at her, seemingly torn, but Annie just waggled her fingers and wandered away. "See you again, maybe."

She was pretty certain she would.

# Chapter 14

Then

"Yes, I will take you to Villa Dolce Vita. But since you are hungry, maybe first I take you to the best restaurant in Positano?" offered the taxi driver Colette found at the Sorrento train station. "If you are hungry, trust Jacopo—I know the best places."

He had a huge gap between his front teeth and his mustache covered half his upper lip as he smiled, yet it wasn't Jacopo's appearance that disarmed her. It was his effusive demeanor. Taxi drivers didn't smile at you in England. They barely turned around to look at you. You were just a fare and they were just a means of transport. Seemed Italians saw things differently.

And Colette was indeed famished. The train journey from Naples had taken longer than she'd anticipated and while she was rapt by the magnificent winding coastal view as they traveled, she wished she'd thought to grab a sandwich back at the station.

But in all her excitement about being here—in Italy—she'd completely neglected her stomach.

"OK," she answered politely. He looked friendly and certainly didn't *seem* like the kind of person who would take unsuspecting British tourists off into the mountains to maim and bury, she joked to herself with an ironic smile.

This was all so new to her, though. The furthest from home she'd ever traveled was across the channel to Paris for a day. This was Italy. Fortunately, she did have one advantage, however: she knew conversational Italian.

Colette's obsession with romantic languages had begun as a child. She loved stories of Ancient Rome and the Italian cadence was so beautiful and lyrical she wanted to learn the language.

She eventually did as part of her studies at university and had hoped to spend time abroad once she'd saved enough money, but her mother's failing health had prevented that. Now, she was finally getting to see the country she'd spent all these years dreaming about.

Jacopo was like something out of a cartoon as he took her huge suitcase and hefted it into the boot of the taxi. Colette now wondered if she might have overpacked, but again she had never traveled before. What did you pack for three weeks in Italy? She'd put in everything she could think of, just in case.

As the car wound along the coast, Jacopo continued to amuse her with stories of his passengers. She asked him to intermittently chat to her in Italian so she could get her feet wet again with the language.

It had been some time since she'd been able to practice and she wanted to test herself before she interacted with the locals. Turned out she still remembered a lot.

"The best restaurant in Positano" was, apparently, a tiny trattoria tucked down the end of a nondescript lane that looked to be in the middle of nowhere.

Jacopo led her inside a place called Delfino and introduced her to whom Colette guessed must be the proprietor, a stout woman with black hair interspersed with streaks of gray, who spoke a mile a minute.

One moment she was behind the counter listening attentively to Jacopo, and the next she had Colette swept up into a warm bear hug.

"Any friend of Jacopo is a friend of mine," she proclaimed in Italian. Colette realized he must have conveyed that she spoke a bit of the language. "I am Mama Elene. I fix a wonderful meal for you. You sit over here," she instructed, leading her to a small table outside on a rear terrace that opened up to breathtaking waterfront views framed by a brightly tiled church dome.

It was…heaven. Everything she'd dreamed about and more.

Colette curled her red hair around her finger as she looked out across the quintessentially Mediterranean landscape, while the warm Italian afternoon sun beat down on the parasol above.

Mama Elene was making her a shot of espresso while she mulled over the menu. Everything looked so delicious she didn't know what to try. She wanted to sample it all.

Thankfully the effusive Italian woman was more than helpful in that department. She set the espresso before her and promptly made her suggestions.

Having settled on her order, Colette sipped her drink and watched people on the myriad streets and laneways below.

Were all Italians so effortlessly stylish? The women who passed by were so impeccably turned out that it made her regard her own attire with a frown. Tousled Italian locks blow-ing seductively in the breeze also didn't compare to her hair in its neat but rather severe bun.

She tended to keep things casual with her jeans, floral blouse and ballet flats. Noelle was always telling her she had to try and make more of herself, but Colette was never sure what exactly was expected. She wasn't the type to wear short-shorts or revealing clothing in summer like her sister. She just liked things simple.

Simple was safe and with all the turmoil in her life over the past few years, safe was exactly what she needed.

It wasn't long before Mama Elene was bringing out her *primi* choice: arancini. The fried cheese and rice balls were crunchy on the outside and gooey rich on the inside.

On the first bite, a string of cheese stretched from Colette's mouth to the remnants on the fork. She chuckled as she caught the runaway strand, looking up just in time to find a pair of dark eyes boring into her gaze.

A handsome Italian man of about her age was standing at the espresso counter nearby, his face propped on an elbow as he leaned against the dark wood.

His pristinely ironed shirt clung to his muscles, the pale blue color accentuating his olive skin. With his jet-black hair and nonchalant hooded gaze, he looked like a character on the cover of one of those classic romance novels—dark and smoldering personified.

Colette couldn't help but stare.

"Luca!" Mama Elene sang out as she emerged from the kitchen, another plate of food in hand. She smacked a kiss on his cheek as she rushed past him on her way to Colette's table. "Where have you been?" she heard the older woman ask in rapid Italian. "And how's your mama?"

This time a portion of steaming bruschetta appeared on

the table as Colette sat silently listening to the exchange between the two.

"I've been busy," Luca answered distractedly, still staring in Colette's direction. Or maybe it was just out at the view, she couldn't tell. Still, she could feel a flush rise automatically up her neck and looked down at her food, doing her best to avoid making eye contact for fear of being drawn even more into the conversation.

But she couldn't help it.

"So busy you can't come to visit your other mama Elene? Shame on you," she said as she smacked his arm playfully. "And look at you. So skinny. Because you don't have me to cook for you, or a wife," she chided. "When are you going to get married, eh?"

Colette couldn't help it, her curiosity got the best of her and her eyes immediately strayed in Luca's direction. Yep, he was looking right at her.

"I can feed myself, so there is no rush to find a wife." He smirked. "Or are you trying to get rid of me?"

"Never!" Mama Elene squeezed his chin and affectionately turned his handsome face toward hers. "You are my boy and always will be. I just want to see you happy."

"Somebody talking about me?"

It was like watching an Italian soap opera. As if on cue, a stunning woman wearing impossibly high heels teetered into the restaurant with a smile on her face and a shock of lustrous blonde hair that reached to her behind. She was wearing a stylish but skimpy outfit that showed off her every attribute— and there was plenty to be admired.

Again comparing herself to yet another paragon of Italian style, and finding herself sorely lacking in that department, Colette promptly stuffed a slice of bruschetta into her mouth.

The flavor of the tomato was rich but not overpowering,

the basil was fresh, and the hint of garlic was just the right mix. Heavenly…

"Lidia," Mama Elene greeted as Colette continued to listen. As ever, she was a silent observer of the lives of others. It seemed that even in Italy she couldn't escape it. Though she noticed this time that the older woman's greeting was not quite so effusive to the latest arrival.

Or was she imagining it?

The trio talked animatedly for the entire time Colette was there (though Mama Elene remained prompt and indulgent in her service of her customers), and throughout three courses they still seemed to have plenty to talk about.

As she finished her grilled shrimp and bresaola, Colette sadly realized she was running out of time to listen as she heard Jacopo's taxi horn from outside on the street, signaling it was time to leave.

She got to her feet and walked toward the trio at the counter. She hated having to interrupt them, but she needed to pay her bill and get going.

"Um, *scusi*," she began politely.

"You're ready to leave so soon? Jacopo is there already?" Mama Elene questioned as she turned to look at her. She rushed to the door. "Ah, yes, he is. I get you your bill."

Colette's finger automatically found its way to a strand of loose hair as she curled it self-consciously.

"So sorry to disturb you," she apologized to the others at the counter as she took some money out to settle her bill. Jacopo was inside before it was paid, and from his exuberant greeting, it seemed the taxi driver was also familiar with the others present.

"You enjoyed your meal?" he asked Colette, hurrying over to her.

"It was wonderful," she replied truthfully.

"What I tell you? Jacopo knows the best restaurant. You come here again, *si*?"

Everyone's eyes seemed to turn in her direction and Colette was sure her face was scarlet by now. "Of course."

"Next time you bring a friend," Mama Elene encouraged, smiling and presenting her with a shot of limoncello.

"Oh, I don't actually know anyone here," she said, staring at the glass, unsure if it would be rude not to drink it. She had no idea how potent these things were and she wasn't really a drinker.

The older woman frowned. "What? You are here by yourself? No family? No boyfriend, even?"

"No," Colette muttered, slightly embarrassed.

"How long is your stay here in Positano?"

"Just a few weeks. I'm not even sure if the place I'm staying is around here actually," she said truthfully, as she had very little information on the villa other than the street address. But she sorely hoped so. The town was picture-postcard perfect and from what she'd seen already, she wanted to explore every inch of it.

"Yes, it is not far," Jacopo told her, "just back up that way—closer to Fornillo."

"And you're here all alone?" Luca said disbelievingly in English.

Colette's tongue twisted in her mouth. She wasn't sure why she couldn't answer, so she just nodded and picked up the limoncello shot, downing it in one.

"Well, *now* you know someone." Mama Elene reached in for another hug. "You come here as much as you like. I let you taste *everything* on the menu."

Colette had to smile, despite the tartness of the lemon hitting her tongue and the alcohol almost making her retch.

Mama Elene was the quintessential Italian matriarch she'd read about, there in the flesh.

Already Italy was living up to everything she'd dreamed about—perhaps even surpassing it. Though she didn't think she'd be consuming any more limoncello.

"Thank you. I'd love to."

## Chapter 15

Then

"Hello?" a timid voice called out, causing Annie to lift her sunglasses and look up from her magazine.

As far as she knew she was the only one at the villa this afternoon. The French students had left around midday, and the German couple had said something about going off for the day to visit the ruins of Pompeii.

They had very politely asked Annie to join them, but wandering around in the heat looking at ancient dead people petrified in molten lava wasn't her kind of holiday.

After last night's exploits, she'd decided to just have a quiet day lazing by the pool. While Valentina had mentioned that there'd be more guests arriving, Annie certainly wasn't anticipating having to do a meet and greet.

Standing up above the terrace now was the mousiestlooking girl she'd ever seen. She had luminous red hair tied up in bun, with plastic-framed glasses on her face, and pale freckled skin.

Her clothes were reminiscent of the kind of hand-me-downs Annie would've worn in her teens, but at least her figure wasn't too bad. She had that and her flaming hair going for her—even if there was little else.

"I'm Annie. Are you staying here?" she asked, jumping up from the sun lounger. Poor thing looked harmless and a bit terrified, to be honest, and instinctively Annie's heart went out to her.

"Colette," the other woman answered in a very definite English accent. "And yes, I think I have a reservation here, but I'm not sure where I'm supposed to check in exactly."

"Ah, things are pretty casual round here," Annie commented airily. "There's no check-in as such, but someone will be coming round later. You the one from England then?"

"Yes."

"Right. I didn't think you looked very American. The manager, landlady—or whatever they call them in Italy—told me that there were two other girls arriving this week," Annie supplied, throwing on a sarong.

She put on her flip-flops, hopped up the steps and led the new girl through the courtyard and into the house.

"Oh. So how do I get my room key?" Colette was still holding on to her humongous suitcase for dear life as they went through to the kitchen. She looked to be a couple of years younger than her and so timid, Annie thought, even in the way she moved.

"Like I said, Valentina will be around this evening. In the meantime, just relax and rest up after the journey. It's hot out there today. Did you have something to eat? Are you here for long?"

"Yes, three weeks. Just a break away from work, really."

"Wow, you must have some job," Annie chuckled, "if you can afford that much time off."

"No, it's not that. It's a family business, a bakery in Brighton. My mother and sister arranged this trip for me as a gift," Colette explained.

"So you're here on your own?" Annie probed, suddenly conscious of the fact that she was the one asking all the questions. Hairdresser's habit. But she was intrigued by the fact that she was a fellow lone traveler.

"Yes, it's a bit of a dream of mine to come to Italy. I meant to after uni but it didn't work out. But I know a bit of Italian, so…"

"Well, you'll be handy to have around so. I haven't a word. In fairness, I was lucky to get through school, let alone learn a foreign language," she laughed. "I work as a hairdresser in Dublin."

"Dublin, Ireland?" a third voice called out then, and Annie and Colette both turned to see a gorgeous blonde standing under the front door arch.

She was naturally tanned, model-thin, and looked as if she'd stepped straight out of the magazine Annie had been reading, with her expensive designer clothes, artfully tousled hair, designer bag on her arm and obligatory Louis Vuitton suitcases at her feet.

All this doe-eyed beauty yet unashamedly sensual, and with a confident air that made Annie feel threatened on sight.

"The American?" she asked rhetorically.

"Yeah, the American," the other woman drawled. "Kimberley Weston. You guys can call me Kim," she introduced herself as she glided into their midst, extending a hand to Colette and then Annie.

Colette greeted her eagerly, a look of undisguised wonderment on her face. Annie wasn't so easily impressed, and she tried to restrain the naked envy crawling up her spine. Colette might not be a trust-fund baby, but this girl certainly was.

Annie had an innate issue with rich people. She wasn't—obviously—and those who were had made her life hell every day for as long as she could remember. Especially in secondary school.

It was bad enough to be the adopted child of a lower working-class family with few lessons in etiquette, no friends and few prospects for improving your situation. The only reason Annie was even at that particular school was because her mother cleaned the parish priest's house and everyone knew it. The mostly well-off pupils took particular delight in tormenting her because of it.

Kim looked exactly like one of those girls who took pleasure in Annie's pain.

"So your own names?" the American asked, sitting down on a stool and crossing her long legs under the countertop. She casually flung her expensive bag on the seat next to Annie's as if it had come from a high-street chain instead of a Fifth Avenue designer boutique.

"Annie O'Doherty," she finally answered as the question began to loom uncomfortably in the air. "And this is Colette. She's just arrived, too."

"Turner," she supplied. "Colette Turner, but Colette is fine."

She really was too sweet, Annie thought as she looked at how the younger woman responded to questioning. Her words were soft, her eyes seemed to seek out anything but the gaze of others. She also watched how the younger girl covertly studied Kim's attire and then her own. There was no comparing the two.

Kim was pure glamour. Colette was pure...twee.

"Where in America are you from?" Colette asked.

"Manhattan."

"New York? Wow."

Annie started to become self-conscious as she listened to Colette and Kim chat easily about their backgrounds and education. Annie couldn't help it, she felt uneasy at being unable to join in the conversation. Grand when it had just been Colette, but Kim was so much more worldly and confident.

Then she thought of something and looked at her watch, having come up with an idea to help find common ground.

"Well, Valentina won't be around for another while yet, and since we're going to be sharing this place, I suppose we might as well get the party started. Drinks, anyone?" She slapped an exuberant hand against her thigh. "There's a bottle of grappa in the press." She winked.

She couldn't help it; it was her fail-safe way of easing her anxiety. A few drinks to help get to know people had always been Annie's social crutch.

And Colette certainly looked like she could do with some loosening up.

"Hey, sounds good to me," Kim chimed in, and Annie automatically warmed to her a little more.

They moved back outside to the terrace and soon she and Kim were drinking up a storm, the alcohol loosening their inhibitions, just as Annie had anticipated.

Colette wouldn't at first. She looked at the glasses of Italian liqueur as if it was some kind of poison.

"It won't bite," Annie urged. She'd promised herself to cut back on the drinking and she had, but she was on holiday after all. And it wasn't as if she was in a position to get sloshed and into trouble. Not here anyway.

"Yes, go on," Kim urged. "Have some fun. We're in Italy, one of the most beautiful places on earth. And I think a toast is in order."

"Great idea," Annie enthused, thinking that maybe the American was OK after all.

The notion seemed to find a home with Colette, too, as she tentatively took a glass and had a measured sip.

"Here's to la dolce vita!" Annie sang, raising her glass to the others.

"La dolce vita," Kim and Colette chimed in return.

# Chapter 16

Now

"Morning, Amanda," Annie sang out a greeting as she walked into the salon, her four-inch heels making a satisfying click against the black-and-white marble tiles as she walked.

Amanda was her new receptionist—the last, a girl by the name of Tori, had failed to live up to her customer service standards and had been let go only two weeks after she started.

The new girl was only a week in but doing pretty well.

#GlamSquad was now one of Crumlin's most popular hair salons. Annie had done exactly what she'd promised Felicity all those years before. A little while after her jaunt to Italy, she'd taken the money the older woman had gifted her and set up a small one-person enterprise in a dingy unit not far from her flat.

Eventually she did well enough at that to afford not only a better place to live but much bigger premises, and was now in a current state-of-the-art salon in a busy shopping center filled with all the best equipment and modern furnishings.

Since then, she'd flourished even more.

She'd taken on staff so she no longer had to style everyone who came through the doors herself, with a complement of four stylists and a (brand-new) receptionist. The place had a string of regulars and plenty of passing trade from the center. In truth, every time she set foot in this snazzy spot, Annie still couldn't quite believe her luck that this trendy salon was really hers.

Her dark hair was twisted into a messy bun atop her head, and her makeup was flawless. Her bag was Kate Spade, her leopard-print dress was from Whistles and her shoes Kurt Geiger. It was a far cry from her TopShop sale-rail younger days.

Now Annie had a glamorous reputation and image to uphold.

She stalked across the salon floor to her office, a small room down the back, close to the washbasins.

Inside, a plethora of photographs lined the walls of her workspace: images of her favorite people and her favorite places—some of which she'd actually visited, like Positano, and others she hoped to travel to in times to come, like Paris and Australia.

She kept those there for inspiration.

Her desk was a minimalist IKEA affair with a comfortable executive chair behind it. Annie settled in that chair now to get started on the latest stock inventory and purchase sheets.

It hadn't been easy building a business on top of all her commitments, and she'd had to learn how to do much of the admin and accountancy stuff herself in between salon appointments and trying to drum up new customers.

She no longer counted stock but she checked the sheets, made the orders, and ensured her business had everything it needed.

The things she could no longer do herself, like VAT and tax, she'd employed professionals to see to, and now, five years on, things were finally working like a well-oiled machine.

She turned her attention to that morning's post, raising an eyebrow when she saw a familiar logo on one of the envelopes and prying it open to find Kim Weston's invite to Villa Dolce Vita's grand reopening in Italy.

Annie smiled. So she'd actually done it then.

Though, as always where Kim was concerned, she felt an instinctive pang of envy, and quickly pushed it aside.

Of *course* she had done it—the same girl never let anything faze her.

Annie also raised an eyebrow at the launch party date, only a month way.

As if she could just swan off to Italy for a long weekend at such short notice. She had a business to run.

She then spotted the flight and hotel confirmations, and how everything had been booked and paid for.

Nice, but Annie was perfectly able to pay her own way. Then she took a deep breath.

There she was getting her back up again—exactly the kind of thing Kim used to always warn her against. She should just accept her friend's generosity and leave it at that.

But Annie couldn't help it. Despite their closeness that summer, there was always a fault line where she and the other two were concerned—and probably always would be.

Right from that first day at the villa, she'd always felt somewhat on the outside and knew she'd never share the same rapport Colette and Kim had, and probably still did now.

But maybe that was understandable.

In truth, Annie was somewhat surprised to actually get the invite. Colette and Kim had kept in much closer contact since that summer in Italy—they had even attended each other's weddings, whereas Annie couldn't make either at the time.

She didn't think they ever resented her for that or anything, but in all honesty, she hadn't really expected their time together to spill over into their lives once they got back home.

It was just a holiday thing. Time and place.

Of course, it was easy to keep up with Kim's life on social media (or at least the version she shared of it) and she knew that she now had a young daughter with her gorgeous husband, Gabriel.

Annie had met the couple briefly when one time Kim was on a business trip to Dublin, and he was exactly the kind of guy the likes of Kim Weston would find herself ending up with—a drop-dead gorgeous hunk with oodles of natural charm and an even greater amount of adoration for his wife.

Again, Annie chided herself for her envy.

Kim deserved this, she'd worked hard for it—yet like everything, the success of The Sweet Life all seemed to come about so easily for her. After that summer, she'd practically fallen into her highly lucrative mindfulness guru and successful social-media-Influencer role without even trying. And with support from the right people aiding her all the way, making introductions, bankrolling her investments, everything...

Whereas Annie had to work her arse off right from the get-go, and even if she continued to expand #GlamSquad, she'd never match the giddy heights of international success Kim had achieved.

But that was life, wasn't it? Some people just glided effortlessly through the water like swans, while others treaded water like demons just to keep afloat.

Annie looked again at the invite. The Sweet Life indeed...

No doubt this new retreat or wellness center—or whatever hippie-dippie buzzword the gullible masses lapped up these days—would also be a roaring success, especially given the location.

And she couldn't help but wonder now what Kim had done with the crumbling old villa. She smiled fondly, recalling how dismissive she'd been of the house initially, calling it an old wreck, when Kim and even Colette had each been able to see beyond the ramshackle disrepair and visualize its former glory days.

No doubt it would be even more glorious now.

Annie exhaled. She wouldn't be going, though—not a chance.

On the one hand she'd love to see the villa, catch up with old friends and visit old haunts, and join in celebrating the latest chapter in Kim Weston's success story.

Yet on the other, the last thing Annie wanted was to revisit that summer that had begun so brilliantly, yet ultimately ended in tears.

# Chapter 17

Then

Kim's eyes were heavy.

The sun was blinding and her head hurt like a thousand spikes were being driven into it. She groaned as she rolled over in bed, the stale taste of alcohol tainting her tongue. Her mouth felt like cotton.

She forced an eye open. *Where was she?*

It was bright, way too bright, and the flimsy gauze curtains on the window stood open, allowing the sunlight free rein. The walls were a garish orange color and there were cracks like rivers across the dingy ceiling.

Painted vines with purple grapes and red-and-white flowers lined the faded trim. It took her a moment to remember where she was and what had happened the day before.

Italy.

Annie, Colette, and *way* too much grappa. It was all a little blurry after that, but she did remember something about dancing outside on an ancient crumbling cabana-type thing under the olive trees.

Or was that Annie? Kim wasn't sure.

She tried to go back to sleep but rest eluded her. Her head was throbbing and the only way it was going to stop was with some pain relief and maybe some food.

But the prospect of getting up to find either seemed the equivalent of climbing Mount Everest without oxygen.

If she was back home she could've just called down for the housekeeper to send something up, but she was in Italy and supposed to be fending for herself.

She groaned again as she forced herself onto her feet.

How she had got to this bedroom in the first place she wasn't sure. She didn't even remember being shown to a room, but despite the hows and means, she seemed to have ended up in one that was hot as hell.

And she might even end up sharing with someone else, she groaned inwardly, spotting the neatly made single bed across the way.

Kim wandered blearily around the landing outside, the intense sunlight causing her even more pain as she padded downstairs and tried to make her way to the kitchen.

Finally she found it and immediately began pulling open creaky old cupboards and messy drawers in the hope of finding something to ease the jackhammer in her head.

"Looking for something?" Colette asked a moment later. She was sitting calmly at the heavy oak table nearby with a cup of coffee.

Kim hadn't spotted her on the way in.

Her voice was ten decibels too loud, though, and she raised a hand. "Not so loud," she moaned. "My head hurts."

"I have some aspirin in my bag upstairs," the younger girl offered, getting up. "I'll get them. By the way, you snore."

*How come she's so sprightly this morning?* Kim asked herself as she settled down at one of the wooden chairs beneath the large rectangular table.

Especially when yesterday her first impression of the English girl was that she was afraid of her own shadow. Unlike the Irish one, who looked like she wanted to beat hers (and everyone else's) up.

And seriously, who made their bed so perfectly like that? Kim groaned inwardly.

Though on the plus side, at least she kinda knew her roommate.

She closed her eyes and laid her head down on the heavy wood, hoping to ease the throbbing.

"Here you go," Colette announced a few minutes later as she placed a pack of painkillers on the table before her. "Are you hungry?"

"Ugh. I don't think I could eat."

"Well, I could," Annie piped up. Kim hadn't even realized she'd come in either.

"How can you both sound so cheery when I feel like a train wreck?" she grumbled in annoyance as she ripped open the blister pack of painkillers. "Thanks." She looked up gratefully at Colette, who'd also put a glass of water down in front of her.

"Won't work," Annie insisted as she moved toward the fridge. "I have the perfect hangover cure," she continued, taking out tomatoes and what looked like it had once been celery from the fridge. She glanced dubiously at the drooping leaves. "God bless French students, is all I can say."

"You make that and I'll do breakfast," Colette said, reaching over Annie and grabbing out some bacon and eggs. "There's a lovely little grocery shop just down the hill. I found it this morning while out on my walk. The owner's been there for over thirty years, she told me."

Kim groaned again. These girls were *way* too perky. Annie looked as fresh as she had yesterday evening, and Colette had been out for a morning walk *and* already made friends with the locals.

Surely Kim hadn't drank *all* that liquor by herself?

"You can cook?" Annie asked, as she began to chop vegetables and drop them in a blender.

"I cooked for Mum every day for years, remember?" Colette answered proudly.

Kim vaguely remembered the English girl telling them last night about her mother being unwell, but that she was better now. They'd all been sitting out on the terrace, sharing stories under the stars.

For her part, she wasn't sure how much or little she'd told them about her own background; last night still felt like kind of a blur.

Annie was about to start the blender, but Kim already knew her head wasn't going to be able to take the noise.

"You two do what you're doing, I'm going outside to lie down for a while. Or no, scratch that," she said, remembering the blinding sunshine. "Maybe I'll try to find someplace in the shade. Call me when breakfast is ready."

She padded out to the hallway, her bare feet slapping against the cracked tiled floor.

She made it to a couch in a living area situated at the rear of the house, facing away from the sun and with little natural light, before the spinning in her head overwhelmed her. She flopped into the worn-though-comfortable cushions without ceremony, and flung an arm over her head to shield her eyes, even though it was satisfyingly dark.

She felt *sooo* bad and wanted to go back to sleep, but with the combination of the pounding in her head and the chatter and cooking noises coming from the kitchen, she knew the chances of that were near impossible.

This was not a good start. Kim had come all the way here to escape her New York party-girl crap and she'd ended up trashed and dancing in the moonlight on her very first night.

So much for changing her life.

"There you are," Annie's voice suddenly resounded nearby. Kim peeked out from beneath her arm. The other girl had a tall glass of some thick red concoction in her hands. She frowned.

"What is it?"

"Bloody Mary, of course. I know it looks rotten, and doesn't taste the best either, but it works. Trust me, I'm Irish. We know the best cures."

Kim sat up. "All right, but if this doesn't work I'm holding you responsible." She narrowed her eyes. "Like I should for last night—as I recall, the grappa was your suggestion. As was the wine and then the beer…"

"Ah, would you stop it, last night was great craic. And the Germans were only too delighted to share their stash with us. Here—" She handed her the drink.

Their chat was interrupted by the sound of singing coming from the kitchen and each gave the other a conspiratorial look.

"How is she so goddamn chipper?"

"I have no idea," Annie replied. "I was full sure she'd be out cold for an entire week after all we drank, but she's better off than either of us. Not a bother on her."

"Think the innocent act is real?"

"Looks that way," Annie said. "Lousy, I know, but when she walked in here yesterday my first thought was: there's someone that could seriously use a makeover."

Despite herself, Kim laughed. "You said you do hair, right? Maybe you could offer her some of your expertise."

Colette announced that breakfast was ready a few minutes later and both Kim and Annie made their way back to the kitchen and the waiting meal.

Kim picked at her scrambled eggs, even though they were really good. The entire meal was. She was impressed. She couldn't boil water without starting a fire. It was fortunate that Colette would be around while she was here; might save her on some of the eating-out expenses.

She remembered now that the English girl had also reacted with considerable enthusiasm last night to her suggestion about the cookery class. Maybe she should just let Colette go along instead, and Kim and Annie could reap the benefits.

"So what are we doing later?" Annie asked eagerly.

Kim looked at her, realizing that, like it or not, she seemed to have made some new friends. She hadn't really considered what she would do while here, she just needed to get away. But maybe some companionship would be a good thing?

As long as they didn't spend all their time partying.

"Dunno," she replied noncommittally. "Did you have something in mind?"

"There's this brilliant place downtown I went to the other night. A late-night bar actually cut into a cave," she enthused, eyes shining. "Great crowd and the music is the biz. We could do our own thing today and maybe meet up later for a bite to eat and head there after?" She turned to Colette for a response.

"Great," the English girl replied with a smile. "Sounds like fun."

Kim nodded in assent. She was happy to check out the town, but she'd already decided that she wasn't going to drink a *single* drop of alcohol.

Time to put her partying days well and truly behind her.

# Chapter 18

Then

The trio ventured down to the center of Positano later that evening.

Annie was right, Music on the Rocks was awesome, but Kim got the feeling that Annie's desire to be there had less to do with showing them a good time, and more with her trying to find someone else, judging by the way she spent most of the night looking around.

Interesting…

Still, they had fun. Over dinner they'd exchanged further snippets of each other's lives, delving deeper into the reasons they were all here in the first place. It was fascinating stuff, especially Annie's upbringing—which was so utterly different from her own, yet they'd both been let down and rejected by their parents.

Kim was kind of embarrassed to admit that hers had basically wanted to marry her off to some guy in England; it seemed frivolous and stupid in comparison to the stuff they'd been dealing with, so instead she'd told them she just wanted to get out from beneath her folks' thumbs for a while.

Later, Annie and Colette confessed to being wiped (particularly after that long trek up the hill) when they got back to the villa, but Kim was still a little wired.

She checked the time and calculated the equivalent East Coast time back in New York.

Realizing that it was the middle of the night there and Natasha would be fast asleep, she decided to upload a couple of photos to the new social media account she'd set up so she and her friend could keep in touch without Kim's parents being privy to where she was.

Her chosen handle was "The Sweet Life," the English translation of the villa's name.

She picked a gorgeous sunset photo she'd taken from the pizzeria they'd eaten in earlier—a golden orb over the water, framed by vibrant bougainvillea trailing the ornate railing at their window table.

It was a pretty good shot if she did say so herself, she thought, as she tagged her friend's account, though her iPhone was brand-new so the camera was top-of-the-range.

"Food with a View" was the rather uninspiring caption Kim chose, but that wasn't the point. She just wanted to let Tash know that she was here, safe, and having a good time.

She still felt guilty about diverting the trip without her folks knowing, though she had sent a message to Spencer Andrews—enough to let him know that there was a slight change of plan and that she wouldn't be coming over this week but his family shouldn't worry.

No doubt Peter and Gloria were already aware she'd gone

AWOL, and she'd have to confront them, too, at some point, but she'd wait till she was better settled here first.

She got a glass of water from the kitchen and ventured around the common areas of the house she hadn't yet had a chance to explore properly.

According to Annie, there were four bedrooms in the villa, three of which were currently occupied by herself and Colette, with Annie in the single room and the older German couple they'd met briefly last night (though Kim couldn't remember much of their conversation) in another.

That parlor-type room off the kitchen in the back which had been her haven that morning was so dark and dreary that it really should be knocked through so as to open out the tiny kitchen and let in some more natural light.

Though perhaps there was some advantage to that; the absence of direct sunlight and tiny windows would at least keep the place cooler in summer. With no air-conditioning in the place, that was definitely needed.

Feeling around for a light switch, Kim couldn't find anything and proceeded further along the wall before stumbling into something. Her shin knocked hard against the side of a piece of clunky wooden furniture and she yelped as pain shot up to her knee.

She kicked at it. "Goddamn wreck," she grumbled, before a thudding sound got her attention.

Creepy...

The hair on the back of her neck stood up and she was about to retreat from the room when she located a small lamp atop the dresser and switched it on.

Yup, this room was indeed long past its prime, with worn interiors and a shabby sofa that looked like it might convert to a foldout bed, which technically made it another bedroom, though she couldn't imagine who would pay to actually sleep in it.

Ugh. Backpackers, probably, or travelers on a budget—like Kim was now. She gulped, reminding herself that she wasn't in Kansas anymore. That would take some getting used to.

But she was pretty sure she could handle it; prove to her folks and herself that she didn't need their money to get by in life.

The windows were open to let out some of the day's heat, and tonight there was a welcome breeze. But other than that there was little else of interest in the room.

Kim reached to turn off the lamp and head upstairs to bed, when something sticking out beneath the dresser she'd knocked into caught her eye.

She kneeled down and fished it out. It was some kind of book. A journal, with some handwriting inside. Beautiful cursive script—a lot of it in Italian.

She flipped through a few more pages, recognizing some words also written in English. Looked like poetry... Actually, no—they were just stand-alone sentences.

*La dolce vita: good food, good drinks, good people. Because life is meant to be lived, and lived well.*

Nice. On a whim, Kim took out her phone and updated her social media caption from earlier.

Much better.

# Chapter 19

## Now

The Grand Hotel Excelsior Vittoria was a famed award-winning hotel located in Sorrento, pure five-star luxury, which was why Kim had reserved it for her family's upcoming stay, and arranged special packages for other overseas guests attending Villa Dolce Vita's official launch.

While she'd stayed at the villa to oversee the last of the preparation of the wellness center interiors and grounds, she'd moved the short distance to the hotel a half an hour away in advance of Gabriel and Lily's arrival.

"Hey, you," she greeted Gabe into the phone, holding it close to her ear as she stood out on the wide terrace of their two-bed family suite. "Where are you now?"

"In Naples just about to take the train. Are you sure you

have time to pick us up? We could just grab a cab the rest of the way."

"Of course I'll pick you up. I'd have picked you up at the airport but I know Lily really wanted to take a train ride and see the views."

"Any view with you in it is the best one for us."

A knot of guilt formed in her stomach. "Hey, I know I've been away a lot…"

"This is a big deal. We both know that."

"It is a big deal but so are you two. I promise, when you guys get here I'm going to make time for us as a family— especially after launch night," she said sincerely. "And yeah, I know it can't be easy having me for a wife."

"As if I'd want any other," he replied with a smile in his voice. "I'm so proud of you, honey. You work hard and you get the job done. But I gotta say, some downtime together will be nice."

Kim's head fell in shame. "How was Lily on the flight?" she asked.

"Good. She slept like a baby most of the way, but was a bit restless and sneezing when we got in. Really hope she's not coming down with something."

"Me too," Kim replied absently, and couldn't help but think: *rotten timing, too.*

Then she chided herself for worrying more about the launch instead of her own flesh and blood.

"I've got some echinacea with me and gave it to her just now," Gabriel continued. "Hopefully nip anything in the bud before it starts."

"Great idea." He was such an amazing father. Echinacea, dental appointments, vaccinations, horse-riding lessons, you name it… Gabe was on top of it all when it came to Lily. Sometimes Kim couldn't believe all the stuff he did on top of his career as a fashion photographer. He'd gone freelance since Lily's arrival, with their nanny picking up childcare duties whenever he was out on a job.

"How long do you think before the train leaves Naples? So I can time the pickup."

"Next one's due in five."

Her phone beeped then, distorting what Gabriel was saying. "Babe, can you hold on a second? I've got another call coming in."

"Sure."

"Hey, Chloe, what's up?" Kim asked her assistant, who was based in her office back in the States.

"Sorry to bother you, Kim, but Hank Bingham is on the line. He says he needs to speak to you urgently."

*What does the head of Legal want?* she asked herself as she waited for the call to be put through. And why now?

"Kim?"

"Hey, Hank. What's up?"

"Are you sitting down?"

"No. Do I need to?" she asked, but automatically moved back into her room and plopped down on the corner of the bed.

"You might."

"Well, I'm sitting now. Tell me what's going on."

"A day ago we received an email from someone who claims that some stuff in *The Sweet Life Guide* is plagiarized. She says she can prove it."

Kim's heart stopped for a moment. She couldn't even breathe as the words replayed in her mind.

"What? Why would someone say that?" she asked, nervously fumbling with the sheets.

"Hell if I know. She says some of the chapter headings in the book are directly lifted from some old family journal she has or something, I dunno. I know they're originally from your social media but because they were reproduced in the book, and thus used for profit, she reckons it's clear-cut plagiarism."

Plagiarism…

"A family journal? Does she have proof?"

"I don't know yet. Obviously I'm requesting all the information now, and not taking anything seriously until I see it. I just thought I'd better give you the heads-up, given the timing."

*Interesting timing for sure*, Kim thought.

"OK, I have to admit I'm a bit blindsided by all this…"

But was she really? This wasn't the first time someone had accused her of being dishonest, she realized, thinking about the more recent negative social media comments.

*The Sweet Life… Don't you mean The FAKE Life?*

She swallowed hard. Could this be connected somehow?

Hank was still talking. "Of course this is probably just bullshit, but I have to ask. Could any of the quotes have been lifted? I mean, I don't know much about all that social media stuff and I guess anything goes, but you know, for the book we would have signed a publisher's release about rights ownership and all that… I'm sorry. I have to ask. It's my job. I'm sure it's just nothing but…"

"Of course," Kim said, neatly avoiding a direct answer. "Look, maybe find out exactly what they have and what they want. Who is this person? Where's she from? Everything."

"Sure. I'll call you back as soon as I have more."

As soon as they disconnected, Kim threw the phone on the bed and put her head in her hands. How in the hell was this happening? And now?

"Oh shoot," she exclaimed when she remembered her husband was still on the other line. "Gabe? I'm so sorry. It was the office and I got caught up…"

He laughed good-naturedly. "Hey, it's not as if it's the first time." Though his tone was light, there was an edge of disappointment in his voice that made Kim feel like an absolute heel.

"I'm so sorry. It's not like I forgot you—"

"You kinda did. Admit it. Anyway, I just wanted to say that we've just got on the train and Lily is really excited. I'd better go."

"I'm so sorry again, honey," she repeated. "And I'm getting in the car right now. See you guys at the station."

"Don't forget the car seat, OK? Or us, for that matter," he added, chuckling. "Lily's putting on a brave face, but I know she's tired after the flight."

Feeling guilty afresh, Kim hung up the call and grabbed her bag and car keys. Her head had begun to pound the moment Hank told her about the accusation and had got even worse when she'd ended up disappointing her husband in the process.

This was a big deal. It was Lily's first visit to Italy and the first time the three of them would be away together as a family in over a year.

Yes, the launch was important, but Kim wanted to make this time special for the people she loved, too. Especially in light of her conversation with Antonio. Gabe and Lily had had to put up with way too many absences over the last couple of years.

Heading out to the hotel parking area, she climbed into the driver's seat of her rented BMW convertible and pulled away, her mind still reeling from what she'd been told.

She rested her head on one hand against the door while she steered with the other.

Why all this negative stuff now? Merely a week away from the grand launch of the villa, the pinnacle of The Sweet Life brand and important tribute to its inspiration.

And that's all those quotes had been—inspiration. It wasn't—*couldn't* be—considered plagiarism, could it? Not when it was just some dumb stuff scribbled in an old journal.

Maybe it was just sour grapes? Or this person was just fishing. Much like the social media haters and trolls she'd become accustomed to over the years.

This was something more, though, Kim knew it in her bones. This was escalating.

A few negative comments here and there were par for the course with a social media presence of her size, and especially since the book was published and she became more visible in the media.

There was also somewhat of a general backlash against the so-called "Influencer" concept now, and lots of bad press and shady dealings. But Kim hadn't done anything wrong.

Had she?

A sickening tug in her gut brought her back to reality.

OK, so she had co-opted some of those quotes in the journal, turned them into social media captions and then subsequently sold this so-called wisdom on to others.

But she'd never intended it that way, had never set out to deceive or (she cringed at the word) plagiarize. And it was really Antonio and Emilia that had taken the whole thing to another level. Didn't that count for something?

A thousand thoughts raced through her mind as she drove and she reached the station before she knew it. She stayed in the car, waiting for Gabriel to call when the train pulled in.

Kim closed her eyes and leaned her head back against the seat, lifting it up to the warm sun. If it went any further and the truth came out, it would ruin not only next week's launch but perhaps even the entire brand.

A potential suit meant her book would be pulled from the shelves. The big-brand collaborations she'd worked so hard to cultivate would automatically cut ties. Her business and livelihood would be gone.

What would Gabriel think when he discovered she'd been keeping this from him throughout their entire relationship? On top of the awful truth about how she truly felt about being a mother.

Despite Antonio's advice, there was no way she could have a full and frank conversation with her husband about that.

Not now.

"He'd never forgive me," she muttered out loud, unbeknownst to herself.

"Who'd never forgive you?" Gabriel's smooth voice appeared in her ear then and Kim jumped in her seat. Her husband laughed as he jokingly raised an apologetic arm in the air, their three-year-old's hand held firmly in the other as they both grinned at her.

"Mommy!" Lily cried out with a big toothy smile.

"Hey, baby." Kim jumped out of the car and went to hug them both.

"What's the matter?" Gabriel asked. "You looked so spooked when we walked up. We didn't mean to scare you like that. You looked like you were sleeping. I know this whole thing has been wearing you down…"

*He had no idea.*

"I'm fine," Kim lied. "I was just thinking. I didn't notice you guys walk up."

"You sure?" he questioned as he studied her carefully. Her husband knew her as well as anyone, but he also respected when she didn't want to talk.

She nodded. "Yep. I'm fine."

"OK. Then pop the trunk and let me get these bags in. You remembered to bring the car seat?"

Kim put a hand to her mouth. "Oh fu—"

Gabriel shook his head but there was a smile on his face. "Lucky I brought a backup." He wrestled with a zip on one of the suitcases and produced a child's blow-up travel seat.

Again, Kim felt like the worst mother in the world. Unsure what else to say—what was there to say?—she picked up her daughter and pulled her close for a hug.

Lily clung to her neck like a limpet, making her feel even guiltier, and combined with the strain she was under and the afternoon heat, Kim felt as if she was suffocating.

She pulled her daughter's hands away, gently lifting her into the rear of the car as Gabriel wrestled with the car seat. Once Lily was buckled up, Kim got back in front and he came around to sit beside her in the passenger seat.

"Sure you don't want me to drive?" he asked before putting on his seat belt. "You do look pretty beat."

"I'm sure." Kim started the engine, eager to get going, desperate to feel the sea breeze on her face once again to cool her a little.

"Wait a second, slow down." Gabriel leaned over to kiss her. "I missed you."

The sensation of his lips on hers had an immediate calming effect. No one had ever kissed her like he did. His lips were always gentle, never rushed or seeking, but patient when she needed him to be. It was as if he could read her so completely and know just what was necessary at any given moment. She didn't want to lose that. She didn't want to lose *him*.

Gabriel's hand remained against her cheek as their lips parted. His thoughtful blue eyes looked at her lovingly.

"I'm here now so talk to me," he reassured. "I know that things have been stressful and you need an outlet. And I know you think you can do everything alone. Just because we're separated by an ocean, it doesn't mean that I'm not there for you. I am. And I always will be."

The words were so timely it was a soothing balm to Kim's panicked heart.

His brow furrowed as he seemed to realize there really was something other than last-minute launch jitters affecting her mood. "Kim, what's going on?"

Lily's hot and bothered cries interrupted the conversation then and Kim was grateful. She didn't want to answer, couldn't answer, his question just then. She couldn't tell Gabriel what was going on, not yet. Not when she didn't really know herself.

She pushed the button to lift the convertible hood back up and give her daughter some shade.

"Everything's fine. Let's get going. Lily needs to rest."

## Chapter 20

Then

"Aren't you getting in? The water's amazing…" Colette, her translucent skin dripping in sea water, ran up to where Kim lay on a towel on the beach. She was dressed in a yellow-and-white polka-dot swimsuit she'd borrowed from Annie, which really accentuated her figure.

A week had passed since Kim had found that little journal full of motivational quotes and interesting tidbits, and since then she'd been dipping in and out of it, finding more stuff of interest to use for her social media captions.

And it seemed to be working. Whether it was the photographs or the captions, the new account was getting loads of engagement. Of course the fact that Natasha, who had a huge social media following herself, was interacting with it probably accounted for much of that.

Kim had to smile when she realized that some of her actual real-life friends from home were now following The Sweet Life account, and she guessed it had to be because of the content, as during their last interaction, Tash had again been sworn to keep Kim's location secret.

In the meantime, she had again been in touch with Spencer, calling him from Annie's mobile phone so as to conceal her location.

"Hey, it's Kim. I need to talk to you," she said as her heart began to race in her chest. She couldn't believe she was doing this, but she was.

She was setting herself free.

"I'm sorry but I need to be honest. I won't be coming to stay with you guys at all this summer. I'm not interested in this so-called arrangement our parents have," she blurted out abruptly. "I barely know you. I don't care how much money your folks have or about your titles. I just want to live my own life. I want to be happy. Do you understand?"

Kim waited for the response. She wasn't sure what to expect, but what she received surprised her.

"Well, I don't particularly want this either. I never did."

"You didn't?" Her heart lifted.

"Of course not. I already have a girlfriend, and this whole affair was something your parents and mine hatched together. I must say, I'm glad to hear you're not so keen either. My mother said you were all for it…"

Kim's eyes widened. To think that he believed *she* was eager to nab him—because of his status. Ugh.

She was glad now that she'd had the good sense to take off. What kind of women was this guy used to? The kind Kim's parents thought *she* was, obviously.

"Well, I hope your folks aren't too inconvenienced," she told him.

"And I hope yours come round."

*Unlikely*, she thought. "They'll get over it."

"Indeed. Well, thanks for ringing, Kim, and best of luck with…whatever you're doing," Spencer said, before ending the call.

"Thanks."

Just what the hell *was* she doing? Kim wondered now. She stared out at the twinkling water, watching Colette and Annie frolic in the waves.

The three had decided that it was a perfect day for a trip to the beach. They were at Fornillo, the smaller sister to Spiaggia Grande, the bigger and much more touristy beach in the center of Positano.

Up till now, they'd spent their days together wandering through the streets and alleyways of the practically vertical town, and visited some of the other popular tourist sites along the coast, as well as a couple of local art galleries.

Well, she and Colette did; Annie told them right from the beginning that she wasn't in the least bit interested in culture or sightseeing, and was far more concerned with getting a tan, which was why she in turn spent most of her days at the villa soaking up the sunshine by the pool.

But today, Kim and Colette had dragged Annie out, and down the perilous 400-or-so-step descent to the beach. Unlike the soft underfoot of, say, the Hamptons back home, the "sand" at Fornillo consisted primarily of sharp rock pebbles and was volcanic in origin, making it hot as hell to walk on.

"Are you coming in or what?" Annie chimed in now, as she approached. The brunette was wearing a light pink swimsuit that flattered her hourglass figure.

Kim looked at her own shape. She knew she was model-thin with a pretty decent body, but Annie had the shape that every woman wanted, and by the looks she was getting from guys on the beach, one that men appreciated, too.

"Must be a real page-turner," Colette commented, nodding at the paperback. Kim flinched a little, thinking she'd spotted the little journal slotted within the pages, but no, Colette was referring to the thriller she was reading.

For some reason, Kim hadn't let the others know about her accidental find at the villa. She wasn't sure why, but she wanted to keep the mysterious journal to herself, at least until she'd got through reading it. Then maybe they could ask Valentina, the villa caretaker, who it might belong to. A previous guest, most likely. Or even the villa's original owner.

In any case, it was an interesting diversion for Kim and she was more than happy to sit on the beach reading motivational quotes and life lessons while she pondered her next move, namely plucking up the courage to call her parents and confess where she was.

But the others seemed determined to get her in the water.

"Maybe later," she mumbled to Colette. "I'm still pretty beat after the trek down here. *And* last night."

The three had hit some of Positano's hotspots again the night before and it was becoming a bit of a habit. One that Kim would need to nip in the bud if she was to have any cash left to continue funding her great Italian escape.

"I was tired, too, but the salt water really brushes off the cobwebs." Colette shivered a little as a light breeze hit her drenched skin. "I'm going back in before I freeze. Coming?" she said to Annie, who nodded.

"In a bit. Just getting a drink." She reached for a bottle of water beneath her things as Colette ran back toward the water.

"I really like her," Kim chuckled as she watched Colette tumble into the waves. "A real breath of fresh air."

"So do I. I have to admit, in the beginning, I wasn't so sure about you, but I was wrong," Annie admitted.

Kim was surprised, not at her candor—she'd learned very quickly that Annie spoke her mind and called it as she saw it—but at the admission itself. "Really? Why?"

She shrugged. "Dunno. I suppose I thought you were this stuck-up trust-funder who looked down on people."

Kim sat quietly. She hadn't expected the bluntness, but she would've been lying if she said she hadn't heard the same before. People always thought they knew who she was—the irony was she barely knew herself.

"Whereas you're actually all right," Annie continued jokingly.

"So are you," Kim replied. "Colette, too. I know we haven't known each other that long but I feel lucky to have met you both. Feels like fate brought us together at the villa." She'd come across an apt quote in the book just now about that very same subject.

*Strangers are just friends waiting to happen.*

The pair lapsed into casual conversation and Kim reluctantly put the book aside. She'd read some more later. Whoever the writer was, the insights penned were well and truly hitting home with her. Stuff about being true to yourself, letting go, and taking risks spoke straight to Kim's soul.

"What's that?" Annie frowned then, as some commotion further down the beach got their attention.

Kim sat forward and screwed her eyes up against the sun.

"I don't know. Looks like something happened." She jumped to her feet quickly then, when she spotted a guy run back up the beach with a woman in his arms.

It was Colette.

The girls rushed down to the shore to meet him and saw that Colette seemed to be bleeding from her temple.

Then all of a sudden, a lifeguard was speaking rapidly in Italian and neither Kim nor Annie had a clue what was being said.

The man who had apparently pulled Colette from the water was speaking with him and before the others knew what was happening, some paramedics and a stretcher had arrived to take their friend away.

"Wait, what's going on?" Kim grabbed at the Italian man's arm.

"It's OK. We follow in my car. We go to the clinic. They take Colette there," he replied.

"Who are you? And how do you know our friend's name?" Annie demanded.

"I am Luca. I explain in the car," he said as he turned and stalked away toward the steps up to the car park.

"Who?" Annie asked Kim as they gathered up their things and moved to follow the stranger. "Did Colette say anything to you about some Italian guy she knows?"

"Nothing," she replied. "I can only guess they got talking on the beach."

"But what the hell happened? And how do we know we can trust this fella?" Annie said.

"How can we not at this point? Do you speak enough Italian to know what's going on?" Kim pointed out.

"Still, are we really getting in a car with him? He could be a murderer."

"We're just going to have to trust that he isn't. And we have to be sure Colette's all right."

"OK, but I'm going to keep my eye on yer man."

Kim looked balefully at her. "For safety or for other reasons?"

As they began the long trek back up the steps, there was no denying that this Luca was very handsome, with his chiseled abs, broad back, and toned strong arms.

She wasn't blind; she'd noticed this Italian male paragon, too, but right now Colette was their priority.

Annie just laughed. "Cut it out," she chided, chuckling at her friend's openly appreciative gaze as they followed along in the hot sunshine behind Luca. "You can ogle lovely Luca all you want later. Once we know Colette's OK and we've figured out exactly how the hell she knows him."

# Chapter 21

Then

Kim and Annie paced the hallway at the clinic as they waited for news of their friend.

Colette had been struck by a Jet Skier on his way out to open water from the beach. This was according to Luca, who'd given them both a lift to the clinic.

"It is my fault," he said, on the journey there. "I called out to her from the shore and she strayed into the wrong area on her way back into the beach."

"But how do you know her?" Annie asked. "I mean, you said you recognized her—how?"

"She had lunch at my aunt's restaurant a while ago—and she is difficult to forget," he said, almost to himself, as Kim and Annie exchanged a glance.

As all three waited in the corridor for news of their friend's prognosis, Kim couldn't help but wonder how on earth she had ended up in a shabby Italian medical center with this motley crew of an Irish girl and strange Italian man, worried about an Englishwoman she'd only just met. It was a world apart from her shiny, soulless, former New York life.

And she decided that was no bad thing.

She was jolted out of her thoughts then by the appearance of a guy in a white coat they could only assume was a doctor, and a pale, limping, but smiling Colette by his side.

They all rushed to her at once. "Oh my God! Are you OK? Are you hurt?"

"Please, sit down," Luca urged, taking her hand and leading her to a nearby seat, while Colette looked overcome and more than a little embarrassed by all the fuss.

Between them, she and the doctor explained that the Jet Ski had managed to swerve away from her just in time, which meant that thankfully her injuries hadn't been terribly serious: just a slight concussion and a couple of stitches to the head.

"Are you sure there is no concussion now?" Luca demanded and Kim was impressed by his insistence that Colette was actually OK before she was signed out.

"No, she is fine," the medic replied curtly, before turning back to Colette. "Please, just rest in your accommodation for a few days, and stay out of the hot sun," he added, glancing at the English girl's sunburned shoulders, which Kim knew Colette had picked up out of complacency about the Mediterranean's UV rays during the early days.

"I will, thank you." Again, she was mortified at being the center of attention, and gratefully accepted Luca's offer of a lift for all three of them back to the villa.

Since her return, the Italian had been a regular visitor.

"*How* is he this hot?" Annie drooled now from a pair of rickety loungers on the pool terrace, as she and Kim watched

Luca pass through the courtyard and inside the house, to where the other girl convalesced amid the cool of the rear living room.

"Dunno, but he sure is burning."

"Burning for Colette, it seems," she replied with some dismay.

Kim chuckled. "Clearly there's a helluva lot more to our girl than meets the eye."

"Lucky wagon," Annie muttered darkly.

"But why should it bother you?" Kim asked, raising an eyebrow. "Don't you have your very own Romeo in the wings?" She watched with satisfaction as Annie flushed a bit and a small smile tugged at her lips.

It was apparent that Colette wasn't the only one being romanced at the moment.

"Mind your own business."

"I am. Believe me," Kim said, lifting up her book again.

Annie rolled her eyes. "You and that bloody book—you're always stuck in it. Must be a good one, though in fairness you seem to have been reading it forever."

"Maybe I just read slowly," Kim countered.

"And maybe my name is Steve." Her response dripped with sarcasm as she stood up and wrapped a sarong around her waist, her boobs bursting out of the skimpy bikini she wore. Kim knew they were completely natural, too, not bought and paid for like so many of her friends back home.

Annie really was the living, breathing definition of voluptuous, though Kim knew the Irish girl had major insecurities about her looks, always referring to herself as a "heifer" and "massive."

Despite Kim and Colette's protests, the other girl just couldn't seem to admit that she had a body most girls would die for. But those assets and, no doubt, Annie's sparkly wit, throaty laugh, and infectious sense of humor attracted plenty of male attention, especially here.

Whenever they went out, their Irish friend was the radiant flame who attracted all of the moths nearby, and since Colette was a little too shy to head off the obvious players—groups of locals or other holidaymakers out for a good time—Kim pretty much played bodyguard on their nights out. She wasn't a complete bore and enjoyed the attention and odd flirtation, too, for sure, but she was determined not to fall back into her old party-girl ways.

"I'm going to head in for a while, before I start getting ready to go out later. Like you said, I have a hot date tonight and I want to straighten my hair and do a bit of a defuzz. See ya."

"Have fun," Kim called after her.

Annie winked mischievously. "Don't worry. I will."

She smiled and shook her head. Between Colette and Annie, she wasn't sure who was the more smitten.

Annie definitely had some mystery man on the go downtown that she seemed especially keen on, given her insistence on taking so much time in getting ready for tonight's outing when it was only early evening and still hours away till dinner.

Colette, on the other hand, seemed completely mortified by Luca's visits.

Kim watched as the guy in question now emerged from the kitchen with a tray of freshly prepared treats. "I leave the food on the kitchen table. Help yourself," he informed her.

She sighed inwardly. You could get lost in the guy's accent, never mind his arms. It was like condensed milk—thick and sweet. Lucky old Colette.

"Thanks."

She lingered for a few moments as she contemplated food or reading. It had been a long time since lunch, but she was so comfortable here. The intense heat of the afternoon sun was starting to dissipate now, enabling her to move out of the shade and bask in the late-evening glow. This was her favorite time of the day to sunbathe and the only time she exposed her skin to the sun's direct rays. Not like Annie, who was only too happy to forgo the parasol and lay out cooking like a wiener on a barbecue all day long.

On the other hand, poor Colette could barely glance at the sun without reddening up like a tomato, and like the doctor had pointed out, it was probably no bad thing that she needed to rest up inside for a while.

Kim's stomach finally won out, and she reluctantly pushed herself up from the comfortable sun lounger and walked back into the cool of the villa. She plated some chicken and pulled a slice of crusty garlic bread from the white paper it was wrapped in, then drifted back out and down to the terrace before curling back into her poolside sun lounger.

Opening the book, she began to once more skim through the words written on the page, as she nibbled on her bread.

*Happiness is like the ocean. It comes and goes. You need to be able to ride the waves of the tide if you're going to stay happy. It means you have to be light enough to float and strong enough to stand up to the breaking on the shore.*

Was she light enough to the ride the waves? Kim knew she definitely wasn't strong enough for the breaking on the shore. How often had she tried to stand up and found herself conforming to what her parents wanted?

Back home, she hadn't been able to ride the waves. Instead she'd drowned in them, and every day sank lower as the waves got higher.

But since she'd come to Italy, the waves had subsided a little.

Maybe little by little she could start to overcome them and perhaps, given enough time here in Villa Dolce Vita, Kim might eventually be light enough to float.

# Chapter 22

Then

Annie had always found it easy to make friends, but what she'd experienced since she'd arrived in Italy was something unexpected. She, Colette and Kim had become almost inseparable in such a short space of time.

She'd already shared with them the story of how she'd come to be there thanks to Felicity Finch.

"It was like something from a movie," she told them over one of their late-night chats on the terrace beneath the stars. "All this time, I was doing this woman's hair, making idle chitchat and thinking I knew her, when I had no idea."

"Such a wonderful gift," Colette sighed dreamily. "Not so much the money, but the freedom, and the opportunity to come here while you figure out what to do with your life."

"What will you do?" Kim asked. "If the old woman meant

for this trip to be life-changing, you've gotta honor that, don't you?"

"And I will," Annie enthused. "I'm going to enjoy myself first and foremost, but when I get back, I'm going to look into opening my own salon." She frowned. "Problem is, while I know hair, I know sweet FA about money or how to manage it."

Kim took a sip of her water. "It's not actually that hard. But before you do anything major like find a premises or buy stock, first find yourself an accountant to have the company registered officially, and give you some advice on how best to plan things when it comes to paying taxes and stuff."

Annie's heart sank a little. She didn't even know she had to consider that kind of thing. But she knew she could learn.

Then there was Colette. Her disarming naivete, openness, and unbridled generosity were more than Annie had ever come across in a person, with the exception of Felicity, perhaps. The English girl was genuinely good-hearted, though a bit immature in her ways, to be fair.

She was hilarious, too, in the way she'd reacted to Luca's attentions after the accident. "It's just so weird..." she confessed to Annie and Kim in the clinic that day, when Luca had slipped out to get her a fresh glass of water. "I just saw this gorgeous guy waving at me from the water, and yes, I *thought* I recognized him from the restaurant... But truly, I couldn't be sure he *was* actually waving at me, because, well...why would he? So I moved closer, and then, bam—next thing I know, I wake up here. Or at least I think I've woken up. Maybe it's really all a dream?" she said, without a trace of irony. "Because it wouldn't be the first time I've conjured up some drama or another in my mind. I had an imaginary friend growing up, you know..." she rambled, sending Annie and Kim doubling up with laughter and considerable relief that their new friend was indeed OK.

Annie couldn't wait to introduce the two of them to Harry. She was a bit disappointed not to see him at Music on the Rocks the second night she'd gone back there with Kim and Annie, but he'd reappeared a couple of nights later when she'd once again ventured down there on her own and, this time, neither of them held back.

"Well, hello there, handsome." Annie grinned when he came up alongside her at the bar. She'd spotted him as soon as she arrived. Gathered in the corner with his friends, and feeling his gaze on her while she strutted to the bar—decked out in a sexy red tassel dress and strappy silver heels—she knew it wouldn't be long before she had company. "Got your dancing shoes on tonight?"

"Depends on if I've got a dancing partner," he replied with a devilish wink that made her go weak at the knees. "Though from what I've already seen, I get the feeling you could teach me a few moves."

Annie smiled, enjoying the open flirtation and the confident way he was pursuing her. "You better believe it."

Back home, lads usually needed a fill of drink before awkwardly trying to cop off. Harry's suave assurance made him all the more attractive.

They'd danced all night and since then had met up casually again a couple of nights, mostly in bars with his mates. But tonight he'd asked Annie if she'd meet him for dinner, just the two of them.

A sure sign that, for him, things were heading beyond just casual. But Annie had kept him under wraps because she honestly wasn't sure if it was just a holiday fling, or whether she was even that interested. And also because she was pretty certain that once he caught sight of Kim, she herself would be forgotten in an instant.

That happened a lot.

The American girl literally dripped with unbridled sensuality and, to be fair, didn't even seem to realize that she was that hot. She certainly didn't play on it anyway. Annie was usually the one who ended up flirting and chatting to fellas on their nights out, while of course Colette wouldn't say boo to a goose. It was funny, but also made her and Kim a little bit protective of her, she thought fondly.

Besides, Colette seemed to have found a new protector in the gorgeous Luca. Man, he was a fine thing. The kind of Italian stallion you dreamed about meeting when coming to a place like this. Annie grinned to herself, suspecting he was exactly that—pure stallion—in the sack, too. She definitely wouldn't mind giving someone like him a go if the chance ever arose.

And speaking of which…

Annie licked her lips. She wondered if tonight would be the night she and Harry did the deed. God, she hoped so. The summer heat here, especially the balmy nights, made her horny as hell and she wouldn't mind working off some of that sexual energy.

They were meeting at a traditional trattoria in town that he had chosen. Arriving at the restaurant, Annie followed the waitress down a short stairway and into a cavernous subterranean dining area.

Arches lined in pale orange brick stood overhead. Square tables lined the walls and the floor was laid in a burnt orange tile. Paintings of the Italian countryside adorned the walls and the tables were decorated in red-and-white check-patterned cloths.

So far, so touristy.

Harry was already waiting at the table and Annie could feel her cheeks rise in a smile as she laid eyes on him. No doubt, he was a fine thing, too.

His sandy blond hair stood slightly askew at the top of his head and she had to resist the urge to pat it down, but it looked so cute all the same, like a bold schoolboy. Instead of his usual rugby-style top or T-shirt, tonight he was wearing a smart blue shirt, but it was his cheeky smile that really got her.

No one had ever smiled at Annie like that. And no fella ever seemed that happy to see her until now.

*Thank you for this trip, Felicity. It's helped me more than you know.*

"Hey, beautiful," he greeted as she approached, stepping out from behind the table to kiss her. His kisses were more intoxicating than any alcohol. It was as if he knew exactly how and where to move his lips so that Annie's insides melted like butter.

"Hello yourself, handsome," she replied jauntily.

"Allow me." Harry pulled out her chair for her and she smiled at the gentlemanly gesture. She'd never had a man do anything like that for her in her entire life.

"Thanks," she said with a smile, lowering herself into the chair.

"I hope you don't mind, but I ordered a bottle of red to get us started."

Annie paused a little. She really should refuse, given her vow not to drink too much and risk losing the run of herself altogether by behaving like a lush in front of him. She wanted to say no, but the eager look on his face made her change her mind.

This was their first proper date after all. She didn't want to ruin it by coming across like a Goody Two-shoes.

"Perfect." She smiled as he poured her a glass.

"So how's your week been?" he asked, and Annie was surprised to find he actually seemed interested to know. Again, most guys she'd been with couldn't be arsed with polite conversation—*or indeed conversation full stop*, she thought wryly. "How's your friend after her accident?"

"She's great—taking it easy, but that's no hardship in a spot like this." She was also touched that he'd asked after Colette. Just went to show that not only did he really listen to her, he also cared about what she said, and wasn't just out for what he could get.

Though, she thought with a grin, she kind of hoped that he was interested in that, too…

"Must say I'm still impressed that you're a solo traveler," he went on. "Though I can't quite imagine taking off on holiday on my own, I can see the attraction in getting time to yourself. The boys are great, but can be a bit full-on…" He shrugged. "It's nice to get away and do my own thing for a bit."

"I get you. Though it's been sort of the opposite for me. I came to Italy alone but I've made some friends since I've been here." She grinned. "Yourself included."

"I'm not surprised—you're obviously the sociable type." Then he reached across the table to touch her hand. "And I'm very glad you chose to socialize with me, though I rather hoped you might consider me a bit more than a friend…"

A delicious thrill snaked up Annie's spine at his touch, and she was sorry when shortly afterward their *primi* arrived and the moment was broken.

Despite the hokey surroundings, the meal was incredible. Harry's posh upbringing had obviously made him well-versed in food and wine, and Annie was enjoying the fruits of his expertise.

On his recommendation, she opted to forgo the Italian old reliables on offer and instead try a French cassoulet, enjoying the rich mix of white beans, duck legs, and melt-in-the-mouth pork. He, in turn, decided on tartiflette, a savory potato dish with cheese, bacon and onions.

For dessert they shared chocolate mousse and clafoutis, a kind of berry-filled cake covered in a flan-like batter. Followed, of course, by two shots of limoncello, which, Annie noted, they pretty much handed out like water in these parts.

She guessed she was probably going to put on at least half a stone with the richness of this meal but for once she didn't care.

Now she grinned as Harry fed her some of the clafoutis and she practically purred over the sweetness and the lightness of the crust.

"Told you you'd like this place." He smiled as he watched her. "Now hurry up and finish that wine, there's somewhere else I want to take you."

She raised a curious eyebrow in his direction. "Where?"

"You'll see," he insisted mysteriously, calling the waitress over for the bill.

Annie looked at her glass. It was her second—or was it third? It was hard to tell when the waiter kept topping them up and it was still quite a way full.

With that and the limoncello, she was already feeling a nice buzz and didn't want to run the risk of knocking it back too quickly—especially on top of all that rich food.

She was kind of sorry he wanted to rush off, too; she was really enjoying their conversation, and the opportunity of getting to know him properly without his mates in the mix.

"Just going to nip to the loo while you finish that," he said, dropping a credit card on top of the bill. "If the waitress comes back, tell her I'll just be a sec, OK?"

"Grand." Annie wondered if she'd get away with just leaving the rest of the wine behind, but she suspected it was an expensive choice, perhaps even vintage, so she'd better not.

Actually… She idly reached forward to check the bill for the price of the wine, glancing at Harry's Visa card as she did so.

Then Annie's heart started to beat a little faster as she noticed something that made her pause and then look twice.

Strange…

"Ready?"

But she had no time to think about it any further as Harry had arrived back at the table and beckoned for the waitress to take payment.

Annie's brain was reeling a little, both from the wine and what she'd just seen. Had she been imagining it? Granted it was so dark in here but…

She shrugged. There was probably a perfectly good explanation, or else she'd just got things wrong from the get-go.

As he put his arm around Annie's shoulders and led her from the restaurant, everything else was very quickly forgotten.

Once outside, his hand slid down to hold hers, their fingers intertwining, and she smiled involuntarily. "Aren't you going to tell me where we're going?"

"I'd rather show you," he replied mysteriously, continuing to lead her along. The pair walked along the streets beneath the olive trees, meandering off the main drag until a cliffside hotel just above Spiaggia Grande, the main beach, came into view.

Annie didn't catch the name of it, not that she had much of a chance to, as Harry started to lead her down some steps cut into the side of the rock toward the beach.

She could hear the water lapping against the shore as they got closer to the sand.

"Take off your shoes," he urged, as he began to slide his feet out of his own. He hooked them over his fingers and offered her the other hand for stability as Annie removed her heels.

Once off, she hooked the straps over her own fingers as they walked onto the sand. Thankfully, unlike Fornillo, the beach was less rocky underfoot and the damp grains immediately worked their way between her toes.

The cool water caressed their feet as they walked hand in hand along the shoreline. The usually packed beach was silent with no one around, only the faint noises from the hotels and restaurants up above.

Annie smiled headily. Now that she'd hit the air, the wine was very definitely affecting her.

He stopped then and turned to face her, pulling her into his arms. "Do you know how long I've waited to get you alone?"

Annie laughed lustfully. "And why'd you want to get me alone?"

He brushed an errant strand of hair from her face. "Why wouldn't I want to have the most gorgeous woman in Italy all to myself?"

She had to laugh. "In all of Italy, huh?"

His hand slid around her waist and then up behind her neck as he pulled her closer, molding her to his body. "More than just Italy, even," he whispered before his lips met hers.

The water cooled her feet as the rest of Annie's body automatically started to ignite.

*Annie. Control yourself.*

She could hear the words in her head but they didn't seem to be getting any further than that as she kissed him back.

She didn't want to take control. She knew it was fast, but she was really falling for this guy. No, she'd already fallen. Hard.

"OK," she said breathlessly when their lips finally parted. She leaned her forehead against his chest. "This is…intense."

"What d'you mean?" he asked, kissing her neck.

"This is just a holiday thing, yeah?" she said, between kisses.

"Don't worry about that now," he replied and Annie groaned as he kissed her neck again. "Right now you're here with me and that is the only place my mind is. I really wish you'd just be here with me."

Her eyes drifted back up to his face. "I don't want to be anywhere else," she said, desire overwhelming her.

"So don't talk about it. You're here with me now and that's all I want. Right this moment. Don't you?"

Annie shivered at the intensity of his gaze and the power in his words.

"Yes," she breathed before his lips silenced her. The passion in his kiss muddled her brain and sent all thoughts of caution scampering as her shoes dropped from her hand into the sand.

"Come with me," he asked as they parted. He was as breathless as she was and the passion in his eyes was savage. He led them back along the beach toward the pier and Annie followed, her eyes wide, wondering if he was actually planning on an al fresco shag.

"Hang on a second. Where are you going? We can't… Not here."

"Not the pier," Harry answered with a grin. "To the hotel… My room."

*Nice one…*

Her limbs trembled with desire as they climbed back up the stone steps and hurried to the hotel.

In the lift, he wrapped himself around her, kissing her with such intensity that she felt like hitting the emergency stop button and going at it there and then.

This was probably going way too fast but she couldn't stop it. And what else was new? Their heads were swimming and both were going under. She wanted him, desperately wanted to be with Harry.

Or whatever his name was.

# Chapter 23

Then

"You really don't have to keep coming here," Colette argued for the thousandth time. "I'm fine now." She sat rigidly on the tatty old sofa in the living room, while Luca brought her food.

She appreciated his efforts but she was sure the man had better things to do.

When Luca smiled it was like the clouds opening on an overcast day, and suddenly the sun came through in full force, making everything brighter.

Colette couldn't help but study him as he moved. He was so cool and authoritative in everything he did. The way he walked with long calm strides. The controlled way he moved to unpack the tray of food he'd brought with him.

However, what really got her was the way he looked at *her*.

His dark eyes seemed to peel back all of her defenses and cut straight through to what was beneath.

"I told you, I will be here until you are fully recovered," Luca insisted as he set a glass of water on a side table and took a seat on the sofa next to her. "Besides, I promised my aunt I would look after you. I would be in big trouble if I didn't."

Colette smiled. Yes, Mama Elene was sweet but fierce, she'd seen that much for herself. "I'm guessing she can be a bit of a drill sergeant," she joked.

"I always thought her more of a general," Luca said as he set the tray on her lap and carefully arranged everything out in front of her. Colette had never been so well looked after in her entire life. Not even her mother had been this attentive when she was a child.

"There is another reason I come," he said then.

"What's that?"

His dark eyes brightened a little as she met his gaze. "You."

Colette felt as if her head was about to explode. She must have misunderstood. "What do you mean?"

He smiled again and took her hand in his. "I mean that I want to get to know you better, my English rose."

"I don't understand," she said, slowly removing her hand from his. "Why?"

Her question seemed to amuse him as Luca began to chuckle. "You really don't see yourself, do you?"

Her brow furrowed at his odd response. What did he mean she didn't see herself?

"Why wouldn't I want to get to know you?" he asked. He folded his arms over his chest and adjusted where he sat to make himself more comfortable. "Tell me. I'd love to hear it."

Colette could feel the heat rising up through her body and she could only imagine what hue her cheeks had taken on as she fumbled for the right response to his question.

"I'm just…not the kind of person someone like you notices," she began with a shrug of her shoulders.

"And what kind of person do you think you are?"

That was a loaded question. Colette had to think for a moment. "Well, I'm not particularly outgoing, or gregarious like, say, Annie," she began. "And I'm not worldly or beautiful like Kim," she added softly. "I'm just…simple, I suppose."

Luca smiled. "Usually the simplest things are the best things."

Colette couldn't help the reaction his response had on her. A large smile spread across her face.

"And you're wrong," he added a moment later.

"About what?"

"You are beautiful," he replied as he curled a strand of her hair around his finger and forced her chin up with another so that their eyes met. "Don't ever say or think that you aren't."

There were wings inside her chest and knots inside her stomach as Colette sat there in amazement. The most gorgeous man she'd ever laid eyes on was telling her that she was beautiful. Maybe she'd hit her head harder than the doctor thought.

"You don't believe me?"

She shook her head. "Not particularly, sorry."

"It's because you don't see what I see," he replied as he leaned closer, one finger still entangled in her hair.

"And what's that?" she asked as she swallowed the lump in her throat.

"I see a brave woman with a caring heart. I see someone who has been through a lot and hasn't let the hardship destroy her. I see someone who doesn't know her own beauty because she thinks trappings like clothing, money, and color from a bottle is what makes a woman beautiful. I don't see any of that. I like my women in their natural state."

Colette almost choked on her food. His women? Was he implying that he wanted her to be his woman?

*Don't get ahead of yourself. He's just telling you what he likes.*

Luca leaned in and, in a low voice, said, "Did you know that you blush a lot?"

"Only around you, it seems."

"Why is that?"

Colette's eyes tried to stay on his but the gaze he returned was just too intense for her. She shrugged. "I don't know."

"I think you do," Luca replied. "I think you know a lot more than you pretend. You aren't like your friends."

"What does that mean?" she asked defensively. She hadn't known Kim and Annie long, but in the short time that they'd been here she'd come to care a lot about them. Each was unique and wonderful in her own way.

"I mean that your friends are who they are because of what they know and see. They aren't their true selves," he replied.

"How can you know that?"

"I've learned to pay attention to people," Luca answered with a smile. "Plus, I have five sisters."

"Five?" Colette repeated as her eyes grew large. How had he survived? She'd barely got through with one sister, far less five. She didn't want to imagine what bathroom visits were like in his house when he was growing up. All that estrogen, too.

"Yes. I was the only boy and firstborn child. I had a great deal of responsibility on my shoulders."

"How did you manage?"

"Very carefully," he chuckled. "I helped my father with his import business and my mother with my sisters until I graduated. Then I went on to get my business degree and follow in my father's footsteps."

"Do you enjoy it? Business, I mean."

"Business is good. We do well with it."

"But you don't love it, do you?" Colette realized. She could hear it in his words. "What do you love to do? What is your passion, Luca?"

He smiled again as he took a forkful of food and raised it to her lips. "This," he said, and Colette opened her mouth to taste it. She hummed her approval. "You like it?"

"I love it," she replied between chews, covering her mouth with her hands. "Mama Elene is such a great cook."

"My aunt didn't make this for you," he replied simply. "I did."

"What?" Colette raised an eyebrow. There was no hiding her surprise this time. "You made this? But I thought..."

"I've always loved to cook. Elene taught me everything I know."

"Then why didn't you become a chef like her?" Luca's expression faltered then, and she knew she'd strayed into a sensitive area. "You don't have to answer that if you don't want to."

"It's fine. I've spent the last few days getting to know you better. It's only fair that you get to know me as well, no?"

Colette didn't reply. If she said yes she might seem too eager, but if she said no it would be a lie. She wanted to know more about Luca. She wanted to know *everything*.

"My father had plans for me. I had a mother and five sisters at home depending on me. I had to do what was right for them," he replied. "That's how I know when a person isn't being their true selves. Because I'm not."

Colette refused the second forkful of food he offered. She leaned in closer as she studied his face. "Why? That must have been years ago surely. Why don't you be who you want to be now?"

"I still have my family to think of. My youngest sister is at school. It will be a few years until she's ready and able to take care of herself."

"So until then, you do what you have to, just not what you love?" Colette said sadly.

"I will be responsible," Luca replied. Another forkful of food was directed to her mouth then and Colette duly accepted it. It was so delicious, perhaps even more so now that she knew he'd made it just for her.

"Why do you feed me like that?" she asked. "I can do it myself."

"Because I like to watch your eyes when you eat," Luca replied. "I like to watch your expressions when you taste what I've made. Especially now you know that I've made it."

"How many of my meals have you made?"

A mischievous glint reflected in Luca's eyes but he didn't respond. Instead he fed her another bite.

"All of them?" she exclaimed.

"Hush, do you want your friends to hear? They'll think I'm doing something inappropriate in here."

Heat flooded her chest and neck once more. "You really did all this for me?"

"I told you: I like you. I take care of what I like."

If he didn't stop soon Colette wasn't sure her heart would be able to take it. No one had ever said such things to her before. She wasn't sure if she should believe it or how she should respond. All she knew was that she liked it. She liked *him*.

"What do you do in your father's business?" she asked as she tried to find something that would keep him talking.

"I'm vice president of Sales," he informed her.

"That's very accomplished. How old are you?" she inquired, realizing she wasn't quite sure of his age.

"I turned thirty-three on my last birthday. What's the matter? Did that surprise you?" Luca questioned as the next forkful of food hovered in the air between them.

"No," she lied, as Luca's phone began to chime. She'd actually thought he was much older.

"You're a terrible liar," he replied. "It did. Why?" He pulled the phone from his back pocket and promptly turned it off. "I hate these things. I would throw them all in the sea if I could."

Colette smiled. She felt the very same way about electronics and was especially glad he'd silenced it in favor of her. "I just can't figure out why you're being so nice to me."

His expression became gentle but his voice was serious. "I can see you aren't a woman who is so easily swayed by words," he replied. "So I think I will just have to show you."

"Show me?" she repeated as he got to his feet, faintly disappointed. "Where are you going?" Usually, he stayed while she ate, and sat and talked with her a while longer before heading back. But today he was leaving early, it seemed.

"I promised my sister I would take care of her children tonight," he informed her.

"You're babysitting?"

*Was there no end to this man's mysteries?*

"My sister and her husband have a new baby and busy lives. It isn't easy for them to get some time alone. I help when I can."

"That's really sweet."

"I'm a sweet guy," he replied as he leaned over and kissed her forehead. "Enjoy the rest of your meal, Colette. I will see you tomorrow. And we will plan what comes next for us when you are well."

*What comes next?*

Colette watched him go, all thoughts of food completely banished from her mind as she tried to figure out what a man like Luca could see in a girl like her.

# Chapter 24

## Now

Excitement woke Colette early. The sky was still dark as her eyes opened. Even though she had just woken, her heart was beating fast with nerves and anticipation.

She turned to look at her husband as he slept on beside her, smiling as she thought of everything he meant to her.

She remembered her promise to cling to the good times, and do her best to forget the rest, even when it was difficult.

Hopefully, though, their fortunes were about to change.

Colette kissed him lightly before easing herself out of their bed. There was something she had to do. Something important that could change their lives for the better.

She padded quietly to the en-suite bathroom, her heart in her throat with every step. This was it. She was sure of it.

This was what she'd been waiting for.

She closed the door behind her and kneeled to open the cupboard below the sink and retrieve what she'd hidden there. Colette unwrapped the small pink box from the bag it had been sold in and stared at it. In the past, these tests had disappointed her. The moment she realized her period was late she'd rush out and buy one, hopeful she was pregnant, but she never was.

Which was why this time she'd waited a full month for her period to appear. It hadn't, so Colette was certain that this time would be different. This time the result would be the one they wanted.

She sat on the toilet and had just put the cover back on the strip when Ed entered the en suite unexpectedly, rubbing his eyes.

"Oh, sorry, I didn't…" he mumbled blearily, then paused when he saw what was in her hand.

Colette froze. This wasn't how she wanted this to go. She had it all planned in her mind. She'd make reservations at their favorite restaurant and then at the end of the meal she'd reveal the happy news.

"What's this?" he asked as he stared at her from the doorway.

"What does it look like?" she replied automatically, gently setting the wand on the vanity.

Ed stepped further into the room. "Darling —" he began, but Colette wouldn't let him finish.

"My period is a full month late," she announced. "I know I always rushed into taking the test before, but I didn't this time. I waited. Still no sign," she said eagerly. "So there has to be only one reason for that."

He looked at her gently. "Well, one in particular, certainly."

"I didn't want to tell you until I was sure," she explained.

He stepped closer and took her in his arms. "You should have, though. I'm keen to know if I'm about to be a dad."

The excitement in his voice almost brought tears to Colette's eyes. She knew Ed really wanted a baby, knew how important family was to him. It was to her, too. She'd wanted to make a family with him for so long. She was sure that time had finally come.

"I'll wait with you," he said, lowering the toilet seat cover and sitting on top of it. He pulled her onto his lap as they waited impatiently for the result to appear.

Colette's leg bounced nervously and Ed placed a calming hand on her knee. "Take it easy," he assured her. "Relax."

She knew he was only trying to comfort her but there was no comfort for Colette at that moment. Within seconds she might finally be able to realize her life's dream.

She was so nervous it was a miracle that it was only her leg twitching and not her entire body. She just wanted this so badly.

Finally, enough time passed for them to check. Before Colette could do so, Ed grabbed the test and looked at it. His face remained still as his eyes moved from the display to her face.

"Well?" she pleaded, desperate for him to smile as she grabbed at it to see for herself.

"I'm sorry…" he whispered.

Colette blinked rapidly. *It couldn't be right.* Her period was a month late. Not days, weeks. A whole month.

"There has to be a mistake. A false negative, maybe," she said as she stood and dropped the test in the bin. She grabbed the box again, scrambling for the instructions, even though at this stage, she knew them off by heart.

"Darling…" he began, gently moving toward her.

"No," she said firmly. "I have to be pregnant." She pulled

out another box. She was going to do the test again. Ed stood by, helpless, as Colette took another wand out of its box.

"Darling, there's no point," he urged, but she wouldn't listen. *This couldn't be right.*

"Of course there's a point."

But a few minutes later, her heart broke afresh as again she was defeated. *Not Pregnant*, read the display. The test fell from Colette's hand and Ed dropped to his knees in front of where she sat on the edge of the bath.

"I'm so sorry, my love."

Her breath hitched as she fought against tears and lost. "Why?" she cried. "Why is it never my turn?"

He wrapped his arms around her and pulled her close. "It will be soon, I'm sure. Just not now."

"Why not now?" Colette argued. "When? When am I going to get my wish? When do I get to be a mother? Like Noelle, or your sisters-in-law, and so many of our friends. What about me? What's wrong with me?"

Now she was weeping openly. There was no hiding or containing the pain she felt. She'd got her hopes up and again they'd been dashed. They were always dashed.

She didn't understand it. The doctors said there was nothing wrong with her. Nothing wrong with Ed either. It just wouldn't happen.

*Why?*

"Come on," he urged as he tried to pull Colette to her feet, but she wouldn't budge. Undeterred, he picked her up in his arms instead and carried her to their bed.

He laid her down on top of the sheets and then sat down beside her.

"All I want is to be a mother," she cried. "I want to give you children. I know you want to be a father, too. I'm sorry that I can't seem to do it. So sorry I've failed you."

"Stop that," he chided, as he wrapped her tightly in his arms. "Don't say that. You have never failed me. Not once. You are everything I ever wanted. The only thing. It doesn't matter about children. I'm sure we'll have them eventually. Just don't ever say that you failed me, Colette. You couldn't, even if you tried."

"You don't understand how I feel," she wept as she looked into his eyes. "Every day I feel incomplete. It feels as if something is missing. I want a child."

She tried to extricate herself from her husband's grasp, but Ed wouldn't let her go. He held her tight as she cried out her pain and disappointment.

She cried until tears no longer came.

Finally she stilled, too tired to move. She stared unseeingly at the curtains. The light of the sun was beginning to show behind them. It was Wednesday. She had to get ready for work but she didn't want to go in today.

Ed stroked her hair. "There you go," he whispered soothingly. "Better now."

Colette was embarrassed. She'd never behaved like that before. She'd never allowed him to know how much pain she was in over her failure to conceive.

"I'm sorry," she began, looking at him.

"Don't." Ed pulled her against his chest gently. "Don't apologize for hurting. But maybe…maybe it's a good idea to just let all this go for a while."

His words gave her pause. "Let it go?"

"You know what I mean. That maybe we both stop trying so hard, and more importantly you stop beating yourself up about this. It hurts you to see the negative result, but it hurts me even more to see how much pain it causes you." He turned her face toward him. "Do you have any idea what it does to me?"

Tears stung her eyes again. "I just want us to have a family."

"We are a family. You and me. I don't need a child, Colette. Quite frankly, if trying for one is going to do this to you, then I don't want it at all." He hugged her tightly. "All I want is you. I'd do anything for you."

She couldn't believe what he was saying. *What about all the talk about family? A big family, with lots of children? Is he really willing to give that up?*

"What about everything we talked about?" she said, still stunned by what her husband had said. It didn't make sense in her mind.

"You're the one who always wanted a family, really. You wanted one, so I wanted one. But if we can't have one, it's fine, too. We don't need it. We have each other, don't we?"

Colette didn't know how to process this. Believing Ed would be so easy. And perhaps letting go of having a child was an easy solution, but it wasn't something she believed she could do. She wanted a child. The desire was deep down in her soul.

She'd taken care of her nieces from time to time, even as she watched Noelle's twins grow from a distance. Among Ed's siblings' children she was a favorite aunt, but that was it. An aunt. Not a mother.

"Always a godmother, never a mother," she mimicked bitterly as her fingers played absently against Ed's back.

"There's nothing wrong with that either," he said. "You are so great with children. Everyone knows that. But maybe it's just not meant to be."

"Don't say that," Colette responded as she pushed herself from his arms. "Don't ever say that. I know I'm supposed to be a mother."

"Colette..." Ed protested.

"No," she interrupted. "I don't accept that. I won't."

She rushed from the bed and over to the bathroom before Ed could reach her, slamming the door behind her and locking it. She could hear him at the door asking to be let in as she sat on the bath and once again began to cry.

How could Ed even say that to her? He knew what she wanted. He knew her heart. How could he just tell her it wasn't for her? She hugged her knees as his voice became more urgent.

"Colette, let me in. Let me in now. Don't do this. I'm sorry. Just open up."

"Just go away," she shouted back.

"Colette, please. This is ridiculous," Ed retorted. "You aren't a teenager. This isn't the way to handle problems. You can't hide away and expect the truth to just vanish. You have to face it. I know it isn't easy. I know it's not what you want, but you have to see what this is doing to you. What it's doing to us." Pain was in everything he said as his tone softened. "You think I want to say this to you? I don't feel good about doing it, especially now, but I have to. I can't watch you rip yourself apart anymore. I can't watch you blame yourself for something that isn't your fault. It just isn't happening and we have to accept that."

More tears erupted as she listened. This might be tearing them apart, but she couldn't let go of it.

No matter how easy it was for Ed to get past this and decide a life without children was OK, it wasn't for Colette. This was her dream.

Exhausted now, she slid onto the floor, resting her head on her arms as Ed continued to knock on the door.

"Just go away," she pleaded softly. "Please go away."

## Chapter 25

Now

It was dinnertime when Kim and her family got back to the Excelsior from the train station.

Lily was hungry and cranky, making eating in the formal hotel dining room an ill-advised option.

Their daughter was small but her lungs were mighty, and when she was upset they resounded everywhere. She wasn't at all badly behaved but when she was off-form she became very miserable and needed more attention.

Gabriel settled her back in the suite while Kim talked again on her phone outside on the terrace.

Hank had called back with some more information on the plagiarism claim.

"I just spoke to the lawyer. This person claims some of the

affirmations were her mother's. They were shared throughout the family for generations. She says you stole them."

Kim's heart hammered as she tried to get a handle on this. "Well, if it's family stuff, did she give any idea of how she thinks I supposedly came by this information to steal it?"

"Her attorney's being sketchy. I think he's trying to feel me out. Rattle us, even, in the hope of a quick payoff. Don't worry. I don't scare easily. And I don't lose either."

"I know," Kim replied. Then she paused. "Does anyone else in the company know about this?"

"You mean Antonio or the investors? No. Just you. I didn't think you'd want anyone worrying, especially with the launch coming up. The only ones who know are the clerk who received the claim, my assistant, and me. Think it's best to keep things quiet at this point until we fully know what we're dealing with."

"I knew I hired you for a good reason, Hank," Kim commented. He was great at his job. She was sure she could trust him to handle this. *If* it could be handled. She sincerely hoped it could.

Her entire life could implode if it didn't.

"Everything OK?" Gabriel called out gently from inside the room.

Kim turned and nodded, flashing what she hoped was a sincere smile.

He turned back to Lily, who was playing on the bed. "Mommy's busy," she informed him, rattling off what Kim recognized as her own familiar refrain. "Can I have chicken for dinner?"

She spoke so well for a three-year-old that people often commented on it. It even surprised Kim how smart she could be sometimes. Gabriel said she took after her, but she wasn't so sure. She didn't feel that Lily got anything from her, except her blonde hair. When she looked at her child she didn't see herself at all. Just Gabriel.

"Kim? You still there?"

"Sorry, Hank, what were you saying?"

"Just that I've also hired someone to investigate these claims. It'll probably be a couple of weeks before we can get better information. In the meantime, don't you worry. I'll make this go away—one way or another. Even if we just have to pay them off to get rid of them, but hopefully it won't come to that."

"Thanks, Hank, appreciate it." She glanced back again at Gabriel and Lily, laughing together in the room. Barely an hour into their family reunion and already she'd abandoned them for work again. What must he think of her? "I need to go. Talk soon."

She walked back into the hotel suite and set her phone down on the dresser. Lily pulled at her dress as she passed by, the bright pink color catching her eye. Kim sat down beside them on the bed and went to cuddle her daughter.

"Hey, honey."

But Lily just ignored her. She was too preoccupied with her dad. Kim felt familiar rejection fill her chest, but she did her best to push it aside.

She could feel Gabriel's eyes upon her as she rose from where she'd been perched. She walked toward the bathroom and closed the door behind her.

Why couldn't she do this? Just be a proper mom. Why did it all feel so…unnatural to her? She could feel the usual sadness rise up and she couldn't stop it.

Everything seemed to be falling apart just now. Just when it all should be coming together.

Tears glistened in her eyes and she shook her head to dismiss them, leaning against the sink vanity. She remained there for a couple of minutes before Gabriel's voice called gently from the other side of the door.

"Honey, are you OK?"

"Sure!" Kim replied quickly and cleared her throat. "Just coming." She flushed the toilet for effect and then moved back to the sink to splash some water on her face. She stared at her reflection in the mirror, and a tired, haggard face looked back.

Room service arrived soon after, and both Lily and Gabriel ate hungrily, though Kim barely touched hers.

When the meal tray was removed, they set about getting Lily ready for bed in the adjoining bedroom. She was fussy and difficult when Kim tried to change her into her pajamas, so Gabriel smoothly took over, telling his wife to head back out to the living area and fix them a drink.

A few minutes later, once Lily was settled, he joined her on the terrace, where Kim again found herself standing by the rails looking out over the water. It was so easy to get lost in the dark depths and forget her troubles for a moment.

Just for a moment.

"Hey," she greeted softly as she turned to look at him. His shirt was off, his feet were bare, and the only thing he wore were the light chinos he'd had on when he arrived. She smiled automatically. He was such a huge guy, tall, strong and built like a rugby player, and she remembered thinking the first time she laid eyes on him that he looked as if he could easily lift her up with one hand.

She loved that, loved how he always made her feel so protected and cherished. All man yet so tender with it. The combination was irresistible.

She really was a lucky woman. And it had been some time since they'd last had a romantic moment together. Gabriel's body was distractingly irresistible, but right now Kim just wanted to lose herself in his strong embrace.

"C'mere," he called, both arms outstretched, as if instinctively knowing it was what she needed. She moved to him, resting her head upon his firm chest, the downy hair soft beneath her cheek.

"I'm so glad you're here," she said as she tried to suppress a sob.

"What is it, babe?" he questioned. "Don't tell me 'nothing,' I know you better. Something's wrong and you aren't taking it well," he said gently. "Usually when something goes wrong, you're all action and solutions. I don't worry then because I know you'll figure it out on your own. Not this time, though. Tell me what's happening."

She looked at him. "You know me too well," she admitted.

"Hey, it's part of my job."

She raised her hand to his face and stroked his cheek with her thumb. "I think someone's out to sabotage me. And Villa Dolce Vita."

His brow furrowed, Gabriel led her back inside to their bed and settled on it, gently pulling her down beside him. "Why do you think that?"

Kim took a deep breath and then explained about the increased social media negativity and backlash, as well as the recent accusations.

"If this gets out publicly, it'll ruin everything."

"Aw, come on, nobody takes notice of online trolls. It's just keyboard warriors hiding in their bedrooms with nothing better to do. The bigger you get, the bolder they become. You know that."

"It's not just that anymore. The plagiarism thing… If the media gets wind of that, they'll have a field day. Especially when there's so much attention on us just now. Bad press for Villa Dolce Vita before it even opens for business will ruin it.

And with pretty much everything riding on this being a success, it could also end up ruining everything I've worked for."

Gabriel pulled her onto his lap and wrapped his huge arms around her. "You're getting way too ahead of yourself now. Hank will work it out, do what it takes to make it go away. That's his job, remember?"

"What if he doesn't, though? And what if this person decides to go public with these accusations—or worse, has proof of them? I'm finished."

"Babe, stop." Gabriel's gaze was fixed intently on her. "Stop working yourself into a frenzy about this. Let Hank do what he does best and you do what you do best. Everything's pretty much ready to go now. Take some of your own advice. Don't worry about what might happen. Deal with right now. Worry often gives a small thing a big shadow, remember?"

Kim smiled weakly. "You really have a way with words, you know that?"

"What are you talking about? They're your words." Gabriel smiled and Kim's heart almost broke in two.

She couldn't admit now that there was some truth to this person's claims. Not when Gabriel was essentially using what he thought were her own words to make her feel better.

"Anyway, it's true. Don't let this get to you. You can handle this. You've handled worse."

"Have I? It doesn't feel like it."

"Yes, you have. And I've been there. Every day since I first met you I've watched you fight for what you want, fight for your passion. It's what you do."

"Why do I, though?" The question was involuntary. Even though it had been rolling around in her mind, Kim hadn't intended to actually say it out loud. "Why is it so important?"

Gabriel was taken aback. "What kind of question is that? What do you mean?"

"I mean, it's not as though I set out to do this—be some kind of mindfulness expert. We both know I sort of just…fell into it, and it's not like I have all the answers either. I struggle as much as the next person."

"Which is exactly why you are so good at this. You're relatable and down-to-earth, not some otherworldly Dalai Lama type. You're just Kim, 'warts 'n' all.'"

"You're saying I have warts?" she laughed.

"I'm saying you're just like everyone else. You have your good days and bad. This is just one of the bad ones and it's inevitable given all you've had to do and think about these last few years. But it'll be over soon and then you, me, and Lily can get back to being a proper family."

Kim's heart sank a little at his words. Could they ever be a proper family when she had no idea how to be a proper mother?

All she truly knew how to do was work, strive, and keep pushing for bigger and better things.

And for what?

Still, she couldn't admit this to Gabriel. Definitely not now. No, she just had to keep going, and hope that what he said was true, that it would all blow over.

And Villa Dolce Vita's grand reveal would be the pinnacle of everything she'd worked for and more.

# Chapter 26

Then

"Do you really think I need *this* much eye makeup?" Colette asked, as her gaze shifted uncertainly between the mirror and her friends.

The three women were in the bedroom she shared with Kim and she was (incredibly) getting ready for a dinner date with Luca.

"Definitely," Annie replied. "It's about time you glammed up your look, if you ask me."

"But what's wrong with how I look?"

"It's a bit…I dunno…like a middle-schooler," Kim replied as she applied more eyeliner. "Annie's right. Time you upgraded and sexed up your style."

"*And* did something with your hair," Annie chimed in. "Your ends badly need a trim and the rest could do with a good deep treatment. Give me a decent go at it, and I could work wonders, honestly."

"Well, I don't want it to be a different color or anything," Colette said quickly, Luca's words from before still lingering in her mind.

"I wasn't going to suggest it—most people would kill for that kind of natural shade. Me and Kim just think there are a few more things you could do to make the most of yourself. You're very pretty, but you hide it all," Annie stated. "You have to show a guy like Luca that there's more to you."

"He seems to like me well enough just as I am, though." She was dubious.

"He does like you as you are," Kim agreed. "But there's way more to you than what he's seen so far. I think it's time he saw that. Don't you?"

"Yep," Annie replied for her. "We are going to make you look so good Luca won't know what hit him."

"I don't want him to like a pretense," Colette argued.

He did like her as she was. For some reason. She didn't mind making the packaging a little nicer, but she still wanted to feel like herself.

"He won't," Kim assured. "We aren't changing who you are, Colette. We're simply bringing out your full potential."

"OK…"

Her friends believed a makeover was exactly what Colette needed and it seemed they were determined to give her one.

Once Kim had finished doing her face, they flicked through her own designer wardrobe for something for Colette to wear.

She was surprised to find that she and Kim were pretty much the same size, though the leggy American's stuff was a good bit longer on Colette's shorter frame.

"He has to see behind all that innocence or else he won't stick around long," Annie stated authoritatively. "A guy like

Luca wants a woman. One who makes him look good and who looks good on his arm."

Colette glanced down at herself. She knew she didn't fit that bill at all.

Luca wore Ralph Lauren polos and Lacoste shorts. She wore Marks and Spencer with the occasional flash of LK Bennett in between. She wasn't a fashionista by any means, but if she wanted Luca to take her seriously perhaps she was going to have to at least show him that she could complement him. And try to hold her own against all the very many glossy and gorgeous women in these parts.

She gulped a little.

"How about this?" Kim asked as she raised up the dress for them all to see. It was a slinky shocking blue knee-length number with a plunging neckline and a daring split up one side. The bodice was fitted and sure to accentuate Colette's curves. But at least the dress's length would look midi on her and perhaps lessen the whole thing's in-your-face sexiness.

"I don't know," she said nervously as she looked at the revealing garment. "I've never worn anything that...color before."

"Perfect! That's just what we want. You trying the unknown," Annie confirmed bossily. "Remember what your mother said. You can't stay in your comfort zone forever. You need to step out and try new things."

They were right. Miriam was always saying there were lots of things out there for her to see and experience. She wasn't going to get that experience staying in her comfort zone.

Colette needed to do what she'd never done before. No more being careful and taking things slowly.

She needed to jump right in with both feet and find out if she could sink or swim.

# Chapter 27

Then

By the time she was ready to leave, Colette couldn't quite believe the sight that looked back at her from the mirror as she smoothed the creases in her dress.

The old mousy girl from Brighton was gone.

The dress did exactly what they'd said it would, bringing out her slender waist and the slight fullness in her hips. It even managed to make her bust seem fuller without looking trashy.

Thanks to Annie, the waves of her hair were completely smoothed out, and the crown pinned up in a neat chignon, while the remainder cascaded over her shoulders.

Despite her concerns, Kim had done an equally miraculous job on her makeup. It felt as if there was nothing on her face at all.

For the first time in Colette's life, she looked and felt subtly, effortlessly…glamorous. It was a heady feeling.

"Ready?" Kim's voice called from downstairs. "Taxi's here."

"Coming," she called back, and brand-new Colette got ready to face the world.

The two enjoyed a lively meal at a small seafood trattoria just outside the main town, somewhere near the water. But Colette couldn't concentrate too much on the food (which, in truth, paled in comparison to Luca's).

He truly had a way of making her feel like she was the only woman in the room, if not the world.

When they'd finished eating, he asked if she wanted to go for a walk "beneath the stars."

She smiled at the romance of it all as he led her by the hand while they made their way down the stone steps to a small bay, and didn't say a word as they walked along toward a nearby pier. In turn, Colette didn't feel the need to fill the silence with unnecessary chatter.

She was enjoying the quiet company he offered, but even more so, she was enjoying the feeling of her hand in his. He had big hands that completely enveloped her own, and they were warm and comforting as his fingers intertwined with hers.

The lights from nearby houses and buildings above the shore reflected on the water as they made their way along to the end of a pier that branched off to the right. The water lapped at the wooden structure but held firm as they stood upon it.

"It's so beautiful here," Colette said softly as she leaned against the rail and looked down into the dark depths.

"Not as beautiful as you," Luca replied, as he moved closer to her, his hands finding their way into her hair and moving the strands back over her shoulder as she turned to face him.

"Thank you," she replied with an automatic blush.

"It's the truth," he insisted, as he gazed into her eyes.

"Why do you say such lovely things?" she found herself asking as she looked at this impossibly handsome man beside her. "Is this a game? Am I a game?"

A tiny smile flashed across Luca's face for a moment before it disappeared. "You really don't see you," he muttered, and gently repeated the words he'd said before.

Colette's breath caught as he moved from her side to stand directly behind her, his arms wrapping around her waist, pulling her against his body. Then his mouth whispered against her ear.

"I won't lie to you, Colette. I've been with a lot of women in my life," he admitted.

Her heart sank. Why was he telling her this? Was it so she could prepare herself for the inevitable letdown in store? Clearly Kim and Annie hadn't transformed her in the way she'd hoped.

"Lots of women," he continued. "But they were all fake. Plastic dolls looking for someone to buy them whatever they wanted. They weren't like you. You are honest about yourself. I remember that first day I saw you sitting in Aunt Elene's restaurant. You didn't act like most tourists, who think that because they've watched a few movies or looked at a few pictures they know everything about Italy and life here. You took my aunt's advice and let her guide you. I liked that." Colette could hear the smile in his voice. "I also liked the outfit you were wearing. Also the face you made when you tasted the limoncello. It was a photograph."

"Really?" Colette questioned as she turned to look at him. It was a mistake. His face was so close that when she turned, their noses met and her breath hitched.

She could feel the heat begin to rise from her neck up to her face as she quickly turned away, much to Luca's amusement.

"You really do blush so easily," he commented as he pulled her closer.

"I can't help it. You unsettle me," she admitted.

"In a good way, I hope."

"I suppose. I've never had anyone affect me this way before."

"Never?"

She shook her head. "Not really. I told you."

"You told me you never really dated in England, but surely there was someone of importance?"

Colette thought about the question before she answered. She didn't have to think too long. There was only one.

"There was someone at university…" she admitted.

"What happened with him?"

"Nothing," she said softly as she hung her head. "He didn't like me."

Luca chuckled. "He was a fool. Then again, he was young, and when you're young you make foolish mistakes." He hugged her tighter. "I'm thankful he did."

"You are?"

"Yes, I am. If he'd seen what was before him, you might not be standing here with me now," he explained. He leaned closer again. "And I like that you're here," he whispered.

Her breath quickened and her heart was racing so hard she could hear it in her ears. "So am I."

She didn't dare turn around again. Luca's gaze was difficult enough to hold when he was sitting a few feet away. When he was only inches…she couldn't imagine what effect it would have on her.

She felt his hands at her waist as he turned her toward him. The moment he did she was caught in his eyes. Lost in the dark pools that looked at her as if she were the only woman on the planet.

"Colette?" he whispered as he leaned closer.

His lips were now getting dangerously close and her heart felt as if it were about to explode. Was she ready for this? How well did she know him? How could she be sure what this really meant to him? To her?

His lips moved closer.

Colette dropped her chin seconds before Luca's mouth would have met hers.

She wanted to kiss him, she really did, but so much fear accompanied the excitement, and at that moment the former had won out.

"I'm sorry," she apologized, mortified. "I can't..."

"It's OK," Luca assured, as he took her hand in his and kissed her knuckles slowly. "There is no rush."

# Chapter 28

Now

Colette's eyes opened blearily and she forced herself up from where she lay against the side of the bath.

She'd drifted off at some point after her tears had drained her.

There was silence on the other side of the door and she wondered what time it was.

Ed was more than likely at work now. Had he called the office to let them know she wasn't going to be in this morning or that she would be late?

She got to her feet and unlocked the door. In the bedroom the curtains were still drawn. She walked to where she'd left her phone beside the bed and checked the time. It was just after ten o'clock.

She ran her fingers through her hair and sighed as she

flopped down onto the bed. She'd made such a scene. She was going to have to apologize to Ed.

Quickly slipping out of her nightgown, Colette headed back to the bathroom to shower. As she stood under the warm jets of water, her hand slid over her flat stomach and she imagined what it would be like to smooth her hand over one with life inside it. How it would feel to have a child moving around, the feeling of little kicks against her hand. She wanted that so much.

She turned off the water, determined to put it out of her mind.

She dressed in jeans and a light cashmere knit, and the gurgling of her stomach reminded her it was long past breakfast time. Going downstairs, she heard Ed's voice still in the house. What was he doing still home? He should be at the office by now. She moved toward the sound and stopped in the doorway of the kitchen.

"I should have more information soon," he was saying. "No, I think that should be enough for now. But let me know of any further developments."

*Another business deal*, Colette mused, as she stepped inside the room.

Ed noticed her immediately and moved to end the call. "Great, thanks, just make sure to keep me up to date."

"What are you still doing home?" she asked.

"I took the day off." He smiled.

Her shock was obvious. Ed *never* took days off for no reason; he rarely even called in sick.

"What do you mean you took the day off?"

"I thought my wife needed me more today than my clients. So I told them I'd be available for calls but wasn't going to be in the office." He set his phone down on the kitchen island and walked toward her slowly. "Unless it's an emergency, I'm all yours."

Colette couldn't believe what she was hearing. "Seriously?"

"Yes," he replied. "I already called into work for you, too, and told them you won't be in, so you don't have to worry."

Ed's approach as he moved toward her was hesitant but Colette wasn't upset anymore. She wasn't going to keep going with the discussion. What was the point? It wasn't as if their arguing about it was going to make any difference. The tests were still negative.

He wrapped his arms around her. "I'm so sorry, my love. About everything."

Colette hugged him back. "I'm sorry, too," she said, a little taken aback by the hollowness in her voice and the numbness she felt as she spoke. The longer she was disappointed and the more absent Ed was, the more alone and empty she felt. She'd hoped a baby would end the feeling, but even that was being denied to her.

"So we're going out for the day," he announced chirpily. "All you have to do is put on some comfortable shoes and we're off."

"Where are we going?" she asked. She didn't understand this. This wasn't the Ed she knew. Her husband didn't just take her out on spur-of-the-moment day trips.

"Don't worry about where. Trust me," he said with a smile. "Today, it's all about us, Colette. Just you and me."

Curiosity got the better of hunger, so she did as Ed asked, got a pair of ballet flats and her handbag, and followed him outside.

His driver was waiting with the car already running when she stepped out onto the street and then her husband followed with a picnic basket in hand.

"Did you pack that?" she asked. If he had then she'd fallen asleep in the bathroom for far longer than she'd thought.

"No," he laughed. "I had something delivered. I'm sure you'll like it, though."

The drive to wherever he wanted to go was a long one. Traffic was especially bad from Belgravia and it took them over half an hour to really get moving.

As they drove along the Mall, Colette glanced up at the Queen Victoria Memorial standing prominently in marble, the golden angels with wings and hands raised to the heavens.

*The queen had nine children.* The thought ran unbidden through her mind. She shook it away, needing to move away from that mind-set.

That was what today was all about, apparently.

# Chapter 29

## Now

The car dropped them off at St. James's Park and Ed took her hand as they walked inside. They'd never done *anything* like this before; he was usually way too busy during the week and what free weekends he did have were usually spent socializing or wining and dining various business contacts.

Time alone as a couple just never really seemed to happen, although Colette got more than enough time alone with herself.

Scarlet oaks and black mulberries were scattered throughout the park, and fig trees bordered the lake, which Ed had chosen as their picnic spot. He draped a light blue blanket on the grass and began to unpack the basket as Colette sat watching him, amazed. He was still unpacking the meal when she noticed the logo on the side of the basket.

"Fortnum and Mason? You really went all out," she commented with a smile.

"Nothing but the best," he answered as he lifted out the smoked salmon. Colette's stomach gurgled afresh. She adored smoked salmon.

Her hunger was soon sated with the selection of mouthwatering delicacies Ed had chosen, each more delicious than the one before. They even shared a bottle of champagne, which they made quick work of before they were ready for dessert.

Colette lay back on Ed's chest and stared at the blue sky. It had been far too long since they'd enjoyed this kind of thing together. It was moments like these that she held on to. Moments she hoped would last. She knew that soon he'd be back to work and life would return to normal again, but hopefully this would keep her for a while. Food for a starving soul.

"Thank you," she said simply.

"You're welcome," he replied. "I know it doesn't make up for this morning, but I wanted you to know that I am sorry. I don't—can't—truly understand how you feel. I suppose having a child means a different thing to you than it does to me, and I'm sorry I told you to forget it. I had no right. I just don't know how to handle seeing you in pain. I just want to fix it."

"You can't fix this, Ed," Colette replied sadly. "It's just one of those things. I want a baby, and we just can't seem to have one. There's nothing that can be done about it."

"Perhaps we could think about adoption…"

"I don't want to," Colette replied quickly. "We've been through this. I want to carry my own baby and I know that seems selfish given there are so many children in this world who want and need good families. I know that. But it doesn't change the fact that I want to experience life growing inside me. I want to feel the fluttering, the kicks, and everything else that comes with being pregnant."

"Including swollen ankles and morning sickness?"

"Yes, even that."

"I wish I could give you what you want, darling. I really wish I could."

She smiled weakly. They ate dessert in relative silence as Colette watched the ducks on the lake. She was surprised at the number of people in the park at this time, midday (didn't they have jobs to go to?), and then figured they were probably wondering the same thing themselves.

After the picnic was over, Colette and Ed ambled through Birdcage Walk. They were silent as they moved beneath the trees, only the sound of the passing traffic there to entertain them. They were about halfway down when Ed's phone rang.

He looked at the display. "Sorry, darling, I need to take this."

He handed her the basket and walked away, Colette watching him as he went. It seemed her husband spent more time leaving her than he did greeting her.

She lingered around the area as she waited for him to return, occupying herself by studying moss growing on the trees and the numerous knots in the barks, almost like knuckles on a hand. There was so much green around her. It was nice to see. Very different to her usual view of dull gray buildings from her office window. She wondered what was happening at work now.

"Colette, I'm so very sorry, but—"

"You have to go," she finished dully. Of course it wouldn't last. His face fell. "I'm so sorry, truly. I'll call the car. I had told him to pick us up later but… Anyway, it shouldn't take him long. I'll have him drop you straight back home."

"Don't bother," Colette replied as she handed Ed the basket. "I don't feel like going home just yet. I think I'll stay here for a while; I was so enjoying it."

"It's an emergency," he told her, somewhat defensively now. "I have no choice."

"I understand," she said softly. "Honestly, go. I'll head back in to watch the pelicans. I love them."

"I know," Ed replied. "I'm sorry I can't come and look at them with you."

"Go—do what you do best," Colette replied sadly. "But I think I need to try something different today."

Saying goodbye, she turned and began the walk back to the lake. She sighed deeply as she strolled, willing the stress and pressure she felt to leave her.

It had been a day of such mixed emotions, most of them negative, but there were still enough hours left in the day she might be able to salvage.

By the time she returned home, it was evening and she found a note from Ed telling her he'd gone to Surrey to see a client and he'd be back late.

For once, she was fine with that. She wanted to be alone.

Colette settled on the couch in the living room with only the side lamp for light, tucked up with her box of memories— things that were always a balm to her soul.

It was not so much a box but an old-style suitcase that had belonged to her mother and one she'd had since she was a girl.

Sadly, and despite her apparent remission, Miriam Turner had died shortly after Colette's return from Italy—something Colette had never quite got over. To think that she'd been lazing around in the sun and living it up in restaurants and on boats, and worst of all focusing on stupid, trivial things like a summer romance, when she could have had three more weeks with her mother.

Three precious weeks she'd never get back.

She cast her mind back to that summer when she'd returned to Brighton, and Miriam had been so full of excitement to know how the trip had gone that Colette hadn't noticed how frail her mother had become in the meantime.

Or perhaps she'd just been too preoccupied with her own stupid worries at the time.

"What was the food like?" Miriam was especially interested to learn all about Italian cuisine, and whether they should take Colette's newfound knowledge and incorporate it into their own business. "We could try a version of cannoli in the bakery, maybe, put our own spin on it...?"

"I think that would go down really well, Mum," Colette agreed, telling her all about zeppole, struffoli and some of the other pastries Luca had introduced her to, but her heart wasn't in it.

When just weeks later, Miriam took to her bed with what Colette thought was just a bout of exhaustion, but passed away within days, life was once again completely upended.

And all Colette could think about was that they never had the chance to introduce the cannoli to the bakery.

She had been inconsolable as she sat by her beloved mother's side while Miriam's life slowly slipped away. Colette felt like the world had spun on its axis twice over.

Then her mother, her rock, was gone. Just like that.

She wasn't prepared for the surreality of it and the absolute numbness she felt once Miriam had taken her last breath. It was like stepping off a roller coaster and being completely unable to find your footing.

Four long years of worrying and keeping things going,

followed by the sheer relief of the so-called remission—she should have known it was too good to be true.

Colette often wondered if maybe her mother had lied about her miraculous remission just to get her to spread her wings and live a little, but she would never know for sure.

She was so devastated and completely useless that Noelle had to step up to make all the necessary arrangements and deal with the doctors and funeral arrangements.

Ed had been her crutch throughout it all, though, and following Miriam's death, a budding friendship that had begun in Italy turned into something more.

The trip had transformed Colette in more ways than one.

Inside the suitcase were various bits and bobs from over the years, important mementos from special times in her life: two tickets to *The Lion King* musical, the first West End show Ed had taken her to, pictures of their summer trip to the Cotswolds a couple of years before.

Then she saw what she was looking for.

Nestled among the various photographs was a picture from that summer in Italy.

She was standing in front of Delfino with Mama Elene and Luca. He had his arm around her shoulders. She looked so happy.

Right then Colette made a decision. She wasn't going to wait until the day of the launch to fly out to the Amalfi Coast, like Ed wanted.

She'd go on ahead on her own, and spend a bit of time with Kim and hopefully Annie before the night of the party, but more importantly in the place where, once upon a time, she had truly felt happy.

"Where are you now? I wonder," Colette whispered as she trailed her fingers over Luca's image on the photograph.

Six years ago, but it felt like it was yesterday. Even now

she could almost feel the weight of his strong arm across the back of her neck and the delicious scent of his skin. She wondered if he still religiously visited Delfino every day for his usual espresso.

And whether she should look for him there when she returned...

# Chapter 30

Then

"Where are we going?" Colette inquired, as she and Luca drove along the coast in the dusk, the lights of the buildings twinkling below them like a group of fireflies swirling around the mouth of a cave.

He smiled mysteriously. "You'll see. It's a surprise."

She smiled as she leaned back in her seat and looked out the window. The smile broadened when she felt Luca's hand move over hers.

She was grateful that he hadn't pushed her the other night, but had been certain that her reticence would be the end of his attentions. In fact, it had seemed to make him even keener.

"Nicely played." Annie had high-fived her, when, mortified, Colette had told the others all about what she'd thought was a disastrous night out. "This Italian stallion has obviously met his match in you."

She seemed to think that Colette was playing some kind of game but truly she wouldn't even know where to start.

She just hoped Luca didn't think the same. She was nothing if not honest and she didn't believe in, or tolerate, deception of any kind.

But she was pleased her resistance hadn't put him off and this time she decided if Luca tried to kiss her tonight she wasn't going to stop him.

"The restaurant at the pier again?" she guessed, when he parked the car in the same location as before.

"Something like that," he mumbled, as he got out and came around to open the door for her. He linked her arm in his. "Your chariot awaits."

"Chariot?" she repeated, laughing, as he led her down to the water to where, this time, a small sailboat waited at the end of the pier. "What's this?"

"Your chariot," Luca said. He stepped on board and then held out his hand to her.

Colette giggled, amazed, as she joined him on deck. "Can you really drive this?" she asked dubiously.

He winked. "I would think so. She's mine."

"You have a boat? Why didn't you tell me that before?"

"I just did."

She watched as Luca cast off and stood in front of the wheel on the upper deck, guiding them out of port. Then she moved to stand beside him as the twilight spread out before them.

"It's getting dark out there," she commented as they pulled away from the reflections below the bay and further into the open waters.

"That's what's so wonderful about it," Luca replied. "Out here the sky and the water become one. You can't tell where one begins and one ends. It's as if there is nothing at all but you and the universe."

"You're something of a philosopher, aren't you?"

"Nothing of the sort at all," Luca replied. "I just know what I like and I spend my time doing it. That's why I brought you out here. Someone I like, to share in something I like." His gaze turned on her as he spoke, and Colette felt a familiar flush rise from the tips of her toes all the way up her body.

"Can I take a look around?" she mumbled, keen to change the subject even though she was pretty sure he wouldn't be able to spot her embarrassment in the darkness.

He smiled. "Please—go ahead."

The boat, though relatively small, was rather spacious on the inside. A small galley kitchen was to the immediate left as Colette descended the stairs, and a food storage area on the right.

Further inside the cabin was a compact lounge area with a table and some banquette seating, a toilet to the side of that, and further in, a double bed occupied the bow area. A nervous lump formed in Colette's throat the moment she saw that, but then the boat jerked in the water so she headed back up.

It was about half an hour before Luca dropped anchor, and once the boat was moored and all was calm, he invited her downstairs once again.

"Have a seat," he requested as he began to roll up his sleeves. "Dinner will be served soon."

He was cooking for her again, but this time Colette would get to watch him work. Luca truly had magnificent hands. The way they flew across the food as he prepared it. He had obviously learned a lot from his aunt. He had everything perfect, from preparation to plating, and Colette was enthralled by it. He could have been a professional. He should have been.

"You're really good at that," she commented as she watched him chop vegetables with deft skill and precision.

"Thank you. I will teach you, if you like. Come here."

She moved into the tiny kitchen space. He handed her the knife and positioned himself directly behind her.

"It's all in the placement of your fingers," he said, his voice low in her ear and sending automatic tingles up her spine. "You must move them like this," he stated as he curled his fingers over hers. "Then the knife is used in a rocking motion, the tip acting as your pivot point."

There was something unashamedly sensual in what he was doing and Colette listened distractedly as she allowed his hands to guide her.

She wasn't trying nearly as much as she was listening to how melodious that accent could make anything sound, and the way he spoke about food with such passion.

She could only begin to imagine what it would be like to feel those hands moving across her bare skin, and realized with a start that she badly wanted to.

Colette swallowed hard.

# Chapter 31

Then

"Why don't you pour some wine and get comfortable back on deck," Luca suggested as eventually heavy beads of sweat began to form on Colette's nose. She wasn't sure if it was from the stove or the heat in her body. "I am almost finished here."

She reluctantly did so, carrying up the cutlery and wineglasses he handed her.

Back outside on deck, the air was completely still and she had no idea where they actually were, though she could still make out the glittering lights of the coast in the distance.

Once again, she was struck by the romance of it all, and she pinched herself, unable to believe she was sitting in the middle of the Mediterranean on a boat with a gorgeous Italian man who seemed impossibly keen to impress *her*.

Up above, the sky was blanketed with stars; constellations she had never seen before lay painted like a canvas above her. It was all so beautiful, truly like something out of a fairy tale.

Minutes later, Luca joined her on deck, placing a mouth-watering plate of food before her.

"If you were to leave your father's business, would you want to become a chef?" she asked as they ate. "You really could, you know."

He smiled a little as he sat across from her. "I don't think that'll happen any time soon."

"But if it did. Would you?" Colette sipped her wine.

"Probably," he replied. "But I doubt I could."

She sensed his wistfulness. He truly did want to do something else with his life, but commitments were holding him back.

The chicken was tender and juicy, the vegetables crisp and perfectly seasoned, and the pasta was perfectly al dente.

"Another masterpiece," she sighed and sat back, unable to eat another morsel. She shivered a little, beginning to feel the late-evening chill off the water on her bare skin beneath her off-the-shoulder top.

"Your approval is always appreciated." He smiled as he cleared the table.

A minute later, a warm blanket slid over her shoulders. "Come," Luca said as he gently took her hand and led her to the front of the boat. Once there, he took another blanket from where it was draped around his own shoulders, and arranged it on the bow of the boat. "After you."

Colette lowered herself onto the softness of the blanket, and looked up in wonderment as she lay down beneath the sky.

"It is beautiful, isn't it?" he commented as he joined her.

"It's incredible."

"You're incredible."

"Oh, stop it," she replied automatically, as a fresh blush painted her cheeks.

"Why do you have such trouble with me saying these things to you?" Luca questioned as he raised his head and propped it up on one arm to look at her.

"I'm just…not used to it, I suppose."

"You should be. You should have people telling you every day how wonderful you are." He put a finger beneath her chin and turned her face back toward his.

"But I'm no one special," she insisted.

"Yes, you are, and I think you could be even more with the right person."

Colette swallowed hard. "And who would that be?"

"Me." He leaned closer, and this time Colette didn't turn away. She kept still, caught between nerves and excitement, as his face hovered over hers and then finally their lips met.

His kisses were sweet, tender yet passionate, and it wasn't long before her hands were touching his face, and she wrapped her arms around his neck, pulling him closer. Their kisses quickly grew deeper and more urgent, and Colette's body screamed for his, unable to believe she could want anyone— or anything—as much as she did in that moment.

As she lowered her hand to the belt of his trousers, a little amazed at her own boldness, he stilled and moved to look into her eyes. "Are you sure?"

She nodded, surer of anything she'd been in her entire life.

Afterward, Luca moved onto his back and pulled her closer to him, nestling her into the crook of his arm, while Colette's body still trembled from the intensity of their lovemaking.

She had never felt so incredible, so alive, as she did just then. As she rested her head against his chest, she felt the ripple of his muscles beneath the fabric and incredibly a fresh wave of arousal stirred.

She smiled to herself in the darkness. This was obviously what people were talking about when they joked about Italian men...

She'd had no idea what she'd been missing.

"What are you thinking about?" Luca asked.

"Oh, nothing," she lied with a grin, snuggling up against him. She wanted to stay here and listen to him forever.

The way he'd made her feel just now, how her insides turned to mush whenever he looked at her, how he spoke to her, and what he said just made her want to lose herself in him and never awaken from that dream.

Despite herself, she was falling for him and she didn't know what to do about it. This could be nothing more than a holiday romance, the ultimate cliché.

But sometimes clichés were a very good thing.

"I never want this night to end," Colette admitted with a sigh. "Is that silly?"

"No," Luca replied. "I am wishing for the very same thing."

She smiled in the darkness, deciding there and then to just go along with it, whatever it was and wherever it might lead.

She and Luca remained there, lying in silence in each other's arms, the picture-perfect sky above them, when the sound of his phone buzzing broke the silence.

Groaning, Luca extricated himself to fish out his phone. He shook his head in frustration, but when he looked at the display she noticed a flash of something, besides annoyance at being interrupted, dart across his face.

"*Scusi,*" he stated, quickly moving away from her and continuing to speak hurriedly in Italian.

He was too far away for her to make out what he was saying, but the secretive way he'd moved to the other end of the boat instinctively made her stomach roil.

"Everything all right?" she asked when he returned.

"All is fine," he replied distractedly.

"Are you sure?" Colette questioned as she studied his face. "I know you hate phones but I hope that wasn't bad news or anything."

But he seemed irritated by her questions, and just like that, the mood changed.

"Nothing to worry about," he insisted, heading over to the wheel of the boat. "Let's get you back."

# Chapter 32

Now

It was an impossibly busy day at #GlamSquad.

Several important clients had appointments all around the same time, which meant all hands on deck and Annie spending more time than usual out on the floor instead of in the office.

Unused to being on her feet these days, by the time four o'clock hit she was exhausted and almost ready to go home and collapse into bed when the phone rang.

"Annie, it's Nick. Can you come over to my office—preferably today? I need to speak with you face-to-face."

Nick was her business manager of sorts, her friend Gemma's brother and a financial whiz kid. Annie was thinking of expanding the business and opening a second and possibly even a third salon, and he'd originally agreed to help her look at the best way to finance it all without putting the current operation under pressure.

But he'd recently ended up having to take a more hands-on role by stepping in and taking over the accountancy side when Annie's previous guy immigrated abroad suddenly.

She checked her watch. "Timing's not great, Nick. Can't it wait till tomorrow? I was just about to head off. Anyway, what's going on?" she teased, her voice light. "You make it all sound so serious."

"It is, actually. And no, I'm not sure it can wait."

She sat forward in her seat, all ears. They had an easygoing, almost buddy-like relationship, and she'd never actually heard him sound so serious.

"Hey, what's going on?"

He sighed heavily. "Well, I'm looking through the accounts for the last three years and I have to tell you, there's something very wrong."

Her heart leaped into her throat. "Wrong how?"

"I really think it'll be easier if you just come here and see for yourself."

"OK. I'll try to be with you within the hour."

"Great. See you then."

Annie was troubled. She was due to meet with the bank soon to help fund the second premises and thus needed the accounts in order before then.

Nick had only been working on them a wet week. What could possibly be wrong? Business was booming. Every single day they were out the door with clients—exactly the thing that made the idea of a second salon a no-brainer.

Distracted, and still feeling more than a little uneasy, she picked up her mobile and fired off a quick text.

Something unexpected's come up so I'll be a bit late. Call me if any issues.

Annie left the salon for the girls to close up later.

She got into her car and headed straight to Nick's office in nearby Kimmage, meeting some annoying traffic on the way. Half an hour later she was seated in front of his desk.

"So what's going on?" she demanded, sitting up straight in the chair, unsure what to expect, but bracing herself for a problem.

In her world, there was *always* a problem.

Nick looked at her, a deeply solemn expression on what was usually an open and smiling face. It was one of the things that had initially made her trust him. And Annie didn't trust easily.

"I honestly don't know how to say this…"

"Just spit it out, Nick. I've never known you not to speak your mind. And you obviously made me come all the way over here for a reason."

"It's not often that I have to tell a client—" his face softened then "—or a friend, what I have to tell you."

Her stomach knotted afresh. Now he was seriously scaring her. "What do you have to tell me?"

"The business…it's in trouble, Annie. Serious trouble. Basically, you're broke. Other than what cash you have in the bank."

Everything froze. She was sure she'd misheard him. "What did you say? That's not possible."

"I'm sorry but it is."

She sat forward and slapped her hand on his desk. "No, it isn't. We do a good six figures in turnover a year and have done so for the last three at least. There's little overhead besides the lease, so profits are very healthy. You're obviously missing something."

"I'm not, truly. You mention three good profitable years but as far as the Revenue is concerned, you owe them back taxes for every penny you've ever made."

"What are you talking about? I put aside a huge lump sum for tax every year—I always have. And I'm up to date with staff insurance and pension contributions…"

But Nick was shaking his head and Annie's heart plummeted again.

He stepped out from behind his desk and perched on the side of her chair. "Your last accountant was obviously creaming the money you set aside for the Revenue. He never paid them a penny, Annie. He's also messed up your cash flow by being late on supplier invoices and racking up some serious interest."

Her mind was whirling. "Frank was stealing from me? But how? Why?"

"I'm not entirely sure of all the ins and outs of it just yet. But even a quick look at the numbers and alarm bells started ringing. I waited until I'd spoken to someone at the Revenue office and knew for sure until I involved you. But it would probably explain why he left so suddenly when you got me in to go over the accounts."

"Oh my God. How much do we owe?" she asked, afraid of the answer. But being a businesswoman was all about facing facts. Not to mention that Annie had never been one to hide away from reality. Better to just face up to it instead of collapsing in a heap about the whys and wherefores. "And how much cash *do* we have?"

Nick's voice was especially somber now. "I'm sorry, Annie. At present, the business owes far more in back taxes, interest, and penalties than it earns. So the short answer is…nothing."

"Don't say that!" Her breath hitched and tears began to fill her eyes. Despite her best attempts at keeping her emotions rational and in check, upon hearing this she couldn't help her despair.

*Nothing...*

What the fuck had Frank done? And why? He'd come highly recommended, so she'd trusted him to keep the books in order when the salon had become so busy that she could no longer do it.

Granted, she'd had a hard time letting go of the reins initially, but that was understandable. This was *her* business, her baby. And Frank had messed it up on her—stolen from her, cleaned her out!

Her knuckles went white as she clasped the side of the chair. She'd kill him. She'd track the bastard down, wherever he was, and there'd be hell to pay...

"It's a horrible situation." Nick was still talking. "And he obviously scarpered when he knew he'd be found out."

"This *can't* be happening..." Annie whispered, almost to herself. "He can't get away with this..."

"I know you're upset and that's understandable," Nick soothed, moving to place a comforting hand on her arm. "This is a huge shock to the system—for anyone. But now we need to figure out what happens next.

"The salon owes the taxman a lot of money—everything. Even if you set up a payment plan, with interest and penalties, you'll be paying it back for years. And the current cash to hand won't be enough to keep paying the staff or indeed yourself a salary for too much longer."

A cry left her lips so suddenly it surprised her. "You mean I'm finished? Gone? The salon is finished?"

She didn't know how to process any of this. She'd worked so hard for so many years to get where she was.

Felicity had *trusted* her to make something of herself.

Now Annie felt dizzy. It couldn't be true. All these years,

all the work—blood, sweat, long hours, and sacrifice—gone. The shock, confusion, and pure disbelief she was feeling then reminded her of when she'd first heard news of her father's death all those years ago. This, too, felt like a death.

It couldn't be happening...

Her mind reeled as she tried to get a handle on the implications of it all.

She wanted to run out of the room, get as far away as she could from Nick's words and this unfolding nightmare.

But she also knew she couldn't do that; from what he was telling her, the situation was critical, beyond that, even. There were decisions to be made, plans to make—desperate measures to consider. She didn't have the luxury of taking off somewhere to cry and lick her wounds.

Nick had made that much very clear.

Still Annie couldn't escape an all-too-familiar feeling of déjà vu. And that, once again, she'd been let down. As always, just when she thought she'd found something good in life, the ax had to fall.

Story of her life.

# Chapter 33

Then

Colette wandered along the streets of Sorrento with a smile on her face and a spring in her step.

She'd never really been desired before. She'd never been anyone's girlfriend either, though she wasn't quite sure she was Luca's yet.

She hoped so, especially after the other night.

It was entirely possible for a man like him to genuinely care about someone like her, wasn't it?

She still had her doubts, but that wonderful evening they'd spent together on the boat had encouraged her to forget her misgivings and just enjoy the time they had together while she was here.

Her copper hair looked like flames as she glanced at her reflection in the passing store windows. Whereas before she would've frowned at her fair skin and freckles, these days, thanks to Luca, she had a greater appreciation for them.

The summer dress she wore—a recent purchase—came above her knees and hugged her neat waist. It wasn't flashy or revealing, still pretty simple, but thanks to Kim and Annie's style advice, a lot more flattering than anything she'd ever dreamed of wearing before.

"Ah, here we are," Colette mumbled happily to herself as she peered up at a sign.

House of Gems was Mama Elene's recommendation when— on a recent visit to the restaurant with Luca—she had asked the older woman for shopping advice. She said it was the best retailer to find quality jewelry at decent prices.

"Don't waste your money in the tourist places," the Italian woman cautioned.

The windows were filled with unusual displays that used everything from driftwood to coffee cups to enhance the appearance of the merchandise.

Inside, the floors were covered in green tiles that looked like marble. They may very well have been marble but Colette was clueless on the subject. Glass display cases dotted the cozy space, while shelves adorned the walls. Colette wandered past a case with a selection of rings and watches, further on toward the bracelets and necklaces.

She was hoping to find gifts for her mum and sister, as well as picking up something small to thank Kim and Annie for their advice, and as a memento of their time here. Onyx, opals, sapphires, and other gems Colette couldn't identify, but certainly looked pretty, lined the display before her.

"Welcome, I'm Anastasia. How may I help you?" a pretty woman with black hair greeted in Italian.

Colette turned to her with a smile and cleared her throat a

little before responding, also in Italian. "I'm looking for some gifts for some special people in my life."

"For a birthday? Or other celebration?"

Colette shrugged. "Just a thank-you."

Anastasia smiled. "You have come to the right place. We have everything you need for every reason." She picked up a silver bracelet with a green stone in it. "Would your friends perhaps like something like this?"

Colette looked at the circles of green mounted in shining silver. It was beautiful, but she wasn't sure it was Kim or Annie. She shook her head. "I don't think so."

Anastasia smiled and moved on to another piece, equally as beautiful, but still not quite what Colette imagined either of her new friends wearing. Kim was elegance personified, whereas something fun or quirky would work best for Annie.

A few minutes later, when guilt began to plague her for the amount of Anastasia's time she was taking up when she still couldn't find something, Colette asked the young woman in English to give her just a few minutes to look around. Everything was so beautiful, which was why she was having such a difficult time deciding.

She turned back to a display case.

"So much to choose from, isn't there?" a male voice commented from beside her.

"Yes, but I just told Anastasia—" Colette looked up and the rest of the words got lost in her throat. Standing in front of her was one of the most attractive men she'd ever seen.

He looked down at her with his arresting eyes and smiled brightly. Colette was lost for words. This part of the world seemed to have a never-ending supply of appealing males.

He chuckled. "Sorry, but I don't know Anastasia."

She felt her cheeks grow warm. "You don't work here,

do you?" she realized, feeling stupid for not recognizing the accent.

"No, I'm afraid I don't. I was just trying to pick out a gift for my mum when I overheard you talking and realized I wasn't the only English-speaker in here."

"You're on holiday here?" she asked.

"Yes, though not for much longer, sadly. Hence the gift-buying. I'm not keen on souvenirs."

"Me neither." Colette smiled. "I'm looking to pick up something unique for my friends, but everything here is so lovely it's hard to decide."

"I'm Edward, by the way," he introduced himself with a smile. "But please, just call me Ed."

Colette studied his open face and smiled back. "Colette."

"Pleased to meet you, Colette."

He was charming and funny, and the way he looked at her made her stomach flop. This was incomprehensible. What could two lovely men like this one and Luca possibly want with her? It didn't seem real.

"Could we perhaps make a deal?" he whispered conspiratorially.

"What kind of deal?"

"I'll help you find something for your friends if you'll help me choose something for my mum? Agreed?"

She smiled. He was nice and had a way about him that Colette knew she could trust him. What was the harm?

"Agreed."

"Wonderful," he answered. "So, tell me a bit about your friends and let's see if we can't figure this out between the two of us."

"Well," Colette began, "one is a fun-loving brunette who seems to have it all under control. She's vivacious and creative, and can do things with hair and clothes that I could only dream of."

"You came here together on a girls' holiday?"

"No, actually." Colette shook her head. "We're staying at the same accommodation and just struck up a friendship. The one I just described is Irish, and the other's from New York."

"A New Yorker, eh. Tough-to-please ball-breaker type, I'd imagine?" he teased.

"Not at all, she's lovely. Though she has expensive taste, judging by the clothes and accessories she has with her. She's also very wise and loves to read."

"So one is a feisty go-getter while the other is a wealthy nerd?" Ed mused with a mischievous glint in his eye.

Colette laughed. "Something like that."

He winked. "OK. I think you've given me enough to go on."

"And what about your mum?"

"Well, she's in her mid-fifties but looks much younger. She's been going gray for years, but masks it by getting her hair colored on a regular basis. She's sophisticated and very sweet, a wonderful mother who is always there for her three children," he mused. "She's a giver, too—always keen to help others."

"She sounds wonderful and would probably get along well with my own mother. She's much the same."

Colette walked back to a display she'd studied earlier and glanced over the necklaces, before selecting one with a trio of pearls set in gold and centered by a diamond dangling from a thin gold chain.

"Here," she said, pointing to the piece beneath the glass. "That one. You said there were three of you?"

"Yes. And that is lovely. Sophisticated, too, exactly like my mother," Ed replied. "Perfect choice."

They both looked up to see Anastasia approach. "Any luck?" the assistant asked with a smile.

"I have," Ed replied, "but my friend's still looking."

Colette looked at him in surprise. "Just like that?" she whispered. "Don't you want to check the price first?"

He smiled. "I'm sure it's fine. Hold on to this for me for a moment," he instructed Anastasia. "I'm still helping my friend."

Several minutes later, Colette walked out of the store with her purchases in hand and a smile on her face.

The selection had been much easier with Ed there to help her. And fun, too. She turned to thank him again as he stepped out the door behind her.

"It was my pleasure." He grinned. "Like I said, us Brits have to stick together. Though I must say, I was impressed when you started chatting to Anastasia in Italian at the end there. I know a few words, but felt like such a clueless tourist compared to you."

Colette laughed. "I studied the language at uni and it's nice to get the chance to practice."

They chatted more then about their respective educations and where they'd studied. As Colette suspected, Ed was the product of private education, which suggested he came from a wealthy upbringing.

Though their roots seemed miles apart, it was still nice to find common ground in their nationality.

"I better get going," she said, shielding her eyes from the late-afternoon sun. The shops were getting ready to close for the afternoon. "It was nice meeting you, Ed. Enjoy the rest of your time here."

"Very nice to meet you, too, Colette, and likewise. Perhaps we'll bump into each other again before we leave."

# Chapter 34

Then

"Heading out with lover boy again tonight?" Colette asked later that evening as she peeked around the doorframe of Annie's room.

"Yep," the other woman answered with a coy smile. "What about you?"

"Luca's usually busy with work on weekdays…" Colette replied, settling herself on the corner of the bed.

Annie thought she noted a hint of hesitation in her tone, but then became distracted by the small purple box tied with white ribbon she was holding.

"What's that?" she asked, expertly running straightening tongs through her hair.

"It's a present."

"From who?"

"Me to you," Colette answered simply.

She laughed in surprise and delight, and went to sit beside her. "A present for me? Why?"

Colette shrugged. "You and Kim helped me so much after the accident, and with Luca, of course. I just wanted to get you both something to say thank you."

Annie took the box in her hands and pulled the end of the ribbon to untie it. She flipped the top open and nestled among soft white satin was a gorgeous silver bracelet with a single oval-shaped turquoise stone at the center.

"You got this for me?" she asked in disbelief. Her life really was full of surprises these days. First Felicity's bequest, then the three girls' unlikely friendship. And Harry, of course.

And now lovely Colette was buying her gifts.

Unexpectedly, Annie could feel her eyes begin to sting and she became overcome with emotion as she ran her finger over the beautifully crafted piece.

"I picked them up in Sorrento earlier." Colette raised her hand to show an identical bracelet adorning her own wrist. "I got one for Kim, too. Something we can all remember this trip by."

"I love it, thank you. But you really shouldn't have… There was no need."

"It's perfect, and so thoughtful," Kim said, stepping into the room, a similar bracelet also on her wrist.

"Almost feels like we're one step away from starting a girl band," Annie joked archly. "The Runaways."

The following morning, Annie paid the taxi fare, trying to ignore the driver's knowing look as he dropped her off outside the villa entrance.

Evidently the walk of shame was a thing in Italy, too.

Though this was different, she reminded herself as she let

herself into the courtyard. Harry wasn't just some random one-nighter, he was much more than that.

Maybe she would get lucky and everyone would still be asleep when she got inside. Strangers or not, she didn't want to advertise to the other guests that she'd spent the night elsewhere.

Typical Irish Catholic guilt. She'd got away with it so far but...

She slipped her shoes off to minimize the noise on the stone floor as she snuck in the back door, closing it behind her as quietly as she could before tiptoeing past the kitchen.

"Good morning," Kim's voice sang out knowingly, and Annie winced.

*Caught red-handed.*

"Hey," she answered airily, popping her head around the kitchen doorframe to face her friend.

"She's home?" Colette called out from behind her. "Thank goodness."

Annie was trying her utmost to be nonchalant. "So what's for breakfast?" she asked, breezing into the kitchen. She moved to the fridge and took out a jug of iced water, waiting for the questioning to start.

Now that it was inevitable, she'd prefer to get it over with sooner rather than later. She wanted a shower. She hadn't intended to stay overnight and when she woke up forty-five minutes earlier in Harry's hotel room, she'd been in too much of a hurry to get back before the others noticed she hadn't come home to waste time on a shower.

"Things went well with Prince Charming last night, I take it?" Kim slid into a seat at the heavy wooden table and looked at Annie with a smirk.

"You could say that," she replied, sitting down beside her and taking a long gulp of water. She was parched.

Kim chuckled. "I'd *more* than say that. This is the third night this week you've stayed out."

Annie looked at her, surprised, and Kim winked. You couldn't get much past her all the same. "Well, who's to say it's the same fella?" she boldly quipped with a wink back.

Colette sat down opposite, looking mildly shocked at this, and Annie resisted the urge to pat her on the head. She really was too sweet and naive sometimes.

"So you've slept with the guy you've been meeting?" she asked her timidly.

"I wouldn't say that we…slept much," Annie replied wickedly, and she and Kim guffawed as Colette turned a brilliant shade of red.

"But you barely know him…"

Her friend's words stuck, especially in light of what she'd discovered (or thought she had—there could easily be an alternative explanation) at the restaurant the other night.

OK, Colette was right, she barely knew Harry, but yet it felt as if they'd known each other a lifetime.

"I know it may seem that way, especially since you guys haven't met him yet," Annie conceded, "however, he's different. He's together, more mature, and I suppose a little more serious than most guys I know. Most importantly, he's serious about me."

"How do you know?" Colette asked.

"Know what?"

"That he's serious?"

Annie paused to think it over. She didn't know how to explain how she felt or where to begin. She just *knew*. But if she'd known she'd be asked to prove why he was different, she would've made a list in advance to save her tired mind the effort now.

"Well, right from the beginning we had a connection—

before you guys arrived, actually," she said, reminding them that she had in fact known him even longer than them. "Just... the stuff he does and says when we're together, I suppose. Even when we're out with his friends his attention is still always on me. And when he looks at me...well, no one has ever looked at me that way," she continued, smiling a little.

"But what happens when he or you go home? Won't everything come to an end?" Colette persisted. But Annie got the sense that she wasn't quite as concerned with Harry's true intentions than perhaps with Luca's.

Aha.

"He says he doesn't want to think about that. He just wants us to enjoy now. What?" she asked, noticing Kim's dubious expression.

"Nothing," she replied, but Annie knew she wasn't really buying it.

*Well*, she thought defensively, *Kim will change her tune once she sees us together.* Not that Annie needed to convince anyone. It was nobody else's business after all.

"Nothing, my foot. What's that's look for?"

"It's nothing, honestly," Kim replied. "You're a big girl and I'm sure you know what you're doing."

Annie's gaze wandered from Kim back to Colette, who looked troubled. "Colette, why all the questions? What about you and Luca—have you two done the deed yet?"

Colette colored and Annie's eyes widened. Well, who'd have thought it? It really was the quiet ones you had to watch.

"It's just..." The younger girl looked uncertain. "It's just we had this...amazing night, but I haven't heard from him since."

"Well, I'm sure he's busy with work. Didn't you already say he had to go to Rome on business?" Annie reminded her.

"Yes, but it's not just that that's bothering me." Colette's eyes shifted uncomfortably.

"Colette, spill. What is it?" Kim asked.

"Something happened that night on the boat…" Her eyes left Annie's face and settled on a spot on the table. "We were having such a…romantic time together and then he got this call. He was really mysterious about it. He hates mobile phones but this time he answered. He jumped up away from me to take it and then immediately afterward we needed to go back. I felt weird about it, especially the way he went so…cold after. And now it's been days since I've heard from him."

Mysterious calls that ruined the mood when you were with a fella? Annie knew those situations all too well. And they usually meant the same thing—you weren't the only one he was seeing.

She looked at Colette sadly. She could tell that her friend was serious about Luca, and that she cared about him.

She hoped for her sake that she was wrong about this, but there was no way to be sure. Especially when dealing with Italian men in summer resorts, where having holiday romances and multiple women on the go was almost expected.

Kim replied before she could. "Colette, if you felt something was strange, did you ask Luca what it was about?"

"I did. He just told me it was nothing to worry about and that he needed to get home," Colette replied.

Another bad sign in Annie's mind.

"Well, if you're concerned that he hasn't been in touch, why don't you just phone him? No reason why you should have to be waiting on him to call you."

"I don't have his number," the younger girl admitted simply. "As I said, he hates phones."

*Oh, come on…*

"Seriously?" Annie said disbelievingly and Kim flashed her a warning look. "He hates mobile phones? Yet he was able to take a call on the boat that night—an important one, apparently."

The writing was on the wall here as far as Annie was concerned. Colette *was* being played for a fool. And she was damned if she was going to let that happen.

"I know," Colette admitted, with more than a hint of embarrassment. "But maybe I'm just imagining things. Maybe that call really was nothing to worry about—a business call or something."

"At that hour of the night, though?" Annie mused skeptically. "Weren't you guys out there well after dark? I mean, it's possible, of course, but it's also just as possible it was something—or even someone—else…"

Colette looked so crestfallen that Annie felt like a heel and realized that she should really keep her thoughts to herself.

Kim obviously felt the same way—staring daggers at Annie now, she put a comforting hand on Colette's arm. "Sweetheart, I think that maybe Annie is trying to suggest that you should take a step back from this whole thing for a bit, just to be sure. It's not that we're saying that Luca's playing a game or anything. We're not. It's just that maybe you should take your time on this?" she assured her.

Colette twisted her hands in her lap. "OK, but if there is someone else…then maybe I'm no better than he is."

"What d'you mean?" Kim asked.

"I mean, I've kind of…met someone else in the meantime." She peeked up from beneath her long lashes.

Annie yelped. "Holy feck, what? How the hell have you managed to snag yourself another fella?"

Colette's face contorted in confusion. "It's not like that," she continued and Annie's mind almost exploded when she told them about a guy she'd bumped into at the jewelry shop in Sorrento the day before.

She had to smile. How in God's name did innocent little butter-wouldn't-melt Colette manage to get two fine things chasing after her in a matter of weeks? Clearly, she and Kim were all wrong about Colette needing to sex-up her look; she was doing just fine without them!

"He was really nice and as we were saying goodbye he asked for my number," she explained. "So I gave it to him. He was so nice. And we've been texting a little, and now he's asked to meet up again for a coffee. He's really sweet... Totally different to Luca."

"*That's* why you're confused," Annie stated, as the revelation hit her. "This other guy is paying attention, whereas Luca's MIA and it's got your mind questioning."

"That's the problem, you see. I'd feel bad for spending time with someone else—even as friends," Colette said.

"But remember these Italian guys are very charming. You've got to be careful," Kim cautioned.

"Ed—that's his name—is not Italian, though. He's a tourist, like us."

"You know, I'm starting to feel kinda left out here," Kim said, laughing. "The two of you have multiple guys crawling all over you and I haven't even come across a single one that's caught my eye."

"That's because you spend too much time sitting around here being zen, and not enough out there painting the town red," Annie teased.

"Well, you know, maybe that's no bad thing. I did way too much partying back home. I'm enjoying just soaking up life here and taking it all in." She sighed. "Be happy in the moment—that is enough."

Annie groaned inwardly at Kim's words of wisdom. Good luck to Kim, but she herself didn't believe in any of that inspirational mumbo-jumbo. She yawned. Hell, she really needed to go back to bed…

"So what do you think I should do?" Colette asked them. "If Luca didn't ever really care about me and this was just a holiday fling, should I go and meet up with Ed, even as friends?"

Annie had to smile. Talk about a turn-up for the books. Who'd have thought shy little Colette, who wouldn't say boo to a goose when she arrived, could now potentially have two men on the go? The change in her was a wonder to behold.

"Well, I know this isn't easy to hear and it's not easy to say, but maybe you have to also look at the big picture and think about what happens after you leave here. I know you like Luca and he seems to really like you, too, but, Colette, do you honestly believe it can be anything more than a holiday romance?"

"Same could be said for you," Kim pointed out, and Annie knew she felt she was being a bit too blunt with the younger girl, but she needed to be.

Colette had to face up to reality eventually.

While Luca seemed nice enough, he was a player through and through, anyone could see that. Especially now after this whole thing about the mobile phone. Who didn't use mobile phones in this day and age?

Someone who had something to hide, that's who.

While Colette seemed to think all the little notes he left for her here at the villa when she wasn't around were old-fashioned and romantic, to Annie her friend's naivete was showing. She'd been around the block enough herself to recognize all the signs. And she truly didn't want to see her get hurt.

If someone didn't talk some sense into her, Colette could end up leaving Italy with a lot more than she bargained for.

# Chapter 35

Then

It was a glorious morning, and Kim could smell the citrus from the lemon trees as she walked through the courtyard and out onto the cobbled path leading down to the center of Positano.

Annie was right: she had been spending a lot of time lazing around the pool and gardens, trying to decide what to do when this trip was over.

Today she was in the mood for exploring, and while she'd asked the others if they wanted to come along, Annie had gone back to bed after her late-night exploits, and she suspected that Colette didn't want to leave the villa in case Luca chose today to come and visit her.

Both had become so wrapped up in their love lives lately, and despite her joke about being left out, Kim truly had no interest in that; not at the moment, anyhow. Romance could be such a humbug, and her life was complicated enough without throwing a vacation romance into the mix. Though she would definitely welcome a charmer like Luca to wine and dine her a little, in order to take the strain off her rapidly depleting line of credit.

She sighed, resigned to the fact that if she wanted to stay here, or indeed anywhere else for much longer, she'd need to think about finding a job.

Thank goodness she'd decided to rough it and that the villa was cheap enough that she could stretch her stay to another few weeks at least.

After that, she'd either have to wing it or head home to her parents with her tail between her legs.

Given her most recent conversation with her mom—when Kim had come clean about her journey diversion—that was the worst possible option. Her parents knew by now, of course, that she hadn't gone to England as planned, but they didn't know where she actually was, and she felt it was unfair to have them worry unnecessarily.

Assuming they cared.

When she'd finally plucked up the courage to call, the phone in their house on the other side of the world rang for a long time, so long that Kim suspected there was no one home. Then, all too soon, her mother's voice could be heard complaining about the hour of the night, and the inconsiderate nature of what Kim had done. No requests regarding her whereabouts or assurances about her safety or indeed any hint whatsoever that they might have been worried or afraid for their only child.

"Mom," Kim had said firmly, "shut up."

The silence on the other end of the line was deafening.

"I don't need you anymore," she continued, having by now

practiced the words a hundred times over. "I don't want you using me to impress your Park Avenue friends or persuade Dad's condescending business associates. I don't want you pulling my strings."

"What are you talking about, Kimberley? You're making no sense. Are you drunk?"

"A little bit," she admitted, staring at the glass of wine she was holding. "But it's not that, it's time and space that's given me the courage to say what I've been afraid to. I'm not a child. I'm a grown woman who knows what she wants and doesn't, and I don't want what you guys want for me. I don't want to have to pay my dues so you can have your heart's desire. I want *my* heart's desire. I'm not the same as you and Daddy, always making deals and manipulating relationships for your own gain."

The silence on the other end of the line spurred her on and soon Kim was saying things she never dreamed she would.

She unleashed it all, thirty years of misery in just a few minutes. Her heart was on a speedway but it didn't matter. It felt good to say it, to let it all out for the first time in her life.

"So that's it. I'm in Italy now and, to be honest, I'm not sure where I'm going next, but I'm going to take some time to find out who I am. I'm going to live my own life on my own terms. Not yours. I would truly love it if you could understand but I don't expect you will. However, I would like you to respect my choice."

"Are you finished?"

"Yes."

"Fine. If this is what you feel and this is the choice that you've made, then I have no choice but to say this. Don't come home, Kim. After what you've done to me and your father—embarrassed this family and shown such disrespect for everything we've done for you—there is nothing here for you anyway."

Gloria disconnected then without another word, not even a goodbye.

Kim was hurt but not surprised. She was a little surprised, though, at the relief she felt.

*The only impossible journey is the one you've never begun.*

And she knew then that she'd be OK.

## Chapter 36

Then

Kim took the bus from Positano down to Amalfi, in the hope that the journey might afford some great coastal views, but the bus was so packed the only view she got was that of a fellow passenger's armpit.

She'd researched a couple of the more popular tourist sights beforehand and began now at the Cloister del Dolce Vita—which she thought was fitting given the name of the villa and her now increasingly popular social media account.

Choosing photographs for it had become an enjoyable pastime, and while Annie seemed to think Kim spent a lot of her time just lazing around, she was actually out and about in the town exploring some of Positano's hidden-most corners and trying to compose interesting shots.

She wondered if maybe she should think about becoming

a photographer as her next step. It was something to consider, but in any case, it was the first time in a long time that Kim felt she was doing something she truly enjoyed.

According to what she'd read about this place, the thirteenth-century Moorish-style cloister was known for its magnificent gardens and religious artefacts.

Outside, a statue of Jesus surrounded by angelic hosts and the twelve disciples stood ready to greet would-be visitors.

Inside, the floors of the cloister were tiled in black-and-white marble and the walls painted white with various motifs chiseled into the stone. Large brown marble columns and smaller ones dotted the interior, with gold being the predominant decorative feature.

The entire structure boasted vaulted ceilings supported by what must have been hundreds of slender double and single columns, and the ceiling frescoes reminded her of the work of Michelangelo.

Kim was so taken by their beauty as she snapped photo after photo that she didn't realize anyone was near until she unceremoniously stepped on someone's foot.

"Oh, I'm so sorry," she said quickly as she turned to the other person—a woman of about her mother's age, who stood an inch or two taller. She was impeccably poised and beautifully dressed in what Kim immediately recognized as head-to-toe Armani.

"No trouble at all," the woman replied in a thick French accent.

"What's that?" a tall, stately man asked distractedly from beside her. He, too, had been so busy studying the frescoes to notice Kim's gaffe.

"I wasn't talking to you, Antonio," the woman said, rolling her eyes conspiratorially at Kim, who smiled.

"I'm so sorry," she apologized again. "I was just a bit mesmerized. Stupid tourist."

"Oh, please, no." The man chuckled easily now, and Kim deduced from his accent that while his companion might be French, he was very definitely Italian. "It is good that you are enjoying the sights."

"This whole place is just incredible."

The man laughed again. "They say that when Judgment Day comes, the people of Amalfi will have no change in life, for they are already living in paradise because of this cloister."

"That's lovely and sounds about right. I'm Kim, by the way."

"I am Antonio, and this is my wife, Emilia."

"So happy to meet you," the woman greeted, lightly taking Kim's hand.

"We would be happy to show you around a little more if you don't mind this old Italian acting as tour guide?" her husband offered.

"Oh, shush, Antonio, I'm sure Kim would much prefer to wander around herself."

"No, please, I'd love that. That is if you don't mind me playing third wheel?"

Emilia pealed with laughter. "*Ma cherie*, we have been married for over thirty years—believe me, I would welcome the distraction."

Their warmth and openness made her take to them immediately. Kim watched them, wishing her parents had the same easiness about them. She observed how loving and tender they were toward one another and how keen they were to include her.

They explored more of the cloister for a while and then Antonio and Emilia insisted Kim join them for lunch.

While the restaurant was amazing and the food the finest quality, the company was the primary reason for her enjoyment.

The couple were each wonderful raconteurs. They talked and laughed and shared stories of their travels all throughout their marriage. Antonio was indeed a native, from Milan where they both lived and worked.

He did something in business while Emilia—a former model—now worked in magazine publishing.

The waiter delivered their main course and the juxtaposition of the colors of her Caprese salad against the backdrop of the ocean was such that Kim couldn't resist whipping out her phone.

"I'm so sorry," she apologized to the couple again as she snapped a quick shot, "I'm going to have to be a goddamn tourist again, but my followers will totally lap this up."

"Followers?" Antonio inquired.

Rolling her eyes good-naturedly, Kim went on to tell them all about The Sweet Life social media account and how she was documenting her trip and sharing it all online.

Though it had since ceased to be so, she neglected to mention that the whole thing had begun as a secretive way to communicate with her friend and hide her whereabouts from her folks.

While chatting, she cropped, filtered, and uploaded the photo, deciding that she'd go back and caption it later. For now, actually eating the damn food was more important.

"What an intriguing idea. So like a photographic travel diary?" Emilia queried and Kim nodded, handing her the phone so she could see the picture she'd just uploaded. "My goodness, you are a talented photographer, these are wonderful—Antonio, look." She showed her husband, who smiled politely but distractedly. He, too, wanted to get on with eating lunch, instead of looking at it in photos.

Kim had to smile but inwardly she was pleased. "No, it's filters that make the photos look that good, honestly. I'm not that great at all."

She tucked into her lunch, but Emilia was still scrolling through her phone. "Seriously, Kim, these are wonderful, especially combined with your beautiful words. Really brings the imagery to life. Are you sure you haven't worked in journalism or even publishing? Perhaps you should."

"Hmm, not so sure about that," Kim laughed and swallowed a mouthful of food. "My parents would definitely kill me for letting my business degree go to waste."

The trio chatted some more over lunch, about other places Kim should visit, both here on the Amalfi Coast and elsewhere in Italy. The couple even very kindly invited her to visit them in Milan should she have cause to be there, but Kim suspected her money would have run out by then.

After the plates were cleared, she excused herself to find a restroom.

"Of course," Emilia replied, directing her to the back of the restaurant. Kim was enjoying herself so much that she made a mental note to try and come back with Colette and Annie sometime before their trip was over.

When she returned to the table, Antonio and Emilia were deep in animated conversation and she grimaced a little, hoping she wasn't interrupting anything.

The older woman looked up and smiled as she approached.

"Kim, I'm sorry, but I have a curious nature. The Sweet Life, your travel journal—I noticed it has a great audience. Your photographs are very popular."

"Oh, not really," she replied nonchalantly. "Compared to some people's—celebrities and stuff—it's nothing."

"Nothing?" Emilia repeated, glancing at Antonio. "I think it is something indeed." She looked at Kim keenly. "The photos are wonderful, but what I read was also very good. Wisdom far greater than is usually found in someone your age. You have some beautiful ideas on life and how it should be lived."

Granted the photos were hers and she'd paired them with what she felt were the perfect anecdotes and captions, but really... Kim could never have come up with stuff like that on her own.

Still, it felt good to be praised. It was a very long time since Kim had been complimented about anything other than her looks.

"Thank you," she said, taking a drink of water.

"Why don't you use this? Build on it?"

"What do you mean?"

"That wisdom. Why don't you share it? You've already created an impressive following in such a short space of time. But people respond even better to people—to faces—and I'd be willing to bet that if you yourself appeared in some of these posts—along with your wise words—people would love it even more."

A small laugh escaped Kim as she listened. "I don't understand..."

"My wife works in magazines, remember?" Antonio reminded her. "She knows of what she speaks."

"The industry is on the crest of a new wave—a huge disrupter," Emilia continued. "Social media is the way forward, especially in the fashion industry. We see it all the time—people like those silly American girls now becoming more popular and influential than some of the world's top models."

Kim made a face. "The Kardashians, you mean?"

"Yes. But I don't mean you should be like those, showcasing makeup and plastic eyelashes. I am thinking something more...holistic."

"Ah, I understand," said Antonio, nodding sagely. "Wellness is a huge industry, growing at an incredible rate." He winked at Kim. "Listen to my wife—she is the greatest business visionary I have ever known."

And as Kim sat in a restaurant in the Italian sunshine, high above the Tyrrhenian Sea, she chatted with two complete strangers about how she could, in fact, monetize the audience she had so far and perhaps turn The Sweet Life into something much, much more than a travel diary.

## Chapter 37

Then

There was no point in denying it. Despite her best intentions, Annie had fallen, and fallen hard.

She'd tried her utmost to convince herself (and the others) that she was playing it cool, but there was no pretending that she really missed Harry whenever they were apart and couldn't wait to be with him.

Had Annie O'Doherty finally allowed her world-weary heart to be melted?

"Out *again* with lover boy tonight?" Kim smirked as Annie got ready to meet him that evening. "Should we wait up or just catch you in the morning?"

"I'll be back later, smart-arse," she replied archly.

"I wasn't trying to be smart," Kim declared, all innocence.

"I was just wondering if we should lock up or leave the back door unlocked for you."

"You can leave it open, I won't be too late. Who knows, maybe I'll bring him back with me," she added with a wink.

"I wish you would. I'd so love to meet this hot stud who's been keeping you so entertained. Between you and Colette, I'm starting to get lonely. Where is she, by the way?"

"Out with Luca. He did indeed call to pick her up while you were out. Maybe I was wrong about him being a chancer. But now I do feel bad for leaving you all on your own, actually. Do you want to come out with me?"

"Don't be silly, I was only kidding. I've had a long day myself so am going to turn in early."

A beeping horn outside the gates from the taxi she'd called sent Annie rushing for the door. "Honestly, I shouldn't be back too late tonight, I promise. See you later if you're still up. And Colette—that is if lovely Luca's not ravishing her on his boat again." She grinned and fanned her face. "Lucky girl."

Kim laughed. "Have fun."

Arriving at his hotel—their agreed meeting spot—Annie headed straight to reception to have them call up and let Harry know she was here, but to her surprise he was already waiting for her in the lobby.

"Hey there, handsome," she greeted, kissing him.

"Hi," he replied with a weak smile. "I thought we might grab a bite here tonight if that's OK."

"Of course."

Straightaway, she knew something was off.

The meal was lovely and perfectly civil, but he kept his eyes on the menu or his plate most of the time, refusing to meet her gaze. Annie's stomach tightened with disappointment and her heart automatically closed over. She'd been around the block enough times to know what was coming.

And just when she'd thought things were going so well.

"Is something wrong?" she asked eventually, as he mulled over dessert options, his face glum and somber and a complete contrast to his usual jokey demeanor.

"No," he replied gently. "I'm just finding it so difficult to choose…"

"I didn't mean the dessert," Annie stated sharply. "I mean with you. You're acting really strangely."

He exhaled. "I just have some things on my mind, that's all. It's back to the real world soon and…"

Annie's heart lightened a little. "And you're worried about where that leaves us?"

"No, I'm not worried about that at all."

Now she automatically felt relief fill her stomach. OK, so he seemed pretty confident about where they stood. That was good, wasn't it?

After dinner, he walked with her down to the beach, where once again they found themselves alone. She couldn't help but reminisce about the first time they'd done this and all that had transpired since.

"It's so beautiful tonight," she commented as they walked. "Then again it always is. Everything about this place is beautiful. I'll miss it when we leave."

"That's true," he replied. "A place where the unexpected happens, wouldn't you say?"

It was. Annie hadn't come to the Amalfi Coast looking for anything she'd found there. New friendships weren't on her mind, and neither was falling in love, but she'd found both just the same.

Or maybe they had found her. Maybe, like Felicity said, this magical place really did have the power to change lives.

"Let's sit," he instructed as he pointed to one of the blue

sun loungers. Annie did as he asked, and he sat beside her, but still seemed tense.

"What is it?" she asked, wondering why the mood seemed so strange tonight.

Was he maybe becoming maudlin that their time together was coming to an end? She hadn't figured him for the sentimental type. He'd seemed quite laddish and macho from the outset, but then again a lot of lads were when they were in a group, weren't they?

And she knew he had a much softer, more romantic side. It was the one she'd truly fallen for.

Now he squeezed her hands gently, rubbing his thumbs over the curve of her knuckles.

"Annie, I'm sorry. I haven't been completely honest with you."

Aha. So he was going to come clean about what had been bugging her since that night in the restaurant.

*Well, this is good.*

"It's just… I'm sorry, because I care for you and I don't want to hurt you."

*Hang on, no.* This was something different. More than a silly misunderstanding or a mistake.

A sickening feeling once again began to fill her stomach and she held her breath for a moment to gather her composure before she spoke.

"What are you sorry about?"

He bowed his head. "I'm afraid there's…someone else."

This she hadn't expected, and instantly she felt her hackles rise.

"Someone else? You're telling me you already have a girlfriend? And you're telling me *now*—after all this time?" Annie was incensed. "Don't you think you should have mentioned something before?"

"I know…and it's been great," he replied. "But maybe things have started to get a little out of hand."

"A little out of hand? It's not as if we just had the odd drunken fumbling one-night stand. We've spent the best part of the last two weeks together and now you're telling me you're already taken. What kind of an arsehole are you?"

"It's nothing like that," he replied quickly. "Believe me, please. It's not that. I don't have a girlfriend, Annie, honestly."

"Then what is it? If you don't have a girlfriend, then what's the problem?"

"It's just… I've met someone else." His voice was soft and his eyes couldn't look at her face.

"Someone else—here in Italy?"

Now Annie felt as if the wind had been knocked out of her. This she didn't expect *at all*. So he wasn't cheating on some poor girl from back home. He'd taken up with another one here.

While screwing her at the same time.

"Yes," he confessed. "Believe me, it wasn't intentional, just a chance encounter, really, but I haven't been able to get her out of my head."

"A chance encounter? You make it sound like something from a romantic movie," she spat. "So you've spent all this time with me, romancing and shagging *me*, then you meet this other girl and suddenly, *bam*! Just like that, everything changed?"

"Something like that. I didn't expect it to, but it did. I'm sorry, Annie, like I said, it was completely unexpected, out of my control. Her spirit is just so bright and lovely that you can't help but fall for it—"

Annie sucked in a jagged breath. "You love this girl?"

His eyes fluttered nervously, but he couldn't look at her. She studied his face. He looked truly penitent.

She'd never seen that before. Every time she'd been dumped

or blown off, the expression on the guy's face was nonchalant—that's if he bothered to tell her at all. Whereas Harry's face now was full of regret and confusion, and somehow that hurt even more.

"Answer me," she urged.

"It's too early to know," he finally replied. His eyes returned to hers. "But perhaps…I could."

There was no holding back the rage now. "So what about me?" she spat. "What about us? What now?"

"Annie, please believe me when I tell you I never meant any of this. When I met you that first night, I thought you so vibrant and alive; it was like a shot of something electric in my veins, and I've loved the time we've spent together. I really care about you."

He was breaking her heart while telling her how much he cared? It made no sense to Annie. His kindness in disappointing her was a million times worse than the harshness she'd received all the times before.

"Obviously it wasn't enough," she answered bitterly. He didn't reply. "Not enough to compete with whatever this other girl could give you anyway."

"She hasn't given me anything. It's not like that. I didn't sleep with her, if that's what you're getting at."

"No, you just slept with me. Multiple times. And now you're just casting me aside because something better's caught your eye."

He didn't even try to deny that. "I'm sorry. I don't even know her that well, to be honest. But there's something there, I'm certain of it. And for that reason alone, I have to be honest with you. I couldn't live with myself otherwise. I think you know that I'm not the kind of guy to mess people around, or at least, I hope you do."

"Damn you, Harry," Annie cried as she marched away

down the beach. That was part of the problem. She did know he wasn't that kind of guy. And because of that, because she knew he was different, she'd purposely held back, treaded carefully, protecting her heart.

And then, just when she'd let her guard down, he'd sucker-punched her.

"Annie, wait—hold on," he called out, hurrying after her as she raced back up the steps. "That's another thing I wanted to tell you. My name's not actually Harry—it's just what the guys have always called me because of my surname. A nickname."

She didn't bother to stop walking. What was the point?

And she had no idea why he was telling this is her now, nor did she care.

Because Annie knew that already; she'd spotted it on his credit card the first night he took her to dinner.

His name wasn't Harry at all, but Edward—Edward Hargreaves.

## Chapter 38

Then

Colette was nervous. Luca said he hadn't been in touch because he'd been called away on business.

But things had definitely changed. Since that night on the boat, she'd started to have serious doubts about whether he was interested in her or, like Annie said, he was playing her.

She'd listened to her friends and their words of caution hadn't been lost on her.

Kim advised her to let instinct guide her decision-making. If Luca wanted a relationship beyond Colette's time here then he'd make that clear. Then it would be up to her to decide if it was what she wanted. Kim also reminded her that there was an ocean between them and those weren't easy hurdles to overcome.

And then there was Ed. In his last text he had straight out asked to meet up soon for coffee.

There's this great little café I found, very traditional, brimming with locals—I think you'd love it.

Colette was intrigued. Ed was so charming and funny that time in Sorrento—the opportunity to chat some more with him would be lovely. She was sure whatever this place he was talking about would be right up her street, too, but to be fair while friendship was all he seemed to want, it still felt wrong to take him up on the offer.

I appreciate the invite, thank you—but I'm kind of already seeing someone...

He responded immediately:

Oh, I'm so sorry, I can see how the invite might have come across. I wouldn't want to step on any toes. I meant merely as friends. And compatriots, of course. ☺

I'm a bit busy this week, she hedged, unsurely. I'll let you know...

Colette wished she had Kim's wisdom and Annie's street-smarts, especially when it came to matters of the heart. The problem was that her heart *was* her guiding force.

She couldn't deny that she was happy Luca had called to the villa today, asking her to come for a drive.

He *hadn't* abandoned her, lost interest in her because he'd got what he wanted, or whatever Annie had been trying to suggest.

He'd also told her to bring a swimming costume, and she wondered if they were going out on the boat again. The thought of a repeat of that wonderful night under the stars filled her with an all-too-familiar desire, and she knew that no matter what—if any—intentions Luca might have beyond this trip, she was already caught in whatever web he had already spun around her.

When Luca's car eventually arrived at Fiordo di Furore, a tiny beach situated low beneath an ornate arched bridge, Colette had at first been a little disappointed that it wasn't the boat. But all too soon she became completely taken by the picturesque spot and aquamarine waters of the fiord.

"Is this it?" she asked from the bridge, steeling herself for the inevitable trek down another of Italy's endless stepped walkways to access the beach.

He chuckled. "It's one of the best places to swim. And also not so many tourists are willing to make the thousand-step descent."

*Thousand* steps? Colette's eyes widened.

Luca retrieved a basket and umbrella from the back of the car and soon they were on their way.

Eventually, they descended onto the pebbly beach and found an intimate spot at the far end, where Luca set up a beach umbrella and towels.

"You brought your swimming costume?" he asked and she nodded. She was wearing the one-piece under her summer dress.

Before she knew it, he was stripping and Colette gulped, trying hard not to stare. Few men in their swimwear looked like Luca did in his, and possibly even fewer without.

Folding her dress tidily on the blanket, she followed him into the water. He kept backing in while she walked toward him.

"Shouldn't you turn around?" she laughed. "How will you know where you're going?"

He winked. "I prefer this view."

The water deepened and soon they were both treading hard

to keep their heads above it. Luca pulled Colette close and held her in his arms. The sudden action caused her to laugh and she wrapped her arms around his neck.

"I am so glad to be back," he said. "I missed you."

Colette searched his eyes. Did he really? He looked back at her, the depths searching hers.

"You do not believe me."

"No," she replied, sighing. "It's not that."

"Yes, it is. I can see it," Luca answered. "What troubles you, my Colette?"

His Colette? She wanted to be.

They bobbed in the water, and Luca picked up her legs and wrapped them around his waist as he supported them both.

"Tell me."

She swallowed the lump in her throat at his question. If she wanted the truth there was no better way to get it than to ask. And no better time than the present.

"That night on the boat, the phone call. You were very secretive about it."

His brow wrinkled. "Secretive? I think I was just annoyed. You know how much I hate those things. I wish they had never been invented, and that Mr. Jobs had stayed working in his garage," he added lightheartedly.

But Colette wasn't to be dissuaded by humor. "Who was it?" she asked, surprised at her own insistence. But she needed to know. "On the end of the line that night."

Luca shrugged. "My father. He and I... Let's just say we do not bring out the best in each other."

She let out the breath she didn't know she'd been holding. She believed him. It wasn't another woman or something he was trying to hide, like Annie had suggested.

He'd already told her that he worked in his father's business more out of duty than anything else. So if the two men clashed, it made sense that a phone call interrupting a personal moment would put Luca out of sorts.

"I'm still confused, though," she admitted. "When I'm with you I feel amazing. Then when you were gone and I didn't hear from you, I wondered what was happening. I still don't know why you're interested in me. What it is that you want."

Luca looked at her thoughtfully. "Is that all?"

"No," Colette admitted, deciding to be honest. "I want to know what we are. What is this thing between us?" she questioned. "Is it just a summer fling, or something more?"

"Summer flings can be wonderful," he mused. He grinned from ear-to-ear until he saw the expression on Colette's face.

"Is that what I am to you?"

His expression immediately became apologetic. "I was just making a joke. You want to know what you are to me. You want to know if there is more than just the time you have left here in Italy."

"I want the truth, yes."

"Well, I cannot tell you for certain." Her face fell at his words. He shrugged. "I do not know what tomorrow will bring," he continued. "I cannot say what will be with any certainty, but I can say what I hope will be."

"What does that mean?" she asked, her voice testy. He was maddeningly obtuse.

He smiled. "Not right now, OK? There is much going on in my life right now. Today is just a day to enjoy the sun and each other." He pulled her closer and whispered in her ear. "I will not play with your emotions. I would not be so cruel. I promise I will answer you, just not now. Now, I just want to be here—with you in my arms."

"That's not fair. Why should I wait around for you to make a decision, to tell me what's really going on?"

"I do not intend to tell you, my Colette. I plan to show

you. Before you leave here, I will make all the arrangements, and soon, you will know. I hope to know also."

"What do you mean?"

"I mean—you are having summer fun right now. When you leave next week, it is over. Italy is gone. But I will still be here. You think you are the only one who wants to know what tomorrow brings for us? I do also. But first, I want you to know your heart. Then, I will show you what is in mine."

"I think I already know what's in mine," she admitted softly.

"Then we have no problem," he replied with a smile, kissing her on the nose.

Colette rested her head on his shoulder.

She just hoped that what they both wanted was the same thing.

## Chapter 39

Then

Kim was about to climb a mountain, literally and figuratively.

As she and Colette began their trek along the gray volcanic gravel trail upward to the crater of Mount Vesuvius, her thoughts were going a mile a minute.

Since she'd met Emilia and Antonio that day in Amalfi, she hadn't been able to stop thinking about the Frenchwoman's suggestion and the notion that with The Sweet Life she just might have something good on her hands, something tangible.

Something she could use as a first step to the rest of her life.

Weeks ago, back in New York in Natasha's bedroom, while she and her friend planned this getaway to Italy, the thought of a different life had really only been a fantasy. But now, purely by chance, a source of change had fallen into her lap.

One that someone actually believed she could accomplish and succeed with.

Kim knew it was all a bit nebulous, but the idea was intoxicating all the same. Freedom and a future?

It was everything she'd ever wanted.

The thoughts were intense but they wouldn't leave her. Natasha had said she needed to do something different.

How different to her old life was this: becoming a mindfulness guru/wellness Influencer?

There were worse career paths, and the photography side was definitely something she could get excited about. She could also perhaps finally put in practice a lot of what she'd learned in her business degree. On her own terms.

Maybe her parents had been right in forcing her to do that much.

Kim knew she had to think this through properly, though. Given the origin of some of the captions and inspirational quotes she'd already used to further her growing social media audience, she figured she needed to see if she could source the journal's origins.

Since Valentina apparently worked for a local property maintenance company and didn't know anything about Villa Dolce Vita's owner, Kim had in the meantime called the agent through which she'd made her original booking.

In fits and starts, given the language barrier, she learned that the house once belonged to an English couple who had passed away many years before. The wife lived in the house alone after her husband died, and according to reports she'd been reclusive, keeping to herself and rarely venturing out.

The story was that she and her husband hadn't been the best of parents and had become estranged from their children back in their home country. When they died, there was some issue with the title deeds, which made the house difficult to sell, so the couple's only remaining relative—a grandchild—had taken over the villa and begun renting it out from afar in order to make some money.

The story was a sad one. Kim couldn't imagine what it would be like being old and alone in a foreign country. She wondered whether that perhaps was the reason the widow had started writing? It made sense given the dual language element of the content.

Had Villa Dolce Vita's former owner written down the things she'd wished she'd been able to change in her life? Were those words of wisdom her catharsis for the mistakes she'd made and the dreams she'd lost? Was the journal that had lately inspired Kim so much been borne from regret? The thought was possibly even more affecting than the book's contents.

However, there seemed little point in her trying to dig any deeper. If the journal happened to have been left there by a guest at some unidentifiable point in the past, then there was no way in hell Kim would be able to track him or her down. And if it had ultimately belonged to Villa Dolce Vita's owner, then that person was long dead and their family didn't care.

They'd probably never read the journal or even knew it existed.

That day in Amalfi, Kim had exchanged numbers with Emilia and the older woman had urged her to contact her for advice and direction in how best to move forward if she chose to do so.

She really seemed to think Kim had something special.

"Be sure to use the number. Don't take it and forget about it," she'd encouraged.

"Please do," Antonio teased, his eyes twinkling. "If you do not, Emilia will never stop talking about it."

Kim laughed. "I promise I will. Enjoy the rest of your stay."

"Likewise," Antonio replied. "Perhaps we will see you again before it is over."

Should she truly consider picking up the phone? Kim wasn't sure. It was a big step. A bold step.

*The biggest adventure that you can ever take is to live the life of your dreams.*

"So what do you think?" Colette was chattering on alongside her as they walked, telling Kim all about the latest with Luca.

Kim wished she had some words of wisdom for her, but there was nothing in the journal about romance, and she didn't really have enough experience herself in matters of the heart to advise.

It seemed as if both of her friends' summer romances had begun to turn—a couple of nights earlier, Annie had returned home from her latest date in a foul mood, and had spent the last few days brooding and moping around the villa.

Obviously, if things were over, her mysterious Prince Charming would remain that way.

Kim and Colette had asked her to come along on today's hike, conscious that their time as a trio together at the villa was coming to an end and there was still so much of the area they hadn't explored, but Annie had flat out refused.

Kim hated seeing her like this. She was usually so vivacious and fun-loving, it was as if her spark had been snuffed out by whatever was going on with her love life. Kim really hoped she'd come out of her funk before her stay was over, or at least before Colette departed at the end of the week. It was a bummer of a way to end what was supposed to be the trip of a lifetime, though Colette, it seemed, was just as wrapped up in her *own* relationship woes as her carefree days in Italy were coming to a close.

"Sorry, what?" Kim asked, turning to her now, and feeling guilty for only really half listening.

"I was just saying that I don't think there's actually anything wrong with meeting Ed for coffee, just as friends. Luca can't complain about it, can he? Not when we're not officially together."

"Sure, I think you're right, and good for you for keeping your options open, just in case."

But when the younger girl looked crestfallen, Kim figured she'd said the wrong thing.

"So you don't think there's any future for Luca and I beyond a holiday romance?" she queried.

"No, no, I'm not saying that at all. It's just…you're an independent woman and you can see and meet who you like. You don't need anyone's approval, least of all a guy's."

But Colette still looked uncertain so Kim decided to change the subject.

"Hey, let's pick up the pace and see if we can reach the next gift shop before Manolo Lady." She indicated with a grin a woman up ahead who was gamely making the climb in four-inch heels.

They'd spotted her on the trail on the way up, and Kim had to admire the Italian determination to remain stylish above all else. She and Colette were wearing trainers, and while the terrain wasn't all that difficult underfoot, she'd much rather keep her fancy shoes for a fancy event.

She was also a bit taken aback to find that, instead of the wholly wild and natural volcanic attraction she'd expected, there were actually three different gift shops at various points on the ascent to the volcano's crater, and worse, hikers had to actually trek right through them to get to the top. She'd thought the theme parks back home were bad, but this was another level.

Still, it was a fun—if blisteringly hot—climb, and the views from the top were pretty special, too.

Half an hour later, when she and Colette had finished their descent and had just reached the bus parking area to meet their transport back to Positano, her mobile phone rang.

Her eyes widened a little when she saw from the caller display that it was Emilia.

"Hi," she greeted, uncertain what the Frenchwoman might want, but equally exhilarated to think that it might be about furthering their conversation about how to turn The Sweet Life into an actual business.

She was right.

"You also said you wanted to learn more about photography and how to do it better?" Emilia said, after they'd chatted a little and Kim told her she was indeed up for exploring things further.

"Well…yes, I think so."

"One of my photographers is coming to Sorrento soon on an assignment for the magazine. He is American, too, and he would be delighted to give you some tips. He says he can come to your accommodation. Tell me your address and I will give him your number also." Kim could hear the smile in Emilia's voice as she continued. "His name is Gabriel Cuminetti. I think you will love him."

# Chapter 40

## Now

Annie had a migraine for the fourth day running, and it was showing no signs of stopping.

She knew what she needed to do, but she couldn't take the time off required to deal with it. Creditors were calling about their unpaid invoices. The end of the month was quickly approaching and there were more and more people looking to get paid. Then there were the usual bills, not to mention her own personal expenses to consider.

"I know we owe you—I just need a little time to sort things out," she recited to yet another supplier on the other end of the line.

She was getting so used to uttering those words they were becoming her own painful prose.

"Annie, I have bills of my own to pay and when I don't

pay, I don't get the stock," John Butler, her supplier, pointed out. "So why should you?"

She sighed. "I know. I just need a little time, John," she repeated. "Please don't cut me off. I know my cash flow problems are not your problems, but I'm asking you to just give me a little more time and I promise that I'll get it sorted."

"I've already given you ample time. If you don't pay the outstanding balances within seven days, I'll hand this matter over to a collection agency. Frank fobbed me off enough times already, so I don't have much confidence in your promises either."

"But I didn't know about the backlog. I assure you if I had known I would've made sure you were paid long ago. I only just found out that there were some delays and I'm trying to rectify that," Annie explained. She closed her eyes and massaged her temple.

"What kind of owner doesn't know what's going on with their own business?" John asked.

His question caused her eyes to snap open. "The kind who trusts too easily," she answered bitterly.

"Where's Frank?"

"He's gone," Annie answered. *And with him most of my company's money and life savings.*

"Can you please give me a little more time?" she implored. "I promise I'll sort this out."

Annie hated the sound of her own voice saying those words. She was begging. She didn't beg, but what choice did she have? If she could keep the creditors at bay just a little while longer, there was a chance she could come up with some kind of plan. If she couldn't, her livelihood and everything she'd worked for was over.

"OK, one last chance, Annie."

The words were music to her ears.

"That's great. I owe you one," she answered in relief. "And I will send some money to you this month. I don't know how much yet, but it will be something. I promise."

She hung up the phone and dropped her head on her desk.

She couldn't bask in that small triumph just yet. There were several more people she needed to call, including the bank. She was definitely going to need another business loan, though at this point she wasn't sure the bank would give it to her.

She needed another coffee. And something for her migraine, too.

Putting on her best game face, Annie headed out onto the salon floor.

"Hello, ladies," she greeted cheerfully. The stylists and customers alike all smiled in return.

"Oh, Annie, there you are—do you have a minute?" Lauren Hennessy, one of her best regulars, called out as she passed the waiting area.

Since day one, Lauren had been coming to #GlamSquad for her weekly wash and curly blow dry, or color treatment and trim, and had even followed her when she moved premises.

The jackhammer in Annie's head seemed to get even louder, but still she flashed Lauren a game smile. "'Course, Lauren. How are you?"

"Privately?"

Annie tried to quiet the discomfort she felt.

*What now?*

"OK, why don't you come back to my office?" She turned to reception. "Amanda, hold Lauren's appointment for a bit. And be a star and get us both a cuppa. Tea or coffee?" she asked her customer.

"Tea, please. And maybe a biscuit if you have one."

The two women walked toward the back of the salon,

Annie's thoughts racing a mile a minute. What the hell did Lauren want to discuss that required privacy?

"Have a seat," Annie said as she closed the door behind them. "What can I do for you?"

Lauren's expression was very still and it only made Annie's anxiety worse.

"Is everything OK, Annie?" the older woman asked.

"Yes, of course. What do you mean?"

"Well, as you know I've been coming to you for a long time, and to my mind this place is one of the best. It's just… I've heard a few things."

"What kind of things?" she asked shortly.

"Well, that you owe people a lot of money. That the business is under fierce pressure," Lauren said flatly.

Annie's heart froze in her chest. How could she know this? Nick wouldn't have said anything, would he?

She stared at Lauren. Words escaped her. If she denied it then Lauren would know she was a liar. If she admitted it then she risked her reputation and that of her salon.

"Who told you that?" she asked.

"One of your suppliers is a client of my husband's at the bank. He mentioned he was having some troubles with a salon who wouldn't pay their bills. I've been a client of #GlamSquad for a long time, Annie. I wouldn't have thought you to be dishonest."

The implication stung and her hackles rose. And with it, Annie's temper.

"Dishonest? How dare you!" she raged before she could stop herself. "I'm as honest as the day is long, which is more than I can say for your husband, talking out of school like that."

"Well…" Lauren's face reddened. "I was only asking because I've been coming here for so long and I thought of you as a friend. But obviously I was wrong."

"Lauren…wait. I'm sorry." Shit, the gossip mill would be

running on overtime now. It was bad enough losing all her money; she shouldn't be trying to lose all her best clients, too.

*Oh fuck*; Lauren's husband worked at the bank where she had her business accounts and might well have some influence over whether or not she got her loan.

She breathed deeply, trying to swallow her pride. Perhaps she could save this and appeal to Lauren's better nature by confessing the true nature of her problems. She hated admitting weakness to anyone but needs must this time…

But the woman was already on her feet and her expression now became cool. "You're a fantastic stylist, Annie, and your salon has always been my favorite, but I'll be taking my business elsewhere. I won't be treated like this and certainly will no longer be associated with someone who doesn't pay their way."

Annie swallowed the lump that was trying to jump into her throat. Her heart was beating so loudly in her ears that she could hardly hear Lauren speak. If she didn't find a way to rescue this, then she was simply speeding along her livelihood's demise.

She couldn't let that happen.

"Lauren, please, this is a stressful time. But believe me, I'm not dishonest, nor refusing to pay my way. I was swindled by someone who used to work for me and I'm just trying to find a way out of this mess. Please, I'm so sorry for snapping. And for what I said about your husband. I didn't mean it."

"Oh, I think you did, actually. And while I meant what I said about your work, to be honest, Annie, your manner has always left a lot to be desired."

With that Lauren swept out of the room.

Annie began to hyperventilate. She stumbled toward her desk and collapsed in the seat as she tried to catch her breath. As she did, her phone dinged and she reached for where she'd left it, wondering what fresh hell was about to be unleashed on her now.

It was Kim.

Hey, I sent you an invite to the launch but noticed you haven't RSVP'd. Really hope you can make it?

For Christ's sake! A goddamn jolly in Italy was the last thing on her mind at the moment.

Annie read the message a few times, resisting the urge to tell Kim Weston to just go and shag off with her big party and her thriving business and her sweet life.

She wanted to lie and say that she hadn't received anything, but the invite and tickets had been delivered to the salon by courier so Kim would know that she had.

She really should have RSVP'd, or at least contacted her to thank her for her generosity, but so much had blown up since.

Oh God…

She kneaded her forehead. There were so many fires to put out and too much stress. Her business was bust, customers were walking out the door, and she had no idea how to rescue this. She had no idea how she was even going to make this month's rent, never mind anything else…

Then Annie thought of something.

She hated herself for it, and had sworn to herself she wouldn't, but she couldn't help it—the pull was irresistible.

She clicked onto social media and scrolled through photos she'd seen a million times before. The perfect life, perfect couple, perfect *everything*—all that she'd wanted and hoped for but could never have. It wasn't fair.

To hell with it, she thought, picking up the phone, her fingers moving quickly over the screen.

Her life was falling apart anyway—what else was there to lose?

# Chapter 41

Now

"Hey, you with us?" Gabriel asked Kim as they strolled through Pompeii with Lily.

The ruins of the great city always stirred her. It was a reminder of how easily and quickly life as you knew it could end.

The remnants of old houses, empty amphitheaters, and perfectly preserved figures spoke of a city whose tragic fall had been told and retold many times before the eyes of its visitors.

"Sorry," she apologized as she took several quick steps to catch up with them. Lily was in her dad's arms and playfully pulling on his nose while also attending to her favorite doll. Gabriel reached out an arm and wound it around Kim's shoulders as she came closer.

"Baby's sleepy, Daddy."

"Is Lily sleepy, too?" Gabriel asked, winking hopefully at Kim, but the little girl shook her head and continued to play.

Kim was still distracted and a few minutes later Gabriel repeated the question he'd asked on their arrival a few days before. "What's going on? You're miles away."

"Nothing," she continued to lie. She wanted to stop, but telling the truth was proving more difficult than she'd imagined.

He sighed. "You're not being truthful, though, are you?" he said, and Kim's heart jumped into her chest. "I know you said you'd have some time to spend with us before everything kicked off, but maybe that was too optimistic."

"No, honestly, it's fine." She refreshed her email again, waiting on more news from Hank, but nothing.

Her mind automatically traveled back to that day she found the journal behind the dresser, and she racked her brains to think who the real owner could possibly be and why they'd chosen *now* to come out of the woodwork.

Well, she could hazard a guess as to why: it was the perfect opportunity to sabotage the launch and publicly humiliate her in the process—which suggested it had to be personal. The timing was too coincidental for it not to be.

So who was this person? A past guest of the villa would surely have long forgotten about it, or if not, would have recognized or identified Kim's usage of various quotes and ideas before now.

It couldn't have been the villa's previous owner either, because when Antonio had made them an offer to buy it, the family seemed more than happy to have somebody actually pay them to take the ramshackle estate off their hands.

Unless it was a disgruntled relative? Who knew how these family things could go?

But there was little point in Kim trying to figure this out herself, she knew. She had to wait until she heard more from Hank and hope against hope that he could make this go away.

"I want to get down," Lily complained, and Gabriel temporarily released his arm from Kim to lower their daughter to the ground.

As always, the moment Lily's feet touched earth she was on the move. Like most three-year-olds she was fearless.

Now, she raced toward the three statues that stood sentinel in the town square. Two of them had no arms and Kim thought Lily might be frightened by that, but nope. She walked right up to the base of the stand on which they stood and stared up, first at one and then the other. She turned to the third. It had the body of a man with small wings and no head.

"Daddy, why are some parts missing?" she asked as she began to move around the stands. "Can we find them?"

Kim had to smile. She'd been such a curious child, too. She'd walk around Central Park with her nanny looking for things to play with.

Though, unlike Lily, Kim's father was never there for her to ask why things were the way they were. Gloria would never set foot in the park either. She was far too sophisticated and important for something so mundane as walking among trees along with the great unwashed.

What Kim was doing now with her husband and child, her family had never done together. So instead of worrying about work, she should really try to live in the moment and cherish this.

Lily grabbed Gabriel's hand and began to run around the ancient piazza, peeking behind the statues one by one. "Come find them, come find them."

"Why don't we?" Kim teased Gabriel.

He looked at her, faintly shocked that she'd agreed to play hide-and-seek.

The afternoon flew by and it was fun; more fun than Kim had had in months.

She understood why Gabriel enjoyed being with Lily so much. Playing with her made Kim's heart feel lighter. She stood back now and watched him chase Lily around the amphitheater, up and down the steps and along row after row, puffing as he went. Her blond pigtails bounced on top of her head as she squealed with glee and waved her doll around frantically as she tried to escape him.

It was wonderful to see and Kim realized with a pang that she was missing out—had missed out on so much of Lily's childhood so far.

That needed to change.

Her phone buzzed in her pocket. She'd switched off the ringer and hidden it in the bottom of her bag in the hope of trying to forget her worries and concentrating on her family for once.

She knew there'd be emails from the office and possibly calls, too, but they could wait.

But this call wasn't from the office. It was from Antonio.

"I've been trying to call you all day. Where are you?"

Her brow wrinkled at the urgency in his voice. "I'm in Pompeii with Gabriel and Lily. Why?"

"I know that's important, but there's something going on you need to know about. I'm sorry to be the bearer of bad news, but we've hit a major snag. More than a snag, actually. This could actually put the launch in jeopardy."

*Oh God, what now?*

Kim's heart began to race. Or was it that Antonio had caught wind of the plagiarism claim and the bad publicity it could generate? Still, it wasn't like him to back down from anything without a fight.

"What kind of trouble?" she asked, holding her breath. "What kind of problem?"

"The licenses for Villa Dolce Vita. They've been revoked."

Kim's eyes widened, not expecting this at all.

"What do you mean they've been revoked? It took us over a year to get those permissions. Which licenses?"

"All of them, actually. Change of business amendments. Accommodation and health and safety permits. Everything."

Her knees buckled, but she did her best to stay on her feet. "Say that again?"

"All of them, Kim. Everything. The authorities are giving some bullshit excuse but I don't understand any of it. Those permissions were granted. Everything was signed off. How could they be revoked now? It doesn't make sense, yes? So I made some calls but still I got the runaround."

It had taken months upon months, maybe even a year, of bureaucratic red tape—never easy in Italy at the best of times—to get everything in order so that the villa could re-open and trade as a licensed hotel and wellness retreat.

Kim had been losing sleep, even hair, over getting those across the line before they could even think about green-lighting the renovations. She and Antonio had attended meeting after meeting and sweet-talked official after official to try and get things signed off. And now he was saying they'd just been revoked, wiped clean?

It was a disaster.

"I don't know what's going on, Antonio. We did everything we were asked. Every form signed, fees paid, calls taken, and meetings had. We did it all. You were there, too, and I know we left no stone unturned." She shook her head in disbelief. "It sounds like someone's out to sabotage us."

"Yes. Something definitely isn't right."

"What do we do, Antonio? We need those permissions to launch, let alone trade. If they're gone, everything we've been working toward has been wasted. Our entire investment... Hundreds of thousands, blown."

"I'll go meet with some of my contacts in Sorrento and see if I can find out what's going on," he reassured her.

"And I'll give Hank a call and let him know what's happening. Maybe he can help somehow." Although her lawyer was already fighting another fire. What the hell was going on?

"Very well. I'll call as soon as I've confirmed a meeting with the authorities. Try not to worry, Kim, we'll figure this out."

"But the launch is this week." She couldn't see how something like this could possibly be sorted in time. "Let me know when you've arranged the meeting. I want to be there, too. I want to look in the eyes of the people who already approved everything and have them tell me why our permits are suddenly no good."

"Let's hope it does not come to that. I will call you back—soon, I hope. Ciao."

Kim hung up as outright anger began to course through her veins. Why was all this happening? Who was doing it? And why? She clenched her phone in her hands as she tried to keep calm.

"What's wrong?" Gabriel demanded when he saw the expression on her face. "And please don't say 'nothing' this time. I can see it in your face."

Kim shook her head, fighting back tears. "Can we just go?" she snapped. The response was unintentional but her emotions were raw, and at that moment the last place she wanted to be was somewhere a population who'd had everything had come to a tragic end.

The parallels were way too close.

"OK, sure. Lily's hungry and she's probably tired, too."

"I'm sorry," she conceded then. "Trouble with the center. Big trouble. I really have to go deal with it."

"What's happened?"

"All the licenses have been revoked. I don't get it," she said angrily. "I just don't understand how this could happen."

"But I thought they were all signed and sealed? They took you forever to get."

"I know!"

Lily's head snapped in her direction and she looked fearfully at Kim. "Why is Mommy shouting?"

"All right. Calm down, we'll talk later," Gabriel urged, giving Kim a cautionary glance, and once again she felt bad.

She shouldn't be taking it out on either of them, but really this wasn't the time or the place to discuss it.

Gabriel drove and Kim was silent the entire ride back to Sorrento. Her mind was full of questions. Ones for which she had no answers and no clue at all how to get them.

Back at the hotel, Gabriel went to get Lily something to eat and Kim returned to their room.

The moment she entered she was on the phone, making calls to the office, Hank, and every government agency and contact she had in Italy.

"I don't like this, Hank," she said to her lawyer as she paced the room. "I don't believe in coincidences, and all of this happening at the same time seems a little too convenient."

"You think someone's trying to sabotage Villa Dolce Vita?"

"Maybe."

"You may be right. I've had my guys looking into those plagiarism claims and while they seem absolutely convoluted, there's certainly enough to bring negative attention and publicity if they decide to go public. Which you truly don't want—not now."

Someone really was out to ruin this—ruin Kim, even.

But who, and perhaps more importantly, why?

## Chapter 42

Then

Annie was going dancing.

She had only one more week left in Italy and she was tired of sitting around moping over some guy's rejection.

Yes, she'd fallen for Edward Hargreaves and was a bit taken aback by how much, but she had to remember she was here on holiday. What did she expect, that he would whisk her back to England to live happily ever after?

But that wasn't what she wanted. Felicity's intention was for Annie to live life on her own terms, not be dependent on some guy to decide her future.

And she was going to do just that. She already had a rough plan of how she would go about setting up her own place. First up, she would do a refresher styling course; years of catering to middle-aged women and the blue rinse brigade's washes and sets had put her out of the game trend-wise, and she needed to improve her offering.

Then she would get some work experience at one of the chain salons, well and truly learning the ropes within a busy popular operation, before taking the plunge and opening her own place.

Taking Kim's advice, she'd also look into doing an additional course in how to set up a small business, getting all the official stuff right from the start and maybe even apply to the Irish Enterprise Board for a grant.

In any case, Annie was determined to do this and do it properly from the start if she truly wanted to make a go of it.

This Italian trip had been a brilliant excuse to let loose and have fun, a fantastic diversion from the humdrum, and she'd even managed to make some good friends on the way, ones who weren't just about partying and getting trashed.

She smiled. After her stinking hangover that first day, Kim had pretty much given up on wild nights out, and whatever mindfulness stuff she'd got going on since really suited her.

She was so calm and always full of good advice—for Colette especially. Annie had got the sense right from the get-go that Kim was running from something other than just boredom, and she figured that whatever it might be, this trip had helped her, too.

The three of them were runaways, really—and as Kim pointed out, it was fate that had led them to Villa Dolce Vita as their means of escape.

Now, Annie looked at her reflection in the mirror with some satisfaction. There was no denying it, she looked *hot*.

Her skin was now deeply tanned from so much time in the sun, and she'd lost pretty much all of her burgeoning spare tire (either from walking up and down those bloody hills, or the lighter Mediterranean diet).

She wore her hair loose, her natural dark curls tumbling sexily around her face. She'd stopped straightening it these days just to give it a break, though she did go heavy on the makeup tonight—full-on glam—and was wearing her best dancing dress. The same figure-hugging number she'd worn the very first night here—one that made the absolute most of her curves and gave her oodles of sensuality.

Actually, with her sun-kissed skin, sexy dress, cascading curls, and smoldering crimson lips, she could easily blend in as one of the locals, she thought with a grin as she slipped into a pair of metallic strappy sandals.

But unlike her first time at Music on the Rocks, now Annie had the good sense to pop a pair of flip-flops into her handbag for the long walk back up from town later.

Or maybe she'd just treat herself to a taxi, depending on how the night went.

However, the club was definitely in her plan tonight, and Annie was going to dance the night away, enjoy herself, and put her latest rejection out of her mind once and for all.

She grabbed her handbag and tottered happily downstairs, smiling as she recalled that old maxim about how to get over one man by getting under another.

Well, maybe she'd do that, too.

Annie hurried outside into the courtyard, and was still smiling when she noticed someone standing under the lemon trees in the golden evening sunlight—a hunky vision even in silhouette—gazing out to the water.

And when he turned in her direction, she saw his eyes widen automatically at the sight of her, his nostrils flare, and his hooded gaze unashamedly travel hungrily up and down her body.

*This is interesting…*

The air was electric and the pull completely irresistible as Annie moved across the courtyard.

"Well, hello there, handsome."

It seemed fate was smiling on her once again.

# Chapter 43

Then

The warm Mediterranean wind blew gently as Colette waited for Luca's arrival at their latest meeting spot.

It was her last night in Italy—she was flying out of Naples tomorrow evening—and he had promised to show her how he felt and to make his intentions known before she went.

In the meantime, he had left another of his romantic notes at the villa, setting out a place and time to meet this evening.

Colette was feeling confident. She was pretty certain he was going to confirm that this meant much more to him than just a summer fling. *She* meant more.

This evening she was dressed in a flowing red summer dress, and the skirt danced around her legs and caressed her calves. It was a halter-style that tied at the neck, and the sash tickled her back as she waited, like a soothing hand comforting her. She checked her watch to see that it was almost eight o'clock. Just in time.

L'Incanto was a beautiful and suitably romantic meeting spot in the center of Positano at Spiaggia Grande, situated right on the beach; though, being honest, Colette would have preferred to spend her last night with Luca at the place where they'd first met. Then she'd also have the opportunity to say a proper goodbye to Mama Elene. Now she walked expectantly inside the restaurant to where a hostess was waiting, and smiled at the young woman who greeted her.

"Table for two for Gambini," Colette declared confidently. "Luca Gambini."

The woman checked her reservations book. "I'm sorry. I don't see any reservation for Gambini here. Are you sure you have the right name?" she questioned.

Colette was confused. The note had definitely said a reservation in his name in L'Incanto, hadn't it?

"Excuse me," she said, stepping back outside for a moment and pulling Luca's note out of her bag.

He'd left it at the villa the day before, when she was down at Fornillo beach with Kim. She read it again. Yes, this was definitely the right place and time, but it seemed there was no reservation. Could there perhaps be another L'Incanto elsewhere? she wondered.

Unless he'd meant to just meet, not necessarily *eat* here, Colette mused then, feeling a bit stupid for assuming.

And doubly stupid for dressing up. Clearly this was another of Luca's surprises.

She waited outside the restaurant for another twenty minutes, and when there was still no sign, Colette cursed herself afresh for not taking Annie's advice and asking for Luca's phone number.

While his aversion to more modern methods of communication seemed quaint and romantic when things were going well, it was an unbelievable source of frustration at times like this when there was a problem.

Colette waited and waited, but still nothing. He didn't show. Deflated and more than a little annoyed now, she wandered down to the beach and, taking her shoes off, dipped her toes in the water.

Luca had promised he'd show her his intentions before the trip was over.

*What if this is how he's showing you?*

She tried to shake the unpleasant thought out of her brain. He wouldn't be so cruel. He wouldn't get her hopes up by asking her to come to some random place just to let her down. He wasn't that kind of man.

But did she know what kind of man he was, really?

Disheartened and soon becoming more than a little concerned in case anything could have happened to him—an accident, even—Colette continued to wait.

A half hour turned into an hour, and she was still waiting. The restaurant hostess even asked if there was anyone she could call, or if she wanted a glass of water, having noticed her loitering beachside in the late-evening sunshine.

It was apparent to the Italian woman, as it was becoming painfully clear to Colette, that Luca wasn't coming.

She was starting to seriously worry that maybe he had indeed been in an accident, when her phone dinged with a text from a number she didn't recognize.

Colette, I am so sorry. You were right: this was just a summer fling. I didn't mean to get so entangled. I will treasure our time together.

She stared at the words, unable to believe what she was reading. It couldn't be true.

Tears filled her eyes as she stabbed at the screen of the phone and called the number back. But there was no answer.

"Pick up," she cried, panicked. "You owe me that much at least."

She dialed the number over and over, but still he never answered. She was almost tempted to call Mama Elene, but she didn't want to involve the older woman and make her uncomfortable. It would be embarrassing and humiliating, and hadn't she already been humiliated enough? The man who'd told Colette he abhorred mobile communication had had the audacity—the absolute *neck*—to dump her by text.

Hurrying away down the shore, away from the restaurant and the pitying looks from the restaurant hostess, Colette lowered herself onto the wet sand, not caring that she was ruining her brand-new dress.

It didn't matter. She'd bought it for a memorable romantic last night with Luca and he wasn't coming.

She didn't matter.

It was all a lie. Her and Luca's time together, his romantic words, his adoring glances, gentle hands—all a ploy to make her fall into bed with him. He'd probably done the same thing to other gullible tourist girls a million times before.

She was such an idiot, falling for his honeyed words and his Italian charm. The ultimate cliché. And when she'd pushed him the other day, asked him outright about his feelings, instead of being honest there and then, he'd told her he'd *show* her.

And he had.

"You arse!" she spat now, wiping tears from her eyes. She'd fallen for him. Despite Annie's words of caution.

Her first time away on a foreign holiday in the land of her

dreams and she'd been taken in—made a complete fool of—by the dashing local.

Of *course* Luca had made her feel like she was the only one—that was how they did it, wasn't it? Years of experience with idiot tourists just like her had taught these guys everything they needed to know. He'd doled out exactly what Colette needed to hear. He'd identified and zoomed in on her weak spots, her vulnerabilities, making her feel like he was the only one who'd ever really understood her, while all the while just trying to get into her pants.

She should never have gone out with him on the boat that night. It was after that, when he did succeed in his efforts, that everything changed.

And then, when she'd tried to pin down his feelings, he'd run for the hills.

God, she was so stupid. And pathetic, too.

Even with the benefit of hindsight, the realization was still devastating. She'd fallen—so hard—for Luca, and along with her heart, her pride had also taken one hell of a hit.

As her anger grew, she continued to try his number.

Let him tell her himself instead of hiding behind cowardly, pathetic text messages. How dare he? She didn't want to believe that he'd be so callous toward her. She'd been so ready to give someone her heart for the first time in her life, and he was just playing with her.

How could anyone do that? *Why* would they?

"Colette?" a male voice called out suddenly from behind her.

She looked up as a bright, familiar grin greeted her, and she instinctively wiped her face.

"Ed," she said in surprise, plastering a smile on her face. "What're you doing here?"

"I thought it was you. I just spotted you from the promenade so I said I'd come down and say hello. I'm just on my way to a restaurant. L'Incanto—do you know it?"

Despite herself, Colette burst into tears.

"Colette, what on earth...?" he asked, concern lacing every word. "What happened?"

She was too upset to speak. The more he questioned, the harder she cried, until finally Ed hunkered down on the sand beside her.

He put a comforting arm around her shoulders and she moved into his embrace.

"Whatever's the matter, you can tell me," he soothed, pulling her into his chest. "Is it the Italian guy?" he questioned, and Colette now wished she hadn't told him about Luca. But since he'd become more insistent about meeting up before she left for home, she'd had little choice but to let him know the details in the hope of letting him down more easily. "Where is he?" Then his tone changed. Concern still lingered but there was something else in his voice now—suspicion. "Did he do something?" He turned her face up toward his, willing her to meet his gaze. "Has he hurt you?"

Colette sniffled. "No, nothing like that. He's not here."

"So why are you here on the beach all by yourself?"

She shook her head sadly, embarrassed afresh to have to admit it out loud.

"He didn't...he didn't show."

"Didn't show? You mean he was supposed to meet you here and he stood you up? On your last night?"

Colette nodded, hurt and shame consuming her all over again.

"What a cock. These bloody Italians..."

"I know," she cried. "I feel so stupid, believe me, for falling hook, line, and sinker for his nonsense that he cared about me and that I meant something to him. But it was all a lie,

Ed. He didn't care about me at all. He never did. How could I have been so stupid? *I'm* so stupid."

"Oh, I'm sure he did care," Ed soothed. "How could he not? You're amazing. But I suppose these guys…well, you know, so many tourists come here all the time and…"

"I know." She turned away, not wanting to hear it.

Now he held her to him and gently stroked her hair. "I'm sorry," he whispered. "You deserve better, you know. So much better."

"I'm not so sure about that. It really is my own fault for being so naive. But thanks for being so nice to me."

She moved away from him now, a bit mortified by her behavior. Nice and all that he was, Ed didn't really know her that well. They'd never managed to meet up for that coffee, and while they'd communicated a bit, it wasn't as though he was a real friend, like Kim and Annie or anything.

"Let's get you home," he said eventually. "I'll call a cab— you said your hotel was called Villa Dolce Vita?"

"It's not a hotel, but you're with your friends," Colette protested.

"Doesn't matter. And we're sort of sick of one another by now," he joked. "Honestly, I'd rather see you home safe and sound. And I really hate to see you upset. I can always drop you off and then pop back. Truly, they won't even notice I've gone."

"If you're sure…" Colette just wanted to leave—to get away from this restaurant, this beach, and indeed Italy. And especially away from the memories of what she'd truly thought was a wonderful romance, but was in reality a complete lie, a sham.

She supposed, in a way, it was a good thing that tonight was her last. She'd had enough.

Colette was ready to go home.

# Chapter 44

## Now

Kim was practically bouncing off the walls as she waited for the council meeting to convene.

In the civic building, she sat outside and tapped her hand on her knee nervously.

"Take it easy," Antonio comforted, as he laid his hand over hers and gripped her fingers.

Kim looked at him. She was so glad he was with her. If not for him she'd lose her patience and quite possibly her temper over this entire mess. She'd called numerous people up and down the coast, as had he, and every time she'd reached someone they'd told her there was nothing they could do to solve the problem of her licenses.

Bureaucracy was a bitch, but Italian bureaucracy was a whole different ball game.

"This is terrifying," she said softly. It was do or die. Villa Dolce Vita was due to open for reservations immediately after the official launch.

If the officials today didn't agree to reinstate the permits then they would simply have to cancel the launch and uninvite all her important business and media contacts—most of whom were already set to arrive in Italy within days. Then they'd need to go through the long and arduous process and considerable hoop-jumping when reapplying. It could set the whole thing back another year, if not more. Kim simply could not let that happen.

"We will work this out," Antonio was saying. "Whatever has happened we will remedy it."

"I'm not leaving here until we do," she said seriously.

"That's the Kim I know," Antonio replied, smiling. "You don't give up until the job is done."

"You bet I don't. This is my baby and I'm not about to let anyone take it from me," she replied with sustained fervor.

"And what of things with your real baby—and Gabriel?"

Kim should've known that Antonio wouldn't have forgotten their conversation from before. And she also knew he was likely using this as a clever diversion away from their current predicament.

She shook her head.

"You haven't spoken to him about it yet?"

"With everything that's been going on, I just haven't had an opportunity—or the time to find one," she replied quickly. "Once the dust on this is settled I will turn my attentions to the personal. I promise."

"I hope you do, or there may be much worse on the horizon than the failure of this venture," Antonio cautioned.

Kim took his words to heart. In all of the years since she'd met him, her mentor's advice had never failed to be accurate.

"I will," she repeated sincerely.

"Ms. Weston? Mr. Berger?" a female voice called. "Everyone is ready."

Kim and Antonio got to their feet immediately. She looked at him for one fleeting moment before shifting her bag onto her shoulder, lifting her chin, and walking into the meeting that could potentially make or break her.

The Italian officials' faces gave nothing away as they both entered the meeting room. They greeted Kim and Antonio cordially, before sitting down across from them at the table. Kim noticed the paperwork spread out over it and wished she could reach across and grab the documents that had landed them in such strife. But she needed to be patient. There was no rushing Italian bureaucracy—this she knew from experience.

However, Antonio was keen to waste no time. He spoke in rapid Italian, asking the officials to straight out explain the nature of the problem.

"Ms. Weston and I are completely confused as to why the permissions for Villa Dolce Vita have been revoked. We did everything you asked all throughout the process, complied with any necessary adjustments and amendments where required. As far as we were concerned, everything was agreed and authorized. What has changed?"

"We did also," one of the officials replied. "But then we received the updated application."

Kim looked at the older man, mystified. "What updated application?" she asked.

"An application for amendments to the licenses," he said, picking up one of the documents on the table. "As such, any changes automatically rescind the previous grant and put the entire project back into the planning process."

"But we didn't request any amendments..." Kim insisted, looking at Antonio, who seemed equally puzzled.

"Show me the new application," her partner requested, and the official duly handed him the document. Kim watched as he read through it quickly and slowly shook his head.

"Yes, this is very definitely a mistake. An oversight from someone in the company—an office clerk, perhaps," he assured them. "Please ignore this request," he said. "There are no amendments planned to the project. This is most definitely a clerical error, a misunderstanding."

Kim let out an inward sigh of relief.

*A misunderstanding... Thank goodness.*

The two officials looked at each other.

"Please," she insisted, her heart rushing into her mouth once again. Surely these guys couldn't insist on holding them to a mistake. These things happened all the time. "Everything remains as it stands. The project is complete and due to open for business within days. We would not and *do* not require any material changes at this point."

She noticed one of the officials give the other an almost imperceptible nod and her pulse began to race in anticipation of what they would say.

"OK, yes. We appreciate that mistakes happen, though in order to reinstate the previous approvals we would need an assurance in writing—"

"Absolutely, I'll arrange to do that right away," she promised them, letting out the breath she didn't realize she'd been holding.

*It was just a mistake. Thank God, thank God...*

She had no idea who in the office would request amendments to the licenses at this late stage, though she guessed it must be as Antonio suggested, a clerical error of some kind. She'd find out—eventually. The important thing was that they were out of the woods.

As Antonio echoed her assurances to follow up in writing,

and exchanged further pleasantries with the officials, Kim noticed him squirrel away the offending documents into his briefcase and made a mental note to examine them herself afterward.

But she couldn't deny her elation and sheer relief that it had in fact all been settled. After weeks of being taken for a ride every which way, finally she'd got some satisfaction.

Thank goodness.

Afterward, when Antonio dropped her off at the Excelsior and she made her way out to where Lily and Gabriel waited for her by the pool, she resisted the urge to skip through the lobby.

Everything was once again *go*.

All Kim needed now was to try and figure out who was behind the plagiarism threat and make it go away.

Then life would be sweet once more.

## Chapter 45

Now

Annie locked up the salon for the day, half wondering if it might be for the very last time. She was out of options. Almost.

There was that one last roll of the dice, but she knew it was a long shot and one that she truly wouldn't have even considered if not for the fact that she was absolutely desperate.

Getting into the car, she checked her phone again for a reply to the message she'd sent earlier, before throwing it onto the driver's seat.

A few minutes later, she pulled into her friend Gemma's driveway, glancing at her phone screen once again under the pretense of checking the time.

She was much later than usual again today, and she felt guilty that the stress and strain of all this was affecting her life in more ways than one.

"Mum!"

Annie's heart instinctively lifted as her little boy rushed out of the childminder's house to greet her.

Charlie was always so happy to see her, and no matter how shitty she was feeling, his happy grin never failed to bring a smile to her face. He was full of chatter, having learned some new football move from Gemma's son, Callum, who was a few years older.

"It's called the seal dribble," he chattered animatedly in the driveway while Gemma waved at Annie from her front doorway. "You do it like this."

Annie watched as he took his scuff-covered football and began to bounce it on his head repeatedly.

"You see? You keep bouncing it like this while you run to the goal. I'm still trying to get it that I can keep an eye on target while I do it."

"That's brilliant, love," Annie enthused as she ruffled his hair. She looked apologetically at Gemma. "I'm so sorry, I'm late again. There was a last-minute emergency at the salon and—"

"It's fine, sure he's no bother. And I hope you don't mind but Nick already told me something was going on."

Nick's sister was a very understanding friend, but Annie never wanted to take the piss. Gemma had been an absolute godsend to her the last few years, taking care of Charlie while she was off working like a demon, trying to get the business up and running.

But with everything that was going on now, Annie worried if she'd even be able to afford her anymore.

Luckily he'd started school last year, which meant that she really only needed a childminder in the afternoons, these days, but who knew how things could change in the future?

At this point, Annie wasn't sure how she was going to get

through even this month with the amount of money owed to suppliers and the staff and business overheads to pay.

She wasn't going to let those worries show, she resolved, as she chatted with Gemma for a bit before bundling Charlie into the car. She wasn't going to allow him to suffer because of her concerns about them either.

When they reached home, Annie stared at the lovely house that had been theirs for the last two years. She'd never felt so proud as she did when #GlamSquad was doing well enough that she'd been able to get a mortgage on a place of their own.

She'd never really lived in a proper house before, not since she was a child at the O'Dohertys', and when Charlie was a baby she'd been restricted to the poky flats offered to single mothers on welfare.

But through her hard work and efforts with the salon, she'd managed to get them out of social housing and into a place with a proper garden where her son could run around and play, where he could have his own room and she'd have a real kitchen—not a few inches separated from the living room by a foot of table.

She and Charlie had that now, but for how much longer?

"Mum, what's for dinner?" he asked as he got out, tucked his football under his arm, and slammed the car door. No matter how many times she told him not to, he always did it.

"I don't know. I'll have to see what's in the fridge."

"But it's Friday! Maybe a takeaway?" he suggested with a grin that always had the power to melt her heart. "Pizza?"

His eyes sparkled with enthusiasm.

Usually, Annie would have insisted they ate a proper nutritious meal prepared from scratch by her, but she wasn't sure how many more chances they'd have to order in.

Memories of the hard times began to fill her mind once again. Days of nothing but tinned beans, tuna, and potatoes—

and whatever cuts of meat were cheapest or on offer in the supermarkets. She didn't want that for Charlie. She didn't want that life again. She couldn't—*wouldn't*—go back to that.

Something had to be done.

The house was a two-bed duplex, and so bright and roomy inside. Annie could still remember what it felt like the first day she walked into it.

There was something about it; something new and fresh and warm, and she knew instantly that this was the place for her and Charlie. This was home.

Now, as she stood in the entrance, she wondered whether whoever came after her would feel the same. Because if the business went under and she had to forgo all her savings to pay her tax bill, she wouldn't be able to afford this anymore.

"Mum, I got the menus," Charlie shouted from inside the kitchen. Sensing her acquiescence about the takeaway, he'd wasted no time in taking charge before she changed her mind.

She ordered two pizzas in the end. Charlie loved meat, while Annie liked to even out her meat toppings with some veg, something her son—like most five-year-olds—hated, though in fairness he was pretty good with food, and—vegetables aside—not at all fussy. In the early days, he'd had no choice but to eat whatever was available. No such thing as kids' menus of chicken nuggets and chips or what have you. And despite her gradual change in income and circumstances, old habits died hard and Annie still insisted he eat what she gave him.

"Don't forget your drink."

"Can I have juice?"

"Nope. Water or nothing."

"Yay, water!" Charlie quipped, without argument. His cheery temperament had a way of making her feel better even when she wanted to indulge in negative thoughts. He truly was her sunshine. He brightened every day, all day.

She badly needed that now.

"Hey, Mum, are we going on holiday?" he asked, picking up the invite to Villa Dolce Vita, along with the hotel info that had been sitting on the kitchen counter since she'd brought it home a couple of weeks ago. "It says my name on this."

Annie's heart turned over. "I don't think so, love."

"Why not? It looks nice. Callum's going to Spain on his summer holidays this year—a big water park with loads of slides. Is there loads of slides there, too?"

"Not really. That hotel is very different to where Callum is going, definitely no water park, though there is a pool. And that's not for a summer holiday either, just a weekend."

"But I want to go."

Annie's smiled tightened. "I'll think about it, OK? Now, eat up and then go and put your pajamas on, and maybe you can watch a bit of *Paw Patrol* before you go to bed."

"Yay!"

Annie didn't rush her shower that evening. She usually did, not wanting to leave Charlie on his own for too long in case he got up to any devilment, but tonight she needed every second of that warm water on her head and shoulders.

A migraine was still lingering, but not nearly as bad as when she'd had angry suppliers (and Lauren) in her ear.

Charlie helped with easing her worries, too. He helped with so much and he didn't even realize it. Her son had the knack of doing the silliest things at just the right time to make her laugh.

Despite all the early hardship, he was her greatest blessing, really.

"Mum, I'm waiting!" he called out from his room now.

"In a sec," she answered as she toweled off her hair and pulled an oversized T-shirt over her head.

She headed toward Charlie's room but stopped short when

she heard her phone beep, indicating an incoming message. Her heart hammered.

Hoping it was the reply she'd been hoping for, she rushed back to check but it was just a text from Nick.

Hope you're feeling a bit better about everything. Just wanted to say that I'll come along to the bank with you next week for moral support if you like?

Swallowing back her disappointment, Annie smiled. Nick was a great friend and she was lucky to have him in her corner.

"Mum!" Charlie called out again. "Hurry, it's creepy in here."

"How on earth can your own bedroom be creepy?" Annie asked, coming in and sitting on his bed.

"It's too quiet, like one of those scary movies."

"Ah, Charlie, I told you not to watch those movies with Callum, didn't I? You're too young for that stuff."

"I know, but I couldn't help it. They were just on. Mum, can I have two stories tonight, please, please?"

"I don't know, hon, I've had a very rough day and I'm tired. I had to make a lot of calls to a lot of people." She sighed. "There are a lot of people angry at Mummy at the moment."

"Why would anyone be angry at you?" he asked, concerned. "You're brilliant."

She smiled, despite herself. "I'm glad you think so," she said as she hugged him. "I wish more people did."

"Nick thinks so," he told her seriously.

Annie looked at him. "How do you know that?"

"I heard him say it just the other day at Gemma's house."

"Really?" She really hoped that Nick wasn't talking to his sister about her financial problems in front of her son. She didn't want Charlie to pick up on any issues. "You heard them talking about me?" she questioned. "What else did you hear?"

"Nothing." He shrugged. "Me and Callum just went outside to play football then."

She tucked Charlie in, snuggling under the covers and nestling him into the crook of her arm as she read him a story while he drifted off.

When he was finally asleep, she stroked his hair and eased herself out from beneath him, studying his face as she watched him sleep.

He looked so like his father sometimes it killed her.

Going back downstairs in her bare feet, Annie padded into the kitchen, then went to the fridge and poured herself an extra-large glass of wine.

After the week she'd just had, it was badly needed.

# Chapter 46

Now

"Mum?" Charlie called out blearily from the bottom of the stairs. It was the following morning and Annie was sitting at the breakfast bar in her pajamas. "You're not dressed."

She looked up and smiled. "I'm not going into work today, love. I'm staying home with you instead."

The look on her son's face said it all. A bright smile lit up his features, causing Annie to smile, too.

"Really? You're not going into the salon?"

"Nope."

The salon was the last place she wanted to be today. Saturday was their busiest day, of course, but there was no point in her sitting in the office, stressing over things she couldn't control. She'd done enough of that.

Besides, there was something else she needed to take care of.

"But you never take a day off," Charlie continued, shocked.

"What? Should I change my mind and go to work instead?" she teased.

"No!" he shouted as he ran and threw his arms around her with a laugh. "No way!"

Again, Annie felt guilty because of all the long hours at the salon that had taken her away from Charlie, but there had been no other option.

She was the only one who was going to provide for him. In recent years she'd managed to carve out more time, but it would never quell the regret she felt for having been so absent in his life as a toddler while she tried to make a go of #GlamSquad.

He was the reason she'd worked so hard in the first place, and why she'd been so absolutely determined to see her (and Felicity's) original plan through, despite her unexpected pregnancy.

"How about a nice walk after breakfast?" she suggested, kissing him on the cheek. "And then maybe a movie later?"

"In the day?" he questioned, wide-eyed. "But you never let me watch TV in the daytime."

"Well, today is a new day," Annie declared, as her phone dinged.

Her breath caught in her throat as she glanced at the screen alert to find a reply to the email she'd sent the day before had finally arrived.

Free to talk now if you like. What's this about?

Followed by a number for her to call.

Annie's heart thumped with both fear and shame as she realized she was really going to do this. She had to.

"Love, tell you what—I've just got to make a quick phone call. How about you chill out for a bit, maybe do some coloring, and then we'll head out for our walk, OK?"

"Maybe some cartoons instead?" He grinned, ever the negotiator, and she distractedly smiled back, her emotions all over the place.

"Just for a little while. But then we go for a walk, OK? It's a beautiful day out."

He scurried off into the living room, pleased at the unexpected opportunity to watch TV.

For a few moments, Annie busied herself in the kitchen with tidying up, hoping that the run-of-the-mill activity might settle her shaking hands.

And when she was sure Charlie was settled in front of the TV and well out of earshot, she dialed the number.

"You told me once that if I ever needed anything for Charlie, that you would help. Well, I need that now…" Annie couldn't believe how normal she sounded as she explained her situation, as if this was no big deal.

She hated, *hated*, lowering herself to this, the idea of being beholden to anyone.

It was possibly her lowest moment yet.

A deep sigh on the other end. "I understand, and I'm sorry but…the timing is not good."

At this she began to shake with fury. As if this was something she could control!

*Well, fuck that. And boo hoo.*

"Are you serious? I never had the luxury of deciding when or if the timing was *good*. No, I was too busy trying to keep my head above water, trying to keep me and Charlie going when we had no one else. And now, the only time I ever ask you for help, you throw it back in my face?"

"I'm sorry. Truly, I'd love to do what I can to help, but like I said, it's just a very bad time…"

She couldn't believe how anyone could be so goddamn cool, so unaffected by her plight or her request.

"So after all your promises, and my keeping quiet all these years so you can maintain your sweet life, you're telling me that you're just going to turn your back on it all now—on your own son?"

Annie was so enraged she hung up the phone without even waiting for an answer. But she'd got her answer, hadn't she? There would be no help forthcoming from Charlie's father, despite his promises and so-called best intentions.

She was on her own. Same as always.

"Mum?" Her son reappeared in the kitchen doorway, concern written all over his small face. "Why are you crying?"

Was she? Annie didn't even realize. She put a hand up to her face, finding that yes, she was indeed crying.

"It's nothing, sweetheart. Someone just upset me, that's all."

"Who upset you? Someone on the phone? Who was it?"

"Just…something to do with work, pet. Nothing for you to worry about."

"But I am worried. You look like Callum's sister when she broke up with her boyfriend. She said she had a broken heart. You don't have a broken heart, do you, Mum? Uncle Nick didn't break up with you, did he?"

*Nick? What the hell was he talking about?*

She knew her single status was a curiosity to Charlie, especially when he was so involved with his childminder's more traditional family, and knew it couldn't be easy for him growing up without a dad when Gemma's husband, Hugh, worked from home and thus was heavily involved in family life.

Annie vaguely remembered what it was like for her without parents before the O'Dohertys and she definitely remembered the void that had been left in her life when her father died when she was a teen.

Charlie had asked only once about his father, though, and Annie had told him the truth, because there was simply no reason not to.

"I met your father in Italy," she'd explained. "I was on holiday there one summer with my friends." She could still recall the melancholy in her own voice as she spoke.

"Was he nice?" Charlie asked simply. "What was he like?"

Annie sighed. "He was nice."

"And what did he look like?"

"Tall and handsome with a smile very like yours."

Charlie grinned happily, showing that same smile.

"Why isn't he here now?" he asked innocently.

Annie tried to choose her words carefully. "The trip came to an end, and I came back here to Ireland. I never saw him again."

"But didn't you love him, the man from Italy?"

Annie took a deep breath.

"No," she said. "I didn't really know him well enough to love him," she told him honestly. She brushed a lock of hair away from his forehead. "It doesn't matter anyway. You and me—we're happy together just the two of us, aren't we? We don't need anyone else."

He had a look on his face that almost broke Annie's heart in two. "I s'pose."

*The man from Italy...*

Thinking about that memory now, she recalled his excitement about Kim's launch invite yesterday and his insistence that he wanted to go.

Had he in his own little way managed to put two and two together?

"I'm sorry if somebody broke your heart, Mum," Charlie

said now, continuing to hug Annie's legs, while she dried her eyes and moved to compose herself.

"Nobody broke my heart, love," she reassured him truthfully.

Instead she was angry—seriously angry.

Annie moved to the countertop and snatched up the package that Kim had sent them.

Before now, the thought of going to Italy for the launch hadn't seriously entered her mind.

But after that call, she just might do it. There was nothing to lose anymore.

Her life was about to go up in flames anyway.

No harm to escape from her troubles for a while. They'd still be there no matter what she did, even if the salon wasn't, she thought ruefully.

She'd go to the bank on Monday with Nick and see if they could secure enough to at least keep them going for another while.

Either way, *to hell with it*. She'd go to Italy for a few days, and take Charlie with her—he'd jump at the opportunity for a rare all-expenses-paid break in the sun.

His very first holiday, and since she might never be able to take him on another...

Yes, why *shouldn't* she go along to the launch at Villa Dolce Vita, Annie decided, and reunite with that summer's old friends.

And foes.

# Chapter 47

## Now

Excitement bubbled over inside Colette as she waited in Naples for the train to Sorrento.

She still couldn't believe she was here, back on the Amalfi Coast after all these years.

She really needed this, perhaps more than she realized. And she was almost glad Ed wasn't going to be able to make it until the day of the party, allowing her more time to relax and catch up with Kim, and hopefully Annie, too.

There was just too much going on at home, and after her last disappointment, it would be a relief to get out of London for a while.

She stood and watched the tracks, waiting for the train's impending arrival. She'd taken the very same ride almost six years before, and she could still vividly remember the emotions that had filled her back then.

Italy had been like a dream, really. She'd been so naive back then, inexperienced in both life and love.

She'd never dreamed that things would've turned out the way they did. That this was the place where Colette's heart had been broken, yet where her ultimate love story had begun.

Ed didn't really see it like that, of course. He wasn't romantic. He tried, but big gestures of affection weren't something that came naturally to him. She understood. It was OK.

That day in St. James's Park had been a nice, though short-lived, diversion. Still, she appreciated the effort he had made.

A little while later, Colette picked up a taxi upon arriving at the station in Sorrento, and found herself chuckling as her driver immediately reminded her of Jacopo that first day when he'd taken her to Delfino.

There was a smile on her face as the memory of that visit to the restaurant returned, when she'd been so unsure of herself and full of wonder and awe at her surroundings.

She wondered if Mama Elene was still there and even whether Delfino was still open. Luca's face suddenly flashed before her then. His incredible smile and piercing blue eyes were vivid in her memories.

Was he still here in Positano? Had he finally done what Mama Elene had teased him about and settled down? Got married to Lidia, maybe, or some other gorgeous Italian girl worthy of his true affections, once he'd got bored of charming gullible tourists?

There was no way of knowing, of course. A lot could've changed and probably had, but Colette hoped at least that the little slice of heaven that was Delfino hadn't.

Impulsively asking the taxi for a diversion from her original destination, she sat back and stared out the window, wondering what the hell she was doing.

"Wait for me," she instructed him a little while later, as she closed the car door and walked hesitantly down the laneway toward the familiar entrance.

It was just the same. Nothing had changed at all and Colette was happy to see that. A large smile painted her features as she stepped inside, fully expecting to see Mama Elene behind the counter.

"Welcome to Delfino. Table for one?"

Colette looked at the much younger Italian woman. "Hi. No, actually, I was just wondering if Mama Elene was here? I'm an old friend."

"I'm sorry, but Mama Elene passed away a couple of years ago. I am Carlotta."

"Oh." Colette's heart sank at the news. She couldn't believe the warm, smiling woman was truly gone. "What about Luca, her nephew? Do you know him?"

"Of course I know him." Carlotta smiled in such a way that Colette knew in her bones she and Luca were romantically involved. Hell, for all she knew the attractive woman in front of her could well be her former lover's wife! "He is the owner of the restaurant now, but he just stepped out. You can wait a few minutes and he will be back," she explained and Colette's heart quickened.

"Oh, no, it's fine," she said quickly, panicking now. "I was just passing and I really need to go anyway. It's no big deal, truly."

"He was only going out for a few minutes," Carlotta insisted. Then she looked behind her, back toward the kitchen. "In fact, I think he might already be back."

"Really, it's OK."

Colette had to get out of there now. She turned and walked

quickly out the door and kept her gaze to the ground as she rushed back to the taxi, terrified of maybe bumping into him on the street outside.

She couldn't see Luca now. She just couldn't. She didn't want to look into that face, those eyes, and not know what she would feel.

Reaching the car, Colette told the driver to take her straight back to Sorrento as originally planned.

No more walks down memory lane while she was here—it was much too dangerous.

From here on, it was all about the now.

# Chapter 48

Now

"Where's your passport?" Annie called as she turned the couch cushions over.

Their flight to Naples was in a couple of hours and things were upside down. Charlie had been playing with his passport the night before; now it was missing and Annie was seriously stressed.

"I'm sorry, Mum. I don't know where I put it," he called down from his room. Annie had sent him up to do another sweep to ensure the essential document hadn't been overlooked.

She slapped her hands on her hips as she looked around the living room and shouted back to him. "It has to be somewhere, so go find it. We can't go to Italy without it, Charlie. If you don't find it, we aren't going."

"No!" her son shouted down from upstairs. "I'll find it."

Annie sighed. It had been a frantic morning already.

She'd overslept when her mobile phone battery had died during the night, and now this.

She flipped over another throw and stuffed her hand between the back of the seat and the cushion. Much to her relief, she felt something slim and leathery beneath her fingers and pulled it out.

There it was.

"Found it!" she called. Seconds later Charlie's happy footsteps were heard rushing down the stairs and the sight of him instantly tempered the brewing storm inside her.

She'd been in rotten form all week, mostly due to the fact that the bank had—despite Annie's pleas and Nick's support—refused her loan application.

#GlamSquad, the salon, Annie's pride and joy, and the business she'd spent the last four years pouring her life, her heart—and all of Felicity's bequest—into, her entire livelihood, was finished.

This trip would be Annie O'Doherty's last hurrah—her last-chance saloon.

If nothing else, the weekend in the sun would be a chance for Charlie to enjoy himself and be happy and carefree before life for them as a twosome changed utterly.

"Come here," she called, her tone mellowing as she pulled her little giant into her arms and hugged him. "I didn't mean to snap at you," she apologized. "I'm just a little frazzled. We're running late and I don't want to miss the flight."

"I know, Mum. It's all right. I'm a big boy," Charlie answered as he looked back at her with his trademark toothy grin. There were very few things that turned Annie's heart to mush but her son's smile was top of the list.

A knock on the door interrupted them.

"That must be Nick," she announced. "Why don't you take your backpack out to the car, and I'll bring the rest of our stuff, OK?"

Charlie nodded and duly grabbed his bag from the floor, tossing it on his back before he ran for the door.

Annie took a deep breath. She was really going back to Italy.

Back to where it all began.

## Chapter 49

Now

"Annie—over here!" she heard someone call out, as she and Charlie came through to the Arrivals terminal in Naples airport.

"Kim, what are you doing here?" She wasn't prepared for this. She'd told her friend they were coming, of course, but she hadn't expected to see her until later, after they'd arrived at the hotel.

*Shite*… Annie put a hand up to her clothes, instinctively straightening the wrinkled T-shirt she'd worn under her zip-up top on the flight.

She'd fully intended to doll herself up to the nines before-hand and appear at the hotel looking and feeling like a film star, but since they were running so late, and she'd been getting Charlie ready, too, she'd barely had the chance to dress herself.

Kim, by comparison, looked like she'd just stepped off a catwalk, dressed as she was in a floaty silk floral top, blinding white capri trousers, hot pink espadrilles, and a pair of Gucci cat-eye sunglasses perched atop her chic blonde head.

"Surprise!" she cried cheerfully, pulling Annie into a huge hug, as Charlie looked on. "And *of course* I'd be here. Where else would I be? I took the day off so I'm all yours—I hope," she added.

Kim released her hold on Annie and then turned to Charlie. "Oh my goodness, you've got so big!" Despite having only briefly met her once when he was smaller, he immediately flung two happy arms around her waist. He was such a friendly child.

"I'm so glad that you and your mom could come for the party. Why don't we get you in the car so we can show you what Italy's like?"

"Yes!" Charlie exclaimed. "Where is it?"

"Right this way," Kim instructed as she placed her hand on his back and directed him to where a snazzy convertible was waiting.

Annie tried to dampen down her inner resentment as Charlie's eyes widened in awe at the open roof.

She closed her eyes and took several cleansing breaths.

Once in the car, Kim's animated conversation and obvious delight at their reunion continued, but Annie couldn't work up sufficient enthusiasm to match it.

Mostly, she listened to her chatter away to Charlie while she watched the world go by, a leaden lump in her stomach as she began to relive the same journey she'd taken all those years before, when she'd thought the world was her oyster.

"Are you OK?" Kim asked, noticing Annie's silence.

She smiled wanly. "I'm grand. Just a bit tired after the flight. How's Gabriel and Lily?"

"All good. They're out and about today but should be back at the hotel later. Lily is so excited about having another child to play with in the pool, which hopefully means you and I will have some quiet time to catch up." She winked conspiratorially. "Aw, it's such a shame Colette isn't coming out till Friday, though—it won't feel real until all three of us are back together."

"She isn't? That's a shame." This was news to Annie. She'd have thought Colette and Ed would be there in advance of the party to support Kim.

"I know, right? Apparently Ed can't get away from work." She rolled her eyes. "I mean, I totally get that, but still..."

Kim chitchatted on about this and that and old times, trying to catch up on everything that had happened in Annie's life since they'd seen each other the year before last.

Of course, Annie didn't utter a word about her business worries or the fact that her life had only recently turned into a complete disaster, and she and Charlie were facing a scarily uncertain future—something made all the more acute as Kim then chattered animatedly about last-minute preparations and hitches with the launch, and all her grand plans for the party.

*Talk about chalk and cheese...*

Conversation ebbed and flowed along the journey until, eventually, they reached the outskirts of Sorrento. The only one really talking by this point was Charlie, who had a thousand and one questions to ask Kim.

His lively chatter automatically quieted Annie's discomfort and mercifully also seemed to distract Kim.

Once she and Charlie were checked into their room at the Excelsior, agreeing to meet Kim back downstairs once they got settled, he was in her ear.

"Can I go down to the pool now? Please, please, *please*?"

"Go on then, munchkin," she teased fondly, as he ran to the bathroom to get changed, then took off for the water at breakneck speed once they got back down.

As she kept an eye on her son from her vantage point beneath an umbrella at a nearby patio table, Annie couldn't believe that here he was, actually running and bouncing around the part of the world in which he was conceived.

How had the time gone by so quickly? It felt like only yesterday that she'd found out about his impending arrival once she'd returned back home, and became desperately worried about how she was going to cope.

She looked up now to see Kim approach with her phone to her ear, and a concerned look on her face.

"Everything OK?" she asked once her friend was off the phone.

"Sure..." Kim replied distractedly.

"OK, let's try that again," Annie said balefully, lowering her sunglasses as she stared at her. "It's me you're talking to, remember? And it might have been a while, but I still recognize that look."

Kim's gaze shifted around uncomfortably.

Yep, something was definitely up.

Her friend sighed and this time looked her square in the eye.

"It's just...there's been a few issues with the launch lately."

"What do you mean? You said in the car earlier that everything was ready to go."

"I thought it was," she replied wearily. "I managed to get round most of my last-minute hitches. But now there's a problem with the caterers I'd booked for the party." Her shoulders slumped defeatedly.

"What? Very last minute, isn't it? What are you going to do at this stage?"

"I don't know." Kim bit her lip.

"Ah, feck it, let's just have a cocktail and you can sort it all out later," Annie suggested, falling back on her default in the hope that it might cheer Kim up.

"Hey," a smooth American voice interrupted them, and Annie jumped a little to see Gabriel standing there, a little girl hoisted up on his hip.

"Hey, Annie, glad you could make it," he said, smiling. Annie didn't know where to look when he reached across to peck her on the cheek. "It just wouldn't have been the same for Kim if you and Colette weren't here, too. Back to where all the magic happened."

He winked at his wife and Annie noticed her shoot him a definite look in return.

"It wasn't magic for everyone, you know. And speaking of which, I really need to see if I can work some magic of my own to try and get this latest snag sorted," she grumbled, putting her phone to her ear once again. "See you guys later, OK?" Kim reached over and gave Lily a quick kiss on the cheek.

"She's tired," Gabriel said. "I'm going to take her up for a nap for a little while."

"Sure…"

But it was obvious that Kim was already miles away, and Annie couldn't help but notice the irritated look on Gabriel's face as he walked away.

Trouble in paradise?

*Now* that *was interesting…*

# Chapter 50

Now

"Oh my God! Colette? You almost gave me a heart attack," Kim heard Annie exclaim behind her, as she put the phone to her ear, and she turned back, unable to believe her eyes. "You're here—already? I thought you weren't making it out until the launch day?"

"Well, I was, because Ed couldn't get away till then, but then last minute I decided to come out on my own and he'll follow. He has a lot going on at work and couldn't get away," Colette explained to Annie.

Kim rushed back to embrace her friends, delighted all three were reunited at last. The strain in Colette's voice was evident, though—as it had been when she'd initially called to explain about her and Ed's arrangements, and Kim suspected that perhaps she wasn't the only one having family issues.

While in her own case there might still be a way to remedy those, she knew in her friend's situation, it wasn't so easy.

There was still no news on the baby front for them then, despite Colette's confession during that call that her period was late—and her hopes that, on this trip, maybe she and Ed might have something to celebrate, too.

Again, whenever she talked to her, Kim felt guilty about how shocked and distraught she'd been when she fell unexpectedly pregnant with Lily, when she knew poor Colette would've given anything for a surprise like that.

"Where's Charlie?" she asked Annie now, and Kim had to laugh when, as if on cue, a dripping-wet child dashed toward his unsuspecting mother and hugged her from behind.

"Ah, Charlie, you drenched me!"

"Oh, he's just having fun." Colette chuckled and kneeled down to say hello. "Hello there. You don't know me but I'm an old friend of your mum's. My name's Colette."

Kim smiled, watching her interact with Charlie on his own level. She truly had a natural way with children, which made it all the more heartbreaking that she couldn't seem to have any of her own.

"So how have you all been?" Colette questioned as she took a seat at the table alongside Annie. "It seems much longer than five years."

"I saw you guys in London just after I had Lily, remember?" Kim reminded. "So not that long for us."

"But I definitely haven't seen you since before our wedding," Colette said to Annie. "Charlie was just a baby then. And look at him now…"

"I know. Again, I'm sorry I couldn't make it," Annie stated. "How's Ed?"

Colette's features twitched infinitesimally. "Ah, you know,

all work, work, work," she mused, as she tried to pass off her obvious unease.

Kim really needed to be getting back to work but she so wanted to stay here and linger over piña coladas and catch up with them for as long as she could. Even if hers needed to be a virgin one. She wrestled hard with herself, unable to believe that there was another snag, yet another fire to put out.

It was getting to the point where it would be a miracle if the launch happened at all.

"Charlie really is growing up so fast, Annie," Colette was saying.

"I can't believe it either. It's as if he was born yesterday."

"He doesn't look so much like you, though. Perhaps he's more like his dad?"

The color seemed to drain from Annie's face at this and Kim was surprised that the topic of Charlie's dad would have such an effect on her friend, given that she'd always been so open about the fact that it was just an ill-fated encounter.

"He's a great kid," Kim put in quickly. "So happy and fun-loving, and I have no doubt that he'll make you really proud."

"He already does," Annie said with a smile. "And what about you, Kim? How are you finding motherhood these days?"

"Oh, where's Lily? Is she here?" Colette chimed in, looking around.

"Aw, you just missed her and Gabriel, but you'll see them later, I'm sure."

"Do you have any pictures? I'd love to see them."

Kim flipped the cover open on her phone case and entered her passcode. She flicked her finger upward in rapid succession as she looked for the most recent photos she had of her daughter.

The further down the list she went, the worse she began to feel. She really was her mother's daughter.

There were tons of pictures of the villa project, some professional shots for social media, and other stuff she'd been sent for approval from the marketing department.

Finally, she found a few from a weekend trip earlier in the year. Gabriel had insisted she take a break from the seemingly endless villa preparations, and the three of them had headed to the Hamptons for a few days.

Kim still had to work most of the time but there were a few occasions when she took an hour or two away to focus on him and Lily.

"We went boating," she commented, as she handed the phone to Colette, feeling a little on edge as she watched her pass the phone in turn to Annie, who seemed even more curious.

"You all take such perfect pictures," she sighed as she handed the phone back, but Kim thought she noticed an edge to her tone. "Lily looks sooo like her dad. No offense, Kim, but I can't really see you in her except for the color of her hair."

"That's probably for the best," she chuckled ruefully. The fact that her daughter looked more like Gabe and called for him when she was frightened or couldn't sleep didn't really bother her. Kim had work to do and she did it. He had more time.

"Kim?" Colette's voice interrupted her thoughts.

"Sorry, what?"

"I was just saying that it might be nice to head over to Positano for dinner for old times' sake later, if you can spare an evening. A good excuse for the three of us to catch up before everything gets too busy for you. What do you think?"

"Ah, for goodness' sake, Charlie!" Annie yelled then, as her son dive-bombed into the pool, sending a huge spray of water in their direction. Kim jumped back just in time for it to miss her but Colette and Annie, who were both sitting poolside, got soaked. "What the hell were you playing at?" she scolded.

Colette laughed it off. "Ah, don't worry, Annie. He was just doing exactly that—playing. It's what kids do."

"Thanks for the advice, Colette, but maybe save it for your own child," she snapped, brushing water off her clothes.

Kim's stomach twisted at the statement. She knew Annie hadn't meant anything callous by it, but still the words had been uttered, and while Colette tried to hide the effect they had on her, Kim had seen the hurt flash in her eyes.

"Excuse me a moment," she mumbled. "In all the excitement, I forgot to call Ed when I got in. I'll be back in a bit."

Kim watched as she hurried off into the hotel building, wondering if she should go after her to check if she was OK. But then she saw her raise her mobile phone to her ear and figured there was little point in interrupting her conversation with Ed.

"Why did you say that?" she whispered harshly to Annie, who looked duly pained.

"It just came out, I didn't mean it. You know I wouldn't hurt Colette, it's just…she doesn't really understand what it is to be a parent. She's used to having children that she can give back when they misbehave, but you can't give back your own child, you know that."

"Still, it was a bit mean, considering."

"I know. I'll apologize when she comes back. I was just a bit frustrated, and tired after the journey, maybe," Annie admitted.

"What's really going on?"

"Nothing." But her eyes turned to her and Kim could see the conflict in them. She waited for her friend to explain as the sound of Charlie's splashing continued in the background.

"Things are a little…stressful just now," Annie admitted finally. She gave a dispirited grin. "For starters, it not always easy being a single mother."

"I can imagine. But I still don't know why you refused to ask his father for help. It could've made life so much easier."

"I doubt that. Anyway, Charlie and I are just fine on our own."

"It's not just Charlie, though, is it? Something else is on your mind."

Annie shook her head. "I'd almost forgotten who I'm talking to. Always Miss Perceptive."

"And you're always Miss Stubborn. What gives?"

"It's nothing—honestly." Whatever was going on, Annie clearly wasn't ready to tell her. Or maybe she never would be. "Anyway, I am who I am."

"I know, and that's why I don't understand this attitude."

"Hey, Kim, give it a rest, OK? You have always got whatever you wanted. Always. You've never had to struggle with anything a day in your life. You have a super successful business, a gorgeous husband and a beautiful daughter, with your big California house, millions in the bank, and now the villa, your crowning glory. What exactly is it about your life that could possibly equip you to understand mine?"

With that, Annie stood up and stormed off to the other side of the pool, where she grabbed a towel and urged Charlie to get out of the water.

*What the hell was that?* Kim thought, reeling as she sat alone, three abandoned, half-finished cocktails on the table in front of her, debating whether she should try to rescue the situation with Annie, who seemed to have flown off the handle for no apparent reason. Clearly something was going on with her, but in time-honored Annie fashion, she was insistent on rowing her own boat. And she had already said she was tired after the flight, so perhaps Kim would only worsen things by pushing it and making her even more irritable.

And it wasn't as if she didn't have enough problems to deal with.

She sighed heavily. This reunion was supposed to be a happy time, reliving fond memories of the summer the three of them had shared, and reaffirming their friendship.

Yet another example of Kim's grand plans going awry.

# Chapter 51

Now

L ater that evening the three friends and Charlie reconvened
at La Cambusa in Positano. The streets were bustling and
the lights of the town were bright, reflecting like stars on a
dark ocean. Located by the water's edge, the restaurant had
been one of their old haunts and a lively local favorite.

Charlie ordered marinara pizza while the others enjoyed
freshly caught seafood. The conversation was lively, and the discomfort of earlier seemed to dissipate with the change of venue.

It was impossible *not* to feel uplifted here on the Amalfi
Coast, Colette thought.

The air was cool and the smell of the ocean crisp around
them. The restaurant was full, but not overly packed, each table
occupied by smiling faces of families and friends gathering together to enjoy time with one another.

Envy wasn't something she was plagued by often, but as Colette sat watching Charlie and Annie interact, she couldn't help but feel that loathsome emotion.

She wanted a child so badly the hurt was visceral. Why was she denied when it had come so easily to Annie? A drunken mistake during which she neglected to use contraception, apparently, and she was pregnant.

How many nights had there been for Colette over the years? How many tests and needles and prayers and still nothing? Would she forever be denied the only thing she truly ever wanted in life?

A cool breeze blew in off the water, chilling her exposed arms. She rubbed them gently. She always got colder more easily than others. It had been the same the last time she'd visited this particular restaurant, though the company had been different.

"This place really brings back memories," she commented absently.

"That's why I so wanted you two to be here." Kim placed one hand on her arm and the other on Annie's. "It just wouldn't feel right to take this next step without you both. You guys changed my life for the better, and for that, I'm eternally grateful."

"Oh, stop, everything you've done has been entirely down to you—we just happened to be here at the start," Colette assured her with a smile. "And I suppose it was a life-changing trip for us all in a way." She glanced from Kim to Annie and then Charlie.

"Yep, life-changing all right," Annie grunted. "At least you two landed on your feet," she added with some bitterness, and Colette glanced at her son, hoping he didn't pick up on anything untoward.

But no, Charlie was immersed in his meal, oblivious to the conversation.

"Is everything ready for the party?" she asked Kim, hoping to change the subject. "Do you need help with anything?"

"No, I think we're good." She grimaced. "Thank God the caterer managed to sort a replacement in the end. Barring any other last-minute hiccups," she added, crossing her fingers.

"Ah, of course all will work out fine," Annie muttered darkly and took a swig of her wine.

Colette inhaled deeply. "Smell that?"

"The sea?" Kim asked as she turned in the direction of the water only a few feet away from where they sat.

"I really miss it," she commented. "I grew up by the water, as you know, but in London everything's smog and exhaust engines."

"Maybe you should move out of the city," Annie commented, chucking back her wine far too fast for Colette's liking.

The thought was tempting, though, and Colette would've been lying if she said it hadn't crossed her mind several times, but it was never the right moment to bring it up with Ed.

Not to mention that he had his career, friends, and family—his entire life—in London. She knew he wouldn't want to move.

"It might be good for a few reasons," Kim agreed. "A change of pace and scenery is always good. Look what it did for us."

"I can't see Ed moving," Annie said then, which Colette thought was an odd comment, given she didn't really know him. "Ah, you know what I mean," she sputtered, obviously sensing she'd spoken out of turn. "The English can be a bit set in their ways."

"Ed's not like that," Colette defended. "He's very open to change, and very flexible about things; probably more than I am, actually."

Again, Annie topped up her wineglass.

"Are you OK to drink that much when—" Colette cocked her head at Charlie "—you know…"

But by the look on her friend's face, she wished she hadn't said anything.

"What? You're trying to suggest I'm a lush now?"

"Sorry… I just… I—"

"Come on, she's on holiday," Kim laughed lightly, topping up all their glasses, though Colette could hear the strain in her voice as she tried to keep the conversation going. "Actually, I think a toast is in order…" But the rest of the sentence trailed off with the ping of an alert on her phone. And by the look on Kim's face when she saw the display, Colette knew it was important.

"Sorry, I need to make a quick call…"

Silence fell over the table as Kim moved away, and Charlie continued to savor his pizza as if it was his last meal.

Annie was smiling tipsily at the waiter, and indeed any other handsome male in the restaurant who happened to catch her eye. Some things never changed.

Did she ever want to settle down, Colette wondered, or was she still content to play the field all the time? It didn't make sense in her mind. Surely it was better to have someone you were sure about, than a trail of random guys you could never commit to—especially with a young child in tow.

But then again, she and Annie were so different. She always marched to her own tune.

Colette only hoped that along the way her friend would find the happiness she deserved and that Charlie would eventually have a more stable family unit than his mother did growing up.

"I need to stretch my legs," she said, getting to her feet. "I think I'll take a little walk along the pier before ordering dessert."

"Suit yourself," Annie replied. "I think I'll stay here and have another glass of vino—if that's OK with you," she asked pointedly, and Colette noticed that while her mouth was smiling her eyes weren't.

Why was she so cool with her? Was it still because of what she'd said earlier at the pool? Colette didn't think her remark was that out of order, but clearly it was for Annie. She'd better mind her own business in future.

"Can I get dessert, Mum?" Charlie asked through a mouthful of pizza.

"'Course you can, pet. We're on holiday."

"OK, well, I'll be back in a bit. Kim's still preoccupied with her call. Whatever it is must be important. Tell her I'll be back shortly."

"Grand."

There was something so wonderfully eternal about this place, Colette mused as she strolled along the promenade on her way down to the steps.

As much as it had changed, it had remained the same. Large gray stone bricks marked the walk from the edge of the promenade all the way up to the coastline. The restaurant's facade was of similar stone and understated compared to the other more colorful buildings that lined the street, but it didn't detract from its character.

Tonight the little bay at Spiaggia Grande was filled with boats, mostly small local fishing craft, interspersed with a few bigger yachts.

She soon found herself on the jetty that extended into the bay. The area was even more crowded with evening diners, but the sea breeze was stronger, too, keeping everyone cool.

Colette strolled at a leisurely pace. The last time she'd been here she hadn't been alone. There Luca was again, finding his way into her thoughts as he had so many times over the years, and even more so since Kim had sent the invite.

It wasn't right, she kept telling herself. She was married. And chances were he was, too, so why was he in her head like this?

Why was she actively seeking out the paths they had walked together and thinking of those times: the way he held her hand, the smell of his aftershave as he pulled her close to shield her from the chill of the wind. The way his strong arms encircled her and the feeling of his skin against her cheek as they stared at the stars and talked about their dreams.

Colette wrapped her arms around herself as she leaned against the rail and looked out over the water.

She couldn't help the smile that crept across her face as she remembered the night Luca had taken her out on his boat. She could still see it like it was yesterday, the town lit up as if it were on fire, soft light illuminating every building etched into the mountainside, the archways and doorways clearly visible, the colors creating an artistic impression.

It had been such a magical night. Being with him then had done something for Colette that nothing else before ever had—given her confidence.

He'd listened to her—really listened, not to correct her or tell her that her views were naive, but because he actually cared about what she thought and how she felt. It had been such a novelty. Up until then she'd spent her life blending in. Which of course was why it was at first so difficult to understand why someone like him would notice her. Why she, out of everyone, had gotten his attention.

*Because you were a tourist, you idiot. Another easy fly-by-night target. You were nothing special.*

But that wasn't strictly true either, Colette assured herself now. Ed, too, had considered her special back then—and still did. Yes, at first he'd merely been her knight in shining armor, offering her a shoulder to cry on after Luca had let her down, but he had turned out to be so much more than that, and he'd especially been a tremendous comfort to her after her mother died.

*Things happened for a reason.*

Still, despite the circumstances of her last visit to the Amalfi Coast, and the entirely new direction her life had taken since, Colette was struck by the notion that being back here truly felt like coming home.

# Chapter 52

## Now

While Colette was off wandering, and Kim was waylaid on the phone, Annie was left to silently drown her sorrows in dessert and wine.

"Are you OK, Mum?" Charlie asked. "You look so sad."

Annie hadn't realized she'd lost herself so entirely to her thoughts. She slapped a smile on her face as she looked back at him.

"I'm grand," she assured him, "just a bit tired after all the traveling today. You finished your gelato?"

"Yes, but I want more."

She laughed. He was growing faster than a weed in spring and had a healthy appetite, but that was his second gelato. "Ah, I think you've had enough now. We don't want you buzzing on too much of a sugar rush on your first night," she teased.

He grinned happily. "It's just so nice, though. I love Italy already."

Feeling pleasantly buzzed herself, Annie sipped her drink and fondly tucked a lock of her son's hair away from his forehead.

"Where's Colette?" Kim asked, reappearing alongside them.

"She went for a walk. She should be back soon."

"Everything all right between you two?" she asked cagily. "I noticed a bit of an…edge."

Annie sighed. "I know—I was probably a bit hard on her over the wine thing. But she sounded so…sanctimonious about my drinking in front of Charlie. What the hell does she know about it?"

"Exactly. But if you don't mind my saying so, you seem particularly touchy. Understandable after the travel but maybe just try and keep it in check a little—at least till after the launch, pretty please? I've got enough on my plate at the moment without the guests going at it."

Annie chuckled, feeling bad now. "You're right. I'm sorry. What's going on now? Another problem?"

Kim rolled her eyes. "It never ends."

"It was good to see Gabe earlier," Annie said. "He looks *hot*. You really did land on your feet there, Kim." She picked up her glass. "Then again, what else is new?"

"What do you mean?"

"Nothing, it's just…he's a great guy—you're really lucky to have him."

"I need to go. Why don't we see if we can find Colette?" Kim suggested, but by her tone Annie knew that, despite her dismissal, she'd somehow managed to piss her off, too.

"You go ahead, I think I'll just finish the wine."

"All right, I'll be back in a few," Kim stated tersely as she got to her feet again and disappeared after Colette.

Once again, Annie felt like the outsider. Colette and Kim had always had way more in common with each other than she did with either of them, yet the three had managed to mesh so well the last time they were here.

But since then their lives had diverged completely, so much to the point that they shared little to no common ground now.

Regret wasn't something Annie subscribed to normally, but right then she was beginning to regret her impulsive decision to come back here, and worse, to bring Charlie with her.

"Mum?" he mumbled then and she could hear the fatigue in his voice before she saw it in his face. He'd had a long day; they both had.

"Hey, come here," she beckoned, pulling him up onto her lap. He snuggled against her collarbone. "We'll head back to the hotel soon."

"I'm tired," he whined.

"I know, love." She stroked his hair. "The others will be back soon and then we'll go. Close your eyes."

A little later she saw his hand reach for the hem of his shirt—a telltale sign that he was about to drift off. Charlie, for as long as she could remember, had always done the same thing to soothe himself to sleep. He'd take the hem of his shirt and suck on it when he was a toddler; as he got older he grew out of that and instead persisted in scrunching the hem into oblivion in his hand until sleep claimed him.

A few minutes later Colette and Kim reappeared at the table.

"Aw, is he sleeping?" Colette cooed, her face softening at the sight.

"Just dozing."

"I'll bring the car round." Kim took the keys out of her bag and headed back out to where she'd parked.

"They can sleep anywhere, can't they?" Colette commented, as she settled back into her seat.

"Especially this one," Annie answered, smiling fondly. As Colette's gaze lingered longingly on her sleeping child, she remembered she had an apology to make.

"Hey, I'm sorry for snapping at you earlier. I didn't mean to upset or hurt you in any way. I was just shooting my mouth off; you know me, I say whatever's on my mind and don't always think about how it'll affect others. And I was a bit tired and cranky in the heat, too. I would never hurt you on purpose. You know that, don't you?"

"Of course," Colette replied, looking relieved. "I'd never hurt you either. And I'm sorry for being a bit pass-remarkable. I should just mind my own bloody business."

"It's grand, honestly. All forgotten about so?"

"Definitely," she replied with a smile, and Annie resolved to hold herself in check over the coming days where Colette was concerned.

Her friend was the only blameless one in this mess after all.

# Chapter 53

## Now

Kim's heart was in her mouth as she drove the others back to the hotel. She was so distracted by Gabriel's message—and the fact that she couldn't reach him on his phone in the meantime—that she was lucky they made it back in one piece.

We need to talk. I think I've figured it out.

What could he mean? And what exactly had he figured out?

Bidding a quick good-night to her friends, Kim quietly let herself into their suite, aware that Lily would likely be asleep, and since she and Gabriel were about to have some kind of… conversation, she definitely didn't want to wake her up.

He was outside on the terrace, a glass of whiskey in his hand.

"Hey," she greeted nervously. "What's up?"

"You tell me." His tone was ominous, a sharp contrast to its usual warmth.

"I'm not sure..."

"Kim, I've always been straight with you, haven't I? No matter what. Right from the start there's never been any secrets between us—on my part at least."

"Gabe, what's this all about?"

"I understood how important this project here in Italy was—this so-called tribute to the roots of your business. And I was happy to go along with that and do whatever it took to support you. But I won't be made a fool of. Neither will Lily."

"I really don't know what..." Kim's mind was reeling.

Had Hank since got a better picture about the lawsuit and told Gabriel everything, including the truth that she was in fact a complete fraud? That she'd used a journal and words that were never hers in the first place and passed them off as her own?

No matter about public perception or bad publicity, the last person in the world she ever wanted to disappoint was Gabriel. He was the only constant in her life—the best thing that had ever happened to her.

She sighed. "I never meant for any of that to happen, honestly. It just seemed to take on a life of its own. And then things had gone way too far for me to stop them. If it weren't for Antonio—"

"Seriously?" His eyes flashed as he glared at her. "You mean there's actual merit to this? I thought it was impossible, that there was no way... Man, I feel so stupid."

She couldn't get over the look on his face, one of complete and utter disappointment in her. It was devastating.

"I swear, for me, it just started out as some fun, a distraction, even. Gabe, I had no idea it would go so far. If I had, believe me, I would never have got so involved."

"He's twenty-five years older than you, for chrissakes. And we have a child! What the hell are you playing at?"

"What? What's Lily got to do with anything?"

"But that's exactly it, isn't it? What's Lily got to do with anything—that's how it's always been for you. She's never considered in your life, always at the bottom of the pile. But this is too much, Kim, way too much. How dare you…"

"I'm sorry," she gasped tearfully. "Don't you think I don't know I'm a terrible mom? I see you two together and I just feel like a third wheel. I'm not even on the same wavelength, and half the time she doesn't really notice if I'm there or not."

"Because you never are!" He stood up in disgust. "And you think this gives you the right to mess up our family, and not just ours, Antonio's, too?"

"What…what has Antonio's family got to do with this?" Kim asked, frowning. "He and Emilia have their own problems to contend with just now."

"And you screwing her husband while she slowly loses her mind is going to help?" Gabriel raged.

Kim's mouth dropped open. *"What?"* she gasped, floored. "You think me…and Antonio… What the hell? How could you possibly think that?" She was seriously gobsmacked that he would utter such a thing. Never mind the fact that Antonio was old enough to be her father, he was also a close mutual friend of both hers and Gabriel. He and Emilia had introduced them, for goodness' sake!

"So you're denying it?" he said, but she noticed his voice had lost some of its bluster.

"Of course I am. Because you are completely and utterly wrong. I am not sleeping with Antonio; he is my friend and business partner and nothing more. Yes, we've had to spend lots of time together over the last eighteen months or so while trying to get this venture off the ground, but it's a business partnership and was never anything else. God, the very thought makes me feel ill. Especially with poor Emilia being the way she is…"

He looked at her. "You're serious."

"Yes. I'm absolutely serious. I would never cheat on you, Gabe. I love you, and to be honest I can't quite understand why you put up with me. But I'm not cheating, I swear."

He was shaking his head. "I don't get it. Emilia was so sure…"

"When did you talk to her? And what did she say?" Kim was baffled as to where all of this had come from.

"She called here earlier to talk to you while you were out with the others. She seemed upset, some mistake with the licenses? She said that Antonio was angry with her and it was all your fault. I tried to calm her down, and then she confided that she thought there was something going on between you two. That Antonio was going to leave her."

Hearing this saddened Kim to the core. "Aw, Gabe, she hasn't been well for a while. You know that. She was just being paranoid." But the mention of the licenses now triggered a memory in her brain.

The way Antonio had been at the town hall meeting, and how he'd squirreled away the planning documents that had caused the trouble without her seeing them, promising her he'd take care of it and find out who in the company had been behind it.

Could Emilia have been behind the new application, albeit unintentionally? She was a company director and signatory on all the plans. Could she have mistakenly resubmitted the applications? If so, then perhaps her prognosis was worse than Kim, or indeed Antonio, originally suspected.

Then another thought struck her. Could Emilia also be the one behind the so-called plagiarism claims? She was the only one who had some sense of the truth; Kim had once confided in her that some of the inspirational quotes might not be wholly original, though she hadn't breathed a word about any journal. But Emilia hadn't seemed to think there was any issue at the time.

But now, because of her (unfounded) suspicions of an affair, could she perhaps be trying to get back at Kim and sabotage the launch of Villa Dolce Vita? It made sense.

Kim breathed deeply, deciding it was time to come clean to Gabriel once and for all about the notebook and how The Sweet Life originally began.

"The quotes—some of the original ones—they're not actually mine," she confessed meekly, explaining how everything had barreled out of control once Emilia and Antonio had come on board. "I never purposely meant to pass them off as my own, or use them to launch the business. They were just…there, and the longer it went on, the easier it was to just keep going."

Gabriel seemed taken aback, but much to Kim's relief, not particularly horrified or upset with her.

"Of course you wouldn't have intended anything untoward, and knowing Antonio and Emilia as I do, I totally get how it all could take on a life of its own. But more importantly, why the hell wouldn't you tell me any of this—let me know what was really bothering you all this time?" he said, reaching for her hand. "We could've figured this out together."

"I didn't know if it *was* possible to figure out. Instead I've just fought fire after fire, hoping that it would all be OK in time for launch night. But I realize now I should've included you from the get-go."

"Yes, you should. We're a team, you and I. In every regard.

But you don't seem to realize it." He put his arms around her and pulled her close. "I'm sorry I accused you like that. I just thought that could well be the reason for your frequent absences, and the...tension...between us since Lily and I got here. That being said, I couldn't quite imagine you and Antonio together but—"

"Ugh. Please don't. I need to talk to him, though. Obviously Emilia's deterioration is worse than any of us thought, maybe including Antonio. He needs to know just in case..."

"Shhh, not now." Gabriel nestled her into the crook of his neck. She couldn't remember the last time they'd been together this way. It felt wonderful and Kim instinctively felt all of the tension leave her body. But then she exhaled.

It was now or never.

"I'm sorry that I haven't been a good wife to you or a mother to Lily," she began. Her heart was beating so hard it felt like a congo drum in her chest. She was so scared he wouldn't understand. That she'd bare her soul to Gabe and he'd just tear it apart.

Still, she continued.

"I know it seems that work is more important than the two of you—especially lately—but it isn't. It really isn't," she assured as she took his hand and began to play with his fingers. "You and Lily are my family, my only family, and I love you. I know you might not think that and sometimes I know I don't act it, but I do. I love you so much."

"I do know," Gabriel replied, as a tender hand touched her cheeks. "And Lily does, too."

Kim swallowed the boulder that had formed in her throat. "I need to tell you something else. Something I've been keeping to myself for a long time because I didn't want you to be disappointed in me. I didn't want you to hate me."

"That could never happen. I love you. I'm always going

to love you. No matter what. Even when I thought you and Antonio… It still didn't stop me loving you."

"You might not feel that once I say what I have to say. I hope you do, but I'd understand if you didn't," she replied as her eyes fell from his. This was the most difficult thing she'd ever had to do.

"OK, now I'm really worried," Gabriel said, sitting back down again.

Kim looked at her hands. "When I got pregnant with Lily, I was terrified. I didn't know how to be a mother. I still don't. Every day I look at her and wonder why on earth anyone would see it fit to make her mine. I'm no kind of mother, Gabe. I couldn't even breastfeed her when she was born. I couldn't get her to stop crying when she had colic. I was utterly useless in her life and I still am. The only person she needs is you and she has you. There's no room for me."

"That's not true."

"Yes, it is. I'm a terrible mother. Worse, I'm my own mother's daughter." The words were bile on her tongue but they were the truth.

"You are nothing like Gloria," Gabriel replied sharply. "That woman should never have had children. Though I'm obviously glad she did."

She couldn't smile at the attempt at levity. "Maybe I shouldn't have either."

His face became still. "What do you mean?"

"I mean I didn't really want Lily, Gabe. The same way my mother didn't want me," Kim said slowly, as if each word was a tooth being extracted. "Look at me. What good am I as her mother? She doesn't even need me."

She was crying now and she didn't even know when it started. She felt so terrible inside but she couldn't stop now. She had to say it all.

"I never wanted to be a mother," she admitted. "But you wanted a child so much…"

Gabriel's lashes fluttered as his gaze turned away from her.

"I'm sorry," she said. "But it's the truth. I didn't want to be pregnant. I just wanted it to be you and me, and then suddenly there was another person in the mix and I didn't know what to do about it. I wasn't prepared. I tried to be happy, but all I felt was fear. I had no reference to what it was to be a good mother. I had nothing to measure myself by except the fake happy families I saw on television. Then after Lily was born I felt even worse. Nothing I did was right for her. Even now I can't seem to get anything right. I'm a failure."

"You don't think you get things right?" Gabriel replied sharply. "But you have to *try* to get them right, Kim. And you haven't done that."

"I know," she said sadly as she hung her head. He was angry. She knew he would be. She deserved his scorn.

"No, you don't, but you're going to," he continued, smiling now. "Don't you stand there and talk about yourself like that and expect me to just sit here and listen. I won't let you tear yourself down and act like you've got a right to do so. Do you know who you sounded like just now? You sounded like your mother, and you aren't your mother. Even though she's out of your life, that woman's poison still looms over you and I'm not about to let it continue." He looked at her. "I probably should have said something before but…this saboteur and the online stuff…I wonder if it might be Gloria?"

Kim's eyes widened at this idea, which, she had to be honest, had never even crossed her mind.

Could it be that her mother was behind all the recent problems with Villa Dolce Vita? Punishing her for rejecting the family by trying to upend the grand launch? It was possible, but Kim couldn't really see it.

Underhandedness wasn't at all Gloria's style, to say noth-ing of the fact that she and Kim's dad had made good on their promise to cut her out of their lives all those years ago.

The Westons hadn't attended Kim and Gabriel's wedding; they didn't even bother to reply to the invite. Which at the time had been hurtful, yet no real surprise to Kim.

Her parents had just got on with their lives, as if their daughter had never existed. So what would have changed in the meantime for her mother to want to mess things up for her, after all these years?

"I don't think it could be her," she told Gabe wearily. "But at this point, I really have no idea." What with Antonio's se-crecy, Emilia's accusation, and the ongoing weirdness between her old friends, Kim wasn't sure of anyone anymore.

It seemed the only constant in her life was Gabriel.

Now he stood up and held her face with both his hands, turning it up to his. "Well, anyone who does try to hurt you has got me to answer to. I love you, Kim. Our daughter loves you, too. You may not be there the way I'd have liked over the last couple of years, I'll admit that, but I know you love us. I also know *you* and have been aware for a long time that you felt inadequate as a mom. I tried to help you, to take it slow and not rush you. But maybe I was wrong to do that. Maybe I should have forced you to face your fears from the start, but I didn't think you were ready."

"What're you saying?" she asked, her voice barely a whisper.

"I'm saying that it doesn't matter what you think you are to us and what failings you think you have. I want you to know that I love you despite them and so does our daughter. You think she knows yet whether you're at work or not or when you're gone too long? She's three years old. She doesn't. As long as she sees you at all she's happy. You're her mother. There is no one like you in the world to her. Don't you get that?"

Kim thought again about her own mother. Even when she'd broken away and moved on with her own life, she'd still loved Gloria and wanted her love in return.

Gabriel's latest suspicions aside, she cared about her mother and father despite the things they put her through, and even though they no longer had anything to do with her, if they came back this minute to say they wanted a fresh start, she would've given it to them.

Why did she think Lily would be any different?

Her daughter was still young. There was still a chance to fix the wrongs she'd made by being so absent in her child's life while she focused on her business. She could fix the things her mother never bothered to. She could be the mother she'd always wanted for her own daughter.

"OK," Kim said. "Thank you. I want to be the parent I need to be. And the woman you need me to be," she replied. "And I'm going to start from today."

Gabriel smiled. "You are already the woman I need."

"No, I'm not. Not quite yet, but I can be. I will be. Just be patient with me."

He leaned forward and kissed her. "Haven't I already?"

She smiled. "I really don't deserve you."

"That makes two of us," Gabriel replied as he kissed her again.

Kim was still reeling at the night's conversation and particularly the accusations of an affair. With Antonio of all people. But at least, she thought, as Gabe took her hand and led her back inside to the bedroom, the mystery of her saboteur looked to have been resolved.

Emilia. She knew there was no malice or reason to the older woman's actions. She had been her great friend and mentor for all these years after all.

But again, Kim realized sadly, of late, she had let her down, too. She hadn't visited Emilia in months, afraid to confront the disintegration of the sharpest mind she had ever known.

And she was wrong to do that.

She would remedy it soon, though. She would talk to her at the launch, of course, but once tomorrow night was over, Kim was setting her priorities straight.

She, Gabriel, and Lily would extend their family vacation by spending a few days in Milan with Emilia and give her old friend the respect she deserved, and also well and truly appease any fears she might have about Antonio, who adored her.

That night, she and Gabriel made love with an intensity that had been missing for some time, and afterward Kim's mind was finally at ease with the sense that everything was going to be all right.

# Chapter 54

## Now

Music filled the evening air and hundreds of glamorous, well-dressed people milled around. Cameras flashed as guests in their finery posed with happy smiles at the grand launch of Villa Dolce Vita.

While there was no doubt that the villa had been well and truly transformed, Annie kind of missed the old crumbling wreck it once was. She used to complain all the time about the state of the house while she was here, but realized now that being so rough around the edges was one of the things she actually loved most about it. Its imperfections were the hallmarks of its history.

Now it was glossy, gorgeous, and glamorous, much like Kim herself. She looked amazing tonight, dressed in a show-stopping pink-sequined gown that Annie was pretty certain was Dolce & Gabbana, her blonde hair up in a classic chignon, and her proud husband by her side.

A picture of success and the ultimate hostess, she was flitting happily from one person to another, while Annie stood alone on the terrace, champagne glass in hand, staring out into the darkness as she leaned against the railings, wondering why she'd come here in the first place.

Charlie was back at the Excelsior with the babysitter Kim had also very kindly arranged. He was having a ball and had spent the day splashing about in the pool with Lily, so she guessed he'd be wiped tonight.

It was no Dolce but Annie's emerald green dress hugged every inch of her body, and she knew she looked good, standing up just as well to any of the stylish Italian socialites and celebrities at this party.

She'd worked hard to regain her figure after Charlie was born and religiously maintained all aspects of personal grooming as her business grew. She went to the gym every day and ate the best she could whenever possible. Tonight, her makeup was impeccable as, of course, was her hair. She looked amazing and she knew it. But she wasn't entirely sure why she bothered.

It wasn't like anyone was benefitting from it besides her.

"Stop kidding yourself, you know exactly why," she murmured to herself, as she drained her drink and stared at the empty champagne flute with disgust.

Flagging a passing waiter, she dropped her empty glass on the tray he carried, and grabbed another.

Happy people, so many shiny, happy, self-congratulatory people. They were making her sick.

Earlier, she'd almost talked herself into not turning up tonight and staying away for everyone's sake, but she'd already come all this way to Italy, back to the scene of the crime, as it were. There would be no avoiding it: the shit was about to hit the fan.

As she waited, biding her time, Annie occupied herself with drink after drink. Several guys tried to talk to her but she was having none of it. Men were her problem in the first place, always had been.

If her father hadn't died then she could have had a normal, happy family life. If it hadn't been for her stupid accountant, she wouldn't now be on the verge of bankruptcy. If it hadn't been for her addiction to men who never had any intention of offering her their hearts, she wouldn't be alone now.

Charlie was the only man in her life who was any good for her, and the only one she needed.

So maybe she should forget about all this and just go now, back to the hotel and the son who needed her?

She'd done her duty, as such, by flying over here to support her old friend, and it wasn't as though Kim would even notice her absence. Despite a plethora of last-minute hitches, her big night was turning out to be a glorious success and everything looked to be going like clockwork.

Annie shouldn't even be thinking about trying to upset the apple cart and ruining it all.

She'd made her decision, and had started wobbling back up toward the house, fully intending to leave, when she saw him, standing idly beneath an olive tree and laughing with someone else, not a care in the world.

Annie sorely wanted to smash the glass in her hand directly into his face, but it wasn't hers and she'd probably have to pay for it, and she couldn't afford that.

"Can't afford anything," she muttered bitterly.

She made her way up the stone steps, the alcohol having taken its hold more than she expected.

She stumbled a little on the top step, going down on her

ankle, and she was sure she was about to fall flat on her face, when out of nowhere a pair of strong arms caught and steadied her.

"It's grand, I'm fine," she slurred as she grabbed on to the front of her savior's shirt and looked up at the sympathetic and all-too-familiar face.

She blinked rapidly.

"It has been a long time, Annie," the Italian said by way of greeting.

"Not long enough, Luca." She pushed away from him, but only managed to unbalance herself again in the process.

Once more his strong arms wound around Annie to keep her steady. "I think I better help you," he suggested.

"I don't want your help," she spat. "Get your hands off me."

"Annie?" Colette's voice appeared out of nowhere then, and she turned to find her friend and her husband standing a few feet away, staring at them.

Great. From Colette's point of view it probably looked like she was coming on to Luca. Annie moved away from him again, forcing herself to straighten up as she tried to fix her hair.

"You're late," she scolded, and slapped a smile on her face as she looked from Colette to Ed.

"*Buonasera*, Colette," Luca greeted calmly, and the raw emotion in his voice made Annie's attention immediately turn back to him.

His dark eyes were staring at Colette as if she were the most incredible thing he'd ever seen. Then she turned and looked at Ed. He was staring at her, too. Both of them still under her spell, even now, Annie realized sadly as she freed herself from Luca's lingering arm and teetered across the courtyard.

"Wait, let me help you," Colette said, once Annie had raised her from her obvious stupor.

Even through her champagne-fueled haze, Annie could tell that the sight of Luca had affected her friend. She was certain Ed wasn't going to like that.

Sure enough, Colette's husband hurried after her as she went to lead Annie back inside the villa.

One moment Annie was navigating treacherous cobblestones in her high heels, and the next she was being flanked by her friend and her friend's husband.

"I'm fine on my own," she complained, swatting them both away.

"I don't think so," Ed insisted, rather roughly tucking Annie's arm into his, leading her inside and away from other guests while Colette followed.

"Better make sure Kim doesn't see this," he urged his wife. "I'm sure she'd be very upset to see someone making a scene."

"Oh, yes," Annie spat. "Of *course* Kim wouldn't want anything ruining her perfect night. Perfect husband, perfect child, perfect life…"

Annie's raised voice was now drawing the attention of some guests nearby. Colette was quick to urge Ed on while she went back to perform damage control.

*Same old Colette, always trying to fix things.*

Annie glanced sideways at Ed. She hadn't planned on him seeing her like this.

She was a mess and she knew it. A drunk, raving mess, and she couldn't be sure what she would or wouldn't say under the circumstances. She needed to get away from him.

"What are you doing?" he questioned through gritted teeth. "You said you wouldn't be here."

"And why shouldn't I be here?" she shot back. "These are my friends."

"You know why. And causing trouble won't help."

"I'm not a troublemaker," Annie slurred, insulted, as Ed

ushered her into what was once the old dark living room toward the rear, but was now a refurbished relaxation area. She slumped into the nearest chair.

Her head was spinning and the ground was wobbling beneath her. She did not feel good.

Ed sat down in the chair across from her. "What the hell were you thinking, Annie?"

"I don't know!" she cried. "Why wouldn't you help me? I've never asked for anything in my life, Ed. And I wouldn't have now either, unless I really needed it."

"I told you, the timing isn't good. I've got some problems of my own, you know."

"No, I don't know. How would I? I'm not your wife. Anyway, I don't care about your problems, just as you never cared about mine. But now, for Charlie's sake, I need you to care. My business is going under," she admitted in a small voice. "My accountant stole everything I have. He stole from my company and left me with months of bills outstanding, and I barely have enough to keep a roof over my head, let alone pay the people I owe. He took everything." She turned to look at him. "You told me once that I could call on you if ever I needed anything. And when I finally do, you tell me to get lost. How do you think that feels?"

"I'm sorry. Like I said, you caught me at a bad time." He looked at her. "Has anything been done to catch this guy?"

"I've tried. But he's disappeared." She sniffed, surprised at the unexpected concern in his voice. "Honestly, I would never have asked if I wasn't desperate."

Ed moved closer. "It's all right, Annie. I'll help you. I know people who deal with this sort of thing. I'll make a few calls on Monday. We won't let him get away with this," he comforted. "I'll make sure he's brought to justice, and whatever help you need, I assure you that you'll get it. I'm sorry, you just…caught me off guard the other day."

He was going to help? He was going to take care of her and Charlie? Annie's tears began to flow freely now.

"Thank you," she said, relief flooding through her, as she felt a tiny inkling of hope for the first time since this all started. She was right to come here after all. She knew that if she got the opportunity to talk to him face-to-face, let him know how truly desperate she was, he would understand.

And he had.

*Thank God, thank God…*

Impulsively, she jumped up and launched herself at him, flinging her arms around his neck.

She wouldn't be on her own. Ed had promised he'd be there for his son if ever Annie needed him, and now he was making good on that promise.

Seems she'd misjudged him after all.

# Chapter 55

## Now

"So sorry about that," Colette was saying as she tried to distract Kim's guests from the scene Annie was making. "My friend has had some bad news." She couldn't believe that Annie had ended up coming all the way back here to just get trashed and make a fool of herself on Kim's big night.

Some things never changed.

"Is she OK?" the couple she was speaking to asked with some concern.

"She'll be fine. My husband is taking care of her now. Please do go and enjoy the party," she urged as she tried to divert their attention from the villa to the main party area back outside. The entire courtyard and terrace had been turned into a reception hall, and even the poolside was hosting guests for the evening. "Can I get you another drink or anything?" she asked the couple, who didn't seem to be getting the hint. Their eyes kept glancing in the direction of the villa.

The last thing she wanted was for Kim to get word of this, especially with all the pressure she'd been under lately.

"That would be lovely," the woman answered. Colette didn't remember their names but Kim had introduced them earlier. They were some wealthy hoteliers from Denmark. The husband was into racehorses.

"Have you seen the pool area?" she asked as she led them back across the courtyard. Along with champagne trays, a bar had been set up poolside to keep the guests well-supplied with beverages.

Hors d'oeuvres were being passed around by the waitstaff and, despite the last-minute catering issue, there seemed to be a plentiful supply of food and drinks.

"Not yet," the man replied.

"Let me show you," Colette insisted with a winning smile. Annie was in good hands with Ed. He'd take care of her. She just wanted to be sure that any unpleasantness the couple had witnessed was thoroughly erased before she left them.

Once she was sure the mini fire had been put out, she headed back up toward the house and was just ascending the steps to the courtyard when she saw him again. She attempted to walk past but he stopped her, reaching out to touch her arm lightly.

"Luca," she said tightly, as her cheeks automatically flushed.

He smiled. "I see you still blush easily."

"It's warm tonight," Colette replied, as she forced herself not to meet his gaze. He still looked the same, exactly the same. As if he hadn't aged a day since the last time she saw him, the day they swam together at Fiordo di Furore.

Right before he dumped her.

Luca seemed to search her face for something. What? She didn't know.

"I was hoping you would be here tonight," he replied.

She fidgeted, unsure what to say to this. "What are you doing here, Luca? I didn't realize you and Kim were close."

"We are not. But there was an issue with her catering company and they needed somebody to prepare the food. I offered to assist." He looked at the throngs of guests surrounding them. "Can we go somewhere quieter to talk?"

"No," Colette said quickly. "I need to get back to Annie— and my husband."

"Please. It will only take a minute."

She didn't know what it was but there was something in the way he looked at her, and the sound of his voice, that made her waver.

But what could Luca have to say to her now that he couldn't have said six years ago?

"Why should I give you even a minute?"

"I think you owe me that much," he replied.

She scoffed. "Owe you? After what you did?"

Luca looked confused. "What I did? You mean what you did."

"What are you talking about?" Colette answered. "I didn't do anything but wait around on the beach like a fool when you were never coming."

"Wait on the beach—for me? When?"

Colette couldn't believe what she was hearing. Was he really trying to pass this off as if it were nothing?

"My last night—at L'Incanto. I waited for you for over an hour but you didn't show. And then you sent me that…text. You didn't even have the decency to tell me to my face."

Luca took hold of her arm and began to lead her away from

the crowd. He guided her to the far end of the terrace where there were fewer guests.

"Colette, I do not know what you are talking about. I never made any arrangement to meet you anywhere close to Spiaggia Grande. For your last night, I asked for us to meet at Delfino."

She was incredulous. "Are you standing here pretending that you didn't send me a note to meet you there, and then while I was waiting around like a fool, send a text telling me that our time together was just a summer fling?"

"I never did any of that," Luca replied evenly. "It was you who left *me*."

"But I didn't do anything! You dumped me. You broke my heart."

"You broke mine," Luca replied with feeling. "I would never have hurt you, Colette. I loved you. I wanted to be with you. I was going to tell you that, and ask you to maybe come back to Italy sometime, or if perhaps I could go to you in England—find some way for us perhaps to have a future together. That night, I had arranged a party in the restaurant with Mama Elene—she was going to help me show you what your life in Italy could be. But you never showed."

Colette was mystified. "What? But this is impossible... I don't understand it. You say you never left a note about meeting in L'Incanto but I know I got one. So who did?"

Luca looked at her, his jaw working. "Annie."

"What?"

"Annie. When I came to the villa the day before, you were out with Kim but Annie was there."

Colette thought back. "You left the note with Annie?"

"Yes, I asked her to give it to you. Maybe she was a little distracted; there was someone else there at the time."

"Someone else? With Annie at the villa?"

Maybe it was him, the guy Annie had been seeing? Charlie's father. Maybe that's why she'd never mentioned the visit?

Luca looked uncomfortable at first, but then something—a realization—crossed his face, and his mouth set in a firm line.

"I need to talk to Annie," Colette stated as she turned and rushed inside. She needed answers. She needed the truth.

Luca's revelation had floored her. Something had gone wrong that last night, and she was going to find out what.

She hurried across the courtyard and back inside the villa, Luca bringing up the rear, and opened the door to the old living room.

To find Annie locked in an embrace with Ed.

## Chapter 56

Now

Kim looked around at the happy, smiling faces of her guests enjoying the party in full swing, and allowed herself a secret smile, thrilled and relieved that everything seemed to be going off without a hitch.

*At last…*

Though thanks to Gabriel's surprising suggestion, she was still half expecting Gloria to appear at any moment, and make some kind of scene in order to throw one final spanner in the works.

The idea that her own mother might set out to ruin such a big occasion in her life made her unnaturally despondent, and she resolved firmly once again to change her ways from now on, and be the best mother to Lily she could possibly be.

She was so lucky (and grateful) that Gabriel had picked

up the slack for so long, but she wouldn't allow him to do so any longer, and was now determined to make it up to both of them. Especially given his surprising assumption about an affair.

To think that he would even *consider* Kim would cheat on him, let alone with someone like Antonio! No, the one thing she could be sure of was that she and Gabe had each other's hearts, and had always been true to one another.

She just wished Emilia felt the same way about Antonio.

*And thinking of Emilia…*

Just then, Kim spotted the couple come through the courtyard entrance, and seeing Gabriel networking with some corporate guests, she headed over to his rescue so that they could greet the couple together.

Emilia looked stunning, as always, in vintage Yves St. Laurent, her hair fastened in her trademark French twist.

"Oh, it's so wonderful to see you," Kim said, hugging the older woman enthusiastically, hoping to allay any potential awkwardness, while Antonio and Gabriel chatted. "It's been far too long and, really, all my fault for not visiting, I'm sorry."

Emilia smiled uneasily, and glanced sidelong at Gabriel.

"Kim… I am so sorry about the other night. I was upset, I don't know why I said what I did."

"Hush, don't worry about it—I completely understand and I know you wouldn't have meant anything by it." She touched her arm. "And I hope it goes without saying, but there is no question of… I mean, Antonio is like a father to me."

Emilia looked pained afresh. "I know that. Which is why I cannot understand why I even thought anything like it, let alone said it out loud—and to your husband, too." Tears appeared in her eyes. "I do not know what is happening to me lately, Kim. I can't seem to…trust my emotions. Or indeed my actions." A low sob escaped from her, and Kim quickly took her beloved mentor's hand and led her away from the crowds to a quieter area further away from the house.

"Please, don't worry about it," she reassured her. "We all get like that from time to time. Things have been so busy in the lead-up to this whole thing, that I've pretty much forgotten which way is up myself."

"But to suggest…to even think about accusing you of something like that—it was unforgivable of me. But Antonio—he has been acting so strangely lately, and when a husband suddenly becomes secretive, you begin to suspect the worst. Also, he was so angry with me about the permits. But I didn't realize I had done anything wrong. In fact, I thought I had done him a favor. The paperwork was in his office, and I thought he had neglected to send it, and that perhaps the project would be in jeopardy. So I sent it instead."

She looked pained. "I don't know why I thought that, since everything was already agreed a long time ago. But I have fallen behind on so much lately, my mind—it is not what it used to be, and I am not sure what is happening…"

She was so truly distressed and painfully aware of her slips that Kim's heart broke for her. "Honestly, it's fine. These things happen. And everything has turned out great regardless. Look around you, isn't it wonderful? I want to give you a proper tour inside the center, too, but maybe tomorrow when there are less people wandering around."

Emilia took her hand in hers. "Yes, the villa looks amazing, and what you have achieved is incredible, not just tonight, but with everything. I saw it when I met you in Amalfi all those years ago—a spark within you. Kim, you should be so proud of yourself. Your parents should be, too, and while maybe it is not possible for them to tell you now, I am certain they will realize it in their hearts in time."

At this, tears now started to form in Kim's eyes as she turned to look at the older woman who had been more of a mother to her than Gloria ever was.

"In any case," Emilia continued, "know that *I* am proud of you, as is Antonio. And again, I am so sorry. I don't know why I even thought for a second…"

"Hush now, please. Forget about that." Kim reached across and pulled her into another embrace. "I hope you realize that all this is as much yours as it is mine. You know that none of it—the villa, the business—would have been possible if it weren't for you, Emilia. I owe it all to you."

The older woman held her tightly, and Kim once again felt terrible for neglecting her the way she had. But that was about to change. Emilia had always been there for Kim whenever she needed her. Now it was time to return the favor.

She would spend some time with her in Milan and then work with Antonio to assess what was best for this wonderful woman they both adored, and how to handle what was to come. They needed to put Emilia's mind at ease, too, and ensure that no matter what happened, she felt secure and loved. It was the least she deserved.

"So for tonight, let's you and I just enjoy the moment and celebrate it together, OK?"

Emilia smiled, now looking much more like her old self, and Kim was about to flag down a passing waiter to get them both a drink, when Gabriel came rushing up, a concerned look on his face.

"There's something going on, hon. Raised voices—an argument—coming from inside the villa. I think we should check it out."

Kim's heart tumbled to her stomach. "An argument? Who?"

"I'm not sure yet. Emilia, Antonio is looking for you." While Gabriel duly led Emilia back to her husband, Kim raced up the steps and back toward the house, with a growing—and all too familiar—sense of unease.

It had to happen, didn't it? Another blow, one final kick in the teeth.

For chrissakes… What fresh hell awaited her this time?

Annie clung to Ed, her fingers hooked into his shirt, feeling for the first time in forever like a heavy burden had lifted.

He would make this OK, he would help her and Charlie. She didn't have to worry anymore.

The smell of his aftershave was rich and familiar. So familiar. She could lose herself in it.

"You still wear the same aftershave," she commented breathlessly.

"Annie, stop," he warned.

"What?" she asked, turning to follow his gaze to the doorway. But there was no one there. "It's just the two of us—we can talk about this…properly now."

"All that was years ago."

"For you, maybe, but not for me," she replied bitterly. "You broke my heart, cast me aside for someone else—but not before leaving me with a permanent reminder."

"I'm sorry. I told you that at the time, and I'm still sorry now, but the whole thing really was…unfortunate."

"Can you imagine how it made me feel to see you outside that day in the courtyard, thinking you'd changed your mind, only to hear that you were there to see Colette? My friend? I loved you, for Christ's sake!"

His head hung in shame. "I didn't know she was your friend, truly. Or that you were staying here at the villa, too. But it didn't matter, by then it was far too late to stop what I felt." His eyes returned to hers. "Annie, I know you cared…"

"I still do. Did you know that there's been no one else since you? No one."

Annie hated herself for admitting that, but it was the truth. The alcohol was like fire in her veins and had loosened her tongue and sent her inhibitions flying. She was saying things she wouldn't normally have said.

Truths she would never have uttered, least of all to herself.

"Annie, this isn't healthy. I believed you when you said you needed financial help, but it seems now that there's a lot more to all this. You need to move on."

"You mean just swap out my heart the way you swapped me out for Colette?"

"That isn't fair. It wasn't like that. I fell for Colette. I'm not even sure why, she was just so sweet and…good."

"And what was I? Evil?"

"No," Ed replied. "You just…weren't what I needed."

*What you needed?* she retorted. "You wanted someone *sweet* and perfect." She laughed mockingly. "Not so perfect after all, though, is she? Colette might have been what you needed, Ed, but she can't give you what I did—a child."

"Annie, I think you better shut up now," he said, trying to extricate himself from her stronghold.

"Not that you cared. You picked her and just dumped me, like a piece of rubbish. And I never said a word while the two of you got to move on, go home to England, and live your happy little lives however the hell you wanted, while I raised our son alone."

Ed's head snapped up, at the exact same time a sharp gasp intruded on Annie's drunken rambling. She didn't even know what she was saying anymore. Everything was just tumbling from her lips. All the hurt, frustration, and anger she'd repressed for so many years was letting itself loose and there was no stopping it.

Her head spinning now, she followed his gaze to find Colette and Luca standing in the doorway. They hadn't been there a moment ago, Annie was sure of it, but there they were now.

*Oh God…*

"What did you just say?" Colette demanded, breaking the silence.

Annie couldn't look at her. She'd never meant for her to ever know the truth. She'd never wanted to hurt her, which was why she'd always explained away her pregnancy to Kim and Colette as just the result of a fling while she was here gone wrong, but she could see the pain and horror in her eyes now.

"What did you say?" she repeated more forcefully.

"Colette…" Luca cautioned, but she threw a hand up to silence him.

Her attention was wholly fixed on Annie and Ed.

"Someone better tell me what the hell is going on!" she shouted, looking at her husband, and Annie startled.

She'd never heard Colette raise her voice before. Not once.

"Darling…" Ed began but Colette cut him off.

"Don't 'darling' me, just explain to me what I thought I just heard. Is Charlie your son? But how…?"

"Sweetheart, she's drunk," he deflected and Annie felt a fresh surge of anger rush through her. How dare he? How dare he deny Charlie now, after all these years?

Years of Annie keeping the truth a secret so as not to mess up his perfect life. Six years of her watching that life from afar: the happy photos of him and Colette together, their wedding pictures, holiday snaps, all the while thinking it could—*should*—have been her.

"I wasn't drunk all those other nights, though," Annie raged as she got to her feet. "The nights you took me back to your hotel and shagged me. When you romanced me on the beach and then dumped me on that same beach later."

Colette gasped. "Oh my God…the guy you were seeing here then, you mean to tell me it was *Ed*? But… I don't understand…"

"It was before you even met him," Annie implored, not wanting her to think that she'd done anything untoward. "And he dumped me when he met you. And then after… I didn't want you to know. I couldn't tell you, Colette. I didn't want to hurt you, not when we'd all gone back to our own lives anyway. He was so good to you in the end. He helped you get over Luca. He brought you back from despair. How could I ever tell you about Ed, when he'd been so much better to you than he'd been to me?"

"And you never thought to say anything when you found out you were pregnant?"

"You and Ed were together by then. I was back in Ireland. Your mother had died, all our lives had moved on, I couldn't…"

"So for all these years you just said nothing?" Colette was trying to wrap her head around it. "And even worse, neither did you." Now she looked daggers at Ed.

"I offered to help when I found out, but at the time she said she didn't want any," he implored. "She just wanted me to know."

"So you knew and you lied—right from the start of our marriage. You knew you'd fathered a child, Ed, and you never said anything? After everything we've been through? *I've* been through? The hell I felt when I couldn't give you a child?"

"Colette…"

"He didn't lie," Annie said, sobbing, unsure why she was defending him. But she couldn't bear to see Colette's pain. "It's just…neither of us admitted the truth."

"And what about that summer and Luca?" Colette said, rounding on Annie now. "Didn't you withhold the truth then, too?"

Annie looked at her. "What are you talking about?"

"The note Luca left here at the villa, right before my last day. What did you do with it?"

"What?" Annie frowned as she tried to think back to the day she was talking about.

"What did you do?" she shouted, and Annie's mind reeled as she struggled to figure out what she was talking about.

"I don't—"

"What the *hell* is going on here?" Kim hissed, barging into the room then, her eyes wide. "Everyone can hear you from outside. What is this?"

"You tell her, Annie," Colette snapped, her mouth tight. "You seem to be full of confessions tonight."

## Chapter 57

Now

"Annie?" Kim demanded.

"I didn't do anything with any note," she told Colette. "I don't even know what you're talking about. I remember telling you when you got back that day that Luca had called and left something for you in the kitchen. At the time I barely noticed him, to be honest."

"Luca remembered someone else was with you that day. He didn't see who it was, though." Colette looked in Ed's direction. "It was you, wasn't it?" she said quietly.

*Now* Annie remembered the day Colette was referring to as clearly as if it was yesterday, because it was exactly when her heart had been well and truly broken.

When Ed had appeared out of nowhere at the villa and she'd spotted him on her way out, her spirits had soared because she'd been so sure he'd changed his mind. And also because she looked so amazing at the time—the perfect opportunity to show him exactly what he'd been missing.

But then she realized she'd never actually told him where she was staying, and when he'd admitted he was there looking for Colette, the penny dropped.

The man she'd fallen for had dumped her for her friend.

It felt like a living hell.

It was then that she'd decided to go home to Ireland, unwilling to spend any more time licking her wounds at the villa, or worse, perhaps even have to see Colette and Ed together, especially when it seemed they'd become even closer in the aftermath of Luca's letdown.

But now she realized something.

"Oh my God," she whispered, looking at Ed. "You did something."

"I did what I had to," he replied calmly, his words unsettlingly matter-of-fact as he looked at them.

"Had to?" Colette questioned.

"He wasn't right for you, darling," he said, referring to Luca. "He was playing with your emotions." Ed crossed the room to where his wife stood, and the Italian immediately pulled her away from him.

"You mean you sabotaged them?" Kim asked, staring at Ed as if she'd never seen him before.

"I took care of her—same as I always have," he replied. "*He* wasn't going to be able to care for her the way I could. The way I have," he said. "To him she was just another in a long line of tourist conquests. I knew he was going to hurt her so I had to stop it. So I took his note and left one of my own."

Colette gasped out loud and put a hand to her head in disbelief.

"When you didn't turn up that night, I suspected he'd

just give up and he did. No man who truly cared about you would've let you go so easily, Colette," Ed insisted. "I never would. So I did what I had to, in order to prove to you that he was no good."

"That's why you were there at the beach that night? Conveniently there to comfort me," she said, looking ill. "And you sent that text—which of course I assumed was from Luca."

Annie couldn't believe her ears. Who knew Ed could have been so cunning? How he could have purposely set out to sabotage and hurt Colette like that, and then swoop in like the proverbial knight in shining armor?

She didn't know where the impulse came from, but one moment Annie was sitting in shock, and the next she'd jumped up, crossed the room, and slapped Ed across his face.

It felt incredibly satisfying and she looked at him defiantly, daring him to say or do anything in return.

Now, Colette was sobbing into Luca's chest and the look on the Italian's face was nothing short of lethal.

Kim stood close by, looking well and truly bamboozled by all of these revelations.

"All this time it was you," Annie said sadly. "It was you who hurt her, not Luca. The same way you hurt me."

"It's not the same, I was protecting her," Ed shot back. "We were meant to be together."

Annie laughed bitterly. "There were so many times I regretted keeping you out of Charlie's life. I believed I was denying him the gift of a father figure at the very least. I thought it was because I was protecting Colette, but now I realize I was also subconsciously shielding us both," she said. "You are no kind of man, Edward Hargreaves. You don't deserve the family you have, and you certainly don't deserve *my* son."

"What?" Kim exclaimed. "Charlie is *Ed's* son? How on earth…"

Colette looked at her. "Yes, something else Annie neglected to share, apparently. So much for her mysterious Italian Romeo."

"Colette, I never once said or implied he was Italian; you just assumed," Annie said. "And I never said anything afterward because I didn't want to hurt you, or interfere with your and Ed's relationship."

"Then why now, Annie?" Colette asked plaintively. "Because it's pretty obvious you've had a bee in your bonnet with me since we arrived. You were openly rude and dismissive to me. Is that why you brought Charlie along? To rub it in my face?"

Kim moved to stand between her friends and put an arm around each of them. "Guys, you're both upset—let's just take a breather for a minute. Maybe you should get some air, Annie," she suggested gently. "And I think perhaps Colette needs to sit down."

"Good idea," Ed said, moving toward his wife.

"You stay away from her," Luca demanded, pushing him back by the chest.

"She's my wife!"

"She will decide that, but right now you stay away. You've done enough."

"I knew coming here was a mistake." Now Ed rounded on Kim. "But you had to do it, didn't you? You had to rub your great success in all our faces. Even though it's a complete sham, and you know it. Tell her, Colette."

Everyone stopped, including Colette. All eyes then settled back on Ed.

"What do you mean?" his wife asked. "Tell her what?"

Ed was glaring at Kim, a self-satisfied smile on his face. "About the notebook."

# Chapter 58

Now

"What notebook?"

"The one you stole six years ago, with all the ideas and words you used to build your so-called wellness empire. They were never yours and you know it."

Annie sat forward. What was he talking about? What else had Ed been up to?

And more to the point, what did *Kim* have to do with it?

"I don't know what you mean…" she began, but Annie noticed she'd gone white.

"Colette, tell her," Ed implored once more, his face smug. "All of this, it could have, *should* have, been yours."

"Oh, for heaven's sake!" Colette looked drained as she turned to Kim. "When I came here that summer, I brought along a diary, silly little stuff I'd written to keep me going when Mum was sick, inspirational quotes to keep my spirits up. But I misplaced it in the house somehow, even though I didn't realize it at the time. I was too busy enjoying myself. Then when your book came out, I recognized some of the chapter headings, and figured you'd come across the diary but never said anything." She shrugged. "It's no big deal."

"No big deal?" Ed raged. "She used your words to get rich, never crediting you."

"Because she obviously didn't know the diary was mine, you idiot," Colette snapped. She looked at Kim. "I mentioned to him in passing one day that I thought you must have found the diary. It's no big deal, honestly. There was no way to tell who it belonged to, especially as I'd written any personal stuff in Italian in case my mother ever came across it at home. And really, it's not as though any of the quotes were even mine anyway—I picked them up here and there over the years."

Annie was floored, although it kind of made sense that this hippie-dippie stuff had come from Colette and not Kim. She was exactly the kind of person who believed in that woo-woo nonsense.

"I swear, I had no idea the book belonged to you—or the words. If I had I'd never…" The words spilled out as Kim explained how she'd tried to track down the journal's origin, believing it to be a previous guest or the villa's owner. "I tried everything, honestly! I stole nothing. Not on purpose anyway."

"I know. And it's not as if I could or would have done anything with it anyway. You're the go-getter, Kim, the one who can turn your hand to anything and make it a success. And you have. I already pointed all of this out to Ed, but it seems he didn't listen."

Then Kim seemed to realize something, too.

"It's you, isn't it?" she said, turning to Ed. "Not only did you sabotage Colette and Luca's romance six years ago, but you've also been trying to sabotage this entire event. Leaving hateful comments on my social media, accusing me of plagiarism, perhaps even going so far as to mess with my permits and caterers, and goodness knows what else! But why go to so much trouble? If you resent me for using your wife's words, why didn't you just come right out and confront me? Why wait until now?"

"I think I know why," Luca put in then. "He did not want this event to happen because he did not want Colette to come back to Italy and discover the truth. And she would—once I got the chance to see her." He put his hand over his heart. "I am sorry for this, Kim, but it is I who upset your catering arrangements, because I needed to be here at Villa Dolce Vita tonight. I needed to see Colette once more, to see if she was happy and if she had made the right decision all those years ago—in choosing him." He shot another dagger look at Ed. "And now I know for sure that it was not."

"He's right. I didn't want you coming back here," Ed agreed, his voice plaintive. "I had to try and stop it. I knew if you came back there was a chance you would realize that you were happier with him than you ever were with me."

Annie shook her head. The person she had once known and adored as Harry was no more. Now Edward Hargreaves was a weeping shell of a man, willing to go to any lengths to get what he wanted. Whatever honor and nobility she had seen in him six years ago was long gone.

Or perhaps never even existed.

"I don't even know who you are…" Colette whispered through tears as she stared at her husband. "But I do know that you never loved me. You knew I wanted someone else back then, and that's the only reason you set your sights on me. It was about winning, wasn't it, Ed? You always have to win."

One look at Ed's face made Annie realize that Colette was

right. He hadn't truly cared about either of them back then. It had all been a competition to him.

Ed Hargreaves didn't care about anyone but himself.

While she had come here expecting fireworks when she confronted Ed about his refusal to help her out of her recent financial bind, she had never in a million years intended to hurt Colette or Kim.

This was the kind of showdown she would never have asked for or imagined, and while she was still angry at Ed for so many reasons, what hurt most was the pain in Colette's eyes when she looked at her now.

"I need to get out of here," she said wearily, and Luca duly moved to usher her out of the room.

Ed tried to follow, but Kim stopped him with the threat of calling Gabriel and having him forcibly and publicly removed by a man almost twice his size.

A proper man.

Annie half wished she could see that happen, though she guessed it was the murderous look on the Italian man's face that had truly given Ed pause.

Now she followed Colette, Luca, and Kim back outside to the courtyard, where down below on the terrace, all the party guests were smiling and laughing as the fireworks show began to kick off.

She noticed that not one of her old friends even glanced upward at the colorful explosions high in the sky off the beautiful Amalfi Coast.

Tonight, there'd been enough fireworks to last them all a lifetime.

# *Epilogue*

## Eighteen Months Later

"And...we're back," Kim said with a rueful smile as she stood on the terrace at Villa Dolce Vita with Gabriel and Lily.

Yet again she'd been transformed.

She'd stepped away from the business to focus on her family and Emilia, a decision she didn't regret. Having more time with the people she loved most had changed her entire outlook on life.

*Family is not an important thing. It is everything.*

Finally, she was taking her own (or, in truth, Colette's) advice.

"The place looks great. I'm surprised Antonio was able to let us have it with the amount of traffic that's been going through here," Gabriel commented.

"Hey, it's still my company so I make the rules." Kim tip-toed up to him and kissed her husband on the cheek.

Antonio had since confessed what Kim already knew—that his wife had mistakenly submitted alternative documents to the planning department, which he'd tried to cover up at the meeting.

"I didn't know for sure until I saw the signatures," he'd told Kim, finally willing to admit that his beloved wife's condition had gone beyond him, and that she needed professional care. Kim assured him not to worry, that she would do everything she could to help. She didn't want to add to her old friend's anguish by telling him about Emilia's suspicions of an affair, as she knew he had enough to contend with.

"You make the rules for the moment at least." Gabriel smiled as he laid his hand on her swollen stomach. "Once this next one comes we won't have nearly as much time for jaunts in places like this."

"I can't wait to see my baby sister," Lily called out. She'd been on the grassy yoga area playing quietly with her dolls until she'd heard her favorite subject being discussed.

"You really think it's a girl?" Gabriel said dubiously. "I was kind of hoping for a boy so that things might even out in this family."

"Nope. I want a girl."

"You're biased, though," Kim teased.

"Boys are icky," her daughter insisted, with a wrinkle of her nose.

"Not all boys. Daddy's a boy."

"Mommy, Daddy's not a boy. He's a *man*."

"But all men were boys once," Gabriel teased.

"They're still icky," Lily insisted.

"Well, I certainly hope you won't feel that way about our little man," Colette's voice resonated from the courtyard. She stepped down onto the pool terrace with a tray of food in her hand, eight months pregnant and absolutely radiant.

"Let me take it," Luca insisted as he hoisted the platter out of her hands and brought it over to the others. "You should not be lifting things."

"It's just a silly tray," she laughed, winking at Kim. She'd begun to waddle a little, something Kim remembered only too well. She'd been like Donald Duck when pregnant with Lily, but thankfully was a few months off that point yet.

She was so happy for her friend, though, and it was wonderful to see her looking so relaxed and happy.

The aftermath of that night had been a difficult time for all three of them, in more ways than one. But their friendship had got them through.

Colette and Annie's heart-to-heart following the party had broken down all barriers, and enabled both women to see the man they both thought they loved for who he truly was.

Annie had been instrumental in helping Colette through her divorce, even offering her a room in Dublin for a while until she felt strong enough to return to London and leave Ed for good. And Colette in turn (and with some financial help and advice from Kim) had helped Annie with getting her business back on track.

Kim was still amazed at the revelations that had tumbled out the night of the party.

Who could have guessed that Ed—of all people—was Annie's mysterious Romeo? And not only that but he had fathered Charlie and had promptly gone and set his sights on Colette before either of them knew about it. Granted, he hadn't done anything behind her back, but for Colette it was still a betrayal. He'd concealed the truth and, even worse, from her point of view at least, was that having promised Annie he'd be there for her if ever she needed him, he'd turned his back on her and Charlie when they did.

He didn't make things easy on Colette either, refusing to let her go, and had tried to drag out the legalities for as long as possible. But Colette, as always, kept things simple. She wanted nothing from him, other than to be free.

Even if she had wanted money as part of the divorce, there was little to share: a series of bad investments over the years on Ed's part had bled their finances dry and left them practically penniless. That was why he'd refused to help out Annie financially, the first and only time she'd ever asked him.

Every time she thought about that, Kim felt for her friend and wished she'd paid close enough attention to their friendship, so that Annie would have turned to her instead. But she guessed if she had done so, then all the secrets they'd discovered that night would never have come out.

She was still bewildered to discover that the journal upon which she'd built The Sweet Life had actually been Colette's, and had since tried her utmost to include her friend in the company, granting her shares and even offering her a place on the board, but Colette was having none of it.

Her motto had, after all, been to follow the simple life.

And she certainly had that now with Luca. Once she and Ed divorced, she had married Luca and moved lock, stock, and barrel to Italy, living in bliss above his restaurant ever since.

Now, with a baby on the way, all her dreams had finally come true.

While Ed had failed in his aim to sabotage Villa Dolce Vita's relaunch and thus thwart their ultimate reunion (while also hoping to make some money on the side through threatening Kim with a plagiarism lawsuit), he had at least succeeded in one thing—finally enabling Colette to live the life she deserved.

"Hey, guys." Annie peeked her head around the entrance gate of the courtyard. She looked amazing. Dark curls tumbled around her head; she wore a pretty floral summer dress and, flanked by a mischievous-looking Charlie on one side and a smiling stranger on the other, she looked…happy.

Kim smiled.

*"Buonasera!"* Colette called out happily, rushing to greet Annie.

"Who's your friend?" Lily asked, pointing to the man with her.

"This is Nick," Annie announced proudly, and Kim knew that this time she truly was head over heels.

Good for her. From what she'd heard about Nick he was a great guy who genuinely cared for both Annie and Charlie, and had also been a huge help in getting her business back on its feet. But for her part, Kim never had any worries on that score. No matter what life threw at her, Annie O'Doherty always came back fighting.

"So—" she looked from Kim to Colette, the old devilish glint in her eye "—are we going to get this party started or what?"

Kim stood up and moved to embrace her and Colette, realizing that their journey had come full circle.

Their friendship had begun here at Villa Dolce Vita, and despite all the ups and downs, it would continue.

Annie had found love and contentment with someone who truly appreciated her, Colette was having the baby she'd always craved with the love of her life, and Kim was finding that true happiness was better to be lived than spoken of.

Life for all three was finally sweet.

★ ★ ★ ★ ★

# Acknowledgments

Lots of love and thanks to Kevin, Carrie, family and friends for their continued support.

Huge thanks as always to Sheila Crowley—my incredible agent and treasured friend.

To all the team at Curtis Brown for championing my work so well—with special mention to Luke Speed for all the massively exciting film and TV stuff that's been happening lately. Thank you so much.

To my fantastic editor, Manpreet Grewal, whose insightful editorial suggestions really brought this story alive, the inimitably wonderful Lisa Milton for her boundless energy and enthusiasm, and all the brilliant HQ team in London.

Big thanks, too, to all the gang at HarperCollins Ireland and MIRA in the US.

Huge gratitude to the fantastic booksellers all over the world who give my books such amazing support.

Last but not least, humongous thanks to readers everywhere. I always love hearing from you so please do get in touch via my website www.melissahill.ie or Facebook, Twitter and Instagram.

I really hope you enjoy *The Summer Villa*.